Howls on the Wind

Howls on the Wind

Book Three of:

The Arcadian Complex

Paul James Keyes

ISBN 978-1-952872-04-4

Published in the United States by Verge Publishing.
VergePublishing.org

Cover artwork by Paul James Keyes and Raven Wade Keyes.
Internal artwork and design by Paul James Keyes.

This is a work of fiction. Names, characters, places, and incidents either are the product of the author's imagination or are used fictitiously. Any resemblance to actual persons, living or dead, events, or locales is entirely coincidental.

You can follow Paul on Twitter (X) **@PaulJKeyes**,
TikTok **@PaulJamesKeyes**,
or visit **ArcadianComplex.com** to become an honorary Arcadian!

"Never trust a man who casts no shadow, for the light may be a mask, hiding the true darkness within."
-Unknown

Table of Contents

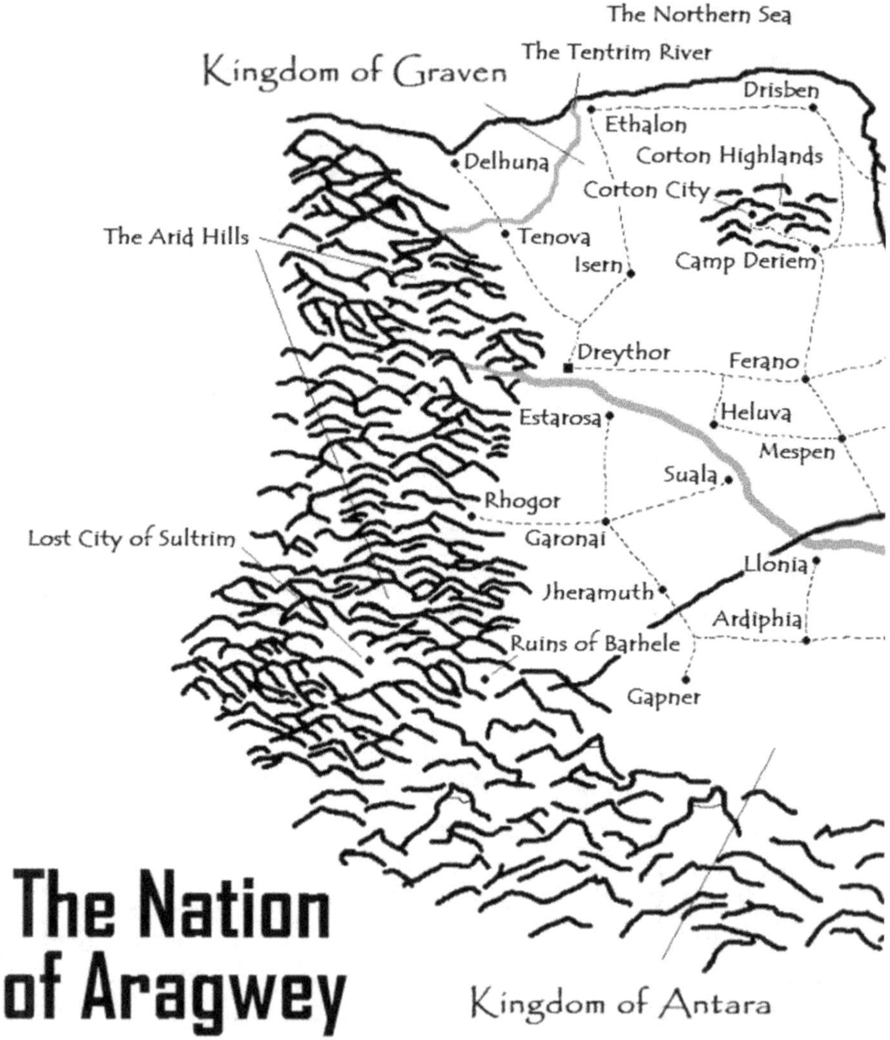

The Northern Sea
The Tentrim River
Kingdom of Graven
Drisben
Ethalon
Corton Highlands
Delhuna
Corton City
Tenova
Camp Deriem
The Arid Hills
Isern
Dreythor
Ferano
Estarosa
Heluva
Mespen
Suala
Rhogor
Lost City of Sultrim
Garonai
Llonia
Jheramuth
Ardiphia
Ruins of Barhele
Gapner
The Nation
of Aragwey
Kingdom of Antara

Kingdom of Taris
Kingdom of Kovehn
N
W
S
E
Ebsdale
Ennen
The Altrese River
Saldrone
Jarum
Besterio
Hordle
Ketsmill
Odenbar
Besbuin
Peninsula
Gulf of Nerim
Darrenfield
Becfield
Felington
Ghromyl
Vermholt
Tavallon
Denherm
Torus Desert
Gestrcho
Melvona
Salenport
Hurspen
Bronam
Telvarse
Silden
Zenbrogh
Cerivon
Benmoth
Rasile
Barslewn
North
Galdren
Bouchen
Yelmis
Whepton
The
Crimson Waters
of the
Minthune River
Tephlona
South
Galdren
Cheslyn
Quono
Ilvanelle
Fort
Bastion
Lithillo
Sarnoma
Parnith
The
Bastion
River
Oeslum
Epero
Nesbern
Mesilo
Aderna
Erotos
Uhlomn
Shian
Point
Lake Baratoa
Faehiln
Anosil
Ersalyn
The Rivers Etto
Elswani Monastery
Shian City
Scar of Phandrol
Kingdom of Phandrol

Hotel Willows
Blue Fox Inn
The Etwel River
The Etwon River
Arcanum Cathedral
The Queen's Palace

Officer Apartments
W
Exam Hall
Candor Fountain
Garson Square
Conset Hall
Laudry Hall
Anshaw Hall
Initiate Dormatories
South Bridge
City of Erotos

Catch me up!
A refresher in case it's been awhile:

Belford awakens in Darrenfield near **Javic Elensol**'s farm. He has the Power to control matter with his mind, but no memory of his past apart from witnessing the destruction of a technological era. He has the Mark of Kings on his arm, which leads him, along with Javic and his grandfather **Elric**, south to **Lord Ethan**—another Mark of Kings bearer.

They flee **Wilgoblikan** and his horde of Whunes, and meet friends and allies along the way. **Salvine**, Javic's what-could-have-been, is transformed into one of their hulking stalkers. **Kara**, a girl Belford meets, is also turned into a Whune. Belford attempts to transform Kara back, but fails....

They reach Lord Ethan in the Glowing City of Erotos. Nearly dead of old age, Ethan starts to help Belford understand his past. Eventually, through meditation, Belford does manage to regain his memories of his past-self, **Aaron Levy**, and his love for **Claire** and his unborn child. They were part of the **Arcadians**, the first generation to use the scientific system now known as the Power, along with all the Mark of Kings bearers (Ethan and the evil **King Garrett** included). Their bodies were memorized by a super computer housed on the moon that controls the Power, and they have been reappearing in Aragwey, staggered over the last thousand years after a millennia within a digital slumber.

Lord Ethan reverts his old age—he shall rule on! Belford goes with him on a mission to kill his rival, King Garrett, but the mysterious **Crimson Stalker** beats them to the kill. Now they fear the young **Queen Havorie** may be his next target.

Javic learns he can channel the Power. At the Ver'ati training academy he befriends **Rylin Gansly**. Both boys are deceived and used by the military. They end up transported to Sultrim, a dilapidated ancient city filled with the Paerto'sul—flying bear chimeras created to protect the city's treasures. Only Javic returns. He has since been raised to Ver'ati and is assigned employment on Queen Havorie's guard.

Havorie seeks to discover the truth about her mother's death when she was a child. It is said she fell from the south tower, but Havorie believes she was seduced by her "nightingale" and pushed to her death.

CHAPTER
1

Pillars of Dust

With his whole body pressed firmly to the stone wall, Rylin Gansly listened for any vibration that might indicate the approach of one of the Paerto'sul. The winged bears had formidable senses of smell—if they drew near Rylin they would hone in on him faster than a bloodhound. Guarded by the bears, the ancient city of Sultrim sprawled far and wide in a maze of tunnels and compounds built high in the Arid Hills. Shafts that ran through the interior of the mountain would occasionally open up into breathtaking views—perches and catwalks precariously etched into the exposed cliff sides. The high passes were treacherous at the best of times and, this time of year, were blanketed by heavy snowfall that made them utterly impassable for a human such as Rylin.

With the Gate Artifact that brought him to the Sun City destroyed by a cave-in, there was no way to leave, at least until the spring thaw.

1

A hollow rumble drew Rylin's attention. It wasn't one of the many quakes that often shook the dilapidated halls. The pattering footsteps of several guardians were drawing steadily nearer to his hiding spot. They'd found him far too quickly.

I shouldn't have stopped moving....

It was too late now. The bears had impeccable hearing as well. If he so much as breathed loudly, they'd be on him in an instant. All he could do was sit tight and hope they would pass him by. The air was stale within the tiny offshoot from the main hallway in which he'd taken up temporary residence. He hoped his scent was contained within the room and did not linger in the hall beyond.

The rumble grew louder. The pattering of the pack moved quickly down the corridor. They were searching for him.

Rylin became absolutely still, focusing on breathing softly despite the surge of adrenaline that was beginning to coarse through his veins. The bears were not easily evaded. Rylin held his breath as they scampered past the opening of the dark chamber. They continued on, maintaining their quick pace. Their motion stirred up the air, wafting the familiar musk of their fur within range of Rylin's nostrils.

If I can smell them, then they can smell me—

The thuds ceased immediately. Several grunts and tongue clicks sounded from down the corridor. The bears could speak Aragwian, but often communicated in more subtle ways when closing in on a hunt.

They turned back around, moving swiftly towards Rylin's hiding spot. The first of the bears burst into the chamber, its claws scraping across the flooring. Rylin slipped his lightglove into place against his palm, sending a piercing beam of light out towards the first approaching bear. It skidded to a halt and reared up on its hind legs. It was just a cub, but still stood as tall as a man.

The bear only paused briefly in the beam before lunging at Rylin. Its huge paws struck him in the chest, taking him to the floor with ease and nearly knocking the wind out of him. It stared down into Rylin's face, taunting him.

"Found you!" Kamila cried out. She licked his forehead before stepping off his chest.

Rylin had trouble distinguishing the bears from one another by sight, but he knew their voices well by now—he'd been living with them for over a month.

Ashran and Besel, Kamila's brothers, were right behind her. Ashran approached Rylin as well and nuzzled his arm. "Rylin found." A pulsing hum, indicating contentment, escaped the young male's throat.

"You guys found me so fast this time!" Rylin laughed, rubbing Ashran's soft nose. "Did you really wait the full five minutes before setting out?" he asked Besel.

Besel flapped his wings, whipping up the layer of Calvenite dust that littered the floor. "We counted to thirty-ten."

Rylin grabbed Besel playfully in a headlock, joke-wrestling the much stronger bear. "I bet you counted too fast!"

"Nah-uh!" said Kamila. "We counted fair. You just didn't hide well!"

Rylin's stomach rumbled with a deep pang of hunger.

Kamila poked Rylin in the belly lightly with her paw. "Mama caught a deer for supper. Wanna go get some?"

"I'm alright," said Rylin. In truth, he was desperately hungry, but he needed to wait for the moon to rise before he could cook the raw meat offerings with the Power. He didn't want to risk falling ill in a place like Sultrim.

The louder thuds of a full-grown guardian sounded from out in the corridor. Rylin and the cubs stepped out of the chamber to see who was coming. Soon, Raljaska, the cubs' mother, stepped around the corner. She focused her black eyes on Rylin as she approached.

"Hi, mama!" all three cubs cried out in unison.

"Hi, babies," said Raljaska. "Hello, Rylin. I need you to come with me. Ma'freit calls upon you."

Ma'freit was the leader of the guardians—a massive bear, wise and ancient, with the strangest ability to see into Rylin's thoughts. When Raljaska first took Rylin in, it had been only upon the judgment of Ma'freit that he was allowed to stay within the Sun City.

"What does she want?" Rylin asked. Ma'freit was an intense presence to be around. Rylin wasn't thrilled to be asked to another meeting.

Raljaska stared at Rylin blankly for a moment. "Ma'freit wants to speak with you." The bears were quite literal and often thought Rylin to be stupid.

"I mean, what does Ma'freit want to talk to me about?"

"You will have to ask Ma'freit," said Raljaska, cryptically. "There is a gathering, and you have been requested."

Rylin gave up trying to get answers out of the bear. He followed behind her lumbering strides as she led him back down the corridor. The cubs trotted along behind Rylin, chattering to themselves about some past hunt, but Rylin wasn't really paying attention. His mind was preoccupied with curiosity over Ma'freit's summons.

Paerto'sul were similar to their natural cousins in many ways. Bears tended to be solitary creatures. Mothers reared their young, but otherwise little time was spent in groups. Gatherings were not common. Whatever sparked the need for a meeting was undoubtedly not good news.

During his first audience with Ma'freit, the old bear gazed into his mind and determined him to be honest and pure of heart. The other bears, other than Raljaska who called the gathering, wanted to kill Rylin for coming to "steal the treasures," as they put it. The guardians were bound to protect the Artifacts housed within the walls of Sultrim.

Rylin was just one of a long line of wizards tasked with pilfering Artifacts through the Gate. The bears were not amused. Fortunately, Ma'freit saw that Rylin had no prior knowledge of the guardians' sacred duty or any intention of continuing to try to steal Artifacts now that he knew of their wishes.

Stealing the mysterious Artifact core was Lieutenant General Cale Fisman's goal—Rylin was just an unwitting pawn, sent on a dangerous task, blissfully unaware.

The corridor became flooded with sunlight as the tunnel opened up to a wide balcony. The crisp mountain air filled Rylin's lungs as he took in the pristine valley far below. Down the range at lower elevations, black spruce and birch trees stretched as far as the eye could see, uninhabited wilderness for countless leagues down into the heart of Antara. Up nearer to Sultrim, the untouched snow blanketed across the many peaks and twisting passes, sparse with vegetation.

Raljaska bowed down. Rylin climbed up onto the back of the giant winged bear without a word. He was used to the procedure by now. Due to the many collapses around the ancient city, the only way to traverse much of Sultrim was by air. Riding the flying bears was terrifying, but exhilarating. Rylin held on tight to Raljaska's fur as the rise and fall of her wing flaps threatened to send him tumbling to his doom. He eased up slightly as he settled in and began to enjoy the ride. It truly was remarkable getting a bird's eye view of the summit.

What would Cormick think of me now? Seeing things no other living person has ever witnessed!

Before Rylin was sent to the Ver'ati training Academy in Erotos, his eldest brother Cormick had always treated him like the baby of the family. At thirteen years old, Rylin was the youngest of five siblings, so he understood Cormick's view of him, though it was still annoying. He missed his family greatly. Leaving home for Erotos had been difficult—he'd never been away before. Now he was on the complete opposite side of the nation! The Lost City of Sultrim, deep in the Arid Hills, was as far from Rylin's home on Shian Point as one could get while still being in Aragwey. A cloud of sadness fell over him as he thought about his mother. The distance between them weighed heavily upon his heart.

Raljaska glided in for a thumping landing in front of the tall structure the bears used as their meeting hall. Rylin climbed down gingerly and made his way with Raljaska and the cubs to the building's entrance. There were dozens of other guardians already present, standing together in rows. Their emotionless eyes followed Rylin as he stepped inside. Raljaska and her cubs hung back as Rylin made his way alone down the aisle of bears.

The meeting hall looked to have once been some sort of court. Tall pillars held up a patchy ceiling—once upon a time it was all indestructible Calvenite, but the stone had since degraded halfway back into the weaker slate from which the structure was originally created. Holes in the ceiling brought beams of sunlight down into the meeting hall. Fine particles of Calvenite dust blanketed the hall with a misting of gray ash. It was like that all across the Sun City. The more enclosed spaces held piles of dust a hand or so deep in places where the centuries had allowed it to accumulate undisturbed. The bears did not have the opposable thumbs required to handle brooms, Rylin figured.

Corshen, Ma'freit's mate, stood at the front of the bears. Gray skin peaked out where old scars all across his body prevented the guardian's matted fur from regrowing. Only another bear could have caused such damage. He was not slowed down by his age, nor the old injuries. Dense muscles bulged from his shoulders where the scarred guardian's massive wings, currently folded at his sides, attached to his body. He was easily the largest of the bears that stood before him.

Rylin looked around for Ma'freit, but she was nowhere to be seen. He stopped beside Corshen and looked up at the elder bear for guidance. "I have been summoned?" he asked.

A deep rumble escaped Corshen's throat. "There is trouble under the mountain," he said.

All of the other bears watched the exchange fixedly.

"Ma'freit wishes to speak with you, but she is preoccupied. Tell me human, what do you know of the earth shakings?"

Rylin glanced at Raljaska at the rear of the meeting hall for a second and then back at Corshen. "The earthquakes? Not much. In Erotos the ground often shakes with Echoes from the Power being used too frequently in the area."

Corshen exhaled a burst of hot breath through his black nostrils. "It is much the same here. In ancient times, the Sun City shook, but after the human's abandoned the mountain, the earth eventually healed and the ground became steady once more." Corshen eyed Rylin closely. "Over the past season, the shaking has returned. Many new collapses threaten to tear the city down. The walls are not what they once were."

Rylin was confused. "I haven't been channeling the Power except to cook food, just as Ma'freit requested," he said.

"We do not believe you are to blame," said Corshen, "but the Power is being used greatly within the city—or more specifically, under the city."

The bears watched the look of surprise fall across Rylin's face.

"Ma'freit senses humans within the earth. They tunnel beneath our feet. They have not yet found the city, but they are growing closer every day. Do you know of this?"

Rylin shook his head. "No, sir," he said.

"The city must be protected," said Corshen. "The human invasion will be turned away once they breach the walls. To that, what do you say?"

Rylin swallowed nervously. The bears could easily decide to kill him if they deemed him to be a threat to their home. "I don't know anything about an invasion," he said. "My people are from far away. The Gate is destroyed. I don't see how they could be responsible for the tunneling. No one even knows where this city is—"

"Lies!" growled a bear standing in the front row. "He is one of them! He is a spy sent to learn the city's layout and defenses. We should eat him."

"Silence, Tanuk!" roared Corshen. "Ma'freit will judge the human's earnestness." He turned towards Raljaska. "You must not let the boy out of your sight until she does." He looked back over the rest of the bears. "Prepare yourselves for the battle to come. Ma'freit will know more about the invaders numbers when she returns from the depths." Corshen turned and walked away without another word.

Tanuk bared his teeth at Rylin. The gnarled guardian continued to eye him as if he were a snack as most of the other bears began to depart from the meeting hall. Rylin stared back, wide-eyed, at the hulking creature.

Kamila, suddenly by Rylin's side, nuzzled his arm to get his attention. "Mama says to come out fast," she whispered to him. "It is dangerous to linger."

Rylin didn't argue. He followed after Kamila with haste in his steps. He felt Tanuk's eyes on his back as he ran all the way down the aisle and out of the hall.

CHAPTER
2

Questionable Alignment

A haze of dark smoke tickled the evening sky. It was coming from the harbor. Belford did a double-take to make sure it wasn't Livian Niern's Black Mist already floating beyond their position. The brain spores were still swirling sleepily around the pyramid like a haze of smog. The smoke above the harbor was something entirely different. With the death of King Garrett, the dangers of Tavallon—namely, its host of deadly Goblikan wizards—were only beginning to rear their ugly heads.

Ethan, at the front of the party, began to push the pace faster. "No… no… no…" he chanted under his breath.

Belford shared looks with Shiara and then Arlin in turn. He wished there was more time before moondown. Its position was already low on the horizon. He dreaded being without his powers.

Thorin's death had left the lot of them gutted, but only Shiara and Belford were presently feeling the emotional pit his

9

absence left behind. Arlin's Talus Shard blade Artifact was now securely back on his hip. It drew out all of his emotion through the palm of his hand as he rested his skin against the crystal in its hilt. It kept him void of distraction—completely combat ready. His over-tightened vocal cords left him unable to express anything at all, apart from the tempered look he now shared with Belford.

When they rounded the final turn and the harbor came into view, all of their worst fears were confirmed. The Rosa Marsa—Captain Bundle's pride and joy, and their sole escape route—was engulfed in flames.

"What is it?" asked Sharith Grine. "Everything looks blurry to me in the distance…."

While Belford had fixed Grine's eyesight to prevent the Ver'konus operative's spectacles from attracting any undue attention, the procedure had left the small-statured man with a severe case of near-sightedness. Belford thought highly of himself, but he knew there were limitations to his abilities and expertise. It was true that he'd trained to be a doctor during a highly scientific era of humanity's history, some uncounted millennia in the past, but optometry had never been the focus of his study. He'd risked Grine's eyes anyway, to lower their overall chance of being noticed by the enemy on their rescue mission. There were always trade-offs like that. He took all of his failures personally, because he knew the weight of his decisions. He'd lost too many friends.

"The bloody ship is on fire!" answered Ethan. He checked the position of the moon, already beginning to set. There was no time to waste. Ethan quickly conjured up a dense raincloud with the Power and positioned it directly above the roaring flames in the distance. The harbor water rose up like a bubbling brew, obscuring the Rosa Marsa entirely.

But it was too little too late.

As the cloudburst dumped on the Rosa Marsa, the smoke grew into a thick black plume above Ethan's cloud. As soon as the moon set, the cloud dissipated into the air. The steamer was still on fire, and now it was half-sunk as well! Ethan's party continued their approach with caution.

Belford spotted Captain Bundles and his cook, Coriva Lethos, huddled together up the dock from their ruined vessel. The captain's son, Eben, was also by their side, as was Vera Ekrin, eyes red and full of tears. Belford's heart twinged at her disheveled appearance.

Many were missing from the group... Ader and Mikel Naffeim—the outlander brothers—as well as the Rosa Marsa's disgruntled deckhand, Garcenus... and the awkward Arcanum steward, Sarbin Raiger... and most poignantly, Wilgoblikan Whune....

When Belford disembarked to rescue Ethan's assault party, he'd left Sarbin unconscious in the cargo hold after he tried to stop him from leaving. Their prisoner, Wilgoblikan, had been all tied-up at his side. There was little doubt in Belford's mind that the dark wizard was responsible for the flames.

Belford ran ahead to reach Vera. She was still coughing from smoke inhalation. "You're alive!" she exclaimed as she threw her arms around him.

Belford embraced her tightly. "What happened?"

Before she could answer, a splash at the Rosa Marsa brought their attention to the harbor water. One of the Naffeim brothers was bobbing about just off the stern of the sinking vessel. A small bit of relief washed over Belford—*Another friend, still alive!*—but it was clear to see there was only one brother in the murky water. Belford couldn't tell which of the Naffeim brothers it was from the distance. Grine and Shiara joined Captain Bundles in pulling him up onto the dock.

Belford was barely able to recognize Ader. His face was severely blistered and singed. Dark streaks blackened his skin and clothes even after his dip in the harbor. "My brother!" Ader cried out. "I could not reach him...." He coughed and retched onto the dock, a combination of smoke and water in his lungs. As much as his burns must have hurt, it was clear the greater pain was from emotional suffering rather than physical.

"They're all dead," Vera sniffled, shrinking against Belford like a frightened mouse. He held back onto her tightly.

For the first time in months, the overwhelming feeling of dread and despair that accompanied his waking nightmares when he'd first materialized near the Elensol farm several months ago washed over him anew. He envisioned the eyes of the dead staring at him, some just outside his peripherals… others were lapped by the oily waters, just beneath the surface. Amongst the many nameless faces from the past, an occasional friend now speckled the ghostly crowd.

So many judging eyes… I need to keep my shit together….

"We need another boat," said Ethan, worry in his voice, but otherwise without empathy.

"And a new captain," said Captain Bundles, shooting Ethan a deathly glare.

"Ader will need Amelioration when the moon next rises," added Grine, looking over the poor man's burns.

Everyone had their own priorities.

Ader's burns were particularly poorly timed with the moon having just set. There would be no reprieve for any of his suffering anytime soon.

"He tried to go back in for Mikel after the rain quelled some of the flames," Vera said with a soft whimper.

Belford's heart ached terribly for them all. His guilt was unrelenting. He rubbed his eyes, attempting to clear out his own misty tears.

"Where's the Goblikan?" asked Ethan.

No one had an answer for him.

Shiara eyed Livian's spore cloud apprehensively. The wind was beginning to shift it in their direction. "If we don't get out of here soon, none of us will even remember why we came here in the first place." No one wanted the spores anywhere near them. There was no telling what memories might be erased or altered.

Belford, personally, had only just finished remembering his past. Claire and his unborn child could be out there somewhere, waiting for him.

I can't forget them again!

That terrible possibility put an edge to Belford's movements. "Let's go!" he cried. "Now!" Although he was still suffering from the smothering hallucinations of the dead, he found himself propelled forward by the prospect of finding his family.

"Everyone listen to Aaron!" Ethan ordered. "We need to escape this city!"

It still felt weird to Belford when Ethan called him by that name. Aaron felt like his past. His memories may have returned, but that time was still very distant to his senses.

Technically, my matter came from quarry rocks, and Aaron died thousands of years ago....

How strange it all was that he should have a dead man's memories, and that they would fill him with such sorrow—a desperate ache. He needed to find Claire. He felt it as a calling, deep in his bones. The pressure of his task smoldered within him, pressing on his core. Claire was lost to the past, but after all Belford learned from interrogating Wilgoblikan, he now knew there was a chance she could still come back to him.

"We ain't going nowhere with you," Captain Bundles spat, eying Ethan venomously.

A glance down the dock made the point moot. There were no vessels left to commandeer, even if Captain Bundles had wanted to help. All the moored ships had quickly disembarked at the first sight of fire. There was no means of escape.

Up the dock, in the distance, the few stragglers who remained in the streets became catatonic as the spore cloud washed over them. The full descent of the mist was imminent.

"We must head west," said Shiara. "Perhaps that silo is air tight." She pointed at a tall structure down the way.

Arlin rushed to the head of the dock and retrieved a baggage cart for Ader to ride in.

As angry as Captain Bundles was, the approaching spores settled any further argument. He helped Arlin and Grine pick up Ader and place him down gently into the cart. Arlin took up the handles once Ader was settled. Ader did not cry out anymore, not even as he was moved, but the pain of losing his brother remained etched on his face as Arlin began wheeling him down the dock. Eben clung to his father and Coriva as they ran ahead of the cart.

Immediately upon stepping off the dock and onto the harbor road, a familiar face emerged from a nearby structure. Wilgoblikan had been waiting for them… and he was not alone. Two more Goblikans, dressed all in black, flanked him in his approach. Whatever was to come next, no one would have access to the Power—not unless they held Power Artifacts, anyway. Belford had come across more Artifacts today than ever before. The right Artifact could give anyone the upper hand. Belford was glad he still had the strange orb in his stomach, stopping anyone—or anything—from affecting him directly with the Power, Artifacts included.

One of the approaching Goblikans was a huge beast of a man, the other, an older woman with a pinched-up face and a too-tight silver ponytail. She scowled in their direction. In a fight, Belford would give the edge to Arlin's blade, even with the muscle-bound Goblikan looking like Thorin's long lost evil twin. The mental comparison to Thorin struck Belford with another twinge of sadness. He doubted the guilt he felt over Thorin's death would ever truly fade away.

Arlin let Grine take over hoisting the cart as he unsheathed his Talus Shard blade.

Wilgoblikan stopped at a distance of about twenty-five meters and pointed at Ethan. "King Garrett's control over my actions ended with his death," he said. "That is true of all of his Goblikans. So let me make myself clear: You and I have several things in common, and one of them is that neither of us wants *that shit* in our lungs." He gestures towards the approaching spore cloud.

"I'm listening," said Ethan. He held up his hand to Arlin to pause any attack.

Wilgoblikan shifted his gaze over to the swordsman.

Belford watched Arlin's expression—it remained stoic and focused like a trained Rottweiler—wishing for permission to attack.

"We all need to escape the spores," said Wilgoblikan, looking back at Ethan, "and we both need to return to Erotos. You for your reasons and me, because that is where you will give me the antidote to the Inhibitor you rightfully injected into my body when I wasn't in control of my actions."

The suggestion that they forgive Wilgoblikan's sins—the death of Kara being the most outstanding in Belford's mind—made Belford want to retch.

"How could we possibly trust you?" Ethan asked.

"The Goblikans are free," said Wilgoblikan. "You may call me Wil, now. My slave name is no more."

Belford wasn't buying it.

Ethan stared Wilgoblikan down. The dark wizard didn't flinch at the scrutiny.

"You cannot possibly blame all Goblikans for the actions of one man," said Wilgoblikan. "I don't wish to kill you any longer, but not all the former Goblikans are fully right in their heads—and how could you blame them after such mental manipulation?—but, nonetheless, there are many who would not agree with forgiving you for Garrett's demise. If you allow me, I will guide you safely from this city and back to Erotos, in exchange for the antidote to my handicap, of course."

The terms were clear. Wilgoblikan wanted the Power back. Belford looked at Arlin, trying to silently transmit his wish for him to attack. His eyes bored into Arlin as he felt his intentions deeply, the way he would when trying to push thoughts across his bond with Claire in the distant past, back when he was Aaron Levy. Arlin, with his sword still held at the ready, did in fact feel Belford's cantankerous energy, though not in a psychic way. He met his eyes and saw his wish—they were attuned through the power of friendship—but there was doubt in Arlin's expression. He held back his justice.

Belford could perhaps see the value of his prudence. There was no telling what the Goblikans could pull out in a fight. But deep in his bones, he knew he could never trust Wilgoblikan.

The hint of a smile on the old Goblikan's face made Belford's own lip raise in a reflexive sneer.

"Now hold on," said Ethan, seeing the tension. "If our interests are truly aligned, I think we should hear him out." He was talking directly to Belford.

Belford felt as if his blood were about to boil.

Ethan addressed Wilgoblikan. "We must escape the spores," he agreed, "or our minds could end up so confused that we may as well slit our own throats here and now."

"Let's go to the grain silo, then," said Wilgoblikan, gesturing with his chin towards the structure they'd already been eying from the dock.

Belford looked towards Shiara for help. He couldn't believe everyone was falling for Wilgoblikan's trap! Nagging at him, the fact that they had already been heading towards the silo fueled his mind with doubt.

What are the chances Wilgoblikan would want us to go where we already wanted to go?

He felt like he was psyching himself out!

Wilgoblikan will always be evil! Right...? He twisted Kara....

"I will gain your trust," said Wilgoblikan, peering once more at Belford with wide eyes.

This is fucking insane!

Wilgoblikan—*Wil, yeah right!*—and his obedient Goblikan cronies led the way towards the silo. A little voice at the back of Belford's mind wouldn't stop screaming:

Don't trust him! Don't trust him! Don't trust him!

CHAPTER
3

Step One: Spores

King Garrett is dead; long live King Garrett.
And Deenan Raughel was the new King Garrett.

With his transformation complete, he now looked exactly like the late King Garrett prior to losing his head and limbs to the Crimson Stalker. Deenan had a fat, plain face now. The golden crown that sat atop his brow was dented from its tumble from the head of its original owner. Its jewel encrusted points gleamed in the oil-lamp light.

Livian Niern missed Deenan's original face.

"Get ready," said Deenan, "this guy's a real nutter. I caught him in some kind of lab attempting to unleash more beasts upon us."

The two Arcanum Illusionists were poised to enter the chamber where Dhron Cain was being held. The moon was recently down. There would be no channeling of the Power to contend with.

Livian smiled at the tenacity of the bald Goblikan. "I wouldn't have expected anything less from Garrett's *Monster Master*," she said mockingly.

Dhron was the only one of Garrett's men to witness the king's death. His cooperation was now at the crux of Livian's plan.

As she stepped into the dimly lit chamber, Dhron turned towards her slowly. He bared his teeth from within the shadows. His gums were grossly dark in color. She could smell his breath from across the room. "Stay away from me, witch!" Dhron hissed. "Whatever you do, I will die a free man!"

Livian made a pouty face. "Death is so final," she said. "I wager you will be of more use to me alive."

She retrieved a vial of specialized spores from the pocket of her petticoat and wasted no time in dosing the unruly Goblikan. Rather than approach and risk losing a finger to the cornered animal, she threw the spore vial as hard as she could at the wall beside his head. As the vial smashed and the wispy tendrils of spores drifted up the dark wizard's flared nostrils, his expression slid into a dazed softness. Even without a menacing grimace, his lack of eyebrows disturbed Livian on a fundamental level.

She approached him as he gazed upon her lovingly. He was her fully devoted servant now. Livian's brain spores were exceedingly complicated, but their application was simple and effective.

Livian always got what she wanted.

She withdrew a tiny bottle of black kohl makeup powder and an adapter stick from the same pocket where she stored her spore vials. Leaning in, she hastily drew a pair of thick eyebrows, slightly too high on Dhron's forehead.

"Now he just looks surprised," said Deenan.

Livian chuckled. "It's still an improvement."

Deenan frowned slightly, and then shrugged.

"Alright, Dhron," said Livian, "now isn't this better than the way Garrett imprisoned your mind?"

"I think I would still prefer to be dead," said Dhron, monotone, speaking with complete honesty. He was deeply devoted to Livian. There was pain behind his black beady eyes.

"Nonsense," said Livian. "I know love has been absent from your mind for a long while, but surely your emotional pathways aren't so closed off that you can't function for me! Did you not once suckle from your mother's teat? You must have known love once. You want me to be happy, Dhron, don't you?"

"Of course, m'lady."

"Of course! And it just so happens that it would please me very much if you would work on changing that dreary attitude of yours. Death is boring. You should search your soul for more ways to be of service. I'm sure that will make you feel better."

"I just want to die. You know I would not lie to you," said Dhron.

"Yes, yes," said Livian. "Now how about you be of service and set up individual meetings for me with each of the Goblikans currently within the capital."

"They will not come," said Dhron.

"And why is that?" asked Livian, an air of annoyance in her voice.

"All Goblikans already know Garrett is dead—our link was severed the moment his head left his shoulders."

Livian and Deenan shared a look. The Arcanum had warned them of this potentiality. It was certainly the worst case scenario for their ploy.

"Some may not come," said Deenan.

"Most," said Dhron.

Livian tugged at her ash-brown braid. "But some will." She had to dig deep to stay positive. "They don't *know* Garrett is dead, only that their link has been severed, correct? Call it a restructuring. Make them fear Garrett's silence as disapproval rather than a loss of control. We will get who we can, and then use them to drag in the rest. It may just take a little longer than we had hoped...."

Deenan grunted.

Livian held his concerns. The moment Garrett died, all of his Goblikans all across Kovehn were released from his control. Most would assume correctly that Garrett was dead. Chaos was imminent.

"Take note, Dhron, new orders to be posted to all garrisons are as follows:" Livian began to dictate. "An invasion by northern barbarians is unfolding." That much was true. "Prepare your forces. A truce must be called across the nation of Aragwey to overcome this common threat. It is a matter of survival. Goblikans are hereby ordered to return to Tavallon for immediate military restructuring. Those of you I have cut off from my thoughts must prove you deserve a spot in my mind once more. Make additional haste in your return to the capital. Signed, Your Beloved King—that's what he would write."

"It won't work," said Dhron.

"Just send it out," Livian insisted.

"Yes, m'lady."

Livian knew she was in way over her head. No amount of training or planning could have prepared her for the task at hand. She needed to fabricate control over the entire Kingdom of Kovehn. Time was ticking away fast. The barbarian invasion was just the existential cherry on top of the shit-cake that had been delivered to her.

Control came down to one thing—the narrative people held in their heads. At the moment, the cloud of spores outside the pyramid-shaped cathedral was in the process of putting all of Tavallon into a fugue state. Later, when the capital city awoke, everyone would be missing the last few weeks or months, depending on how quickly their immune systems managed to purge her spores. It was a science, but not an exact one. Spore density within the environment played a significant role—the results would vary. More certainty would have required Aerologists manipulating airflows around the city. Livian dabbled in Aerology, but there was little time and much to be done. The spores would roll through with the wind.

Mast help anyone who receives more than their fair dose.

Her micro-fungi could turn a brain to mush given enough time or too high of a concentration.

"Don't just stand there!" exclaimed Livian. "Go send the orders, and then find me some more Goblikans to convert!"

"I love you," said Dhron as he ran from the chamber.

Livian rolled her eyes.

"Those eyebrows look stupid," said Deenan. "I'm going to go find some supper."

"Just like the real Garrett..." Livian quipped. "Quite the thespian you are proving to be."

"It's been a long day," said Deenan, face drooping. "I didn't know I would be impersonating such a young man." The real Garrett's reverted age had been yet another surprise for the Illusionists to contend with. Insurrection was never easy. Deenan may have looked to be in his twenties now, but his body still felt all his years.

Livian waved him off. As talented of an Illusionist as Deenan was, his only job was to pretend to be the megalomaniac prick that was Garrett. Livian's duties were far more nuanced. She had stepped into the role of Garrett's top advisor. False memories of her presence throughout Garrett's reign were already embedding themselves into every citizen, guard, and Goblikan that encountered her spore cloud outside the pyramid. Successful memory implantations would occur ninety-nine out of a hundred times, while the remainder would experience confusion similar to advanced dementia.

A failed assassination attempt was all anyone would remember from Ethan's incursion on the realm. The general narrative would be enough to keep the average person nullified, but Livian had a lot more hearts and minds to control if she was to have any hope at preventing a Goblikan insurgency.

Garrett had ruled these lands with an iron fist. Now that his link to the Goblikans was severed, all of their twisted minds were free to pursue their own dastardly ends.

And then there was the Crimson Stalker. Livian's assumption was that the mysterious assassin with all the Power Artifacts was a part of the northern invasion. Most of the leaders of Aragwey were already dead, their armies headless as the foreign threat bore down upon them all. The decades of infighting across Aragwey had left them with their pants down now as the northern barbarians proved to be far better coordinated and well-manned than previous reports had suggested. The Arcanum analysts were not usually so far off on their risk assessments. The barbarians had been but a minor inconvenience to the northern kingdoms in the past. This coordinated invasion was taking them all by surprise.

The Crimson Stalker managed to kill nearly all of the palace guards on his hell-path to the throne room. A single partial regiment of twenty-three men was all that remained. They were outside during the attack and thusly had already consumed enough spores to believe Livian to be their superior. Several of the men walked with her now, guarding her as the rest searched the pyramid and surrounding grounds for any remaining threats. Livian hoped the Crimson Stalker would stay gone. A flurry of severed body parts remained in his wake. The gruesome cleanup would take days.

Livian made her way to a grand balcony above the main entrance. She wished to get a wide view of the city to see how the spore cloud was progressing.

One of her guards placed a hand out to stop her just shy of the balcony. "The mists—they are unnatural... and smell of... cinnamon...?"

The spores would not affect Livian—a pivotal safety feature she had been apt to include during her engineering of the mind-altering substance—but it was sweet of the guard to worry over her. "What is your name?" she demanded.

"Sir Kierington," the guard answered.

A real sense of duty in this one….

She didn't respect his follower mindset but people like him could still be useful. "Kierington," she said, "that smell is cardamom, not cinnamon. Now step aside, I'll be fine."

He moved his arm out of Livian's way. She memorized the soft features of Sir Kierington's face before stepping out onto the balcony and taking in the sights. The sprawling capital was covered in her spores—a hazy cloud that lingered in the evening stillness. Across the way, a dense spout of black smoke rose up from the harbor, marking a stark contrast with her spore cloud. The smoke and spores swirled together.

To the southeast, a group of Goblikans was creating their own wind with some sort of Power Artifact. They cut a path through the mist, moving towards the smoke. There was nothing she could do for Ethan's entourage anymore. Hopefully Mast would be on their side.

An explosion to the west made Livian flinch as it shook the city, rattling through the dark panes of glass that lined the grand balcony. The shockwave formed ripples across the mist. The chaos caused by the free Goblikans was already beginning to unfold.

CHAPTER
4

BOOM

Belford awoke in a ditch. His head was pounding, his ears ringing with a high-pitch whir. Flames danced across the sky. The air smelled strangely like some sort of savory holiday cake—he couldn't quite put his finger on it—toasted bread and spice. His body wavered with the shock of an explosion. Waking up disoriented was troubling given Belford's history of amnesia, but he was pretty sure he still knew who he was, so that was something at least.

Cardamom…?

He pushed himself up onto his elbow, peering dizzily into the sky as it dimmed and filled with black soot. The last thing he remembered was Ethan and company following Wilgoblikan to the nearby grain silo….

He knew he was missing some time. A crater resided across a torn-up street. Chunks of stone littered the walkway. The plume from a massive explosion formed a small mushroom cloud that hung eerily in the sky above him.

We failed our assassination attempt on Garrett! The thought struck Belford as odd. *No... Livian's Black Mist....* His mind was all out of whack. Belford felt vastly uncertain about the events of the day. *Livian is one of Garrett's top advisers....* Wrong again. *She came here with us on the Rosa Marsa! Garrett is dead! Thorin is dead... Mikel is dead... Lieutenant Canbel... all dead....* Other than Garrett's demise none of those were facts Belford particularly wanted to cling to. The flames of the grain explosion had purged the air of spores in the vicinity, but not before he had breathed in more than a few. He could only hope that whatever falsehoods had been embedded into his memories would be easy to root out.

Arlin appeared by Belford's side and silently helped pull him to his feet.

"I don't know what happened..." said Belford, his own voice sounding hollow to his nearly deafened ears as the words escaped his mouth.

If Arlin knew any better as to the series of events that had transpired, he certainly had no voice with which to explain it to Belford now. Belford glanced around, searching for Vera, Shiara, Ethan, anybody! But no one else from their entourage was present.

Did Wilgoblikan just blow everybody up?!

His heart, already pounding, began to beat faster. He frantically searched his surroundings. After taking several steps in the direction of the crater, Arlin grabbed him by the front of his shirt and slapped him in the face to get his attention. The shock brought Belford back to his senses. Arlin glared at him sternly then pointed at a group of approaching Goblikans.

Belford counted five of them through his blurred vision. They were partially obscured by what looked to be a bo staff, spinning unnaturally in front of the group like a propeller. No one was holding the stick as it spun—it was clearly a Power Artifact. It whipped up the distant misting of spores to form an airstream which the Goblikans ran through. They were closing in quickly on Belford and Arlin's position.

Belford reached for the curved blade that should have been lashed to his hip, but it was gone. With bits of his short term memory missing, he had no idea how he'd managed to misplace the weapon. It wasn't on the ground around him. The moon was down, leaving him completely helpless in the face of a fight.

As he quickly scanned the area for his blade, he noticed a pile of nearby rubble beginning to shift. When the ringing in his ears finally faded, he could hear pained grunts—somebody was alive and moving in an attempt to unbury themselves from the pile of stones that had once been a wall.

Belford's eyes grew wide with apprehension as a large figure began to emerge from the pile. It was the huge brute of a Goblikan that had been accompanying Wilgoblikan. His face was awash with blood and caked in a thick layer of grime and dust.

Arlin rushed to the man's side and helped lift him to his feet.

Not an enemy then, I guess....

Belford wished he could remember what had happened. His brain felt so damn foggy.... He fought back a wave of vertigo. It nearly knocked him from his feet. He tried to steady himself.

"Get him out of here," the large Goblikan said to Arlin, pointing at Belford. The other Goblikans were nearly upon them. The large man's only weapons were his fists—he wore black fingerless gloves with short spikes at the knuckles.

Arlin nodded to their unexpected ally before turning to Belford once more. He grabbed him by the nook of the elbow before pulling him onward down the debris-filled street. A fight broke out behind them. The large Goblikan grunted as he punched the spinning bo staff out of the air. The other Goblikans split up, three staying on the large Goblikan while the other two pursued Arlin and Belford.

As unsteady as Belford's legs were proving to be, there was little chance of escaping on foot. Arlin recognized as much. After rounding a corner they stopped and turned to face their attackers.

The Goblikans were upon them in an instant.

They looked like twins. Both had shaved heads and intense, dark eyes. Their light armor was made from dried hide. Short blades protruded from each of their sleeves, strapped to their forearms like extensions of their appendages.

Arlin's blade had the reach advantage, but it was still four blades against one. Arlin didn't wait for them to make the first move. Placing himself between Belford and the Goblikans, steel immediately clashed as they struck at one another. Arlin's attack was deflected. The Goblikans were well trained. They flowed through stances and struck back in unison. Arlin's chainmail saved his organs as a flurry of stabs cut through his outer shirt, shredding it into confetti. He grunted as he shifted back on the balls of his feet.

Belford empathetically dipped and shifted along with Arlin. He knew how it felt to hold the Talus Shard blade. As agile as the pair of Goblikans was proving to be, the instincts of a thousand battles flowed through Arlin's sword.

A parry and a kick later, and Arlin managed to knock one of the Goblikans down onto his back. Arlin struck again, launching himself on top of his downed foe. He hacked at him, aiming for his neck.

Belford didn't stand by idly. While Arlin fought he picked up a chunk of stone debris and threw it deftly at the other Goblikan. The stone struck the man across the temple just as he made a move to stop Arlin from landing a killing blow. Arlin's attack was brutal. Belford's distraction sealed the deal. A gargling cry was short lived as Arlin nearly removed the downed Goblikan's head from his body.

Belford felt numb inside. He'd seen far too much gruesome death for one day.

The remaining Goblikan kicked Arlin in the face a moment later, sending him sprawling out onto his back. The Talus Shard blade, slathered in blood, slipped from his fingers and scraped across the stone street, stopping outside of Arlin's reach.

Dazed, Arlin did not even raise his arms to protect himself. Death stared him in the face, and surely would have taken him if not for their large Goblikan ally bounding around the corner of the building just in the nick of time. Bloody and battered as he was, the massive man had still managed to best his attackers.

He barreled into their remaining foe like a freight train. A gust of wind from the bo staff Artifact—the brute of a man had taken it for himself—sent Arlin and the Goblikan flying apart. Next, a rain of spiked fists landed across the remaining Goblikan's face, dislodging teeth and smashing cartilage until there was no chance he would rise again.

The beast of a man stood up slowly. He eyed Belford with a flat stare. "Thank Gord," he said in a grunt.

It took Belford a moment to realize the Goblikan was giving him a command, and not weirdly expressing his own thankfulness. "Your name's Gord?" he asked. "I've actually met a Gord once… little gypsy boy… he was much smaller than you."

"It's a very common name," said Gord. He continued to stare at Belford. Gord's look filled him with unease.

"Uh, thank you, Gord," said Belford, realizing the man was still waiting. Adrenaline from the fight heaped atop the trauma of the day to fill Belford with a jittery energy. Gord's spiked gloves dripped with dark blood as he extended his hand for Belford to shake.

Arlin climbed back to his feet and retrieved his sword before joining them.

"Here," said Gord, handing Belford the bo staff Artifact. As soon as Belford took it from him, Gord turned and started walking away.

"I think I have a concussion," said Belford. "What happened at the grain silo?"

Gord stopped and looked back with a slow turn of his head. "It blew up."

A man of few words....

Belford nodded to himself. "Yeah, I got that part. But where is everyone else?"

Gord turned around again and continued walking without giving him an answer. Arlin patted Belford on the back as he limped past, following Gord. Arlin must have received more than a few bruised ribs by Belford's measure, not to mention that kick to the head!

Belford shook his own head before following the two silent warriors. He hoped he could trust Gord to continue being on their side. The prospect of trusting a Goblikan made him almost as anxious as he was over the holes Livian's spores were chewing into his memory. He felt like he had a head full of worms as he raced through the dangerous streets of Tavallon.

CHAPTER 5

Unchained

In the Glowing City of Erotos, the rising and setting of the sun did not define the flow of the day. At the stroke of midnight, with the moon high in the sky—though it was hidden behind an imposing curtain of dark storm clouds—Ver'ati all across the city were fully awake, managing their research and delving into the arcane arts while the Power was accessible. Students over at the academy in the east city would be finishing up their first classes of the night. As difficult as Javic Elensol's time at the academy had been, he very much missed his days with Rylin, Baxton, and Sima, studying and learning new skills to pass his exams. Nothing had gone how it was supposed to. He could hardly fathom that he was now a full-fledged Ver'ati, raised by the Arcanum for somehow surviving his Dance of the Elements.

Javic's black Ver'ati robe came back from the tailor fitting perfectly this time around. His official garb had been redelivered to him with a note attached from Arius Vanton, wishing Javic the best of luck in his new role within the Queen's Guard. His former professor had kindly placed the garment alteration order for him and seen to its delivery at his last official address—Mallory Worvon's apartment at the Blue Fox Inn over the Etwel Bridge in the west segment of the city. Mallory had inked a small heart on the back of Arius's note along with the words "I'll see you soon" in impeccable handwriting. She forwarded the package to the palace.

After his awkward encounter with Mallory during which Javic realized Mallory was pregnant with Arlin's child, the thought of seeing her again stirred a complicated mix of emotions inside both his heart and mind. He'd fallen for her because she'd mothered him. Deep down he still cared about her greatly, and she obviously cared for him as well, but Javic couldn't see a future with her that made any sort of sense. Ultimately, he felt betrayed and strung along, but it had been his own stupid assumptions that caused him to feel that way. Mallory owed him nothing. She was just a kind soul that he had clung to during a time of emotional turmoil. A pang rocked his heart—guilt for reducing their connection to such terms in his mind, but what else could he think? She was having Arlin's baby!

He had been feeling a lot of guilt lately. His grandfather, Elric, was still absent. He knew his grandfather's departure from the city had not been his fault—Professor Vanton pointed Elric towards the Lost City of Sultrim, where they'd believed Javic to be trapped—but he still felt terrible over the way things had been left between them.

Grandfather was right about Erotos.

The powers that controlled the Glowing City had tied so many strings to Javic that he was left dangling like a marionette, strung along completely at their mercy. Belonging to the Arcanum and to the Ver'konus military academy would have, at one time, brought him such pride—the institutions' reputations preceded them, holding such hope for a better world, that even before Javic knew he could touch the Power he had blindly thrown his support behind their goals.

They were supposed to be the good guys....

Only now that he belonged to both organizations did he see the corruption that poisoned their highest ranks. Morality played little role in the decisions of any of the men in charge. At this point—after losing Rylin and nearly being killed himself on multiple occasions—being a part of the Arcanum and of the Ver'konus made him feel icky, like there was an oily residue coating his soul. Working for Queen Havorie, at least, was a much nobler endeavor in his mind.

Lord Ethan's glowing orbs lit the city, nearly blocking out the stars with their brilliant shine. Even inside the palace, a retrofitting of wires and bulbs brought light to the dead of night. The only place not lit by the orbs was the condemned south tower, supposedly dangerous, currently locked by a thick Calvenite chain to stop anyone from entering. In reality, it was there specifically for the queen and her cohorts.

Javic moved towards the tower with quick footfalls, stepping as quietly as possible to avoid drawing any notice. At his side, Queen Havorie's young maid, Ervia Sindel, accompanied him. Her drab maid's uniform helped her blend in with the dark walls of the palace almost as much as Javic's Ver'ati robes did for him. The queen's head of security, Damian Sarvo kept changing up the patrol schedule, purposefully complicating their efforts to conduct their secret investigation into the death of Havorie's mother.

Queen Nestra's death had taken place some fourteen years prior. The trail was cold, but Havorie was adamant that they were closing in on a culprit. Javic wanted to help—it felt like the right thing to do—but he couldn't shake the feeling that by joining the queen's team he had only multiplied the dangers he faced within the politically tumultuous city. An unknown killer and Havorie's secret mandate to unmask him was not the first conspiracy Javic had been thrust into since coming to Erotos. General Guther Aldune and Arcanum Councilman

Tanner Cresdale—two of the most powerful men in the city—both would have preferred Javic to be dead. It was only by Havorie's extension of a job offer that he hadn't wound up a ward of the Archive Historians, where he was fairly certain a terrible "accident" would have soon befallen him. At least at the Archives he would have known who his adversaries were.

Everyone.

Poking his nose around the palace, there was no telling who had murderous intent.

As Javic and Ervia rounded the final corner before the south tower, Javic prepared his mind to begin manipulating the Power. The only way they were getting past the unbreakable Calvenite chain was with magic. Fortunately, Javic had become quite proficient at dealing with the unnatural material during his time with the Ver'ati Builders in Anshaw Hall. Working with Calvenite and carving the slate that preceded it came more naturally to him than other applications of the Power. He knew what he needed to do—convert the dark material back into slate, snip it apart, slip inside, and then carefully re-hook the chain so that they could go about their business without notice.

A trailing glance out the tall windows that faced the central gardens informed him that he was short on time. Beyond the storm, still raging with its howling winds, movement on their floor across the way on the other side of the palace could be seen through the glare of the rain and garden lights. He couldn't tell who it was, but if their course stayed true they would be upon him in a mere minute or two.

Ervia noticed the movement as well. "Another patrol so soon?" she asked, exasperated.

Javic's mouth tightened.

They had just wasted half an hour in a linen closet when the last patrol lingered in the western corridor. Javic was used to being stuck in closets from Professor Vanton's class where he hadn't been allowed to participate because of his emotionally-driven connection to the Power—at least now he had finally found his anchor. Thinking of riding through the meadows on his horse, Olli, helped settle his mind into a peaceful state that allowed him to commune with the Power more consistently.

He didn't like hiding away in closets, but at least this time he had Ervia to keep him company. Ervia was a quiet little thing. She was about the same age as him—sixteen going on seventeen. While she hadn't opened up much to him in the short amount of time they'd spent together, she was polite. The thing was… she always watched him with overtly wary eyes. He was pretty sure he made her nervous. They'd both needed to remain completely silent while waiting in the closet for the patrol to move on. There really was no predicting the patterns Damian had put in place for the palace guards. It felt to Javic like the man knew exactly where he needed to be—the south tower—and was doing everything he could to make his life difficult. Their only choices were to either call off their search for the night and sneak back through the halls, or hurry the hell up! Javic wasn't about to fail before he'd even started.

He tried to steady himself to draw in the Power. His mind went to what was once his happy place—riding Olli across the countryside—it was the best way he knew to make the connection possible. Unfortunately, the anxiety he felt over the rapidly approaching patrol sent ripples across his attempt at calmness. After wasting nearly half his time trying to steady his thoughts, he caved to the urgency of the situation and began reaching for an emotional charge instead. Professor Vanton would not have been impressed.

He started by conjuring up images of the fields of tall barley back home in Darrenfield, swaying in a warm breeze that rustled the golden grasses together. The sound of the grass would always soothe his nerves back then. Now, knowing his farm was burnt to the ground by Wilgoblikan, the memory of home was tinged in sadness and something more sinister— hatred for Wilgoblikan and the Whunes.

They killed Salvine.

She'd been the first girl he'd ever truly loved.

Wilgoblikan took everything away from me.

His jaw tightened and his face pinched up as the strength of his anger allowed the Power to seep into his bones. It soon filled him to the brim, sharpening his senses with a deep awareness of his surroundings. He could make out the patrolling guardsman's footsteps in the near distance. The buzz of the energy tingled in his fingertips as he set himself upon the Calvenite chain blocking their entry.

The conversion to slate was simple. The chain's dark façade faded into a dull gray on one of the links. He left the rest intact. Once the link was weakened, he blasted it with a kinetic force that shattered it into a dozen tiny pieces.

"Mast almighty," whispered Ervia under her breath.

"Sorry," Javic whispered back as they went about scooping up all the fallen bits of debris. They couldn't leave a trace of their breaking and entering behind.

Ervia slipped the chain loose from the double-door's handles and pulled the right side open just far enough for each of them to pass through. Javic held the chain in place as he entered. In the darkness of the south tower on the other side, Ervia used one of Havorie's Power Artifacts, lent to her by the queen for their mission. It allowed her to look through the wall and get eyes on the approaching guardsman. Its appearance was unusual—a scroll made of transparent material, which then lit up with a view of the hallway beyond when Ervia pressed it squarely to the wall.

"Ten seconds," Ervia warned in a harsh whisper.

Sticking his hands through the crack between the doors Javic pinched the two loose links together with his fingers. He didn't have time to reform a new link or anything fancy like that, so he used a process called Seaming to glue the two links together quickly. Their molecules intertwined at their point of contact, fusing permanently—or at least until he was to reverse the process upon their exit.

He pulled his hands back and slowly clicked the door shut without a moment to spare.

Ervia held up her arm, pointing in the direction of the guard on the other side of the wall as he passed. After the patrol rounded the next corner, the young maid finally allowed herself to take a breath.

"Just because we're here on the queen's orders doesn't mean there won't be repercussions if we get caught," she said, her eyes shining in the light of the Artifact's film. "We could very well lose our heads just for setting foot here after Captain Sarvo's mandate."

Damian Sarvo really didn't want them in the south tower. This was where all of Queen Nestra's remaining possessions had come to rest after her death—dusty linens atop finely carved furniture and crates, stored and forgotten. The tower was once Nestra's sanctuary just as it had become Havorie's before Damian condemned the structure. If Queen Nestra's locket still existed, it would be here.

Javic knew the stakes: The locket contained the evidence Queen Havorie required—a photograph of her mother's suitor, taken shortly before she was lured by said suitor to the top of the south tower and pushed to her death. Havorie only knew the locket and photo existed because of a coded entry in Nestra's old diary. Finding the photo was the only way to identify the killer.

A single photograph was not ample evidence of the wrongdoing, but it would suffice for Havorie. She was still in the 'identifying the threat' portion of her 'retake control of her kingdom' plan. There was still a very long journey ahead.

Using Belford's novel technique of creating a bubble of energy to light his path, Javic formed a nearly weightless orb in the palm of his hand. He took moisture from the air to create its layers of tightly woven particles. It didn't require much mass at all, but it could not hold its form without a constant supply of energy. He began grabbing at the heat from the air around him to feed its endless hunger. A spark appeared at the orb's center, quickly growing in brilliance like an acutely oxygenated furnace. The shine soon filled the gloom of the south tower's stagnant air.

"Do you think the Charisms can detect my channeling from this far away?" he asked Ervia as he thought about how illegal his actions were. The Power Artifact orbs at the palace's entrance were always monitored by at least two Queen's Guard.

"Probably…" said Ervia. "But they're always lighting up from some Ver'ati or another channeling outside the palace grounds as well. Just keep it dim and keep away from the windows."

Javic wasn't one for scavenger hunts—he wasn't really there to search—that was Ervia's job. He was just there to get Ervia into the tower and light her way. He followed along behind her, keeping the shine of his orb tamped down to a simmering ember of its potential luminosity as she made her way up the spiral staircase at the back of the tower.

The higher they climbed, the more Javic could sense the swaying of the tall spire. The wind was ferocious! After having witnessed Laudry Hall being devoured into a massive sinkhole, not even the unbreakable Calvenite brought Javic much comfort. The shifting motion left him with uneasiness in his stomach that made him feel like he was back aboard the Rosa Marsa, bobbing down the Crimson Waters.

A boom of thunder overhead rang out as the wind and rain beat against the side of the tower. The Aerologists had predicted the storm, and could have done much to ease its magnitude, but the risk of an Echo was deemed too high to justify such use of the Power. Ultimately, that made tonight the most perfect night for banging around in the dark despite Javic's concerns.

As much as he absolutely hated the anxiety that came along with sneaking around, he would have been lying if he said it didn't also give him something of a thrill. His body was flooded with adrenaline from nearly being caught at the door. The Power inside him kept him focused but his body was buzzing in a deliciously tactile way. His light orb flared up slightly as he breathed deeply, feeling all the sensations that the Power afforded him. He could sense the space around him in a deeply intuitive way when he put his mind to it—feeling the wood of the cabinetry, the fibers of the moth-eaten rugs beneath his feet, the grain of the boards of the floor and the never worn Calvenite stone that encased it all—he was connected to everything at the very core of his being. It was all clay to his fingertips.

He could form, change, or do just about anything he desired—anything for which he understood the process, anyway. It was difficult not to let that fact go to his head.

I'm the most powerful Ver'ati in the city!

Perhaps it already had gone to his head…. His strength with the Power was the whole reason Queen Havorie invited him to the palace—the reason she picked him to aid her. He was exceptional. It was a good feeling. It gave him hope for a brighter future. He thought about his grandfather. Elric had trained with the Paerto'radam swordsmen, and then given everything up to live as a farmer. Javic couldn't imagine making that choice after touching such greatness. How could he be fulfilled anymore by tilling fields and sowing crops? He often did miss the peace and quiet of that simpler time, but he could control the Power now. He could control anything! It brought an excited tingle to his belly.

"Keep pace," Ervia chastised.

He'd been lingering. The sense of agency that the Power delivered when first grasped was intense, but also fleeting. He knew in reality he was still a novice, no matter his rank. His skills with the Power were rudimentary, though he did have great potential. He hurried to Ervia's side.

Before the tower was sealed Ervia had already inventoried most of the rooms in service of the counting house—the Royal Estate's accountants. Nestra's recently rediscovered coded diary had been in a hidden compartment in an old desk.

When they reached the high-up storage room where Ervia's inventorying had been prematurely cut short, she went about pulling the linen covers free from a line of furniture along the far wall. Javic turned up the brightness of his light orb—there were no windows here to worry about. The air chilled around them as the orb ate up the ambient energy.

Glancing across the pieces of furniture, it looked to be a full royal bedchamber set that Ervia had uncovered. She began knocking on panels in the drawers of an ornate dresser. She dumped the yellowed cloths contained within the drawers onto the floor, scouring every bit of the decoratively carved cabinet for hidden secrets.

Her thoroughness reminded Javic of the guards in North Galdren measuring the widths of the floorboards of Shiara and Thorin's little blue wagon in search of contraband. It felt like a lifetime ago that he had become aware of the poverty the systems of the ruling class imposed upon the less fortunate. The greed of the elites held no bounds, carried in their sedan chairs on the backs of servants to vast estates while massive slums sat just on the other side of the wall. Starving children were forced to steal food in order to have a bite to eat at all. The guards kept them in line harshly while King Lodrin—now dead for all the good it did him—collected his tax through blood and sweat. The war machine was always ticking and it needed funds. Anything to keep up with the threat of the Kovehni military.

Given the opportunity, any Ver'ati could have fixed everything! So many people were suffering for no reason. Better homes could be built; food could be planted faster and more efficiently with aid of the Power. But if the people weren't starving, convincing them to sign up to be military fodder would have been much more difficult. It was a story as old as time. Nothing ever changed.

He hoped he was helping the world a little bit now in his own way by aiding the queen. He may have been a powerful Ver'ati, but political power was an entirely separate beast.

Politics was the last thing a former farm-boy like him ever expected to be sticking his nose into. It was all so disingenuous and cold. He really didn't understand Havorie's world on a fundamental level, although he'd gleaned glimpses of the powers at play from watching Belford's whirlwind experiences upon first arriving in the Glowing City.

He tried to make himself useful, heading over to inspect an old vanity nearest the stairwell. Its built-in mirror was tarnished, his reflection faded around the edges. He imagined the last person to use it may very well have been Queen Nestra. The wood felt tacky to the touch as he slid the main compartment open with his fingertips. A golden locket, shaped like a heart, sat dead center on the little shelf within.

"Wait… no way. Is this it?" Javic reached in and snatched it up. He began to fumble with the clasp as Ervia shuffled over.

She nabbed the locket right out of his hands. "That's for the queen's eyes only." Pools of shadow darkened her expression—an effect of the flat light of the orb. She studied the simple piece of jewelry apprehensively. The locket was rather plain for a queen. "You can't possibly have found this here…" she said shooting a wary eye towards the vanity.

"Sure I did," said Javic, "right there." He pointed at the little shelf.

"That doesn't make any sense. I've checked this vanity before," said Ervia.

"I don't like this," said Javic. "We should get out of here." He didn't know what it all meant, but the scene felt staged. The locket was just sitting out, almost in the open, in the closest piece of furniture to the entrance—right there in the first place they'd come to look. It was all far too convenient.

Ervia nodded curtly, then rushed ahead, back down the stairwell to the base of the tower. Her head shifted back and forth, ahead of her as she sped down the remaining steps. At the base of the stairs she stopped and pulled the locket back out of her pocket. She unhooked the clasp and pried open its tiny compartment.

"What happened to '*The queen's eyes only*'?" asked Javic.

"Oh, shut it. Look!" Ervia held up the open locket. There was a picture of Queen Nestra on the left side, but the right side was empty, missing the picture of the suitor.

Javic cursed under his breath.

Across the south tower's entrance room, the double-doors clicked as they were pried open. Javic's breath caught in his chest as he instinctively cut off the flow of energy to his light orb. The sparks inside shot outwards in one final burst. He flung the quickly melting ball of goo from his fingertips at the same time, splattering it against the nearby wall.

There was nowhere to hide.

They were immediately bathed in the light of a lantern.

Ervia shoved the locket back in her pocket as Javic grabbed her from behind and spun her towards him. He did the only thing he could think to do and planted a gratuitous kiss squarely across her trembling mouth. Her jaw remained stiff as their lips collided. She stared back at him with wide eyes. Javic put his hand up towards the light as it shined across them, trying to play off their many serious indiscretions as a simple juvenile romp. He put out his tongue a little bit and Ervia immediately bit it.

He pulled away and turned towards the light.

Ervia was blushing deeply beside him. At least that would help with the narrative they were about to have to sell.

All Javic could think about was how angry Havorie was going to be that they'd been caught. Ervia definitely wasn't who Javic wanted to be kissing. His own cheeks began to blush as he thought about the little crush he had on the queen. He knew it was stupid. But she was just such an interesting person—commandeering and strong in the face of such challenges.

It certainly didn't hurt that she was also super cute!

Once Javic's eyes adjusted to the lantern light being aimed directly into them, he wasn't the least bit surprised to see the man behind it was Captain Damian Sarvo. Damian stormed over to them, keeping the light pointed in their faces as he approached.

"Corporal Elensol!" Damian exclaimed with indignation. "And Ms. Sindel—why am I not surprised to see the two of you out of bounds? And what is this?" He snatched at the chain of the locket, still hanging out of Ervia's pocket. "Stealing?"

"No, sir, I swear!" cried Ervia.

Damian grabbed her by the wrist and began dragging her towards the open door. "I'll deal with you later," he said threateningly over his shoulder to Javic.

Damian wasn't a wizard, but he was a competent swordsman, and he was also Javic's direct superior.

Javic followed him out of the south tower while searching his mind for the right words to get them out of trouble, but he wasn't sure there was anything he could say. They'd been caught in a trap. The biggest unknown was whether or not Damian was involved in the conspiracy.

The captain relocked the chain around the handles, not noticing or at least not commenting on the two Seamed links. As Damian started down the hallway with Ervia still in his grasp, Javic raced for the nearest voice box—the advanced system of intercoms that linked many of the rooms of the palace together.

He smashed the button sequence for Queen Havorie's chambers.

"Report," ordered Havorie's voice, transported through the walls and out of a series of tiny holes at the center of the box. She'd answered his call extremely quickly, preemptively seated by the box on her end in anticipation.

"We found it, but it was empty—Damian has it now, and he's taken Ervia!"

"Go stop him at once!"

"I don't have any authority here! What do you want me to do?"

"I don't know! Please! If he takes her, we will never see her again! Get her back at all costs!" Havorie sounded to be in a complete panic.

Javic rushed after Damian and Ervia not knowing what under Mast's raging sky he was going to do once he caught up to them.

He was not moving quietly.

Damian stopped and turned around as Javic approached like a bumbling buffoon. "What is the meaning of this?" he asked pointedly.

"May we speak privately, captain?" asked Javic, still without a clue as to what he was going to say next.

Damian narrowed his eyes, reading the serious expression on Javic's face. He let go of Ervia's wrist and left her standing alone at the side of the hallway as he followed Javic far enough away that they could speak quietly without being overheard.

"I can't let you take her, captain," said Javic.

Damian's expression darkened.

"She didn't do anything wrong," he continued before Damian could cut him off. "It was my fault, I made her come here with me, and she didn't steal anything! That locket is a gift."

"You gave her this?" he spoke quietly so that Ervia could not overhear his words.

"Yes, captain."

"And yet you were caught in the south tower amongst all of Queen Nestra's possessions—may Mast rest her soul."

"Such a simple locket," said Javic. "You are not implying that something so plain could have possibly belonged to a queen?"

As Damian lifted the locket up to his eyes, Javic reached out with the Power and boiled the inside of its compartment with his thoughts, flash burning the photograph of the former queen. Damian flipped open its compartment to a small puff of black soot.

"Hoping to sway her into relations?" he asked. His tongue made a *tsk* sound. "Maybe not a queen's locket, but this still looks rather expensive. I dare say a Ver'ati such as you shouldn't need to try so hard for the attention of a maid. How did you afford something like this, anyway? I know who you are. I know you have no money to your name, boy."

Javic's eyes grew wide at the intense scrutiny.

"And don't you try to lie to me!" Damian raised his voice. "I'll know it in an instant!"

Ervia craned her head in their direction, listening intently.

"I made it!" The words escaped Javic's mouth even as he knew it was the worst thing he could possibly have said. "I made the locket…."

Damian gasped. A smile appeared on his lips a moment later. "You must be aware the creation of gold is illegal under Arcanum law. Punishable by death."

It was indeed a grave offense. Javic had just been trying to get the blame off of Ervia. Creating gold undermined the stability of the economy and was taken very seriously.

"I… please, captain…" Javic stammered.

Damian let out a snickering laugh. "I'm just messing with you, corporal," he said, clasping Javic's shoulder firmly. "We both know the Arcanum does not rule within the walls of this palace." He paused. The fact that Javic was technically an Arcanum representative within the palace was not lost on either of them. "Because of course, the queen is in charge."

"The queen…" Javic nodded slowly.

"By all rights I should report you to the Arcanum, still." Damian's smile dropped as he returned to his usual serious demeanor.

Javic tried not to let his fear show on his face.

"But I won't do that. Assuming you become and stay useful to the Guard—no more of these out-of-bounds shenanigans." He pointed at Javic knowingly as he walked away.

Javic was left with his mouth hanging open. Ervia rubbed her torqued wrist as she looked on in worried confusion.

Damian slipped the golden locket into his breast pocket before disappearing down the hallway.

CHAPTER
6

Into the Depths

High in the Arid Hills, Rylin felt the hospitality of the Paerto'sul bears wearing thin. Raljaska had been ordered to watch over Rylin—and she remained friendly, as did her cubs—but the rest of the bears viewed him as more of a snack than a friend. Particularly, Tanuk was of great concern to Rylin. The fully-grown male had a thick hide, rippling muscles, and claws like daggers. The hot-tempered bear believed Rylin to be an enemy and had the ability to bite him in half in one snap of his jaws. It was not the healthiest of combinations.

While ferrying Rylin away from the dilapidated meeting hall, Raljaska glided across the bitter updrafts back to the section of high-up tunnels and chambers that she and her cubs called home. The bears required him to have another meeting with Ma'freit to prove his loyalty was with them, and not with whatever humans were tunneling under the mountain, causing all the Echo-induced earthquakes.

The idea that the humans might rescue him from the Lost City worried Rylin as much as it filled him with hope. Ma'freit could read his thoughts and feelings. He had to pray that his ignorance of the so-called invaders would be enough to save him from the bear's damnation. Rylin just wanted to go home.

Rylin's wariness of Tanuk proved to be well-founded when the lumbering beast landed upon Raljaska's peak shortly after their return. Raljaska heard his approach before Rylin was aware of the danger. Her ears perked up. Rylin noticed her attention drift.

The great bear spoke in a low boom: "Kamila—lead Rylin into the depths—you must find Ma'freit."

Rylin, still oblivious to Tanuk's approach, questioned Raljaska's command. "I thought we were supposed to wait until Ma'freit came back up top-side?"

A blood-chilling roar echoed down the hallway from outside on the snow bank. Rylin's expression drooped as he recognized the approaching peril.

"I will attempt to slow Tanuk's advance," said Raljaska. "Make haste."

Kamila's brothers hid amongst the crumbling crossbeams of the roof as she and Rylin raced from the den. Rylin did his best to keep up with the young cub's quick legs. Raljaska's chambers were connected to the larger structure of Sultrim's tunnels. Kamila galloped ahead. "I think I know the way…" said the cub.

Behind them, more terrifying roars rang out. Several ground-shaking bangs brought down a misting of Calvenite flakes from the ceiling as the two behemoths began to tussle about within the close quarters of the den.

The hallways were long and twisting, and rife with cave-ins. Luckily Kamila knew this portion of the tunnels by heart. They continued on at a tear until a cave-in within the main tunnel forced them down a side passage.

"Your friend did that," said Kamila, gesturing with her fuzzy head towards the cave-in. The bears had not been pleased by

Javic's antics—causing cave-ins and bridge collapses all over the run-down city, not to mention stealing their treasures. Rylin knew Javic tried to find him, but then ended up breaking the Gateway, leaving Rylin trapped as Javic escaped back to Erotos with the Artifact core that Lieutenant General Cale Fisman so desperately desired. Rylin didn't blame Javic for running from the Paerto'sul, but the outcome certainly hadn't landed in Rylin's favor.

He liked to think of himself as mature—and a mature person wouldn't be seething with pent-up rage at having been abandoned callously by his best friend. In a lost city filled with man-eating flying bears, at that! Rylin was almost fourteen— practically an adult by his standards—though he was admittedly quite small for his tender age.

I'm not mad. I'm just disappointed.

Those were the words he thought to tell Javic, assuming he lived long enough to see him again. He'd never had one of the bears try to attack him before—not in all the weeks he'd spent living amongst the Paerto'sul.

As he ran on, he passed alcoves of floor-to-ceiling shelves filled with Power Artifacts. They lined the hallway on both sides. Kamila kept looking back, silently urging him to pick up his pace. She pulled ahead steadily as they continued towards the massive underground chamber that Rylin had taken to calling the Hub. As much as the Artifacts that surrounded him intrigued him, he knew not to disturb the bears' treasures. The Hub contained a series of bridges, partially collapsed, that connected most of the sections of Sultrim together like an underground superhighway. The gate room through which he'd arrived in Sultrim was completely destroyed, but on the wings of a bear one could quickly travel to any number of places across the ancient city.

Rylin had never tried to ride Kamila before. She was larger than him, but only just. A nervous flutter formed in Rylin's belly. Due to the severity of the collapses, once they reached the bridges, traveling by air would be their only option.

A deep rumbling earthquake made the halls shudder. Rylin aimed the beam of his oversized lightglove up at the ceiling as more flakes rained down from above. He was winded by the time they reached the open air of the massive Hub chamber. Here, the ceiling was too high for his light beam to illuminate. Never before coming to Sultrim had he even considered that such a large chamber could possibly even exist! It made him feel exceedingly small.

"I don't know if I can lift you," admitted Kamila. "But I should be able to glide, since we are going down."

Rylin looked over the edge of the abyss. He'd never been down into the depths, as the bears called it. "How deep does it go?" asked Rylin.

"Deep," said Kamila. "It gets hot down there."

Isn't heat supposed to rise…?

Rylin felt like he was straddling an excessively hairy potbelly pig as he climbed on top of Kamila. He knew better than to make that comparison aloud, though. He barely had room to wrap his legs around her as she spread her wings. He leaned forward and gripped her with his arms in a headlock, desperate to hang on.

"Not so tight!" she complained. "I'm just a baby!"

The realization that he was indeed about to ride a baby bear down into the abyss was disturbing. A mighty roar from behind them solidified his resolve to push forward. Rylin loosened his grip and briefly reflected on the terrifying absurdity of his predicament. If he managed to ever make it back to Erotos alive, he knew one thing for certain: He no longer had any intention of continuing on with the Ver'konus after graduating. Any childish cravings for adventure he once held were well cured.

Mast, burn you, Lieutenant General!

Pilfering the Lost City was no task for an initiate. He'd been used, and he was angry about it, but that did him absolutely no good as Kamila dove headfirst over the ledge.

The bear kicked off the platform one last time and then—*Whoosh!*—Rylin gritted his teeth. It took everything he had not to cry out as his stomach lifted up into his throat. The Paerto'sul could see in the darkness, but Rylin found himself completely blind as his lightglove sunk into the bristly fur of Kamila's thick neck.

"Not so tight!" Kamila roared again.

Rylin tried to relax as they soared downward at a jarringly steep angle that put his butt well above his head.

All I can do is trust....

Rylin closed his eyes and felt the air blast across him. They continued on in a near free-fall until the sensation of the weightlessness settled into his bones. It was as petrifying as it was exhilarating!

Kamila flapped her wings quickly several times.

Rylin gripped on tight again.

"Hold on!" Kamila cried.

Rylin squeezed even tighter with his knees. He could feel Kamila extend her wings out further. The air caught them, shifting their angle of decent. Rylin's head was back up where it belonged, but they were still falling fast.

After nearly a whole minute of falling, Kamila began a frantic flap. Rylin's fluttering stomach dropped hard, and didn't stop slipping until it reached his gonads. Gravity returned abruptly. He was smushed against Kamila. Her paws slammed into the ground unexpectedly, hard thuds slapping upon what sounded like compact sand with her long bounding steps. Rylin felt like he was riding a skipping stone as they bounced several times. The steps picked up in pace with each bounce until Kamila was running in a desperate gallop.

There was nothing he could do as Kamila's feet suddenly faltered.

Rylin shrieked as he tumbled forward, losing his grip with his knees. His legs flipped over his head again, but this time he found himself flying free from Kamila. The flight was much shorter this time, ending in a painful slam that left him splayed out flat on his back against a beach's worth of compressed Calvenite flakes.

Somewhere far above, a massive roar answered his shriek. Tanuk was hot on their trail and closing in fast.

Kamila reappeared at Rylin's side, nuzzling into his ribs painfully. "I'm sorry!" she cried out in a panic. "We must run!"

Rylin's chest was tight—the wind knocked out of him. He gasped for breath as Kamila bit onto the hem of his shirt and dragged him along. He felt like there was a boulder sitting squarely over his lungs. His heart pounded in a desperate twang, his blood pressure rising with every passing moment that his breath remained caught in his chest.

He knew if he did not get up and move soon, he would be dinner.

"Please get up!" begged Kamila. "I'm sorry!"

Rylin fought against the strain, finally managing a meager gasp of breath that kickstarted his lungs into functioning properly once more. He rolled to his side and then onto his knees. Kamila urged him to his feet with a tug of his sleeve. Rylin pressed his palm snugly against the metal disk inside his lightglove, once again producing a steady beam that cut though the gloom. He shined his light ahead as they ran.

The bears had cut paths through the deteriorated Calvenite piles over the course of centuries. They'd managed to compress the flakes into trails that flowed between the dune-like mounds. Here and there, large chunks of stone littered the cavern floor, fallen from above.

Kamila led the way, bounding towards a narrow tunnel that sloped downward, leading even deeper into the Earth. The tunnel was carved into the compressed Calvenite flakes, which maintained a sandstone-like structure. Claw marks all across the curved walls and ceiling of the tunnel indicated it had been formed by the bears themselves, rather than the original wizard builders of Sultrim's founding.

As they approached the tunnel, Rylin could already see more passages splitting off from the main one. Some of the pathways were wider than others, branching in seemingly random directions like the trails of an anthill.

Rylin ambled after Kamila as she scampered headlong through the main tunnel's opening. Tanuk was large, but he would still be able to fit inside.

A ground-shaking bang sounded as Tanuk slammed down hard just outside the tunnel entrance behind them. "You cannot hide from Tanuk! I will crunch your bones!" threatened the angry bear.

The tunnel was tight, slowing Tanuk down to a walk as he followed Rylin and Kamila inside. Many of the diverging pathways bubbling off from the main tunnel appeared to be dead-ends—empty dens of bears long absent.

Rylin was fairly convinced he was about to die, but he focused on forcing his feet to press onward. He could hear Tanuk grunting as he squeezed himself through the tunnels behind them. Kamila rushed through a tight passage ahead.

"Must go deeper… right, left, straight, left… then I forget," said Kamila.

Rylin dared a glance back just as Tanuk reached the tight portion of the tunnel. The great bear was forced to his belly. He clawed the floor, cutting deep grooves as he pulled himself forward.

Kamila ran ahead, leaving Rylin to follow her previous directions. He took the right-hand passage. The tunnel grew wider again. Another split in the tunnel—Rylin cut left. Tanuk's lumbering strides picked back up again as he finished scraping through the narrow portion.

More diverging pathways left Rylin briefly questioning which path Kamila considered to be the straightaway, but a brief pause allowed his ears to pick up on her distant scampering coming from the tunnel with the steepest downgrade. He pressed onward.

He caught up to Kamila after the final confident left turn. The young cub was standing in a wide chamber with no less than eight passages leading off in various directions. It was a complete maze of nonsense to Rylin's eyes.

"There are multiple ways down," said Kamila.

There was no time to think as Tanuk barreled towards them. One path looked exceedingly tight—too small for Tanuk to follow. "What about that one?" asked Rylin, pointing his light beam at the steep slide of a tunnel.

"That path is forbidden…" warned Kamila. "It leads to the Great Device."

Rylin didn't care if it led to the bottom of a latrine as long as Tanuk couldn't follow them.

Kamila didn't complain much as she too weighed their options. "Mama's gunna be mad," she said.

Rylin shoved himself into the hole behind Kamila just as Tanuk reached the chamber. One last angry roar shook them as they slid down into the depths of Sultrim.

CHAPTER
7

Shallow Breaths

Blast you, Belford! Where are you—you sad sack of potatoes!?

Shiara regretted not making Belford stick with her when the group split in two.

Every time I take my eyes off of you, something bad happens!

The explosion had not been subtle. She feared the worst. Ethan and Captain Bundles took turns kicking in the door to a small residence with street access once it became clear they wouldn't be able to outrun the fog.

Shiara cupped her firestone earring Artifact within the palms of her hands, rolling the still-cooling gem around as if it were a prayer bead. The gem was no longer searing hot as it had been immediately after draining the energy from the giant lizard-beast that crunched Lieutenant Canbel during their initial assault on the pyramid, but it was still uncomfortable to the touch and not quite ready to be utilized again. She blew on it within her hands in an attempt to speed up the cooling process. It looked like she was getting ready to roll a pair of dice.

Shiara didn't believe in luck—superstitious acts did little to comfort her. She was a follower of Mast, but not a particularly devout disciple. The typical prayers and rituals taught by the Ek'radam monks were merely a holiday tradition for her, to be practiced only on one of the few holy days each year. She'd missed the last day of prayer—winter solstice—too distracted by her mission to assassinate King Garrett to notice the occasion's passing.

She chose to believe that everything happened for a reason, but even within that hope, she held a contradiction in her soul. Deep down, she was a realist. She knew life was purely what one made of it. Nothing more, nothing less. She'd fought for every scrap she'd ever gotten out of this world. Life was often unfair. Existence was pain. Suffering. Chaos. She knew she was fighting against the natural order of things by resisting tyranny.

At the same time, fate was the only explanation she had for Belford crashing into her life.

She supposed she'd ultimately gotten exactly what she wanted out of coming to Tavallon—the destruction of King Garrett—but at the cost of no less than her whole heart. Her protector was dead. Thorin was gone. He had been closer than family to her. She would have swapped places with him in an instant—his absence pained her terribly! She never thought she would lose him. He'd always been the one to keep her grounded and even-tempered.

While Belford had stripped most of Thorin's blood from her skin and clothing, she could still smell the metallic scent in her sinuses. Her hair had a dried matting of it crusted up against her scalp. Dark flakes fell like dandruff as she scratched desperately in an attempt to remove them from her body. The gurgle of Thorin's last breaths would haunt her forever, she had no doubt. She'd kept her eyes squeezed tight, but the stickiness of his blood as it washing over her… that horror was unavoidable.

As grim thoughts of Thorin tumbled through her mind she squeezed a bloodied square cloth in her pocket. It was dry now, and crusted stiff. It was also all she had left of Thorin. She wished she had Arlin's Talus Shard blade within her reach to draw up all the dark emotion back into the void. The stoic mindset it imparted was a kindness she'd immediately longed to experience again ever since she'd released that hilt from her grasp.

When Belford, Arlin, and their Goblikan escorts didn't return from scouting out the grain silo, there was little doubt they were in trouble. Then, when the violent explosion rocked the city, she knew her fears to be true. The group had no choice but to hunker down in the nearest structure and try their best to seal off the windows and door. Livian's spores descended upon their position like a dense fog, blocking out the outline of the sun with a gloomy sky.

Damp towels and other linens were stuffed in every crack. The occupants of the residence they'd ducked into were terrified, huddled together in a back room as Wilgoblikan led the efforts to fill the gaps.

Trusting Wilgoblikan had definitely not been Shiara's call. With the rest of Wilgoblikan's cohort missing along with Belford and Arlin, *Wil* was the only Goblikan left amongst them. The fact that he was barking orders in an authoritarian tone irked Shiara deeply, though she tried not to let it show upon her face.

The foul man had directly attempted to murder her months ago in Felington, and yet now he refused to even impart a passing glance in her direction. If he was aware of their past crossings, he wasn't showing it. He pointedly ignored her as if she were of no consequence. She felt like she had disappeared into the tacky wallpaper at her back. By all rights, Wil was their prisoner. His command of the Power was suppressed with Inhibitor. He was just a begrudgingly useful old man amongst their party of all-powerful Ver'ati, Shiara included. Even Captain Bundles—no power to speak of and an ample jiggly belly to boot—looked capable of dominating Wil in a physical fight. Wil's pale, malnourished body was covered by the scars of Ethan's torturous interrogations during the journey north aboard the Rosa Marsa.

And yet he continues to dole out commands!

"Press those sheets more firmly, you dullard!" Wilgoblikan barked at the captain's son, Eben. His spirit was far from broken. "We'll all be breathing spores and forget what we're doing here if you can't manage it right!"

Captain Bundles glowered at Wilgoblikan from across the flat. He was busy blocking off a different window. The captain was at his wits end with the whole lot of them. Shiara had no doubt the Rosa Marsa's crew would be choosing to find their own way forward the moment everyone was clear from the dangers of Tavallon. They certainly had no reason to stick around. Shiara genuinely respected each of them, though she was under no illusion that they liked her back to much of a degree. She had imposed greatly upon their lives. They certainly did not deserve their losses. Half the crew had wound up dead or missing since the first time Shiara laid eyes on their round captain.

"Get another bucket of water over here!" Wil yelled over his shoulder. The aged Goblikan was about as trustworthy as a viper as far as Shiara was concerned. Alas, it was not up to her. It was not her place to question Lord Ethan's decisions. Wilgoblikan was smartly showing submission to Ethan, and Ethan alone. While it was true that Wilgoblikan's mind had been controlled by Garrett during his brutal reign, it was difficult to see Wil as an unwilling participant in the carnage for which she knew him to be responsible. The calculating bastard spent many decades in service to King Garrett and the Goblikans. Shiara believed in second chances, but she very much doubted anyone could come back from the atrocities Wilgoblikan had partaken in. The man had acted as a monster!

There was no chance he wasn't mentally damaged from such evils.

Everyone remained in their positions, waiting on bated breath as the mist descended. Shiara pressed the bedsheets in her hands into the gap beneath the front door.

The city outside fell eerily silent. The birds overhead ceased their squawking and dropped grossly to the street in a series of quick thuds. After the last one fell, the silence returned. There was nothing to do but wait. No one spoke, matching the hush that surrounded them for quite some time, until Captain Grine sent out the first alarm:

"It's seeping through!" he cried. "Look, you can see it in the light!" Sure enough, wispy tendrils were accumulating upon the windowsill. His damp towel was stretched wide over the gaps in the window shutters, but the fabric was too thin. The spores reached up at him, riding the subtle airflows within the room.

"More linens!" Wilgoblikan barked again. "They need to be wetter!"

Coriva, manning the bucket, sprinted for the faucet, but stopped prematurely within the doorway to the back room. "It's seeping through the floorboards!" she exclaimed.

Vera appeared in the doorway with more sheets, but lingered at Coriva's side. "This is the last of the sheets…" she said. It wasn't nearly enough to cover the floors. The building was breathing. And soon the spores would be in their lungs.

The fine mist lingered at their ankles. It looked like steam above a boiling pot. Shiara stopped pressing her sheet to the door gap with her hands and promptly stood. The light from the windows illuminated the leaking floorboards. To the crew of the Rosa Marsa, it must have felt very much like being aboard a sinking ship once again—that's how it felt to Shiara anyway—like each breath might be her last.

"Fight for every clean breath!" ordered Ethan. "Focus on blocking the windows and keep your heads high!"

It was a losing battle—they all knew it.

CHAPTER 8

No Honor Amongst Goblikans

Belford jogged alongside Gord and Arlin down the hazy cobblestone street. The peculiar bo staff Artifact they'd taken from the dead Goblikans at the grain silo spun freely at their lead, blowing a momentary tunnel through the mist. The workings of the Artifact were a mystery to Belford. It maintained its distance at the lead of the group regardless of their speed. When they slowed, it slowed. When they stopped, it ceased forward movement entirely, but continued to spin in a blur like an old airplane propeller. Moving fast behind it was the only way to maintain a *mostly* spore-free pocket of breathing space.

All Belford had to do was toss the bo staff into the air—it hovered into a superposition in front of them. The way it floated reminded Belford of how superconductors could be locked in place with magnetic fields. That was called quantum locking, but he recalled that it required extremely low temperatures to lock a small amount of matter in superposition.

He was a little fuzzy on the science behind that phenomenon. Whatever the explanation, the bo staff spun like a perfectly balanced top as they cut their path.

"Where are—?" Belford began.

"—Breathe less," grunted Gord.

Belford just wanted to know where everyone else was!

He couldn't quite recall why Livian Niern had been on the Rosa Marsa with them… she was Garrett's top advisor. The contradiction in his memories hurt his head. Remembering anything felt like pushing through sludge—his brain was fogging over as much as the street. He wasn't entirely certain what they were even doing running through the fog in the first place. The spiced scent in the air was strangely pleasant. He felt almost like he was in a dream as they dashed through the cloud. Everything but the present moment was washed out, faded by the mist. He was fairly certain he wasn't actually dreaming… he could still count his fingers, anyway… he couldn't usually do that when he was asleep….

The bo staff shifted its path as Gord angled to the right. Belford wasn't sure who was controlling the Artifact's trajectory. It seemed to be locked to the sum of their masses.

Ahead in the mist a tall figure stood motionless. The black robes of a Goblikan solidified as the wind of the bo staff blew across him. He stood, plain-faced and emotionless, frozen like a statue. The man's mind was gone. Gord pounced on him, attacking without hesitation or mercy. He knocked the hapless wizard to the ground and began pummeling his face into a pulp under his spiked gloves. Bones crunched with every solid blow he landed.

Belford turned away, sickened by the brutality of the kill.

No honor amongst Goblikans….

Gord was only satisfied once the unfortunate wizard's face was turned into a soup.

He stood up and continued forward as if that hadn't just happened, pushing the bo staff onward with his motion.

Garrett's gaudy pyramid loomed above in the haze, barely visible in the distance.

I watched Garrett die....

Belford had to keep reaffirming his memories in order to stop them from fading into obscurity. He'd seen so much death....

Gord and his brawny mass made a sudden right turn as the street before them crossed with a larger throughway. The bo staff stuck with Gord.

Catatonic citizens—eerie ghosts lingering in the cloud—stood dazed in the street. Their minds were deep under the spores' control. Gord scanned each one as he passed. None were Goblikans. Belford was glad for it. He did not wish to witness another slaughter.

The spore cloud drew thinner as they reached the edge of the harbor and continued alongside the water. Visibility along the promenade increased with every step they took until they suddenly burst from the cloud entirely.

Gord ceased his lumbering strides, breathing hard. He turned back around to face the mist for a moment, shaking his head. He spat on the ground in disgust, clearing the taste of the spores from his mouth. He continued on at a slower pace for a moment before reaching out and snatching the bo staff out of the air with a perfectly timed swipe.

"Where are my friends?" Belford demanded to know now that they were clear of the fog. He was unable to recall the last time he'd seen Shiara, Vera, or any of the others. A sinking feeling tugged at his heartstrings.

Arlin put a consoling hand on Belford's shoulder. He tried to speak, but his over-tightened vocal cords rasped at the strain.

Gord didn't look back. "There's no saving people from that," he said. "If they escape, they will head west."

Belford hacked a lungful of mucus onto the ground—yellowed, as if full of pollen. He was too deep in his confusion to argue as Gord and Arlin ushered him further from the mist.

CHAPTER
9

Escaping Tavallon

As the lowly flat slowly filled with spores, the desperate situation Shiara and company found themselves in was quickly coming to a head. Soon, there would be no clean air left to breathe and they would all fall into a catatonic stupor.

"What will happen if the other Goblikan's find us here?" asked Eben, the shortest amongst them. He was already beginning to look glassy-eyed. He would be the next to succumb to the spores. The surviving Naffeim brother, Ader, was already well into a daze. Propped up against the wall, his burns oozed with clear plasma. His shivers continued, but his pained grunts ceased the moment the spores overtook his senses. Perhaps it was a mercy for him.

Wilgoblikan, for once in his miserable life, looked fearful—yellow, wide-eyed panic consumed his face. It would have been amusing to Shiara had the danger not been such a threat to them all. "We should place the towels over our faces and make a run for it!" Wil suggested, stepping over to Eben, intent on taking the towel from the boy's window to use for himself.

Eben shouldered Wilgoblikan away from him.

"Touch him again and I'll bash yer head in!" Captain Bundles growled angrily.

Wilgoblikan stepped back, throwing his hands up in exasperation as he paced the floor like a cornered rat. "Your merry band of assassins will not find the freed Goblikans to be merciful. If we are caught, we will be executed. I was a member of the Special Guard—highest amongst the Goblikans. We ruled harshly. I daresay the others will not forgive me either." He was speaking directly to Ethan.

Ethan silently took stock of the linens available to them. He approached Grine with an intense stare. "The towels will work better than the sheets," he said solemnly as he placed a hand on the edge of the towel in Grine's window. "We've held the spores off as long as we can. You and you—" he pointed at Grine and Shiara, the only other Ver'ati in the group, "grab towels and let's go."

"There's no way that's going to work!" cried Grine.

"We can't just leave these people!" Shiara blocked the door with her body.

"That was an order!" shouted Ethan.

Wilgoblikan took the moment of discord to shove Eben aside and rip his towel from the windowsill. "Every man for himself!"

Ethan did the same to Grine, selfishly taking the window covering and holding it over his nose and mouth as he rushed at Shiara. Wilgoblikan got to her first. Shiara squared up with the Goblikan, but Ethan joined him and together they threw her from the doorway. It all happened so fast—before she knew it, the door was pried open and the two reprehensible men disappeared into the fog.

"Mother-loving cowards!" yelled Captain Bundles as he ran to his son's side.

"They've doomed us all," Grine lamented, shocked by the suddenness of the attack against him. He picked himself up off the floor as the mist poured in unabated through the uncovered windows and doorway.

Shiara placed a finger against her firestone earring—it still wasn't completely cooled yet, but it was usable to some degree. She had an idea. "Everyone stay close to me!"

Captain Bundles hefted Ader up over his shoulder and joined Coriva, Eben, Grine, and Vera, already at Shiara's side.

Shiara's understanding of the spores was that they were tiny living creatures—a modified psychoactive fungi. She had no idea if her firestone earring would work to disable them, but it was all she had. She focused her thoughts through the Artifact and into the encroaching fog. The gem dangling from her lobe began to glow as it activated. Normally, she would pull all the energy out of an area and the affect would linger as a dangerous static field. This time, she refined the gem's hunger into tiny bursts that she shot forward until the gem's reach waned. The cloud before her responded with an electric shimmer. The airborne spores dropped to the floor like grains of falling sand. She had no idea how many shots she would get.

"Let's go!" she cried as she ran out through the cleared path.

Another blast from the earring sucked the energy out of the spores in a streak down the street. Everyone stayed close behind her as she fine-tuned the Artifact's draw. The last thing she wanted to do was accidentally drain herself! She could still taste the spores in the air despite her best efforts.

They hadn't gone more than fifty paces before they found Wilgoblikan and Ethan standing side-by-side, their towels heaped on the ground before them. They did not respond to the group's approach, already lost to the spores' influence.

Useless pricks.

She shot another energy-sapping wave past them. There was nothing anyone could do for them now. The rest of the group continued on through the Artifact's wake, moving back towards the harbor. Shiara could tell the gem was starting to get hot again as it bounced painfully against her upper neck on a smooth patch of previously burned skin.

They were yet to reach the edge of the fog when they came across a row of baggage carts at the top of one of the docks. Shiara eyed the carts with a grimace.

"Don't you even think about going back for them," said Grine upon seeing her lingering expression.

Just beyond the dock, a large drainage pipe jutted out from the rocks along the water's edge. A steady airflow—spore-free—blew from the tunnel. Shiara glanced back at the baggage carts, her heart pounding as she considered her duty to the Ver'konus.

"They wouldn't do the same for you," said Grine.

Shiara closed her eyes, steadying her wavering thoughts. "Our chances of making it back to Phandrol are better with them," she said.

Grine turned to look at Vera and the remaining Rosa Marsa crew, squinting through his nearsighted eyes. They were already making their way into the drainage pipe's opening. His shoulders drooped—a sad, puppy-dog expression falling across him. He knew Shiara was right. "Let's make this snappy," he said.

Shiara sent another blast back towards the carts. The fog had already flowed in to fill the gap she made previously. The paved ground in front of them appeared to shimmer along with the air. At first, Shiara thought it was an effect of her firestone earring, but she quickly came to realize it was her own vision that was wavering. The spores were winning the battle for her mind.

They moved fast, wheeling the carts back towards the arrogant fools they'd left behind. As they passed a tree standing in a planter, the limbs appeared to form an arm, waving oddly at Shiara as she passed. Everything was dancing around her with a disorienting wiggle as she bounded along desperately behind her cart. Her mind was beginning to escape all reality and reason.

When they finally reached Ethan and Wilgoblikan again, Grine helped her shove the idiots into the carts. They fell with unceremonious bangs against the wooden interiors.

Shiara's vision began growing dark around the edges, but soon the darkness was replaced with flashes of brilliant color. If it wasn't so concerning, it would have been beautiful. Her feet nearly tripped her up as she began to lose control. She could barely focus as she ambled back towards the harbor once more.

The last thing she remembered was trying to send another burst out from her earring, but feeling it resist—its capacity full to the brim. Swirling colors and strange thoughts that weren't quite her own streamed through her beguiled mind. A wild trip overtook her perception as she left her body behind and fluttered after a shimmering fairy that slipped into the distance down a forested path. All the rocks and leaves to either side of her laughed joyously. She continued further away from herself, absorbed by a giant mandala of geometric shapes that flashed in sequence, rewiring the very synapses of her brain.

CHAPTER
10

Ain't No Captain

Vera gripped the hem of her dress anxiously. Shiara and Grine had been gone for far too long. The drainage tube flowed with a steady stream of ankle-deep gray water. The smell was less-than pleasant, but the lack of any cardamom notes in the air meant they were safe from the spores, at least, for now.

The crew of the Rosa Marsa lingered in the darkness as Captain Bundles fumbled around in his coat for the box of matches he carried alongside his pipe.

"They're goners," said Bundles as he struck up one of his matches. A permanent dark glower was etched upon his brow, illuminated by the tiny flickering flame.

"What are we gunna do, papa?" asked Eben. "Ader needs healing."

Bundles puffed out his cheeks as he lit his pipe. A wisp of smoke trailed down the tube and out into the harbor. "All the

Ver'ati are lost," he said stoically through the pipe's mouthpiece. "I'm 'fraid Ader is lost too."

The hopeless stillness on the captain's face was terrible to witness. Vera had the same hollow feeling in her gut. Without a healer, Ader was as good as dead. The poor man was propped against the side of the pipe, eyes open, but not present in the least with his mile-long stare. There was no telling if the spores would clear out of his system on their own. At least his catatonic state appeared to mask awareness of his burns.

"'Least the air is clean," said Bundles. "Let's continue on and pray we find our way out of this deathtrap of a city."

Coriva held Eben to her chest as he softly cried.

Bundles lit another match for light after the first one burned away. He took several steps deeper into the tube before Vera spoke out: "You're just going to leave him like this, captain?" she asked. "He's part of your crew!"

"He was," Bundles retorted with a snap. "Now he's dead because of you lot. And don't call me captain! I ain't no captain, not with Rosie sunk."

"But he's not dead yet!" Vera couldn't believe his callousness. "We need to wait until the fog clears and go back for Shiara and Grine, it's his only chance!"

"He's as good as dead," said Bundles. "They all are. The spores have taken their minds! Can't you see it, girl?!" He gestured sharply at Ader. He took another puff off his pipe. His shoulders slumped. "We have to escape the spores—get outta this city—there ain't any other choice to be made." He was clearly resigned in his decision to abandon Ader.

"I can't leave him like this," said Vera, "it's wrong!"

"Do what you must," said Bundles. "I'm gettin' my family to safety." He turned away again and began walking deeper into the darkness.

Eben continued to sniffle. He stepped over to Ader one last time and shook his shoulder. "Come on, wake up," said the boy, but Ader's mind was deep inside itself.

Coriva grabbed Eben's wrist and pulled him into her once more. "Come on, sweet boy," she said, hugging him tightly before steering him after Bundles into the darkness.

Vera stood, mouth agape. Tears welled up in her eyes.

Coriva turned to her before departing. "Good luck," she said softly. "I pray you'll find Ader the help he needs." Her mouth tightened into a tight frown as she departed.

Vera sat in silence for a long while, staring across the tube at Ader as she contemplated the misery of life. The air remained clear in the tunnel as the lingering spore cloud outside only grew more dense.

After some time, her training kicked in and she grabbed at the pouch of herbs cinched around her waist. She always carried it with her. She had been Ethan's nurse for years when he was still an old man. She knew how to treat a burn.

She didn't have any aloe, but she did have ground marigold powder and a fresh roll of gauze. Typically, ointment was not administered for the first day to avoid sealing in a burn, but Ader was in a bad way. His oozing skin would become infected if she did nothing. He didn't respond at all to her touch as she gently wrapped a selection of his burns. The severe ones still needed to breathe. The risk of his skin sloughing off was too high on his left arm and shoulder in particular. She could only hope her treatment would bring some relief if he managed to reemerge from the spores' influence.

She stayed at Ader's side as night fell. There was little she could do to keep him warm apart from shimmying up close and provide him with as much of her own body heat as possible. The darkness of the night was so dense she could barely make out his hunched form as she shivered in the darkness by his side. Her feet fought against the curved edge of the tube. The strain in her toes was becoming increasingly painful.

Beyond the tube, the moonless, spore-filled sky made her feel lost in the darkness. Eventually, the moon arose in the early hours of the morning, but only the rising of the sun brought a reprieve to her sleepless purgatory. With the daylight came winds, gusting from out of the east. Slowly but surely the spores began to dissipate from the tranquil streets. Many hours later, once the air beyond the tunnel became completely clear, Vera finally dared to venture out to see what had become of the lost Ver'ati. To her chagrin, several Goblikans had already found them first. Shiara and Grine had nearly made it back to the pipe—they were hunched over the handles of their baggage carts just shy of the head of the dock.

Vera stayed low against the rocks as she cursed her misfortune. If only she had ventured out sooner when the spores first began to thin! The Goblikans placed Shiara and Grine roughly into the carts already containing Ethan and Wilgoblikan and began to wheel them north.

She briefly prayed to Mast for Ader's safety. At least the sky was clear—there would be no rain to wash him away! She stayed far back, but began to trail after the Goblikans.

The city was slowly rousing from the stupor of the spores. Civilians peeked their heads out of windows and doors, confused expressions abound.

Vera knew there was not much she could do against a Goblikan—let alone a city full of them!—but even so, she kept them in sight. Everyone's lives were riding on her now.

CHAPTER 11

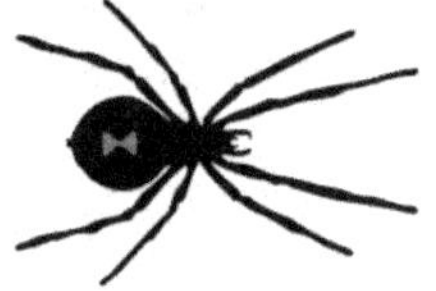

Step Two: Expand

King Garrett's residence within the pyramid cathedral was located at the exact center of the structure. It was perhaps the gaudiest display of power and ego to have ever existed. Livian's eyes lingered upon the four-story-tall relief carving that resided across from the indoor promenade on which Garrett's golden bed was perched like a dais before a god.

The carving—an unrealistically handsome version of Garrett's face—was sculpted into a seamless slab of white marble. A dark layer of Calvenite sat behind the polished stone, providing contrast and security. Garrett's face smiled down at her menacingly. It was even creepier at night when the uplighting brought out the deep shadows across the massive façade. The flickering flames really brought his presence alive.

She did have to admit that the sounds of the vast fountain basin beneath the carving did at least make for pleasant white-noise as she tried to sleep—unsuccessfully—on her first night within the pyramid. A waterspout show repeated at the strike of every hour. This strange place was hers and Deenan's refuge now.

The only natural light that made it to the center of the pyramid came from a singular shaft constructed entirely from a clear, sturdy material. The shaft encased a mechanical lift that Garrett used in place of stairs to move vertically from the pyramid's great depths, all the way up to a transparent room at the very tip of the imposing structure.

Monster Master Dhron was proving to be a very helpful servant to their cause. He'd given Deenan detailed instructions on how to better impersonate Garrett. The former king had a daily ritual of riding the lift up to the pinnacle where he would masturbate over all of Tavallon, drizzling down the front of the structure like a nasty little bird shit.

Dhron's hand gestures added to his visceral description.

Deenan refused to partake in the despicable practice, but he didn't want to deviate too much from Garrett's typical routine. The view from the top was mightily impressive. He was up in the tip now, getting acquainted with the place. Garrett's strong sexual appetite was officially on hiatus, though. Deenan ordered Dhron to send away all of Garrett's mistresses and personal servants. Livian hoped life would treat the women more kindly going forward.

As the hourly fountain display completed, Livian felt the moon descend beneath the horizon, taking with it her control over the Power. This was the perfect time to dose more Goblikans with spores. Barring any unexpected Power Artifacts, the Power was unreachable by all, but her spores did their work no matter the position of the moon. It was much less dangerous to dose wizards when they had no way of fighting back. Livian thought of herself as a black widow spider—her special poison made her the apex predator. She was yet to find anyone who could counter her attack. Dhron's terrible lizard had been her closest call.

With the spore cloud above Tavallon dissipated, Livian's efforts to create a network of loyal Goblikans began with a great boon, but soon stalled out. Twenty-eight trained dark wizards wandered into the Pyramid around first light with the spores' passing, but in the hours that followed, the new arrivals ceased. Counting Dhron, Livian had twenty-nine Goblikans on her side by the time she was done with their realignments. They were each madly in love with her now. It was a good start, but there were hundreds of Goblikans in the city she still needed to convert. It would be interesting to see how many would answer her "restructuring" declaration. Her turned-Goblikans were staying close at hand, guarding the cathedral grounds. Concernedly, the chaos Livian had expected to arise did not entirely manifest. She knew order did not just maintain itself. Someone was controlling the rest of the horde.

It soon became clear that the free Goblikans were amassing an alliance. They refused her minions access to the larger city of Tavallon. It was worrisome that they were surrounded by Garrett's former puppets. Regardless of whether or not they believed Deenan's version of Garrett to be legitimate, they all had reasons to despise Garrett and the Arcanum alike.

"Don't you think the King should be finished by now...?" asked Sir Kierington, pacing the walk between the central lift and the main gallery corridor—Garrett had a lot of wall art. Sir Kierington was now captain of the guard. "Will you ride up with me?"

"Maybe he's trying for a two-fer," said Livian. Even though Deenan probably wasn't masturbating, she knew he would prefer to spend his downtime without disturbance.

Kierington was insistent. "He will be less angry if we go together. I have an important report to give him." While the knight had not been dosed with love-spores like the Goblikans Livian was collecting, she could sense that he had a naturally strong affinity towards her. She enjoyed teasing him. The attraction went both ways. It was a natural flirtation. Kierington was strong and capable, and far more grounded—less brainwashed—than Livian had anticipated from any of Garrett's guard. He was a fighter at heart, perhaps a little simplistic for Livian's taste, but his intelligence was still within the standard range. She enjoyed how his hardened demeanor was belied by softer undertones when he spoke with her.

Livian obliged his request, joining him on the see-through lift. It started its rise at the press of a button; machinery whirred as tightly woven cables lifted them straight up into the air.

"I've been meaning to ask…" said Sir Kierington. "I've seen what you've done to the Goblikans. The mist…."

Livian tensed up at the change in conversation. Her right hand, already deep in her petticoat pocket, began fumbling around for the correct vial of spores to end the line of questioning before he had a chance to even begin.

"How does it make them love you?" he asked pointedly.

Her fingers fumbled over her restocked stash of various spore varieties. She felt across the ridged caps with her fingertips. The wrong vial could kill them both instantly in such an enclosed space. It was important she chose the right one.

Sir Kierington turned towards Livian, observing her as she internally panicked over not being able to find a suitable vial fast enough.

"I just want to know how it works," he said. "It's obvious you are not Compelling them like the King—he needs his scepter to remove their defenses for that—yet, still, the wizards all just accept you as their leader… they love you."

Perhaps Kierington was less simplistic than Livian assumed. As the lift reached the top of the chamber and slid into the ceiling, they were bathed in sunlight from the clear pinnacle above.

Livian's fingers finally found the correct vial—the subtle curve of a heart was etched upon the stopper. "I can show you," she said calmly, withdrawing the clear tube into the open.

Kierington looked on with curiosity.

"You see," said Livian as she began working on removing the tightly wedged rubber end, "the spores tell you a story—my story." The stopper finally came loose. "They implant some of my memories into your mind. Enough that you are able to truly understand me on a deep, personal, fundamental level." The spores were dense—they remained mostly in the vial as she held it up, only small tendrils reaching above the lip as she jostled the tube.

"Unnatural..." said Sir Kierington, shifting backwards on the balls of his feet away from the open vial.

"On the contrary," said Livian. "It's the ultimate dose of empathy and intimacy. We love ourselves—well, most of us do anyway—and so by taking a whiff of this you integrate me into your understanding of yourself. What's more natural than love?" She shifted the vial closer to Kierington's nose. He pinched up his face, rejecting the offering.

The lift reached its stopping point and the door began to slide open automatically. Sir Kierington stepped free before the door finished opening all the way. "I've seen what you've done to Dhron," he said warily. "Would you really want to change me like that?"

Livian let out a genuine laugh. "He did receive perhaps a bit too much! How about just a little sniff, then? It won't harm you. It's actually a very enlightening experience." He had too many questions. Livian would be dosing him one way or another.

"I must decline," said Kierington. "I'm not one for collectives. Besides, it would be best if we all kept our heads straight and focused for the moment at hand."

Livian's eyes took in the rest of the pinnacle chamber. The tinted glass diminished some of the harshness of the sun. She looked for Deenan in the hopes of backup with her attack on Sir Kierington. She was disturbed to find additional guests.

Three Goblikans in specialized suits that gave them artificial gliding wings stood perched beside Deenan.

They must have flown up and entered through the balcony before moondown!

They were decked out in light-armor and goggles. Short blades attached to their arms protruded out from under their suits. One Goblikan had his blade held to Deenan's throat. A glance back at Kierington showed a pointed lack of surprise in his expression. He'd played her. She'd been a fool. A lamb led to slaughter.

"Put the stopper back in," Kierington ordered. "You've already been inside my mind enough. You aren't really King Garrett's top advisor, are you? And that's not even really King Garrett!"

She glowered at Kierington as she fumbled with replacing the stopper.

A gesture from one of the Goblikans dismissed the knight. He met Livian's eyes as he stepped back into the lift.

"And here I thought things had been progressing jovially," Livian said dryly. She blew a kiss gently over the top of the stopped-up spore vial, aiming the air in Kierington's direction. She knew it was a useless gesture with so few spores having spilled, but Kierington was less certain. He cocked his head nervously as the door slid shut and the lift dropped from view.

She turned her attention back towards the winged Goblikans. The man she presumed to be the leader of the pack approached a bench. "Join me," he said.

Livian's coat jingled and clinked as her spore vials jostled together in her pocket with her movement.

The lead Goblikan's facial skin was leathery and cracked from sun exposure. He slid his goggles up onto his forehead, revealing pale skin underneath. He had piercing blue eyes and an unkempt bush of a beard—jet black with several streaks of gray. He wore a hawk emblem on a patch on his right arm. His unit's reputation preceded itself. He was a Night Hawk, an elite aerial fighting unit. There were very few Night Hawks, because their method for flying was excessively dangerous and led to a decrease in life expectancy. The level of physical fitness and skill required to finesse the winds was very high. To be part of this unit was a great honor to the Goblikans before her. It spoke to a fearless mindset, as well as a sort of *unhinged* competency.

"Finally, the person who is actually in charge," said the Goblikan, eyes locked on Livian. He pointed over at Deenan. "Very convincing, but I knew the real Garrett well."

"I'll take our ongoing existence as a sign you are a reasonable man," said Livian as she took a seat beside the Night Hawk.

Deenan grunted as the Goblikan at his back roughly trimmed a few neck hairs off of him with his arm-blade.

"We see the value in your deception," said the lead Goblikan. "We may allow it to continue. But do not mistake that for weakness."

"Let's not get off on the wrong foot," said Livian.

"My name is Nal Viershin. My cohorts and I represent the Free Goblikan Alliance. We will not be re-subjugated—by anyone. We have no interest in joining the odd haram you've created here."

"Understood," said Livian.

Nal's hardened stare was deadly serious. "You are alive because we do not wish for the kingdom to fall apart. Your cooperation will make that goal more attainable." Nal abruptly slapped his leg, making Livian flinch. "Alas, agreement amongst the Goblikans is proving difficult to attain! I believe your skills may be of assistance." Nal stood up and offered out a large callused hand to Livian.

Livian furrowed her brow as she allowed Nal to take her hand. As he pulled her back up to her feet he twirled her around in an effortless spin, during which he ran a thin rope around her middle and hooked it back to himself with a clasp on the front of his outfit. "Place your ass on me," he said. Livian turned on her own this time, hesitantly. Nal attached an additional harness over her shoulders like a backpack. He pulled her rope tight, bringing her posterior against his pelvis. Livian felt his girth and broad legs pressing up against her through his light armoring.

Nal readjusted his goggles back over his eyes before walking her over to the opening to the balcony.

"I really don't care for heights!" cried Livian. Everything was happening so fast!

"Stay rigid, or we'll drop too quickly from your drag."

"Can't we just walk out the front door?!"

Nal let loose an amused chuckle as he dragged Livian up and over the edge of the balcony like a doll in his arms.

"It really is a perfectly good door!" Livian let out a high-pitch scream as Nal jumped and spread his arms and legs wide. The cloth of his suit caught the air and kept them aloft, barely above the angle of the pyramid as they descended until an updraft finally gave them some additional lift.

Livian continued to scream. The vials of spores in her pocket banged together dangerously as she soared beyond the royal grounds on the belly of a Night Hawk.

CHAPTER 12

The Great Device

Rylin slid on his butt down the lumpy tunnel. The air did indeed become warmer as the passageway descended, plotting a meandering spiral deep into the Earth. In the lead, Kamila slowed as she noticed a low vibration in the stone beneath her paws. The rattle was barely audible. Rylin recognized it as the ambient sound of machinery in the distance. It reminded him of the old metal tooling factory back home in Shian City, servicing the large shipyards.

Kamila proceeded apprehensively.

"Who made these tunnels?" asked Rylin. They were clearly too small for all but the bear cubs to pass through.

"Mama says this is where the last of the humans once lived," said Kamila.

Rylin couldn't imagine why anyone would want to live so deep underground—*Unless they were hiding....* "Did the Paerto'sul kill all the humans?" he asked pointedly.

Kamila paused and glanced back at Rylin with a slow turn of her head. The bears did not have obvious expressions like people did, of course, but Rylin felt uneasiness in her dark eyes. She turned back around without answering. "We shouldn't be going this way," was all she said.

Tanuk hadn't exactly given them much of a choice in the matter.

As they scooted along in the dark, Rylin couldn't help but succumb to claustrophobia. His breath quickened. It was too warm to have the tunnel walls pressed right up in his face as they were. He'd rarely felt such a panic before in his life—one time when he was eight he'd been rolled up in a rug by his sister Ellis. She was the closest in age to him of all of his four siblings, but she was still six years older than Rylin. She hadn't always been the nicest to him, but he would have done anything in that moment to see her sweet face again.

Another time, when he was ten, he'd hidden in a trunk during a game of hide and seek, accidentally becoming stuck for several minutes. It felt like a very long time to him in the moment. Screaming out his hot breath left him sweaty and hoarse in the throat. Not being able to stand up in the tight tunnel now was triggering for him.

At the same time, he was grateful for the small space—it kept him out of Tanuk's jaws—but the suppressive feeling made him long for the open air of the sea. He closed his eyes for a moment and pretended he could smell the salty mist of the morning fog back home, but try as he might he was unable to trick his mind—there was simply too much dust and heat filling his nostrils. The warmth of their breath added to the already humid air of the tunnel.

By the time they reached a wider chamber it felt like a furnace was venting into the room. "Why *is* it so hot down here?" Rylin asked.

"The Great Device," said Kamila, as if that answered anything.

Rylin shined his light across each chamber they moved through. He noted the rooms were becoming progressively larger as they went on. The heat continued to grow, but at least the walls were not so tight anymore. The dust that littered the floor was undisturbed, so he wasn't expecting any surprises, but there was only so much he could relax knowing that Tanuk was still out there somewhere, hunting for him.

Rylin led the way now, Kamila walking sheepishly in the rear. She didn't know the way forward any better than he did at this point. They were in a forbidden place, after all. There was no telling how the passages intertwined. He had to assume Tanuk knew his way around the depths better than they did. The ambient hum continued to grow louder the deeper they stepped into the ancient bunker until Rylin could feel the vibrations shooting right up through his feet.

The source of all the rumbling and heat was finally revealed to him when they reached a wide, spherical chamber. A contraption at the center of the perfectly carved cavern measured about sixty paces wide and stood equally as tall. The untarnished construct of metal rings, cables and vent tubes rattled mysteriously beneath a host of deteriorating Calvenite fittings and catwalks. Rylin froze in place as a series of clicks sounded from within the strange machine.

He knew without a doubt that he was gazing upon the Great Device. The lack of degradation on its parts told Rylin that the device was an enormous Power Artifact. There was no other way that Rylin could think of for it to have outlasted its Calvenite fittings. The clicks clanging out from inside the machine warned him that it was reacting to his presence.

Several massive silver rings along the outside of the chamber connected back to the central device by rods that ran horizontally through the contraption's center like spokes on a wheel. The rings began to turn slowly, rotating freely from each other's axes.

Rylin and Kamila both had to stand clear as the outer rings periodically shifted across the chamber's openings. The speed of the rings was slowly increasing.

"What's it doing?" Rylin asked Kamila, in awe.

A booming voice rang out, startling them both. Words rolled through Rylin's head simultaneously, sounding in a harsh whisper inside his mind. *"The Heart of Sultrim beats once more."* He instantly knew it to be Ma'freit. The telepathic bear was reaching into his thoughts to implant the words as she spoke. He would have heard them even without ears.

Kamila yelped and tucked her tail as the de facto leader of the Paerto'sul entered the chamber on the opposite side of the room.

CHAPTER 13

The Endless Spring

Ma'freit was not the leader of the bears simply because she was the eldest. Nor was it her telepathic abilities—though that certainly didn't lessen her claim, others amongst the Paerto'sul had inklings of that talent as well. The bears had chosen Ma'freit to keep order because she was the biggest, most ferocious Guardian of the Sun to have existed in several generations.

When fully grown, female Paerto'sul were always larger than their male counterparts. Tanuk would have barely stood to Ma'freit's shoulders if they both were to stretch up on their hind legs. Tanuk's head would have fit snuggly in her jaws as well. Ma'freit's fur, deep brown and shiny with natural oils, was thick and bristly. She had few scars, unlike some of the other bears, simply from the fact that few throughout her life had dared to challenge her supremacy. For many years she had commanded the bears by sheer might and fortitude.

Ma'freit may have been the eldest of the bears, but she was only thirty-five years old. Rylin had been surprised to learn from ten-year-old Raljaska that the Paerto'sul usually had a lifespan of around forty years, only really slowing down from age in their final year or two of life.

Kamila, hiding behind Rylin from Ma'freit's dead-eyed gaze, was well-spoken for a cub of just one and a half years old. The bears were frighteningly brilliant. Given their intellect, it felt a little odd to Rylin that their society respected physical prowess more than anything else. He resolved that it was simply in their nature. Each bear was a formidable force all on its own. Ma'freit… she was truly a terrifying tank of a beast.

Rylin swallowed a glob of thick saliva at the back of his throat as the old bear eyed him flatly. The rings of the churning machine at their side continued to accelerate in their motion.

"Come," Ma'freit grunted. "Or we'll soon be trapped." She turned around, pausing briefly to allow one of the Great Device's metal rings to pass in front of the opening before quickly trodding out of the chamber.

Rylin and Kamila followed after the large guardian. As they strode past the device, Rylin noticed his body fill with a static charge. His hair began to stand up as the current flowed through him. Kamila's fur behaved similarly, lifting to one side to line up with some unseen field the device was generating.

"Tanuk has been trying to eat us," Rylin mentioned as he hopped through the opening before the next ring arrived. His hair continued to stand on end, even as they left the chamber behind. His skin tingled all over.

"Tanuk is wont to doing things the old ways," said Ma'freit, not pausing in her stride.

The old ways referred to the physical laws of nature—survival of the biggest and meanest….

"To kill a cub is against my laws," Ma'freit continued. "I very much doubt Tanuk would have eaten Kamila."

Rylin frowned—an anxious bubble forming in his gut. *Is she not going to protect me??* He had hoped for at least a little reassurance!

"You must earn my protection, human-cub," said Ma'freit. She did not glance back.

She's already reading my thoughts!

"Ma'freit knows all," confirmed the great bear.

Kamila eyed Rylin momentarily.

"We have arrived," said Ma'freit as she passed through an archway and out onto a grand embankment.

The ceiling disappeared above them in the wide cavern. Rylin shined his light across the sloped stone and then out at the sprawling reservoir of still water.

"The Endless Spring!" cooed Kamila, frolicking down to the water's edge like an excited puppy.

"This is where our kind come to birth our cubs," explained Ma'freit. "The salt cleanses all."

An underground salt lake....

Sultrim never ceased to amaze Rylin. The water may not have actually been endless, but it was wide enough for his light beam to disperse into obscurity rather than illuminate the other side.

"We will have to suspend our practice. Your presence here has reawakened the city," said Ma'freit. "The Great Device senses your Ver'ati blood. Now this basin is charging with energy."

Kamila, who had been about to enter the water, took a step back. Her fur was standing on end again, this time being drawn towards the basin.

Behind them, down the tunnel to the Great Device, a sequence of clicks carried their way. Artificial lights sprang to life, shining brilliantly with a blue hue despite the centuries of stagnation. Rylin turned and watched as the glow brightened—additional sources gleaming from recessed positions within nondescript holes in the rotting Calvenite ceiling of the passageway. They continued to turn on one-by-one until the sequence split in two at the tunnel's arched exit. From there, they began to wrap around the outer wall of the saltwater basin.

The walls curved inwards, forming a giant circle that Rylin could now see as the lights ran their illumination into the distance. The lines eventually connected back together again on the other side of the gap. The distance made the spots of light look like stars on the horizon.

"Do you know why we're down here?" asked Ma'freit, unfazed by the changes.

Rylin slipped his lightglove into his pocket. He wondered what else might have been powered on across the city. The founder of Sultrim, John Graven, was said to have introduced many miracles to Aragwey. Much had been lost to the tides of history.

Ma'freit was staring into his soul.

"—Uh—sorry… yes, Corshen said you sensed humans tunneling beneath the mountain with the Power. It's what's causing the earthquakes."

Ma'freit turned her massive head to gaze back over the basin. "This is the closest point within Sultrim's caves to the humans' tunnel. They are still too far away for me to read their intentions, but I have assessed their presence. What would it mean to you to learn their numbers include many entities that are not human?"

Rylin narrowed his eyes.

"Their auras are dark—their drives easy to ascertain," Ma'freit continued. "They crave only two things: To please their masters, and to cause pain—suffering. They are tormented slave-creatures."

"Whunes…" said Rylin. There was no doubt in his mind. The humans coming to Sultrim were not there to rescue him. They were Goblikans.

CHAPTER
14

Perfectly Pragmatic

Today was the anniversary of the death of Queen Nestra Elveres—Queen Havorie's beloved mother. Few cared to recall the occasion. None referenced it to Havorie, at the least, but she always felt the day coming about a month in advance. Her darkest hours were always this time of year. Today was an even more somber day than usual, given that she'd fallen straight into Damian's trap.

She'd felt it in her gut for some time now, and with an ever increasing certainly—Captain Damian Sarvo was toying with her.

Who else could have placed the locket there for my people to find? No one else but the killer would have even known to remove that old photograph.

A million questions were running through her mind, but only one explanation.

86

It's a warning.

He wants me to return to being a puppet.

A defiant spark flashed inside of her.

Javic and Ervia stood at her front, side-by-side at the center of the informal meeting hall. A massive version of the royal crest—a blue-and-gold fox—was engrained with actual gold beneath their feet. It encouraged Havorie's attendees to keep their eyes pointed downward. It was an impressive space for an informal meeting hall. Havorie found informal meetings went better when people were reminded clearly of her status. As belittled as her station had become, she was still the queen.

Ervia smartly stared at the floor. Javic, conversely, stood with his fists balled up behind his back like a soldier in a military lineup. He ignored the eye-catching crest as he tracked Havorie's every movement.

Havorie cared little for the anxiety she was causing them as she paced back and forth. She was deep in thought, and had not spoken a word in several agonizing minutes—agonizing to her subjects anyway. Havorie was just trying to think. The looks of shame on their faces at having failed in their task of retrieving the locket were unhelpful to her concentration.

"You burned my mother's photo."

The queen's words after such silence startled Javic. It was funny to Havorie that this well-meaning boy was the most powerful Ver'ati in the city. At this point, he was but a lion cub. She hoped she could still tame him once he reached his full potential.

"I apologize, my queen," said Javic. "I couldn't think of another way of freeing Ervia from Captain Sarvo."

Havorie had briefly lost her composure over the voice box and had indeed ordered Javic to do whatever it took to free Ervia. She just wished that what he had chosen to do had not ended in them losing the only piece of evidence she knew to exist.

"And you're certain there was only the one photo—none of the suitor?" she asked.

"Quite certain," Ervia spoke up.

Havorie's eyes flicked towards the maid. It was possible Damian was not the killer, but he was certainly aiding and abetting the culprit with his actions. He must have gotten to the locket first, removed the photograph of her late mother's "nightingale," and then replaced the empty locket for them to find. But then he'd taken it from them again the moment after they found it…. Havorie didn't know what to make of the puzzle. She was back where she started with no evidence or clues to guide her investigation.

She paused her pacing and glowered at Javic. "You told him you 'made it' with the Power?"

Javic's head drooped in further shame.

"He was obviously the one who placed it there for you to find, which makes what you said such a bold-faced lie. You gave him everything he needs to hang you—which I'm not entirely convinced he won't do, by the way—and then you just completely lied when he already had you caught red-handed."

"I didn't know what else to say. He was taking Ervia."

"Well, he knows you were lying to him since he set the whole thing up. Literally, saying anything else would have been better. All you did was give him even more power by further incriminating yourself."

Ervia chimed in: "Granted it does sound bad, Javic did the best he could in the moment. Lest you forget, Damian was already in control."

Havorie turned towards the young maid in guarded amusement. The mousy girl had been growing bolder with every passing day.

Ervia blushed slightly under her gaze, but continued speaking. "He knows Javic was lying. He knows the locket was your mother's. Anyone who sees it would notice its aged tarnish. It was always obvious that Javic didn't form it with the Power. His lie was just ridiculous enough to get Damian to let us both go. Javic's silly confession only sounded compromising—no Arcanum charge would have held up under closer scrutiny."

Havorie was impressed—Ervia's logic was sound, but her adamant defense of Javic still drew the queen's ire. "And now we are left with nothing," said Havorie.

Ervia lowered her head again whilst Javic's snapped back up defiantly. "We still have each other—Damian would have made Ervia disappear, just like you said he did with your last maid."

Havorie hated when people threw things back in her face. "You are dismissed," she said. "Get out." She turned her body away from the pair and pointed toward the door of her chamber. She knew Javic was right, but she did not want to give him the satisfaction of watching her dig herself into an even deeper hole. They had been in the south tower on her orders. She told Javic to rescue Ervia at all costs. Havorie was responsible. They were her friends and allies—and she needed them now more than ever—but she was also their queen. She needed to maintain her composure.

Their footsteps echoed off the decorative floor until they reached the doorway. There was a creak as it opened, then a pause. Havorie held her posture, refusing to turn back, though the delay was curious.

"You go on," said Javic.

The door clicked shut as Ervia departed without another word.

"I told you to leave," said Havorie.

Her eyes widened in surprise as the young Ver'ati's hand gently grabbed onto her shoulder. She let out an audible gasp as she was drawn around to face Javic.

The disrespect! He released her shoulder at once but remained close—*Inappropriately close!* Havorie nearly opened her mouth to chastise him further, but the scared look on Javic's face quelled her tongue, if only for a moment.

"I'm so terribly sorry that I've failed you," Javic said in a rush. "Sometimes when I'm put on the spot I feel like only the worst possible words come out." He suddenly dropped to one knee and bowed his head, as if only now remembering who he was standing before. "Honesty is really important to me, so I just feel like I need to say this to you—"

Havorie raised an eyebrow as Javic spoke with his gaze lingering just above her knees.

"I kissed Ervia," he said.

Havorie blinked several times.

"In the south tower, when Damian rushed in, we pretended like we were embracing."

Havorie raised an eyebrow. "How is this my concern?"

"It didn't mean anything to me," insisted Javic. "I just did it because I had to. But the whole time, all I could think about was you—" His head tipped back, their eyes meeting again as if for the first time. Javic's face reddened into a deep blush. "—Of getting the locket back to you," he amended.

Havorie frowned. Javic really was a smitten little pup. Havorie reached out with her fingertips and caressed his chin. Javic's expression remained serious. "You should grow some scruff," she said. "You would look much older."

A knock at the door signaled her next meeting was already upon her.

Her eyes remained locked on Javic's for a moment longer. The young Ver'ati intrigued her—from his impressive grasp of the Power, to their quickly evolving rapport. "Enter," she ordered with a boom in her voice. She withdrew her hand from Javic's chin. "Go," she said softly.

Javic snapped to his feet and bowed quickly. He passed Caspin Byron entering with a thick leather ledger under his arm. Javic looked back only once as he closed the door to the chamber behind him.

Caspin, grandson of Havorie's head steward, old Resoldo, kept perfect posture as he approached his queen. There had not been many children in the palace while Havorie was growing up apart from her and Caspin. She'd always been friendly with him. People called him simple, but Havorie knew his mind just worked differently than most. Now, he had grown to be one of her greatest allies.

The large white scars that ran the length of his face where General Aldune smashed him with a glass of brandy were somewhat faded by the work of the Ameliorators. It had taken several sessions, but he was beginning to look less disfigured. The scars would never entirely fade, but Caspin took them in stride.

"Are you looking at these little things?" Caspin asked, running the thumb of his free left hand down the length of his deepest scar—forehead to chin—the slice had just barely missed his eye.

"You look very distinguished," said Havorie with a small smile.

"You should have seen the other guy. He was a bear."

"A brute, I'm sure," Havorie agreed.

Caspin patted the ledger resting under his arm. He looked excited.

"Is that it?" asked Havorie.

"This is it," said Caspin. Havorie followed as he stepped over to a table at the side of the chamber and placed the thick tome down. "January of year eighty-six of the fourth Cycle of the Mark."

The final month of Queen Nestra's life. Today was January twenty-seventh—fifteen years to the day of her mother's death.

"And that contains all of the transactions?"

"Everything. This is the master ledger for the counting house for that month."

Havorie flipped open the ledger. The oiled leather squeaked as the binding stuck to the wooden table beneath. "And you've already perused the whole lot?"

Caspin nodded. "There's nothing out of the ordinary—at least not at first glance. Typical requisitions. The palace needed many supplies that winter. Most purchases were necessities—wheat, corn, barley—but there are also several outliers. I found that the royal photographer you asked me to look into arrived on the second of the month. Unfortunately that's a dead end. He's deceased. But I did discover another oddity." Caspin edged in front of Havorie and flipped through the pages to a specific entry in the back half of the ledger. "Here," he said, pointing with confidence. "This one."

Havorie leaned in to read the tiny scrawl. The line detailed the final payment for a statue, commissioned the spring before by Nestra herself.

"Phens Strouslan," said Caspin. "That was the sculptor."

"What do we know about him?"

"Also deceased."

Havorie frowned. "Why is this curious?"

"Other than the fact that your mother commissioned the work personally?" asked Caspin. "It says the statue was to be placed in the central garden atrium. I've never seen a sculpture by Phens Strouslan in the gardens. It would have been installed mere days before…."

Before Nestra's death. The unspoken words sat heavy in the pause.

"That is curious," admitted Havorie.

"I told you."

"Thank you, Caspin," said Havorie. "I don't know what I'll do with this information, but thank you."

Caspin bowed formally as he scooped the ledger back up under his arm. "You should walk the gardens and see if you can find it," he added as he made for the exit.

"That's… a suggestion." The thought of visiting the gardens on the anniversary of her mother's death was perhaps the most awful idea Havorie had ever heard uttered before in her life, but it was also perfectly pragmatic.

She couldn't decide if she was amused or annoyed to find Javic waiting for her when she stepped out of the meeting hall.

"I assume you still want me on your personal detail today?" asked Javic.

Havorie paused in her steps, looking the poor fool up and down. "You don't know what today is, do you?"

"Tuesday?" asked Javic.

"Are you asking?"

"It's Tuesday," said Javic.

"Today's the day my mother died," said Havorie. She began walking again while Javic's jaw dangled askew.

He had to move double-speed to catch up.

"It's fine," she said. "Why would you know? You're not even Phandolian."

Javic shook his head. "Tarisian," he said. "I grew up on a farm."

Havorie shot Javic a look of consternation. She'd known everything of consequence about him from reading his file before she hired him. Somehow, he still found ways of leaving her speechless. "How delightful," she said.

"I mean, I've done more things than just farming," said Javic. "I'm a really good archer… and um…."

"Just stop," said Havorie. "Stop talking."

Javic's brow wrinkled up, saying a million more words without opening his mouth. Havorie ignored his expression. She continued walking towards the central garden atrium. At least he stayed silent.

Havorie found that the closer she got to the gardens, the slower her legs allowed her to move. By the time she stepped out into the light she felt like she was wading through water. Her whole body was resisting taking her closer to the south tower. She refused to look up at it as she began to walk the winding paths with the solitary goal of locating the commissioned Phens Strouslan statue.

The gardens were beautiful during the spring and summer— well manicured and bright with floral arrangements and a charming mix of both native and foreign vegetation. This time of year, however, the sky was gray and gloomy, and most of the flora was deciduous, so barren sticks with scraggly branches stuck out of the still-damp soil from the previous night's storm. The light would only be good for another hour at best, so she got to her search straightaway and did not dally.

Havorie didn't spend much time in the gardens usually, even during the prettier months. Nestra used to bring her here all the time—fresh air for her fresh baby lungs, but that was a lifetime ago. There wasn't a whole lot to do other than sit on one of the benches and reflect upon life. She usually preferred to be up in one of the towers taking in the views from up high.

Falcon stirring in the deep....

She'd never ceased to feel like a little bird trapped in a cage.

Javic walked along silently behind her as she meandered. The gardens held many statues. At least with all the leaves gone, the various sculptures were easier to locate.

A chiseled doe and buck endlessly drinking from an algae-filled pond had been there her whole life. Moss grew upon their backs and the pond looked scummy. Things used to be better maintained around here. The lack of attention wasn't just due to the offseason. The Crown employed many servants working many jobs all across the city, but there was only one gardener trusted to the task of servicing the grounds, and he was becoming rather aged.

It was a large garden for one man to prune. Responsibilities like cleaning out the pond algae were probably better suited for a younger back than Mr. Einar Banneth possessed. The royal gardener, Einar was an old timer, already tending to the flowers well before Havorie was born. Havorie knew all the old timers and did her best to keep them employed. Einar's talents were unquestionable but his efforts were dwindling with each year that passed. It was not his fault that he was slowing down.

Havorie could hear the gentle whisks of a straw broom hard at work on the other side of the gardens. She continued her search for the Strouslan sculpture.

Girl with Offerings was next along the path. The statue depicted a young child with two plates—one, an offering to Mast, and the other, gifts to the old gods. Mast loved gold, while the old gods preferred berries. Most references to the old gods had been eradicated many centuries ago during John

Graven's reign. Havorie would never admit it around the Ek'radam monks, but she had always had a soft spot for the ways of the old gods. *Girl with Offerings* was definitely not the Strouslan sculpture.

Further ahead, Havorie stepped off the path, making a beeline for the next set of stone figures. They were deep in the brush and obscured from view.

"My queen, your dress," said Javic with an annoying amount of concern for her garment.

Havorie didn't bother looking down as she hiked her dress up farther to avoid the mud. The statues she'd seen in the distance ended up being a series of animals—a stone cat stalking several stone toads on suspended lily pads within a cracked stone basin, empty despite the rain. They were old, but not Strouslan's—a plaque read: "Ferra Gherani."

Havorie sighed. She decided to stop wasting her time and go ask the one person who knew the gardens better than anyone. The sounds of Einar Banneth's sweeping stalled as he eyed the queen's approach. He removed his hat and bowed deeply as she trod down the path towards him.

"Hello, Mr. Banneth," said Havorie.

"My queen!" he exclaimed. "I did not expect to be seeing you on this day!" His cheeks were rosy from the cold. A pile of debris—leaves, bark, and broken limbs—sat beside him. "I must apologize, the storm last night wreaked havoc all across the gardens, I am afraid," he said with a wrinkled frown etched upon his deeply tanned face.

"It is quite alright," said Havorie. "I was actually wondering if you might be able to point me in the direction of a specific sculpture?"

Einar puffed out his cheeks, his face shifting into a grin. "Well, of course, my queen. I know these gardens like the back of my hand."

"Good, good," said Havorie. "The sculptor whose work I seek is named Phens Strouslan."

Einar's grin dropped immediately. "Uh, I'm so sorry my queen, but the sculpture you seek is no more."

Havorie perked up at his immediate recognition. "But there was a statue?"

"Of course," said Einar, eyes wide beneath his wrinkled brow. He turned his head away from Havorie, looking south, and pointed with his broom in the direction of a nearby patch of brambles.

Havorie strode past the old gardener, Javic hot on her heels. Einar watched them go, his cheeks puffed out again as he gripped hard onto the handle of his broom. The sound of sweeping did not return as Havorie stepped off the path once more and skirted the edge of the brambles.

"Is it just me, or was he acting really strange?" asked Javic.

"Quite peculiar," responded Havorie as she forged ahead. She did not stop until she arrived at the edge of the garden, met by a stark Calvenite wall.

"Under there," said Javic, pointing at the spiky stems of a rose bush, its tendrils reaching like vines up the side of the wall. There were no buds this time of year, only thorns. Beneath the bush, remnants of a broken stone pedestal could be seen.

"Help me pull those back," she ordered Javic.

He sprang into action, using the thick sleeves of his Ver'ati robes to shield himself from the thorns as he pried back the vines so that Havorie could get a closer look.

A plaque with Phens' name resided at the base of the broken pedestal surrounded by dead thorns. She had to lean in close to read the rest of the writing. According to the plaque, the statue had been named "Nightingale," but nothing remained of it apart from the cracked stone of its base.

This is it....

Havorie's heart began to beat faster as a terrible realization soon settled in. She took a step back from the bush of thorns as a dreadful haze fell across her. Craning her neck up, her eyes followed the tall wall before her. As they drew higher, she knew what she would find. She was standing directly beneath the south tower balcony, right where her mother had fallen all those years before.

CHAPTER
15

A Little Bit of Everything

There was a glaring lack of answers in the search for Queen Nestra's killer. They'd reached a dead end in the royal gardens—*A literal dead end.* Javic stood shirtless at the back of one of the palace's laundry rooms scrubbing at a mess he'd made out of his Ver'ati robe. A red spattering of tomato soup had sloshed all down his front while carrying the bowl back to the guards' barracks. *One careless moment.* He couldn't even manage to eat lunch in peace.

The truth felt tantalizingly close, but it remained elusive, just out of reach. The narrative told by all the evidence had not changed. The secret suitor, Queen Nestra's Nightingale, had ensured that every clue led back to the same hopeless point, dashed at the foot of the south tower. The idea that their investigation was being actively hampered by the murderer wasn't helping Javic sleep at night.

There were select few individuals that he could trust. He could never let his focus drop. Today it was soup, but he knew

98

very well that all of their lives were at risk if he faltered more severely. The constant paranoia—founded or not—was already beginning to wear on Javic's psyche. Despite a comfortable feather-stuffed mattress on his cot in the barracks, Javic had hardly slept a wink at his stationed residence. Only during his shifts protecting the queen was he able to nap for an hour here or there. She understood his anxieties and did not fault him for the less-than-professional demeanor. Havorie went about her business as usual while Javic reclined on sofas or chairs, or rested his head atop one of the large round cushions in the Royal Library.

He was tired. It made him reckless. A stubbly beard of short facial scruff was beginning to take ahold of his chin. Growing the beard hadn't been intentional; he simply hadn't the time for self-care. He didn't have time to be doing laundry either, but here he was. He wondered what Havorie thought of the stubble—she hadn't mentioned anything about it since suggesting he grow it—his hairs were still a bit sparse, which is why he usually shaved them off. Gazing into a mirror on the near wall, he had to admit that the stubble did indeed make him look older.

He flexed his arm muscles, rotating around to view them from different angles. He was already beginning to weaken from his months away from the farm. He frowned at the unfortunate reality. He was still strong, but his shoulders in particular were beginning to look less rounded. His new sedentary life was quickly catching up with him.

He dipped a sponge into the sink at his side. The soapy water was tinged with red from the spilled soup. He continued scrubbing away his reckless indiscretion. He could have pulled the mess out with the Power in an instant, but he was trying to avoid breaking any more laws than were already necessary in his service to the queen.

A rustle of fabric within the sheets strung up all across the chamber behind him brought his attention around. Havorie appeared in between the linens. Her golden curls bounced in tight spirals, framing her pristine face. Her downturned eyes were absolutely seething with irritation as she swept through the sheets.

Javic hoped she was not mad at him. He knew she was frustrated from the lack of answers in their investigation as well. He was certain he was not yet late for his shift at least.

Her expression brightened as she took in his shirtless appearance. "There you are," said Havorie.

"Is all well, my queen?" asked Javic.

"Better now," said Havorie. "I've just finished my meeting with Aldune." Her mood needed no further explanation. The general was never pleasant. Havorie waved her hand dismissively. "I had all the servants stay clear, and keep all the alcohol hidden with them," she said. "You should have seen the way he glowered at me!" A mischievous grin flashed across her face.

Javic beamed back at her. Anything that upset Guther Aldune was a bonus for his day. The general had had it out for him ever since he disobeyed by following him into the Erotos Underground to protect Belford when they first arrived at the Glowing City. That was before Javic joined the Ver'konus. If he were to commit such disobedience now, it would be seen as treason.

"How'd you find me?" asked Javic.

Havorie flashed him a view of her Detector, strapped to her wrist. One of the dials was glowing brightly and pointing directly at Javic. "I can always find you," she said, her brilliant green eyes flashing as she spoke. "You could be anywhere in the city and my Detector would still point right at you. I quite like the certainty, really." She looked Javic up and down with a raised eyebrow. She must have noticed how tired he looked. "When was the last time you bathed? Are you unwell?"

Javic squeezed his eyes shut, dying of embarrassment. "It's not been that long…." He lifted his arm, sniffing at his armpit.

Havorie took a step back.

It wasn't that *bad!*

"I bathed two days ago when you were meeting with the Gravish ambassador," he said confidently.

"That meeting was three days ago, hun," said Havorie, wrinkling her nose in a combination of amusement and scent aversion.

"Wait…" said Javic, realizing a deeper irony in his folly, "what day is it?"

"Saturday?" asked Havorie.

A twinge of sadness struck Javic's heart. "So today's the fourteenth," he said with a quiet disappointment. "That means it's my birthday."

Havorie's eyebrows rose up. "You didn't know it was your own birthday?"

The pity in her voice only made Javic feel worse. Being apart from his grandfather—his only family—was making him feel terribly alone. Sending the swordsman, Orris Fen, to find and retrieve Elric had eased Javic's worry for his grandfather's safety at the time, but with no new news, his absence still weighed heavily upon him.

Havorie could see the sadness all over his face—there was nothing he could do to hide it from her. "It's my grandfather," he said. "I've never been without him on my birthday before."

"I'm so sorry!" cooed Havorie. "Did he pass recently?"

Javic felt his cheeks flush from embarrassment. "Oh, no, nothing like that! He's still alive. He left the city to try to find me when I was transported to Sultrim." Havorie already knew all about Javic's escapade stealing the Artifact Core to the Orb of Parphim right out from under the watchful eyes of the Paerto'sul—he'd gushed about it on one of their first evenings together. Something inside him told him he could trust her. She had, after all, saved his life by choosing him at his Dance of the Elements. "I sent a man to find him, but I've yet to hear anything."

Havorie nodded in understanding.

"He'd usually wake me up early with a special breakfast including my favorite—pancakes—and give me a gift." Elric would finally bestow upon Javic the present he'd acquired during the Autumn harvest festival. They would spend the day playing together and make a big dinner before ending the night telling stories to each other by the fire.

"He sounds like a loving man," said Havorie. "A grand breakfast is exactly what Old Resoldo always arranges for me on all my birthdays as well." A glossy-eyed expression briefly fell across her face.

Javic knew Havorie understood his traumas on a personal level. Separation anxiety was just a fact of life for people like them. They'd both experienced the loss of their parents at a young age. That was not something the body easily forgot. Understanding his affliction did little to lessen his fears of inevitability losing his grandfather one day.

Before Javic realized what was happening, Havorie stepped backwards through the hanging sheets, surveying their surroundings. She came back with focused intent, leaning in and planting a small kiss on the corner of his mouth.

Her lips were so plush and soft! Javic's blush darkened even further as his stomach fluttered deeply.

"I know you're not Phandolian, but a birthday kiss is tradition here," said Havorie. A small amount of color appeared upon her own cheeks as her gaze lingered over his lips. Her eyelashes fluttered momentarily. "Oh, I've just had the most wonderful idea!" she exclaimed. "Follow me!"

Javic quickly threw his damp Ver'ati robe back on over his head and shuffled after Havorie. The queen didn't wait as she exited the laundry room and strode off down the hall. "Where are we going?" asked Javic, his stomach still fluttering with butterflies. Her kiss had perked him up in an instant!

"Hush now," said Havorie. "It's a surprise!"

They rounded the corner by the palace's anteroom, quickly passing the Charisms chamber as they continued down the long corridor, not stopping until they reached the entrance to the northwest tower. She made Javic wait inside while she made a quick call on the voice box in the hallway. He could have used his heightened Ver'ati senses to overhear her if he wanted to, but he plugged his ears instead to maintain the surprise. Soon, Havorie tapped him on the shoulder. They continued on up the stairs until they reached the highest balcony and sat down in front of a narrow table to take in the breathtaking view of the city.

The air was crisp, but the sky was clear. The sun shined down upon them with a glorious radiance that warmed their faces. Far below, the intricate stained glass windows of the Arcanum Cathedral reflected a thousand different colors back up at them. The domed roof held hundreds of ornately carved figures—too small to distinguish their details at such a distance. No one could really see them from the ground either—the artistry felt almost wasted by their placement, but the scope of the detail still inspired awe in Javic as he gazed upon the curved roof.

Beyond the cathedral, the obelisk that greeted approaching vessels was visible atop the defensive battlement wall. Its tip glinted with a golden glow in the sunlight, shining like a beacon. The height of the battlement blocked out the downstream view of the Etto River—a safety feature of the palace's placement—but as Javic traced his eyes up the Etwel branch of the Etto he found he could see all the way to the harbor. The tall masts of some of the ships rose up, framed by the snow-tipped peaks of the Scar of Phandrol beyond, piercing high into the sky far to the south.

The Glowing City was impressive from above—a bustle of activity was abound with First Sense having occurred only an hour before. The moon appeared hazy in the bright blue sky, still fairly low along the western horizon.

"I've always loved the views from up high," said Havorie.

It truly was beautiful!

It was a fact that most people spent their whole lives on the ground looking down. Javic didn't think he would ever tire of a view so grand.

They'd barely had time to chat when a procession of kitchen servants appeared behind them, carrying heaping trays of breakfast food in their arms, despite it already being past noon. The twinge of guilt Javic felt at the extravagance was overwhelmed by the gratitude he had towards Havorie for implementing the kind gesture. It was far too much food, but the massive mounds of pancakes on one of the silver platters were a truly impressive feat for how short of an amount of time they'd spent out on the balcony! It was a feast beyond anything he'd ever experienced in his life.

The sausage links were glistening with fat. The steam rising off of them in the crisp air brought the delicious scent of their drippings to Javic's nostrils. Fried eggs drizzled with a spicy smelling brown sauce had runny yokes begging to be burst. A warm loaf of dark brown bread, sliced and ready to be grabbed, sat in a wicker basket. Its yeasty scent added to the overwhelmingly delicious aroma rising up from the feast.

Honeys and jams sat next to a wide bowl of fluffed up whipped cream beside the mound of pancakes.

"I didn't know if you preferred syrup or a berry compote, so I asked them to bring a little bit of everything," said Havorie.

"I've only ever tried plain…" said Javic, his eyes as wide as saucers. "Are they shaped like crowns?" He was in absolute awe.

"Ah, yes," said Havorie, "they do that."

Javic's eyes danced across the assortment of sides. He approached the whipped cream and used his finger to scoop up a dollop.

Heavenly sweet.

His eyes met with Havorie's as he swallowed it down. "Thank you," he said, his heart filled by her thoughtfulness. "This is amazing!" Javic grabbed a plate and began to serve up. He loaded it with more food than he could eat—the display hardly looked touched.

Havorie sat watching him with a smile.

"Aren't you going to have anything?" he asked upon noticing her lack of interest in the food.

"Oh, no," said Havorie. "I'm quite alright. I don't eat lunch. I usually fast until supper."

Javic scoffed. "Nonsense!" He put his plate down in front of Havorie anyway and began to load up a second portion on a new plate. "All this effort... I can't be the only one eating!"

Havorie narrowed her eyes at the tower of pancakes on the plate before her. Javic finished loading up a second plate and sat down by her side.

"What will they do with what we don't eat?" asked Javic.

Havorie hesitantly cut out a bite with the edge of her fork. "I've no idea, honestly," she said.

"I swear if they just throw it out...."

Havorie scooped a bit of the berry compote on top of her bite. She chewed slowly, deep in thought.

"You should have it given to the poor," said Javic. "Order Damian to serve it up!"

Havorie put her hand in front of her mouth, grinning as she finished chewing. "An angel and a devil all at once, Javic Elensol? You know, I don't think I've ever met anyone quite like you before." She speared up a big bite of pancake slathered in whipped cream, then guided her fork over to Javic's mouth instead of her own. "Take it! You've put way too much on my plate!"

Javic nearly choked as she shoved the bite back too deep. "Easy there," he laughed through the food. "Oh no!" he feigned, staring at Havorie's lips. "I think you've got something right *there*!" He scooped up a teeny bit of whipped cream from his plate and booped it across her lips and the tip of her nose.

She gasped, her jaw falling open as her eyes grew wider. "I don't even think they brought napkins!" she cackled boisterously.

Oh, thank Mast, she's laughing!

"Well that's just a terrible oversight…" said Javic, grinning ear to ear.

Havorie's eyes darted towards the heaping bowl of whipped cream.

"No! Don't you think about it!" cried Javic. The wild streak he was beginning to recognize in Havorie flashed across her face. She dove for the bowl, but Javic—less encumbered in his robe than Havorie was in her dress—got there first on the other side of the table. He yanked the bowl away from her fingers.

Havorie bit her lower lip. "You can't do your queen like that!" she flirted. She put one hand on her hip and extended her other across the table at Javic. "Give me the bowl!"

Javic was grinning so hard his cheeks hurt. "I can't do that! The table is too wide!" He held it slightly closer to Havorie.

She lunged at the bowl but Javic pulled it back again just in time, laughing. He put another dollop on his finger and flicked it at her. It missed to her left, but started them both on a mad dash around the table as Javic tried to keep away from the queen.

Havorie pounced on him as soon as he let her catch up. The whipped cream was too thick to spill as she tackled him to the balcony floor. She playfully scooped up more cream onto her finger and lowered it towards Javic's mouth. He licked it off slowly, their eyes locked all the while. The charge between them was palpable. It made Javic's heart race. He sat up on one arm, holding onto her waist with the other so as not to buck her off.

"Are you just going to stare, or are you going to help clean me up?" she asked.

Javic could have sworn he was floating. His actions hardly even felt like his own as he leaned in closer to Havorie's slightly parted lips. An exhilarating rush overtook his head. Their lips met passionately—the whipped cream melting between them. He felt her tongue reach out, tasting the sugar that had already fallen into his mouth.

Javic closed his eyes as Havorie moaned softly into him. Their kiss began to grow in intensity, tongues becoming more bold as they twisted and played with each other.

Havorie moaned again, this time louder.

Much louder….

Far too loud….

Javic opened his eyes. Havorie wasn't moaning, she was crying out in fear. It hadn't just been in his head, they really were floating! They were already higher than the railing, but thankfully still on the right side of it.

"Stop this at once!" Havorie screeched, her eyes wide with terror.

The moment of realization—that he was levitating—an act known to be deadly for a wizard to partake in—was enough to snap Javic back to attention. He released the Power that he had inadvertently grabbed. The floating turned into falling as Havorie screamed atop him.

They landed hard in the middle of the pancakes, sending half the trays of food tumbling to the balcony floor in a clamor of bouncing silver.

Javic groaned as his lower back took the brunt of the hard landing. Only the fluffy pancakes saved his spine.

Havorie was still straddled on top of him—gripping on for dear life with her thighs.

Several guards stationed nearby ran out onto the balcony to see what the crashing was all about. They shied away again upon seeing Havorie on top and seemingly in control of the situation.

She hopped off of Javic, her face void of emotion. She shot him one last fearful glance as she silently departed from the balcony.

Javic felt like he was going to throw up as he watched her go—her dress covered in a smattering of compote, jams, and jellies.

CHAPTER
16

Official Arcanum Business

Mallory Worvon did her best not to look like a tourist as she walked beside Tyris Orensten through the wide doors of the Arcanum Cathedral's entrance hall. She'd heard about the painted ceiling—it was famously the vision of a master painter brought to life high above her head on the domed ceiling—but she had yet to venture into the sprawling cathedral to witness the artistry firsthand until now. The Arcanum was a place for wizards, not for ordinary people like Mallory.

Tyris, still a mere initiate within the Ver'konus, would not have normally been allowed to enter either, but for the official Artifact Requisition Form clenched between his fingers. It was their badge of entrance to the lavish cathedral. Official Arcanum business.

Their true task was one of subterfuge. The Artifact requisition was just an excuse, penned and stamped by Professor Arius Vanton so that Mallory and Tyris could meet with one of the professor's former students—an ex-pupil by the name of Lyle Stronghelm, once an aid to Councilman Tannel Cresdale, now reassigned to the Archive Historians.

Being an Archive Historian was said to be one of the most deadly jobs within the Arcanum. Pouring over old texts was only part of their duties. The Power Artifacts they worked with—painstakingly deciphering their abilities—were known for their unpredictability. Accidents when dealing with such unknowns were unfortunately common. Being sent to work with the Historians had been a slap in the face to Lyle. Such a transfer was a known way that Councilman Cresdale liked to deal with Ver'ati that no longer fit into his agenda.

Normally, Mallory would not have agreed to anything resembling espionage against a powerful institution such as the Arcanum, but Professor Vanton's design was to discover the truth behind Javic and Rylin being sent to Sultrim. The lingering conspiracy was threatening to pull Javic back in. That's what Mallory and Tyris had gleaned from the professor during a closed-door meeting behind an anti-eavesdropping Artifact. Mallory wouldn't know what to do with herself if Tannel got his way and Javic ended up dead.

Professor Vanton was being watched too closely, so it was up to Mallory and Tyris to meet with Lyle and see what new information he could provide. An unscrewed luminescent bulb to the east of the cathedral had signaled across the Etwon that an urgent meeting needed to be held.

Mallory wished she could have lingered below the painted dome, but alas the best way to avoid unnecessary scrutiny was to keep moving towards the corridor that led to the vast Archives beneath the cathedral's foundation. They already looked too out of place as it were, being the only people not dressed in black robes.

Tyris's muscled physique reminded Mallory of Arlin. She never ceased worrying about his safety. The child growing in her womb was a constant reminder of the man to whom she owed everything. She felt tears welling in the corners of her eyes as she thought about his dangerous journey. Her hormones were all out of whack from the pregnancy, leading to bouts of heightened emotion at the most inopportune moments. Her mind went from Arlin to Javic and back again. She knew she'd hurt Javic by not telling him about her pregnancy sooner, though that had not been her intention. She hadn't expected Javic to latch onto her the way that he had. Until recently, Javic was the only person Mallory even knew in Erotos.

She had, admittedly, clung back onto Javic for support. All her feelings were a tangled mess. She probably shouldn't have kissed him that night when he was getting handsy in her bed. It was a pity kiss mostly, but in the moment she'd also felt the need to know how it would make her feel—if the feelings she was having were true... and the problem was they were! The kiss stirred something within her. Javic wanted her desperately—she could feel his intensity. It was a sensation that Arlin rarely chose to foster within her. For everything that Arlin excelled at, being emotionally open was not one of his strengths. Arlin's absence still ate away at Mallory, though not quite as literally as the baby within, hungering for her very life essence. The calcium in her bones was being stripped away by the life growing inside of her. She wished Arlin had never left, but deep down she knew his choice to be inevitable. He wouldn't have been Arlin if he didn't honor his own deepest convictions.

Tyris's keen eyes picked up on Mallory's emotion. She shook her head dismissively before he could comment. The affable initiate held much empathy in his expression as they continued on despite him knowing nothing of her internal struggles. The silent support from someone who was still practically a stranger to her only added to the confused mass of emotions in her core. She didn't know how she was supposed to navigate any of it. She felt so alone, despite knowing she would never be alone again. She placed her hand over her abdomen, feeling the tightness of her quickly changing body. She was not yet showing, though she was expecting the pregnancy to pop any day now. Her breasts were already starting to grow larger, becoming more tender than she'd ever experienced before in her life. It wasn't fun, and the worst of it was yet to come.

Damn you, Arlin! Why aren't you here?

She missed him with a deep ache that swelled inside of her.

Tyris smartly kept his mouth shut. Mallory was grateful for his silence. They walked without words down the slanted corridor. It took them steadily underground. The ramp ran around the outer edge of the cathedral. Stained glass windows up high let light in as the floor continued to dip lower until they were several stories beneath the surface. After rounding what felt like the full circumference of the cathedral, the high ceiling was replaced by a dark hole ahead of them. It looking like the opening to a crypt as the passageway ran even deeper into the earth.

All the artistry that exuded from the lofty architecture of the rest of the cathedral was abandoned at the entrance to the tunnel passage. They'd been directed to take the corridor and just keep on walking. Mallory had severely underestimated just how far they would have to go to reach the Archives.

Gray stone bricks spackled with plaster formed the walls around them as the angle of the floor drew steeper. The repairs were not recent—additional cracks had since crumbled some of the bricks away entirely, reducing them to powder. Dirt peeked through, forming long-ignored piles of mess that eroded Mallory's preconceived notions of the Arcanum. The pristine erudite surface was built above crumbling catacombs that made her feel claustrophobic to traverse.

By the time they reached the start of the Archives they were at least half a dozen stories under the surface. A Historian station with a counter and wooden turnstiles blocked off a series of long passageways that stretched out in every direction into the distance. Luminescent bulbs lined the passages beyond, illuminating them with their steady glow. Wires strung between the bulbs were completely exposed, not tucked away like they were at surface level. Alcoves lined the walkways, housing all of the Power Artifacts in custody of the Arcanum—a vast library of wizardly tools.

They approached the Historian station and rang a little bell sitting atop the counter. Still gazing down one of the long tunnels, Mallory was startled by a Ver'ati suddenly sitting up behind the desk as if rising from a coffin. The wizard frowned at the interruption to his nap.

"Lyle Stronghelm?" Tyris inquired.

"Please place your Requisition Form on the counter," said the man, ignoring the question.

Tyris placed the paperwork down and pushed it towards the man.

Scooping up the form, he eyed the stamp closely. "I am Lyle, but you are not Arius Vanton," he said.

"Professor Vanton couldn't make it himself," said Tyris. "He's sent us in his stead."

Lyle immediately slammed his own stamp down on the form. *Rejected.* "Does Arius think lightgloves grow on trees?" Lyle asked. "Our stock is low."

"Speaking of lights…" said Tyris, leaning in closer over the counter, "a certain bulb was out…."

"I've already told you," said Lyle, "you are not Arius Vanton, so I have nothing to say to you."

Mallory felt her jaw tighten at his rudeness. "The professor is being watched. He hasn't the means of meeting with you, so you can drop the sour attitude," she said sharply. Her raging hormones were readily taking control over her tongue. "You know why we're here, but we still do not! So how about filling us in? You called this meeting."

Lyle's eyes shifted over to Mallory slowly, clearly unimpressed with her bark. "I trust Arius," he said. "I don't trust you. I don't know you, and I don't owe you one lick."

Tyris exploded forward with surprising ferocity. He grabbed a fistful of Lyle's robe and yanked him halfway across the counter. "That's not how you speak to a lady," he growled.

Stacks of paperwork went flying. The whites of Lyle's eyes flashed in fear of Tyris's wrath. "Hey now!" he cried out, holding up his hand submissively. "I didn't mean anything by it."

Mallory was shocked by Tyris's outburst just as much as Lyle was, but she managed to temper her reaction.

"I can tell you about the Gate," Lyle offered in a rush. "It's broken!"

"We already knew that," said Tyris, yanking on him again.

Tyris allowed Lyle to struggle free after another moment. Lyle squirmed back up off the counter and pointed an accusatory finger in Tyris's face. "Then you know as much as I do," he said. "I can't tell you anything more! My other news is much too *sensitive*. I will only speak to the professor—right to his face—*with his sound blocker*—so you better go tell him to figure things out and come and meet with me himself! No amount of threatening is going to change my mind!"

"We're on the same damn side, you conch-blowing fool!" Tyris growled again. "You're really not going to tell us anything?! We've just trekked all the way down into this dank musty hole to find you!"

Lyle glowered back. "You know I was once a steward to the Arcanum Council? All I can tell you now is both the Arcanum and the Crown are involved. It's big—I dare not speak one more word of it until I see Professor Vanton!" He stepped back so that Tyris couldn't reach for him again. "Not one more word!" He hit a button on the wall beside him and a Calvenite blast door dropped from the ceiling as fast as the blade of a guillotine. It blocked them off entirely from Lyle and the Archives.

"That did not go well," said Mallory through pursed lips.

Lyle's muffled voice carried on through the blast door: "Now leave at once, before I call somebody to remove you!"

Tyris glowered at the black polished wall, staring at his own dark shimmer of a reflection with gritted teeth.

"Let's go," said Mallory, tugging on his sleeve. "He's clearly not going to tell us what we came here to learn."

"I hope the roof caves in on you!" Tyris shouted to Lyle before allowing Mallory to pull him away. His face was still red hot with rage.

Mallory wished Tyris had let her do more of the talking. His shift in mood proved an unhelpful turn in the conversation. He was missing a certain amount of tact that might have come in handy for a more amicable conclusion.

An ominous cramp took Mallory's stomach. It only lasted a brief moment. She sighed as she took a deep breath, instinctively placing her hand over her abdomen as she did so. She was only here to help Javic—in the hopes of getting answers before anything else bad could happen. There would be no answers today. Professor Vanton would have to find a way to meet with Lyle himself.

* * *

Professor Vanton heard the footsteps approaching his office from down the long hallway in Conset Hall for only a brief moment before the moon set and his senses diminished along with his connection to the Power.

He was just starting to dig into a steaming bowl of noodles he'd warmed up just before the moon set. Classes were over for the evening, but occasionally students came by to speak with him after hours. After a minute, when he still had not heard the footsteps pick back up again, he set down his supper on his desk and stepped gingerly around his towers of earmarked research books to peek out his door.

The flash of heat hit him before he reached the hallway. All at once, flames burst from the dry papers all around him. The searing pain of a fiery explosion only lasted a moment before the intensity of the inferno flashed even hotter, rendering Arius and everything in his office to a burnt up pile of ash.

CHAPTER
17

Hornet's Nest

When the cloud of spores first faded from the streets of Tavallon, Vera did her best to keep a low profile. The Goblikans carted her unconscious companions through a wide plaza. She hobbled along at a distance, wandering slowly amongst a gaggle of disoriented citizens as she scouted out the area. The city was still trapped in a mental fog despite the clearing of the air. Those caught outdoors remained frozen in place—wavering bodies, lost in a stupor.

Vera watched as her companions were wheeled through the front gates of a fancy estate. She couldn't go any farther without being conspicuous. She stood within the plaza at the edge of the estate grounds. Her anxiety became difficult to manage as the square drew in more black-clad Goblikans by the minute. They came piling out from the surrounding government buildings. Their eyes shifted about, wary and alert as they mingled. She'd stumbled into the middle of a kicked hornets' nest!

A plaque on the side of a pillar labeled the area as the Governor's Square. Her Ver'ati companions had been taken into the Governor's Mansion. Vera didn't risk lingering any longer as the plaza quickly filled with the remnants of Garrett's twisted hierarchy. She continued north of the mansion to a residential area. There, citizens were just beginning to venture out to retrieve their beguiled loved ones from the streets.

A young man skirted past Vera, scampering between the afflicted. "Eaume!" he shouted as he searched the frozen crowd. His short beard hid a worried scowl. "Have you seen an elderly woman in a blue shawl?" he asked Vera.

She shook her head. "No, sorry."

"I told her that fog wasn't natural, but she insisted she could make it to the market and back. Always so stubborn!" The man continued on in a huff.

Beside a back entrance to the Governor's Estate, Vera eyed a group of four young servants striking up matches for their smoke sticks. She wandered closer and leaned up against a wall beneath their stoop, pretending to be afflicted with spores. She could barely make out their hushed words.

"How are we supposed to just keep working?" one of the young men asked the group.

"It's an uprising!" another agreed.

"Calm down, they're only killing the officials, not the staff."

"I'm not going back in there," said the first man. "I saw what they did to the governor's family…."

A pair of maids fled the servants' entrance behind them, pausing briefly to sniff at the air for any hint of the aromatic mist before joining the young men. The girls' pallid faces had trauma etched all across them. Vera took note of the maids' uniforms—plain gray aproned dresses tied with a loose green ribbon and an under-layer of white frills that peeked out from the bottom. Both maids looked just about ready to abandon their posts as the men shared their tobacco with them.

"They've ordered a platter of steaks," said one of the girls.

"We're to fetch more meat from the market," added the other.

The man who'd witnessed the slaughter of the governor's family grimaced at the mere mention of meat.

"No shop owner in their right mind is going to be open today in this mess."

They deliberated amongst themselves before one of the young men set out with the two maids, accompanying them on their quest for steaks amongst all the turmoil. Vera followed behind the entourage, keeping her distance.

The smell of smoke in the air tickled at Vera's nostrils. She assumed, at first, that the odor was coming from the meat market, but after further observation, a dark plume was rising up farther to the north. Upon reaching the market, she was surprised by the size of the crowd of shoppers and merchants. The people of Tavallon were out en masse, panic buying everything in stock in a series of lively auctions. All of the spore-frozen individuals in the area had been sequestered into a tight cluster and placed off to the side, out of everybody's way. The young man searching for his Eaume squeezed his way between the dazed bodies, working towards a blue shawl in the back corner of the pack.

The mansion servants briefly gawked at the relative normalcy of the market—no one was looting anything. Order held firm. Commerce paused for no man. The servants made for the premium butcher with fists full of Goblikan cash, apt to please their new masters.

Vera didn't know what she was doing anymore. She was just following the maids because she needed a maid's uniform if she was to have any hope of sneaking into the Governor's Mansion. She couldn't exactly ask the girls to strip for her… and she wasn't about to plan some sort of ridiculous heist either. Vera bit her lip.

Perhaps sneaking off into the countryside with Captain Bundles would have been the more prudent option.

She knew it would have hurt her heart to leave Ader to die, but whatever was to happen next, Ader wouldn't survive long without receiving some Ver'ati healing.

The maids were just finishing their transaction and stepping out from their shop of choice when Vera's attention suddenly became transfixed upon a pale, shirtless man. He had greasy blond hair that ran long, well past his shoulders. The man looked like a scrawny awkward teen with his gangly petite frame, but for the wrinkled yellow eyes of a crazed Goblikan beneath his brow. Most notably, he wore a black prosthetic limb at his side—his right arm cast entirely in dark metal.

The Goblikan strode down the line of shops whistling to himself. His eyes flashed across Vera and he immediately stopped his tune. A wide grin spread across his thin lips. He turned away, laughing obnoxiously loud. His antics caused a hush to fall around him as others within the crowd grew wary of the Goblikan's presence.

Vera backed away slowly. She didn't like the way the dark wizard leered at her. He looked utterly unhinged.

Off to the side, stepping out from the catatonic crowd, the young man had found his Eaume. He had her hefted up in his arms. The rest of the crowd wavered in place around them.

All those poor souls should really be off their feet... they must have been standing all night!

The Goblikan's focus shifted to Eaume and her bright blue shawl. He cackled as he pointed his metal fist in her direction. The old woman's shawl, along with the rest of her clothing, slumped into a heap in her grandson's arms. Poor Eaume's body liquefied, melting into a goopy stream of matter that flew towards the Goblikan's outstretched fist. The ooze compressed into a ball of dark brown fluid which surrounded the man's prosthetic arm momentarily before igniting into sticky flames. The Goblikan then sprayed a fiery geyser all across the bustling stands behind him. The fire stuck to everything it touched—flesh or stone, it mattered not—searing all like flaming tar.

The sky above the market was filled with dense black smoke. The melting crowd and all those who had witnessed the madness immediately erupted into screams—cursed howls on the wind.

The Goblikan just kept on laughing, gasping with a manic cackle while he sprayed everyone with his unquenchable flames. It was so shocking to witness that Vera nearly forgot to run! Only when one of the maids fled past her did she turn to follow suit.

The unhinged Goblikan continued to cackle with glee as he looked once again in Vera's direction. His supply of Eaume-goo was exhausted. He pointed his fist towards Vera next. The maid in front of Vera squealed with a panicked hiss as the air was forced from her lungs by the liquefying effects of the Goblikan's process. Her dress tumbled to the ground unmarred and empty as the girl melted into a brown soup before Vera's eyes. Her remains streamed back to the Goblikan.

The ooze once again ignited as the madman directed the spray across Eaume's grandson and the sequestered horde of spore-afflicted individuals. Their silence as they burned and melted into smoldering piles of ash chilled Vera to her core.

She scooped up the empty dress as she ran by. She didn't stop running until her calves were burning hotter than the flames at her back.

CHAPTER 18

Step Three: Survive

Nal Viershin of the Night Hawks was a flippant, cocky son-of-a-bitch. Livian had experienced her fair share of misogyny in her life—it was no secret that institutions like the Arcanum were rife with pissing contests—but the Goblikans respected one thing above everything else: Physical prowess.

Being able to beat the shit out of others became even more important to the Goblikans' social structure when the moon was down—as it was presently. The female Goblikans may have been perfectly capable wizards, but their presence was scarce in the plaza where most of the Free Goblikan Alliance had taken up residence. Livian supposed the women were keeping low profiles to avoid their more domineering counterparts.

The way the men eyed Livian like dogs salivating over a plate of meat was concerning, to say the least. She knew she was utterly and irreparably screwed. Ultimately, she could use the spores in her pocket to kill herself and everyone around her, but she hoped it wouldn't come down to that.

The air smelled of smoke and charred meat as Nal led her through the plaza and into an adjacent estate which appeared to have been the home of someone very wealthy until recently. The polished stone floors bore the evidence of a violent overtaking. Streaks of blood made slick patches that the Free Goblikans avoided as they immersed themselves deeply in the residence's bountiful stash of liquor.

Past a grand stairway and down an oil-painting-lined hallway, the estate's parlor had become headquarters to the alliance's leaders. The excited chatter of the drunken Goblikan commanders ceased the moment Livian stepped into the room behind Nal.

A ruggedly handsome Goblikan with a Talus Shard blade strapped to his hip stood up from where he was seated upon a finely upholstered leather sofa. He stepped in front of Nal and Livian, blocking their advance.

His eyes flashed yellow in the parlor's dim light as a wide smile stretched across his face.

"Do my eyes deceive me, or is our dead king's most trusted advisor, Livian Niern, actually alive and breathing before me?"

A blade-brother, a wizard, and a smooth talker.

Livian was abashedly impressed. She had never heard of any wizard's amongst the Paerto'radam. Her eyes lingered over his chiseled chest, partially exposed beneath a loosely buttoned dress shirt. His pectorals were hairless and glistening. She wondered how often he oiled them.

"I daresay I've made her panties wet," said the Goblikan with a smirk.

His sexual appeal quickly evaporated at his crassness.

Nal turned to look at Livian. He grunted a laugh. "She's looking at your sword," he said, "she thinks you're a blade-brother!"

They both burst out with grunting laughter.

"They call me Redbone. Ives Redbone," the Goblikan introduced himself. "And I'm sorry to disappoint you sweetheart, but I'm no blade-brother."

"Clearly," said Livian. "Every blade-brother I ever met was a gentleman."

"I'm certainly no gentle-man, though I have killed many a gentle-fool," said Ives. "This blade—" he tapped the Talus Shard's hilt, "—I took it from a blade-brother's cold dead hands." He stared Livian down.

"If you're trying to intimidate me, it's not working," she said.

"Just know, I don't appreciate witches messing around in my head. You best watch your step or you'll learn why they call me Redbone."

Livian narrowed her eyes.

Ives drew his stolen Talus Shard out of its scabbard and held it up between them, displaying the yellow wrappings around the sword's grip. The tip of the hilt was tinged with a disgusting dark stain. Blood. Ives ran his tongue down the length of the wrappings while staring Livian dead in the eyes.

Livian grimaced as Nal pushed her past the man—*The dead-eyed freak!*—and directed her towards a closed room at the back of the parlor.

"I would like you to appreciate everything that is at stake here," said Nal. He spoke casually, as if Ives had not just threatened to penetrate Livian brutally with the hilt of his sword.

Few things in life frightened Livian. Ives made her skin crawl. Her hands shook in her pockets as she clutched a fistful of vials. She glanced a daring look back at the psycho. What would have been a disarming smile on Ives' face had she not known better was now a sinister mask to her eyes.

"I understand the stakes," said Livian.

Nal paused at the closed door and turned to look at Livian with a raised eyebrow. "Obviously your own hide is on the line," he said. "But this conversation we're about to have… well, it concerns no less than the future of Aragwey."

He pushed open the door and directed Livian to head down the narrow stairway beyond. The Goblikans in the parlor remained silent, leering in her direction with their yellow eyes as she stepped through the opening. The hard soles of Livian's shoes clomped against the hollow wooden steps as a cool draft breezed past her. They descended into a windowless wine cellar. Lamp light flickered across the rows of dusty bottles.

When she reached the bottom of the stairs, the sight of Lord Ethan, Wilgoblikan, Shiara and Grine all unconscious and laid out in a row upon the stone floor was an unfortunate discovery. Livian recognized her spores in action.

Bloody fools! They were supposed to get clear!

Ethan's Mark of Kings was exposed. The Goblikans knew what they had. It was a disaster!

"They are alive," said Nal, "for now." He gripped Livian's shoulders from behind and pinched them in a tight massage. "Whether or not they remain that way will depend entirely on how helpful you can be to us."

Livian shrugged away from his touch. She immediately spun around to face him.

Nal held up his palms. "I'm not your enemy here," he said. "Some will vote to put you all down—but I think you can be of use. And as for this lot," he gestured at the spore-riddled lineup. "I see one bargaining chip against the Ver'konus, anyway." He pointed at the Mark of Kings on Ethan's arm. "Tell me who this is."

Could the Goblikans really not know who they have?

Livian was worried Nal might just be testing her honesty, but she decided to lie to him anyway. "That's Aaron Levy," she said, trying to keep her expression as neutral as possible. It was unlikely the Goblikans were aware of Ethan's rejuvenation. It was a reasonably safe lie.

Nal nodded slowly as he looked upon the prisoners. "Ah, so then Wil finally found his charge, but failed to kill him." He tsk'ed his tongue. "He'll definitely be killed," he said of Wil.

"All of the king's former Special Guard are forfeit. That was the one stipulation the rest of us immediately agreed upon."

Livian's eyes lingered over Nal's expression as he mused over his fellow Goblikan. He'd bought her lie! He was none the wiser.

"There are a lot of personalities in this little democracy we're starting to build here," he continued. "If you think Redbone's bad…. There are some who think even I was too high amongst the king's ranks! Imagine that!" Nal laughed. "So, you see my dilemma? If I kill them all, there won't be enough of us left to resist the barbarian horde." Nal started to walk back up the stairs to the parlor. He gestured for Livian to follow.

The barbarians were an existential threat to all of Aragwey. Livian saw the fine line everyone was treading—the true stakes at play. Nal needed to rein the rest of the Goblikans in if any of them were going to survive the war that was coming their way. Just as much, he would be needing assistance from the rest of Aragwey.

"So you want me to use my spores to convince the others to vote with you?" asked Livian.

"Not exactly," said Nal, continuing his walk up the stairs.

Returning to the parlor brought the uncomfortable stares of the other Free Goblikan commanders back upon Livian. At least Ives had moved on. Livian would have been glad to never see that freak ever again.

"I do want you to use your spores," said Nal, "just not on these fine folk!"

The silence in the parlor was deafening.

"No," said Nal, "It's the crazies I'd like you to dose."

They all look crazy to me….

They exited the parlor and proceeded back through the mansion, then out into the plaza. The sun was shining bright in the blue sky, not a cloud in sight. The edge of the square opened up through archways to a wide mezzanine below. Down the stairs and back against the wall, wrought iron bars blocked off prison cell alcoves, carved into the stone of the plaza's foundation. A wide wooden stage stood across from the cells—that was where Garrett once held public executions.

Goblikans stood guard over the few prisoners present at the moment.

"These are the crazies we were able to catch today," said Nal, pointing to the line of prisoners. There were six mad Goblikan's in total. Five of them were men, three of which were stripped nude and stained with dirt and filth. "We found that one in the latrines fishin' for a snack," he gestured to the naked man on the end who was in the process of waggling his short erection between the bars at Livian. "Don't get too close, he's still covered in shit."

It was one of those days where it would have been better had Livian not gotten out of bed at all.

"They are now all your mental patients," said Nal. "Cure 'em, knock 'em out, or kill 'em—and do it by moonrise! Each day, you'll be brought more as they're caught. The more you save for the barbarians, the happier you'll make me."

Livian already had spores on her that could kill or incapacitate, but curing them of their crazies was another challenge altogether. "My technique does not completely override the individual within," she said. "Even with my spores, I'm afraid of what that one might do," she said. She didn't need to indicate which one. The man on the end was trying to toss his ejaculate in their direction.

Nal frowned. "Probably more trouble than he's worth...." He waved a guard over and ordered him to retrieve a pike.

The madman danced back and forth in his tiny cell as the guard repeatedly stabbed at him. He was surprisingly agile, laughing the whole time as he hopped back and forth between his feet. Eventually, his luck ran out and he caught a blade to the abdomen.

"Now I've done you a favor. Don't make me regret it," said Nal, pointing at Livian as if they'd just struck a deal. "Save the rest, and maybe I don't cull all your Ver'ati friends."

CHAPTER 19

Step Four: Thrive

As far as Night Hawk Nal was concerned, Livian was doing exactly as she was told. What he failed to realize was that rewiring the Goblikans was precisely what she'd aimed to do in coming to Tavallon in the first place. Curing the broken minds of the mad Goblikans did not have a one-size-fits-all solution. However, with the masturbatory latrine gremlin put out of everyone's misery, using the love spores was still the best way to reign in the violent disobedience of the others. She dosed each of them thoroughly, not wanting to take any chances of a rejection.

The more feral the Goblikan, the more important it was that all of her implanted memories stuck deeply in their consciousness. She couldn't have them humping her legs like dogs—they needed to see the whole picture of her design and understand her wants and desires. She needed them to strive to be useful. Her love-spore stash was nearly depleted, but she had five additional loyal subjects in the end, ready to lay down their lives for her.

The two surviving naked men ceased howling at each other like wolves. All it took was a whiff of her spores and they dropped to their knees, cowering against the stone floors of their cells. They shook in fear of her displeasure, trying their best to cover their genitals with their hands.

They'd fallen into deep shame. All it took was their understanding of her disgust. They would not grow resentful of her revulsion because they understood from Livian's point of view why they were revolting. They also knew that it was within their own power to change their ways. Only by being perfectly devout servants to Livian might she ever forgive their sins.

She was their one true god now.

Each one of them was willing and ready to lay down their very lives to save Livian from harm, or even simply to propel her agenda. They would do anything for her, just for the chance of receiving a sweet pardon from her cherry lips.

She had their undying loyalty. It was love—a truly beautiful sentiment! When their maligned brains went to make decisions, their first thoughts would always be: *How can I aid Livian and her well-being?*

Livian was impressed by her handiwork. She'd used her memory-implantation method to control many a wizard back in Phandrol. Every time she ran into a roadblock in her career, the people standing in her way soon fell for her lovable charm. At this point, half the Arcanum loved her to some degree or another because of her manipulation. Perfecting her art had taken much trial and error.

Her first and greatest stroke of genius had occurred when she was a young teen, still studying for her Dance of the Elements at the academy in Erotos. Fungus was capable of facilitating changes inside the human brain. A batch of mushrooms she'd consumed on a dare ended up giving her that epiphany.

She befriended an Arcanum researcher and used his microscopes to look closely at the mushroom spores to learn how they worked. Thus began her experimentations. The Power gave her many hints as she worked, providing an emotional release when she successfully imparted her will upon the spores. They still looked the same to the naked eye when she was done with them, but she learned that inside every spore, a packet of information existed—many packets, really— each telling the spore how to form on a cellular level.

When she concentrated on imparting her own memories, she could use the Power to encode the experience into the mind-altering signals released by the spores. What most people didn't understand was that on a fundamental level, everything was chemical. The intricacies of her work were vast, but the Power handled all the precise, minuscule changes across the cells as long as she directed the process adequately with her greater understanding of the truth behind the physical world.

Testing first on insects and subsequently rats, she learned how to use the mind-altering spores to control simpler minds before working her way up towards human beings.

The spores told people a story and then told them how they felt about it afterwards. Her love spores—as she called them— were her most potent memory spores yet. They told the story of her upbringing. There'd been many struggles growing up poor within a war-torn town along the Minthune. She was the result of forced relations upon her mother by a Ver'ati stationed nearby to her village. Testing positive for the Power changed Livian's life. It allowed her to escape, and it gave her the ability to touch others.

Her memories were imparted in excruciating detail by her spores so that the recipients would understand her and her worldview; her ultimate design. After that, the spores flooded their brains with the perfect concoction of chemicals to convince them that they loved her story—that they loved her. They wanted nothing more than to see her succeed. That was their greatest wish, and deepest fantasy—to help Livian attain everything she wanted. It brought them the greatest joy in life. It brought them peace. She didn't torment her subjects. That was what the Goblikans all experienced with Garrett's traditional Compulsion. Instead, she awarded them with fulfillment.

Interestingly, the positive reinforcement method seemed to work particularly well on the Goblikans. Now free of Garrett's grasp, they could not fulfill their base need to satisfy their master. They still held all that anger and pain, but now the ones that Livian altered were able to find a new purpose. Garrett had been so cruel to them. The switch from a stick to a carrot had the Goblikans desperate to please her, if only for the good feelings it brought them. They'd been starved of positivity for so long.

She knew the creation of Whunes and chimeras was a similar process to her alteration of spores. She did her work a level of abstraction away from the intended changes. Her method of control was much more subtle than Compulsion, and she preferred it that way. She wasn't a maniac like Garrett—she was just a practical woman who understood that control was necessary to enact her will upon the world.

Her wish was to change Aragwey for the better. She wanted to fix it for all the kids not fortunate enough to be born with the Power in their blood. The best way to do that was to go straight to the source of the problem—first Erotos, and now Kovehn, the Goblikans, Tavallon, Garrett—and start enacting the change she wished to see, one monster at a time.

Nal really was doing her a favor by helping deliver the worst of the Goblikans into her fold.

If my spores work on this lot, I just may yet succeed!

The efficacy was looking even more promising than she dared hope. The sniveling men on the floor weren't exactly the hardened obedient soldiers that Nal had requested, but at least their hearts were now in the right place. They'd gone from wild to obedient, and that was half the battle.

She would need to work up a new batch of spores after moonrise now that her stash was nearly depleted—it was easier to propagate more by duplicating an existing batch than it was to manufacture a new set from scratch. Otherwise, no two batches ended up exactly alike. After creating her love spores, she knew she'd come as close to perfection as she was apt to achieve. She kept the strain alive through cascading generations like a baker maintaining yeast for a signature loaf.

She had her mind set on dosing Nal and the other Free Goblikan commanders as soon as possible. Only the sexually violent ones like Ives Redbone really worried her. An experience with a particularly aggressive professor during the early days of her experimentations had required extreme measures to fix. His brain proved unswayable from its disgusting proclivity of finding joy in corrupting the innocent. He'd gotten off on his position of power over his female students. Falling in love with Livian only made his obsession stronger.

She was forced to kill him, and that led to her needing to erase him from the minds of all the other students and staff. It was a messy situation—not how Livian liked to work.

She paced before the cells, taking stock of her new subjects. If all went well, eventually she would attain control over the majority of the Goblikans in Tavallon. From that point on, the rest who managed to resist her charm would be more easily exterminated for the good of Aragwey. Influence and power were synonymous—her accumulation of support need only remain steady. The balance would tip and the rest of the pieces would fall in place all at once.

She stopped her pacing in front of her lone female recruit. The woman had remained still at the center of her cell since Livian's arrival. She was muscle-bound and stout. Her shaved head was covered in both old and new scars. She gazed back upon Livian with a glint of jealousy in her almond-shaped, bloodshot eyes. That was a problem that sometimes arose when dosing other women. They always wished they could be her, and not just serve her. "What do they call you, and what's your story?" she asked. She needed to sort out what changes might be required in her future doses.

"I'm Tora Bacielle, but they call me Terrible Tora. A few came to poke me, so I sliced their bits off," she said.

"And that made you one of the crazies!?" Livian exclaimed. "Mast forbid you protect yourself!"

"I made a necklace out of 'em," Tora added.

"Oh," said Livian. She glanced over at one of the guards standing nearby the cells, close enough to overhear everything. His heightened tension quelled any doubt. "Did that work well as a deterrent?"

Tora shrugged.

"Well, don't do it again," said Livian, "unless you have to."

Tora took a bow, a smirk on her lips.

"This one's cured," Livian announced, "you can release her." The guards ignored her. They were waiting for Nal's return. "It was worth a shot."

She continued on down the line. An obese man with a sad scowl was next. "What about you—no necklaces, I hope?"

"That's Klain," said Tora. "He can't speak—he wouldn't stop screaming in the mist so they took his tongue."

"I see," said Livian. "You're quiet now, and ready to take orders?"

Klain bowed his head.

The naked wolf twins were in the two cells to follow. They weren't really twins, but they were both blackened with soot and dirt. "And you two, you're going to work on civility, aren't you?"

They both grunted in response, remaining prone before her.

"I'm sensing a lot of nonverbal here," she said. "If you act like dogs, the other Goblikans are going to treat you like dogs."

They prostrated even harder.

At least they were her dogs.

The last of her motley band of crazies was still seated cross-legged at the back of his cell. His right arm was a prosthetic formed out of dark metal. The scrawny pale man reminded her a bit of Dhron, but with stringy, long blond hair instead of a bald head. "And you," said Livian.

The man glared up at her with his head still downturned, his chin tucked. He had a seething fire behind his yellow eyes.

"Name and crimes," Livian insisted.

"Merrik Firefist," he said, cocking his head to the side.

Livian glanced once again at his black metal arm. "Your mother never told you not to play with fire, did she?"

Footsteps approaching down the stairs of the mezzanine drew Livian's attention to Nal, back to check on her progress. "It's his work you been smellin' all afternoon," he said. "He barbecued the north barracks and then roasted a bunch of folks at a meat market. He's been on a rampage ever since he was released from his mental chains."

"A firebug? Never would have guessed with a name like Firefist. Bad boy!" Livian exclaimed. "No more flames!"

"Unless it's against the barbarians," added Nal.

Merrik stared back at them both with a blank expression.

Livian was in command of a bunch of psychopaths. It was less comforting than one might hope.

Nal glanced over at the wolf twins, still prostrate on the stone. "Everyone's being so well behaved. I'm impressed!"

Livian curtsied.

"We're tracking another bomber, but they managed to hide before moondown," said Nal.

"I need time to make more spores anyway, once I can reach the Power again," said Livian.

"Just as well we haven't found the mad bastard, then," said Nal. "Do I need to worry about this lot?" he asked.

Livian shook her head. "They will remain obedient," she said, glancing across each of them for any signs of descent. "No more slicing, screaming, or burning anything. If you embarrass me, no one's giving you a third chance."

Nal continued to praise the quick turnaround of Livian's charges as he led her back up to the plaza, returning her to the mansion of the alliance headquarters. This time he led her up the grand stairway and into a servant's quarters at the end of the hall. "You'll be staying here for now when you're not working," said Nal. "Should be comfortable enough."

It was a poor trade from staying in Garrett's residence at the pyramid.

"And one last thing," said Nal. "Sorry, this will hurt a bit." He pulled an egg-shaped device out of his pocket. It looked like a metal seedpod with about twenty small pea-sized spheres attached across its dimpled surface. Nal pressed the top of the egg and the tiny spheres all dislodged from the dimples and fell into the palm of his other hand beneath. He clicked the button on top of the egg again while holding it up to Livian's forehead. The spheres moved with precision, rising up from Nal's hand and floating over towards Livian.

The balls drove themselves against her flesh, stinging as the pressure increased. Livian cried out as the pain grew unbearable. The spheres continued pressing steadily against her until they tore through her skin altogether, forming twenty different bore holes all across her body.

"Now that this is paired with you, if you try to channel, the holder of this part will feel your intentions. If you mean to disobey, a long press will recall the spheres straight through all your major arteries," explained Nal. "Probably shouldn't test it."

The burn of the spheres only receded when they finished moving inside her, taking up residence at various spots throughout her body.

"Someone will come and get you when you're needed again—best not to channel at all before then. You wouldn't want any misunderstandings, got it?"

Nal left Livian to ponder over her predicament. The restrictive Power Artifact was another major obstacle on her path to domination. There would be no removing the spheres if Nal didn't agree to it first. But, if the Goblikan allowed her to make more love spores—and later those spores just so happened to adjust Nal's point of view on the matter—perhaps the channeling restriction wouldn't be as much of a deathblow to her ambitions as she feared.

She'd been risking it all every step of the way on this mission. Nothing had changed in that regard, though the pain of her pierced skin did shake her nerve. She turned down the oil lamp and reclined upon the small cot to try to get some rest. After several hours, as sundown approached, a scratching at the door brought her back to her senses. A jingle of keys was followed by a click and the door swung inward.

A young man with a messy mop of hair stood in the doorway. He was no older than fifteen based on his scrawny frame. "Livian Niern?" he whispered into the darkness.

Livian sat up, narrowing her eyes at the intruder.

"Dhron sent me," said the boy.

About damn time....

She sprang up from the cot and rushed towards the boy, already fishing through her pocket for a specific vial she wished to hand him. He stood his ground with wide eyes as she frightened him with her haste. She didn't want to waste a moment! "Take this," she said, stuffing a vial of clear spores into his sweaty palm. "See that Dhron gets this to Lord Ethan and the other captured Ver'ati in the wine cellar! It's just through the parlor in the west wing."

"I know it, ma'am," said the boy, his pupils dilating as they locked onto Livian's eyes in the dark of the room.

"Those spores will help wake them up," she added. "They must escape! Deliver this message to Dhron at once!"

"Yes, ma'am," said the obedient little boy.

As he backed away from the doorway, a slow clap sounded from down the hallway. Nal and Ives appeared from around the corner smiling at her like she'd won the biggest idiot award. The mop of a boy strode proudly over to the dangerous men. He held up the antidote spores to Nal's outstretched hand. "I knew you wouldn't disappoint," said Nal. "*Lord Ethan* will be of much more use to us awake than he is in his current state." He slapped the vial against his palm several times before swirling it in a circle and holding it up to his eyes. There was nothing to see, the spores were extremely small. The clear vial glinted in the lamplight from the nearby hallway fixture.

Livian felt like a complete imbecile.

Nal handed the vial over to Ives. "See to their awakening, and to their Neutering."

"My pleasure," said Ives as he departed.

"Wouldn't want any heroes thinking they can fight their way out of this." Nal pointed towards Livian with a jovially smile. "Thanks again," he said before closing her back in to her room.

CHAPTER
20

Vera snuck into the Governor's Mansion shortly after nightfall. She hoped the short-staffed estate wouldn't notice her intrusion. The back door was clear as she pulled the lever. The handle was locked, but the strike plate was blocked with a wad of paper to prevent the servants from accidentally locking themselves out during their smoke breaks. Security was lackadaisical—it didn't cross any of the Goblikans' minds that they should look twice at a lowly maid. They thought so highly of themselves that they couldn't comprehend anyone being desperate or stupid enough to walk straight into the middle of their hornets' nest.

Vera grabbed a mop from a servants' closet and walked the halls quickly as if she knew where she was going.

She did not.

The layout of the mansion was straightforward. There was an east and a west wing, and several stories above her. The Goblikans kept mostly to the main floor, banging around and throwing quite a rumpus of a party in what was formerly the governor's elegant dining room over in the east wing of the mansion. The party had spilled out into the hallway beyond, wreaking havoc on the study and nearby library as well.

Stacks of books were being used to stoke a grand fire—a crude kiln-like structure had been erected by one of the Goblikans in the center of the library. Its exhaust tube protruded like a metal spike through the mansion's wall, venting the smoke of the burning books out into the plaza. Vera avoided the madness after hearing a woman's scream and briefly peeking in.

The cries of the abused servant chased her back down the hallway with an extra dose of dread in her steps. There was nothing she could do for the unfortunate girl. It pained Vera to walk away. She was a survivor. Lord Ethan had abused her for years—his treatment of her only growing worse recently when his age reverted to that of a virile young man. She hated Ethan. She hated that ultimately she was risking death and worse for her abuser, but to her, there were varying degrees of evil. The servant's cries fell silent, though the grunts of the Goblikan continued. Whatever Ethan was, the Goblikans were unequivocally worse in Vera's eyes.

Shiara and Grine were good people, and Ader was relying on Vera as well, but seeing the horrors around her made her want to curl up into a tiny ball and cry for hours on end. She didn't have that luxury. Vera *was* a survivor.

The bodies of the governor's people were gone, but streaks of blood remained on the polished floors as she continued her search for the Ver'ati.

She swapped the mop in her hands for a pitcher of wine and immediately withdrew the kit of herbs she always carried with her from out of her pocket. She broke the wax seal around a vial of dried oleander. She'd kept the highly poisonous herb on hand for the better part of the last three years. A potted shrub of the rose-colored laurel was gifted to her by the Gravish ambassador in hopes that she might use it to end

Ethan's lingering life. She'd dried the plant and ground it herself, keeping it alongside her assortment of medicinal herbs. She'd considered slipping the poison to Ethan on many occasions but had never been able to work herself up to taking that plunge.

She poured the entire vial into the jug of wine and swished it around vigorously in a circle until it mostly dissolved. It was enough to kill a train of oxen, but death would not be instantaneous.

The chatter of less raucous voices drew Vera forward past a curved staircase and into the west wing. Only the Goblikan commanders would be seated around calmly plotting with this brutality as a backdrop. She gave her deadly wine jug one last swirl before setting forth to fill the glasses of the terrible men in charge.

The parlor was a tad informal for a meeting room, but the comfortable furniture made for the perfect place for the Goblikans to recline and shortly die. Vera didn't miss a glass as she circled the low table in front of the seated commanders.

When she was finished distributing her liquid justice she stood at the edge of the room and silently tracked how many sips each man consumed. As long as they drank most of their glass, they would be dead within the hour. It was a kinder ending than she dared say any of them deserved. All of the commanders were gruff, strapping men—physically strong enough to dominate their competition and take control.

In total, Vera counted eleven soon-to-be-dead men. She wished she could end all of the Goblikans throughout the whole mansion—the whole city! Lord Ethan's hard stance against King Garrett's evils had been pretty much the only reason she'd been able to come up with to stay her hand whenever the thought of permanently ending his abuse had crossed her mind. Killing the leader of the Ver'konus would have been suicide for her, but she'd still considered it on the worst days. She was glad now that she'd saved the poison for even more terrible monsters.

Every man in the parlor arose to show their respect as two more Goblikans entered the room. One was wearing an awkward winged suit, while the other looked to be a blade-brother, though he was definitely a Goblikan as well—his eyes flashed yellow as they locked with Vera's. She lowered her gaze immediately as the Goblikan swordsman zeroed in on her. Vera's breath caught fearfully in her chest. The swordsman was the first person to acknowledge her existence since she'd entered the mansion.

The man in the bird suit stepped between them, breaking the swordsman's intense stare. "Boy, oh boy, have we got some news," he said, a huge grin spreading across his dark sun-kissed face, creased beyond his years. "The witch confirmed it: Our guest of honor is none other than Lord Ethan himself!"

The Goblikans burst out into a chorus of foul words, punctuating their distaste of the resistance leader.

"Let Nal speak," demanded the swordsman.

The room quickly quieted back down.

"Thank you, Redbone," said Nal—bird-man was apparently the alpha of the group. "Ives here has the antidote to wake 'em up."

Several of the commanders chugged their wine in celebration. Others did not look so happy. "Why even wake them up?" one commander asked loudly. "If it's Ethan, we should just slit all their throats and be done with it!"

"Hear, hear!" another commander agreed.

"Are you really going to make me hold a vote on this?" asked Nal.

"Every commander gets a say!" exclaimed the dissenting Goblikan.

"Fine," said Nal, "a show of hands, then." He kept his thick arms crossed in front of himself. "All in favor of killing the prisoners?"

Six hands shot up.

"All in favor of reviving them, and then Neutering them before moonrise?" asked Nal, raising his own hand.

The swordsman, Redbone, along with the five remaining Goblikan commanders raised their hands as well.

"Six to seven—Neutering, it is," said Nal.

While the Ver'ati being killed would have been inarguably the worse outcome, Neutering was no better for Vera's hopes of saving Ader.

Neutering was the Goblikan equivalent of Inhibiting wizards from the Power—the difference being that Neutering was a physical procedure, and it was permanent, whereas Inhibitor could be reversed with the right serum.

She'd spent time with several Neutered Ver'ati years ago at Fort Bastion, back before she was Lord Ethan's nurse. She was just a fresh field medic at the time, working at the warfront. There was always demand for medics. Ameliorators were preferred when the moon was up, but a good medic could stave off death during the powerless in-between times. She enjoyed being able to help minimize the casualties, and the trained position paid reasonably well considering it was far less dangerous than being a soldier.

The neutered wizards in her ward were a sad sight to see—no visible wounds, but being cut off from the Power caused a terrible pain that lingered in the absence of their cherished connection. They would howl horribly when the moon rose, the loss stinging deeply all throughout their bodies like fire trying to escape from their veins. The Neutered Ver'ati's visitors stopped coming when it became clear they were mere ghosts of their former selves.

It was not a fate to wish upon anyone but the worst of enemies.

Redbone pushed past Nal and made straight for Vera.

Could he know I'm an imposter?

Her heart was pounding out of her chest! But then the swordsman grabbed an empty wine glass off the table and held it up to her expectantly. Vera filled his cup, accidentally pouring the final dregs of undissolved oleander from the bottom of her jug as she emptied it.

Redbone leaned in close to Vera and sniffed slowly at her dark hair. "You smell like meat," he said harshly before turning away again.

The foul scent of the liquefied maid from the market lingered on the uniform. Vera's legs trembled softly beneath the stolen dress.

A bald Goblikan who had already downed a second glass of the deadly wine suddenly projectile vomited violently across the low table.

"Disgusting, man!" exclaimed Redbone, jumping back to save his shoes. He sloshed out half his wine with the movement.

Vera held her breath as she scanned her eyes across the ill expressions of the other Goblikans. No one had put the pieces together yet.

Redbone sneered at the horrified vomiter before going in to his own glass with a big gulp. He shoved his nose in, drinking deeply, but then spit back up as soon as he noticed the thick dregs at the bottom. "Tannins! This tastes like shit! It won't do at all!" He tossed the rest of his wine on the fine rug.

Vera hoped he drank enough.

"You—pretty girl—come with me," said Redbone, staring once again at Vera with his hand rested atop the discolored hilt of his sword.

Vera stared back at him with wide eyes.

"I saw a special bottle in the cellar I want you to open."

She swallowed hard, doing her best to look unperturbed. Her brow was furrowed. She couldn't remember what a normal expression felt like anymore.

Redbone made for a door at the side of the parlor, only looking back once he had the handle held within his grasp. Vera quickly stepped over the dying Goblikan's vomit. The stupid fool still didn't know what had hit him. She hurried after the creepy swordsman as he started down a set of wooden stairs that led into the cellar.

The wall of fine wines was expected. The line of unconscious Ver'ati plus Wilgoblikan was a surprise. Redbone pulled a vial out of his pocket that Vera recognized as one of Livian's rubber-stopped containers. He unstopped the spores and wafted a bit into the faces of each of the prisoners.

They all immediately began to rouse as if from a deep slumber, grinding against the ropes that restrained their hands and feet, though their eyes remained squeezed tight.

"If this works fast enough, we'll have an audience!" Redbone said excitedly as he tossed the empty vial aside and reached down to untie his pants.

Vera's eyes grew wider as she realized the Goblikan's true intentions of bringing her down here. He was already erect as he pulled his pants partway down. Vera backed away slowly, his girth alone turning her stomach.

"I don't need you to like it," said Redbone, "in fact, I prefer it if you don't." He stepped towards Vera, his evil yellow eyes feasting upon her terror.

"Please, you mustn't!" Vera begged.

"Feel free to scream," said Redbone. He took such pleasure in her distress.

Vera had nowhere to go as the sick man shambled forward at her, trapping her against the side of the stairwell.

Shiara's eyes opened slightly, glancing around the wine cellar in a groggy haze. There was nothing she or anyone could do to stop Redbone.

He grabbed Vera's wrist with a firm hand and pulled her down roughly to her knees in front of him. "I hope you can hold your breath," he said, "I'll slap you awake if you pass out. I don't want you missing a thing."

In a desperate act of preservation, Vera's hand grasped ahold of the stained grip of Redbone's sword. The wisdom of a thousand swordsmen immediately coursed up her arm. Her body was filled with the skill and experience of every holder of the Talus Shard to have come before. Her fear drained away in an instant, though she couldn't help but shed a tear for the many women who had died terrible deaths after being viciously pummeled on the hilt. She knew her fate if she failed to stop him.

Redbone's eyes went wide as he realized his folly. Vera gripped his testicles and shaft with her other hand as she drew his sword out and across them in one quick motion.

Redbone howled as his bits severed away cleanly. He fell backwards, utterly shocked as blood began to spout from his neutered nether region.

Vera discarded the shriveled genitalia with a sick plop. She quickly rose to her feet, astutely raising up the sword in case Redbone made another move for her. He grabbed at his crotch with both hands instead, trying to hold in his blood. She stood over him without sympathy. His squeals were pathetic. Vera wanted him to die, but she didn't want it to be too quick. She stabbed into his abdomen slowly, feeling the shifting tension on the blade as it pierced his organs. He cried out again with a grunting gurgle as he scooted across the wine cellar floor. If the poison didn't get him, the blood loss would.

Vera cut the prisoners free from their bindings with precision. Shiara sat up, rubbing her wrists. By the time everyone was fully roused and had managed to climb the stairs back up to the parlor, eleven dead Goblikan commanders decorated the room. The poison had worked even better than Vera dared hope.

Nal stood up from where he'd been crouched over the last of the dying commanders. He gestured with his arms, allowing two short blades to protrude from out of his sleeves, but simultaneously backed away from Vera as he took in the image of the girl who had defeated them all.

Vera spit at his feet. The wobbling prisoners at her back skirted the edge of the room, avoiding the slew of bodies as they exited the parlor.

The ample wisdom of the blade told Vera to choose her battles carefully. She backed out of the room, joining Wilgoblikan and the Ver'ati as they made their escape.

CHAPTER 21

A Puzzle to Solve

The sun was getting low over the crystal clear waters of Lake Baratoa by the time Elric Elensol and Cormick Gansly decided to end their failed fishing excursion prematurely and make their way back to their little camp. It wasn't from lack of knowledge or effort that the fish weren't biting—Cormick, after all, was a skilled fisherman. The simple fact was that the lake was fished out. The Antarans, whose diet consisted primarily of fish, pulled most of their harvest from the Great Minthune, however, each year after the algae bloom turned the waters blood red, fisherman traveled far and wide in search of alternative sources of protein to feed their families. Although the Crimson Waters soon returned to its usual murky brown and the fisherman were long gone from Lake Baratoa's banks, the lake was left depleted for the season.

"So much empty water," lamented Cormick as he broke down his fishing rod. "I could have caught supper thirty times over by now anywhere else."

"I've no doubt," said Elric. With no money left to speak of for the remainder of their travels, they were fast running out of options. The road weighed heavily upon Elric, though he tried not to let it show. Cormick, too, was feeling the strain, despite his youth. It had been three days since their last proper meal. Lake Baratoa was supposed to be the answer to their plight.

Elric's heart grew heavy as he compared the minor discomfort of his rumbling belly to the true hardship Javic and Cormick's brother Rylin must have been facing, trapped in the Lost City of Sultrim. There was no way to know if Javic was still alive, but every day that passed certainly decreased his chances of survival in the harsh mountain terrain. The urgency of Elric's journey made sleeping at night difficult. All he had in this world was his grandson. There were no lengths to which he would not go to find Javic and return him to safety.

Cormick's eyes, sunken from lack of sleep as well, held the same heavy weight behind them—worry for his little brother. Elric was glad to have the fisherman in his company, even if there were no fish to be caught. Cormick's determination matched his own. Family was all that mattered. Their parallel pursuits bonded them in a way deeper than mere traveling companions.

Elric stuffed a pinch of dried tobacco from a pouch on his hip into his old clay pipe. He didn't often smoke, but the process was calming to the senses. He lit the bowl with a match and filled his mouth with the smoke, tasting the earthiness of Darrenfield once more on his tongue. He'd meant to live out the remainder of his days in Darrenfield. It was unlikely now that he would ever return.

He offered Cormick a puff from the pipe once the fishing rod was packed away. Cormick accepted. He glanced out over the lake once more with a disheartened shake of his head as he exhaled. They began a slow shuffle back to their campsite, just up from the water's edge.

The pack horses nickered at Elric as he approached. He patted each of their noses in turn as he looped their feed bags around their heads. The horses were the only ones still eating well. He retrieved one of Professor Arius Vanton's research journals from his saddlebag and sat down on his bedroll before pawing through the pages in search of the spot he'd left off from that morning.

The journals were dense and scholarly, containing every reference to the Lost City of Sultrim from across the ages that Professor Vanton could find. The closer they got to the Arid Hills, the more important deciphering the professor's notes became. Many expeditions had attempted to rediscover the path to Sultrim over the years. Elric and Cormick *needed* to succeed where the rest failed.

Cormick picked up a second journal. Together, they studied the notes in silence for as long as the dying light would allow. There were still many volumes left to read through. Once they reached the treacherous passes to the west, there was no telling what might prove to be of importance.

With dusk quickly approaching, their empty stomachs were making it hard to stay warm. The chill of another winter night threatened to temper their bones. Elric began to build a fire as Cormick rustled around in his pack for a handful of nuts that had fallen loose earlier in the journey. It was all that was left of their food supplies. Cormick solemnly passed a few over to Elric. He ate slowly, crunching each one into a fine paste before swallowing it down; savoring every morsel.

Lantern light through the trees, out on the nearby road, caught Elric's attention. A large caravan was approaching the lake. Elric ceased his campfire preparations as hopes of traveler hospitality danced through his desperate belly. No less than two-dozen coaches rolled into view before the newcomers took notice of the tiny campsite and came to a halt. Elric and Cormick shared a quick look to confirm their next move before stepping out to greet the strangers.

Elric almost didn't notice the murals on the sides of the coaches in the dim light, but even if he hadn't, the flamboyant garb of the travelers would have been enough to tell him they were gypsies. The driver of the lead coach craned his head down towards Elric and Cormick, a nervous look appearing on his pinched face as he turned his lantern upon them.

"Hello, fellow travelers," said Elric with a friendly wave.

The lead driver did not return the greeting. Instead, he turned in his seat and banged with his fist on the wooden paneling at his back.

Elric stood in silence as the back of the coach opened up and a matronly woman stepped down into the road.

"Elric Elensol," cooed the aged gypsy woman, "I did not think to be running across you again."

"Illiyna Mek'Verona," said Elric with a smile as wide as his face. He would have recognized her long silver hair anywhere, even without the one-of-a-kind set of facial jewelry that spiraled across her left cheek and brow. "It is good to see a friend on such a day!"

Fortune smiles!

The gypsy caravan was the same one he'd briefly traveled with on his journey south to Erotos from Darrenfield.

"And a new face with you," said Illiyna, eying Cormick with a sly smile. "Come—I have many questions, but such things are best discussed over a hearty meal."

Elric and Cormick's bellies growled in unison. Illiyna's smile widened as Cormick hustled over to the coach at the prospect of food, trodding past Elric in his excitement.

"The name's Cormick Gansly," the fisherman said as Illiyna offered out the back of her hand. Cormick lifted it to his lips and planted a small kiss.

"A charmer, aren't you?" The silver-haired gypsy feigned bashfulness. "Don't worry," she whispered to Elric when he reached her side, "I learned long ago that men only get better with age." She gave him a not-so-subtle wink.

Elric didn't remember Illiyna being so flirtatious the first time they met, but as the rest of the gypsies went about their business and a table was readied for the matriarch and her guests, a nearly empty bottle of wine was placed at Illiyna's seat, answering all of Elric's unasked questions.

"What brings you to Lake Baratoa of all places?" Illiyna asked.

Elric was caught with a mouthful of rabbit stew. He hastened to swallow but Cormick stepped in with an answer before Elric could speak again.

With as few words as possible, Cormick filled Illiyna in on the unfortunate circumstances of their quest. Illiyna kept her pale-gray eyes locked on Elric the entire time Cormick was speaking. The spiral of gems on her face shined in the lamplight in mesmerizing fashion, like a dance of fireflies. Elric had seen facial art like Illiyna's being done once when he was a boy—dozens of tiny piercings. While sneaking where he did not belong, he'd witnessed a young gypsy girl receiving the piercings from her elder. She hadn't so much as flinched as the beads of blood appeared; hole after hole driven into her flesh. The thought of being turned into a human pin-cushion had unsettled him in his youth. Elric was unsure of the cultural significance of such designs. Perhaps they were purely ornamental—the gypsies weren't apt to share.

Elric suddenly realized he'd been staring at Illiyna for far too long. He diverted his eyes, but he was certain she'd already noticed.

The rest of supper brought a barrage of flirtatious energy from Illiyna in Elric's direction that was not wholly unwanted, but felt mildly inappropriate in the wake of his quest. Illiyna seemed oblivious to Elric's resistance. When it came time to turn in for the night Elric was worried Illiyna might make an advance on him. Instead, she offered to share camp with the two travelers for the extent of the gypsies' stay on Lake Baratoa's shore.

The next day, Elric and Cormick were able to spend their time scouring Professor Vanton's notes while the gypsies dragged nets across the lake. They were far more successful than Elric and Cormick had been. As glad as Cormick was to have food again, Elric could tell the fisherman's pride was bruised.

At midday, they gathered with the gypsies for a small meal. The lake's bounty had been generous; preparations for a supper feast began almost as soon as lunch was finished. All the gypsies, men and women alike, cleaned and gutted the morning catch while a group of younger men dug out ovens in the clay-heavy soil.

Illiyna, insistent on hosting, wouldn't let Elric or Cormick help at all in the preparations, but when Elric saw a young women hefting heavy buckets of water up from the lakeside to be boiled into drinking water he couldn't ignore his chivalrous callings.

She instantly grew wary at his approach.

"Those look awful heavy," he said. "Please, allow me to take some of your burden."

She glanced hesitantly in the direction of Illiyna's coach. No one was watching.

Elric realized he may have unnerved the girl. He flashed a smile to try to put her more at ease. "I apologize if I offend," he said. "I just seek to be of service. May I?" He extended a hand to take one of the buckets. The young gypsy woman's mouth twitched up into a brief smile in response despite her apparent reservations. She allowed Elric to carry one.

"I don't mean to intrude," said Elric, "I just couldn't sit by doing nothing whilst you toiled away under such strain."

"I'm not supposed to talk to strangers," the young woman said quietly.

Elric was surprised by her odd speech inflection. She didn't sound like a gypsy. Once they reached the fireside and poured the buckets into a large boiling pot Elric examined the young woman more closely. Her eyes were green, not pale gray like Illiyna and her ilk. The girl's black hair matched the predominantly dark-haired gypsies, but faded marks on her scalp suggested it had recently been dyed.

A woman on the run....

She muttered a quick "Thank you," before shying away from his curious gaze and trotting off beyond the group of gypsies still gutting fish.

Quite the enigma....

Her skin was far fairer than the other gypsies, which became apparent when viewing her side-by-side with them. Elric put the oddities surrounding the young woman aside as he got back to work on reading the Sultrim texts with Cormick. He did not see the young woman again until later that evening during the feast.

That night, the gypsies placed all of their tables together end-to-end to form one long row. Elric and Cormick were sat once again beside Illiyna. Elric found his mind drifting as he gazed out across the way at the out-of-place young woman. Being more sober tonight, Illiyna was quick to notice Elric's wandering attention. She scowled when she saw towards whom Elric's focus had diverted. Upon seeing Illiyna's expression, Elric's curiosity grew even stronger.

"That girl...?" Elric started. He wasn't one to pussyfoot around a subject.

Illiyna sighed. "Pay her no mind," she said. "Rose has been traveling with us for some time now. It would be best if you didn't mention seeing her to anyone else. It's a sensitive matter, you understand?"

Elric had no idea what to make of the cryptic warning, but said "Of course," to Illiyna's wishes.

The subject of conversation was quickly changed back to Elric and Cormick's journey.

"A lofty quest," said Illiyna. "The Lost City of Sultrim has been well sought after for centuries due to the fables of treasure believed to reside there. What makes you think the two of you can find your way through the twisting mountain passes where everyone else has failed?"

Cormick's jaw drew tight at the pointed inquiry. "Those other people may have *wanted* to find the Lost City, but I *need* to find it," he said. "It's my little brother out there...."

Illiyna nodded, although she was clearly unconvinced of their chances.

Despite Illiyna's wishes for Elric to pay Rose no mind, her interactions—or more accurately, her lack of normal interactions with the gypsies, kept drawing Elric's attention back to her. When Rose went to retrieve her dinner portion, the gypsies avoided her. When she returned, no one joined her at her table segment. She ate alone.

Cormick began watching her now as well. He leaned in close to Elric and whispered in his ear. "So strange—they're leaving a gap around her like fish around a shark. You ever seen that before? The way a school of fish will clear just enough space for a shark to pass amongst them and avoid interaction? It looks like fear… But of such a shy young woman?"

"She's an outsider," Elric whispered back.

"So are we," said Cormick, "but you don't see them avoiding us like we're blighted."

Elric knew Cormick's evaluation to be true. Something still didn't add up with Rose.

She sat eating slowly with a bored expression on her face.

Cormick's curiosity waned and soon he was back in conversation with Illiyna. "I have more than just my determination to help me succeed where others failed," he said. "We have texts—journals from a professor in Erotos who studied the Lost City. He gave us volumes of information—every reference made about the city throughout the ages compiled together. No one else had anything like that before."

Everyone indulged in wine with supper. By dessert their tongues had all grown much looser for it. Elric was deep in conversation with Illiyna.

Once again, Illiyna's facial piercings were lit beautifully by the array of lanterns sitting across the line of tables. The tiny gems shimmered and twinkled with a hundred different shades of dark purples and reds before shifting in spectrum to brighter blues and oranges—the colors changed depending on the angle of her face to the lights. Elric couldn't help but stare. "I would never ask this," he said, his tongue slightly lethargic from the alcohol, "but the piercings—what do they mean? And who designed yours? I don't know if that's rude to ask..." he admitted. "I only mean to admire." He couldn't help but feel nervous like a young man again. He could have chuckled at himself. *Wine.* It did have a way of heightening his emotions.

Illiyna stared back at him for a short moment with a straight face before bursting out into jovial laughter. "Do you intend to inquire about my age next? Or perhaps my waistline? Yes, those are incredibly rude questions to ask a woman!" she chastised him, but never stopped laughing.

Elric's face was already flush from the wine—he hoped it would not change to an even darker shade. *At least she's laughing!*

Illiyna held her hand up over the left side of her face, blocking the piercings from Elric's view. She was still smiling behind her palm as she played coy.

Cormick nudged Elric with his leg. At first Elric thought his traveling companion meant to suggest he lessen his flirtations, but a glance at Cormick showed his eyes were narrowed upon Rose. She was no longer seated. She stood with her head craned towards a nearby copse of trees, looking the image of a spooked deer.

Rose released a long-held breath, and with it a white ball of lightning shot out from her chest and traveled in a crackling wave pattern towards the dark thicket. The ball-lightning spread out in an explosion of sparks upon entering the grove. "Somebody is watching us!" cried Rose. She looked to Illiyna for forgiveness for using her abilities.

A wizard! All of the oddities fell into alignment within Elric's mind.

The sound of a body collapsing in the brush proved her strike to have been a success.

Cormick jumped to his feet and was the first reach the copse. He disarmed the stunned man of his blade. A glint coming from the hilt piqued Elric's suspicion.

"Bring that here," he asked of Cormick as several gypsy men moved in to surround the uninvited guest.

As soon as Cormick drew nearer to Elric, any doubt he had about the sword quickly evaporated.

A Talus Shard.

A steely-eyed expression fell across Cormick's face as he held the blade up in his hand. The stunned eavesdropper must have been a decorated blade-brother of the Guardians of Truth.

The gypsies dragged the unconscious man over to the line of tables. A dose of smelling-salts was administered and the blade-brother's eyes shot open. His beleaguered expression fell across Elric.

It took a second, but then suddenly Elric realized who he was looking at—a face he hadn't seen in nearly two decades. "This is Orris Fen of the Paerto'radam," he announced.

Orris sat up sputtering. "I have news of your grandson," he wheezed as he latched onto Elric's tunic. "He wishes me to recall you to Erotos. Javic lives."

CHAPTER 22

Blood and Sand

Belford was less than pleased to be on the back of a horse again. It was giving him flashbacks of his journey south with Javic the previous autumn. His backside was already growing sore from the firm saddle. Beside him, Gord's stolen stallion looked like a pony beneath his massive frame.

Belford feared for the safety of his friends—Vera and Shiara in particular. The unrest in Tavallon had sent a steady stream of evacuees out in every direction from the capital city. He, along with Arlin and Gord, kept to themselves and stuck to the main highway as they traveled west towards the city of Vermholt—the last hub of civilization before the rolling sands of the Torus Desert.

Other refugees from the north coast crossed their path, bringing news of barbarian sieges and cities razed to the ground along the Northern Sea. The barbarians were ruthless in their campaign, slaughtering all those who remained behind. The carnage sounded awful—starving caravans of ill-prepared city folk sauntered slowly across the countryside. Every town they passed was overwhelmed with people seeking refuge and aid of every kind. Foraging was impossible along the border of the desert.

Belford was going on three days without a proper meal. The sun made his head feel woozy, threatening to pull him from his saddle as his stomach made a deep, disgruntled growl. His blood sugar was dangerously low. Every day that passed added to Belford's worries. Their horses were even starting to slow down as they approached the outskirts of Vermholt.

"We should stop for water," Belford complained.

Gord gestured widely around him. "At what stream?" he asked.

Belford frowned at Gord's dismissal. He was no expert at survival, but he knew it had been far too long since anyone had hydrated.

"We can drink once we reach the city," said Gord.

"Will the horses even make it that far?" asked Belford. They were still quite a ways out.

"These are desert horses," said Gord. "They'll be fine. Just suck on a pebble or something."

Belford sighed. His mouth was so dry! Sucking on a pebble might make him salivate, but it was a pointless gesture if he didn't add new moisture to his system. He wished the moon was up so that he could transmute some water out of the useless sand, but moonrise wouldn't be for several more hours, and by then they would already be in the city with any luck.

Gord kicked his stallion in an attempt to make it move faster, but the dehydrated beast only slowed down with the blows. After several more heel jabs, the poor horse stopped entirely, knelt to the ground, and then keeled over, dead on the spot.

Gord stood up, balking in dismay. Even desert horses had their limits. Belford smartly said nothing.

Before continuing on, Gord used one of his spiked gloves to puncture a hole in the expired beast's neck. He filled his canteen with its thick blood and began to sip on it as he walked beside Arlin and Belford on their mounts. He offered the canteen up to Belford, who pointedly refused. Belford felt his stomach turn at the mere thought of drinking horse blood, though he knew it was a practical move on Gord's part. Arlin passed on it as well.

The silent swordsman massaged his neck along the scar left behind by the Crimson Stalker's razor blade. Belford had opened him back up the previous day, attempting to fix Captain Grine's rushed Amelioration work. He'd taken the mangled structures and realigned things as best as he could, but it would still take time for Arlin to get used to the changes before he would be able to comfortably speak once more.

Belford walked his horse up alongside Arlin's. Their brown mares were far less impressive than the steed Arlin had left behind in Erotos. Belford cleared his throat. "I remembered something else about my past that I haven't told anyone yet," he said.

Arlin perked up, looking over at him.

"Claire was pregnant the last time I saw her," he said.

Arlin raised his eyebrows and pointed at Belford.

"Yup, with my kid—a daughter," he said. "Claire could sense her inside her womb."

Arlin nodded solemnly.

"It's hard to even know what to think, you know?" Belford mused.

Arlin continued nodding.

"I haven't really told you that much about my past, and I'm not going to bring it all up now with Gordy over there listening in—" he glanced back at Gord and caught him rolling his eyes, "—but if I find Claire… we're having a baby… a human child! Like, what is that! How can anyone just casually bring a new life into this world?!"

Arlin was smiling to himself. His hand was resting on the hilt of his sword.

"What are you doing right there?" asked Belford. "Your hand—you're touching your sword. I know what that does. You're masking your feelings."

Arlin removed his hand from his hilt at once. He glared back at Belford with indignation.

"I knew it!" exclaimed Belford. "You're terrified of having a baby with Mallory!"

Arlin's scowl became more downturned.

"I don't even blame you. I get it now," said Belford. "It's like a crushing elephant of responsibility that wasn't there before is suddenly standing on my chest making it hard to even breathe. I have to find them both. I don't know how to live without them...." Belford locked eyes with Arlin. "Elephants were really large land animals back in my time—the biggest! I'm not sure if they still exist."

Arlin nodded an affirmative.

"That's good!" said Belford. "They were nearly extinct in my time. I'm kind of surprised they made it."

Arlin shook his head, 'No.' He tapped his chest over his heart, and then reached over and tapped Belford's chest as well.

"Oh, you're saying I was right about your feelings."

Arlin grimaced as he nodded again.

"So then elephants really are extinct."

Arlin shrugged slightly, uninvested.

"You'll be a great father," said Belford. "You have to know that. I've seen your courage many times. You don't have anything to worry about. Any kid of yours is going to be a true warrior."

Arlin raised one eyebrow, giving Belford a side-eyed glance as he rode slightly ahead of him. He pulled out a pad of paper and a pencil that Belford had formed for him with the Power shortly after setting out from Tavallon. He scratched away at the pad for a moment before holding it up to Belford.

"'I hope my child is just like Mallory,'" Belford read the note aloud. "You and me both, buddy. We can only hope they turn out like their mothers."

Arlin growled to clear his throat, and then rasped three heartfelt words: "We'll—find—them."

What a great friend.

Belford smiled at him warmly.

They kept their horses moving slow so that Gord, on foot, would not be left behind. The horse blood dribbling down his chin was enough to keep the passing refugees at a comfortable distance. Belford's head was on a swivel—he looked back every time he heard the sound of hooves behind them. He always hoped to see their lost companions riding across the flats, but all he ever found were more strangers fleeing the madness of the freed Goblikans.

When they reached the outskirts of Vermholt there were no tall structures to greet them. The whole city was built into a split gorge of jutting sandstone—the exposed cliff-sides housed a series of hand-carved caves which served as residences for the population. Only a few larger slab structures were scattered throughout, mostly at the opening of the gorge.

The moon rose just as they passed the last outpost before the city. Having access to the Power again would have come as a comfort to Belford, except that he immediately noticed a change in his usual perception of his psychic connection.

It was weak.

And instead of growing stronger as the moon shifted fully into view, his connection floundered further with every step they took towards the gorge. His ability to sense the matter around him was covered in a blanket of *nothingness....*

He'd heard about the dead spot for the Power that the Torus Desert held within its sands—a remnant of the blast from the fabled Orb of Parphim that ended the Cleansing by vaporizing Garrett's Goblikan horde about a century before. His intuition told him now that the mechanism of the Power that usually replicated the matter markers—the Virus Replication

Protocol—must have been damaged or destroyed by the orb's blast as well. The sand here was just sand now. No markers remained for him and the computer to use in enacting his will on the environment.

Even when the moon was down, Belford could always somewhat sense the presence of the markers around him. Here, the few remaining markers were too diffuse for him to get a clear picture of the terrain in his head. He felt like he was an old cell-phone antenna with spotty service. He was still connected to the computer on the moon, but he could do nothing without an adequate presence of matter markers around him. The rolling sands, carried by the wind, spread the corruption outward from the original source of the orb's blast.

Belford's memory since being exposed to Livian's spores was spotty. He was missing chunks of time here and there, sometimes many hours in a row where he couldn't recall a thing, as if his body had been on auto-pilot or something. The mental fog worried him, but at least his regained memories of the Arcadian Project and his life before Aragwey remained intact.

"Why do they call this place Vermholt?" Belford asked. "It sounds like some sort of gothic hell-scape, but it looks more like the Valley of the Kings to me." He knew Gord and Arlin wouldn't get his references, but he didn't really care.

"You sense the fluctuating Power?" asked Gord.

Belford nodded.

"That used to start many leagues to the south. Vermholt was once the last city where the Power remained strong. This was where the masterless Whunes that rove the desert stopped their advance—where the vermin halted."

"Halted?" asked Belford. "Past-tense?"

"That gorge is a major crossroads," said Gord. "It still holds the line. Warriors keep it safe from the scourge of the desert. It's just more difficult these days with the expanding sands."

They continued on to the mouth of the ravine. Gord was met with scrutiny from the armored guards, more so from the blood staining his mouth than the fact he was a Goblikan. No one could consistently reach the Power here so that wasn't a worry. The guards let them pass after confirming Gord wasn't in some sort of murderous stupor.

They had nothing to trade but their skinny dehydrated mares, which they hocked for a hearty meal and several draughts of light ale each. The alcohol content was low, but it was the best way to hydrate while avoiding getting dysentery from the well water.

They waited throughout the day, seated outside a tavern in the shade where they could keep an eye out for their lost companions.   As night fell, Belford's worry grew.   He previously had dared to hope they'd all made it out of Tavallon around the same time.

Maybe they're just traveling slowly....

Ader's condition certainly might have delayed them some. He didn't want to think about the alternative. His brain was full of holes but he was astutely aware of the mess they'd all gotten themselves into as the spores descended. They were with Ethan, the most powerful Ver'ati alive.

They have to be alright....

When it became clear another night apart was in order, they used the remainder of their coin to rent a couple of tiny cots. Gord was too large for the beds and chose to sleep on the ground instead, using a rolled up sack for a lumpy pillow. Belford couldn't imagine the Goblikan's discomfort—the sand flees nipped anything that wasn't lofted.

After a second day without the others showing up, Belford's worry turned into deep, nail-biting concern. He never should have allowed Gord to convince him to abandon his friends! Ethan was powerful, but so was Belford. He could have done more—should have!

An anxious knot squeezed his insides. They all ended up bit-up on the ground the second night. Belford couldn't sleep a wink. Arlin and Gord kept their focus on practical survival— boiling water from the well and cleaning their clothes in a large pot loaned to them by another band of pitying travelers passing through from the coast.

On the third day, Gord and Arlin traded their labor for enough money to buy supper for the group, but with so many refugees, the price of a bed was still too high to afford. Belford kept watch for their companions as the sun began to set in the west.

One coach finally rolled in, chasing the sunset. Belford glanced up from where he had been snoozing as the sound of the horses caught his ear. He rubbed his eyes, clearing out the dusty sand from the corners as he tried to make out the coach's driver in the dying light. Two dark-haired women sat in the front seat. Belford's heart leapt as he recognized Vera and Shiara's pinched scowl from the distance.

"Arlin!" he shouted behind him into the tavern where the swordsman was lending his strength to move crates of supplies for the establishment. "They're here!" Belford jumped up and ran in their direction to greet them.

Vera spotted Belford first, pointing him out to Shiara before handing off a sword to her that had been lying across her lap. She reigned in the horses and then hopped down to greet him as he approached the coach's stoop.

They met in a wordless embrace. Vera buried her head in Belford's chest as Shiara climbed down on the other side of the wagon. Sharith Grine poked his head out of the back and gave a little wave.

"Is everyone here?" asked Belford.

Vera shook her head. "Bundles and his family… we parted ways. Ader is with us, though—he's doing a lot better now— he's in the back resting. The spores really got into him deep. The effects are still wearing off."

Shiara stepped up behind Vera, one hand on her hip, and the other clutching the sword Vera had handed her.

"You have no idea what a relief it is to see you!" Belford exclaimed with a boyish grin. "Thank you for not dying!"

"Yeah, well, no thanks to you," Shiara responded. "I thought you'd come back for us."

Belford's face turned beet red in an instant—he could feel the heat rising in his cheeks. He knew he'd messed up.

"You should be thanking Vera, anyway," said Shiara. "Without her, every one of us would be dead, or worse."

The gem in the hilt of the sword caught Belford's eye. It was glowing the same way Shiara's firestone earring occasionally did when it was overfilled with energy. "Is that a Talus Shard?" Belford asked, gawking at the blade's familiar appearance.

Arlin caught up to them, stepping up beside Belford. He held up his own sword. The gem in its hilt was glowing as well. The shine grew in intensity as he moved closer, bringing the blades together.

"It's Vera's," said Shiara. "She earned it."

Belford was confused but also impressed. He knew Talus Shards were rare and powerful Artifacts. "You must have an interesting story," he said to Vera.

"It's certainly a long and unpleasant one," she responded.

Belford hung his head in shame. "I'm sorry I wasn't there for both of you. The spores… we had to get away—they were eating our brains. Everything is still hazy…."

"Well, we're fine now," said Shiara.

"We made it," added Vera.

"Just do better next time," said Shiara. "Ask yourself what Thorin would have done, and then maybe try doing that instead of running away with your tail between your legs." She eyed Belford and then Arlin harshly in turn.

Always so ruthless….

Belford was absolutely gutted. Shiara, with her hand on the emotion-sucking blade, couldn't have cared less about the sting her words caused.

Arlin, emotion masked by his own sword, grimaced with chagrin.

Vera gripped onto Belford again, squeezing him once more in a tight hug. Her fingers clenched onto him desperately throughout the long embrace. Belford cupped the back of her head—he could feel the tension drain out of her as he did so. It was apparent that she had faced great adversity in his absence.

He felt like such a selfish prick.

Every decision he'd made since he and the other Arcadians had their bodies memorized by the computer on the moon—everything he'd done since reappearing a millennia later in Belford Quarry next to Javic's farm—had been done to improve his chances of staying alive in the vain hope of one day finding his way back to Claire. His unborn child only added to his desperation. The issue was, he'd consistently ignored the well-being of every other person he cared about every step of the way. While his last few days were full of holes—as if his mind had been eaten up by worms—the love and desperation that filled him was an ever-swelling mass of twine. Since Thorin's death, he knew he had lost his way. He was losing himself.

"I'm sorry," Belford said again. "Truly."

Shiara fixed him with a steady gaze.

"I can't lose anyone else," he said. And he meant it. He'd lost Claire—along with his whole world. The Arcadians had thrown their fates to the wind. At times he felt like he was just a reflection of his former self. He needed to remember he had his own agency. He was still standing when so many others had been lost to time. He couldn't change his past, but if he didn't hold tight to the ones he loved now, he knew he was destined to wind up all alone again.

Ethan stepped down from the back of the coach, stretching his legs as he took in the dusty sunset over Vermholt. Wilgoblikan was still present as well, Belford was less pleased to note. While Ethan and Wil's deal was their ticket to safety, Belford had no grace left within him for either man. At one time, Ethan had represented hope of understanding the past.

Now, Belford just saw him as another asshole with a loose moral code.

Ethan had always told Belford that by regaining his memories he would understand why Garrett deserved to die. But now with all his mental pathways revitalized, he wasn't sure what he believed anymore. Garrett had certainly been a piece of work—there was no question about that—but the downfall of civilization was not caused by one man alone. The situation with the Arcadian Project had been a tangled disaster from the beginning. It was all more convoluted than he would ever truly be able to unravel from just his memories.

He knew now that dwelling on the past would only lead to more pain and suffering—both for him and for the people around him. Simultaneously, the lingering feeling that he would never truly be able to escape it all remained omnipresent—an ever lurking danger that threatened to pull him back into the darkness.

CHAPTER
23

The Originals

Beep.... Beep.... Beep....

The sound of a heart rate monitor chirped over the steady roar of the recycled air that filled the windowless hospital room.

"What's left of a bloke once you tear him down to nothing—and I mean really nothing—to the point where he doesn't even recognize his own reflection?" Travis stood beside Aaron's recovery bed, staring at himself in the mirror on the far wall. The skin on his bald head, once covered in self-drawn tattoos, was now blistered and peeling from radiation sores. The sores oozed with plasma, glistening under the harsh lights of the EAC medical facility in which the Arcadians now found themselves captive.

The medical center smelled heavily of disinfectant. Aaron hated the stink of bleach, but it was inescapable. He was barely strong enough to even lift his eyelids—it was hard to believe Travis was already on his feet! All of the Arcadians had received what should have been lethal doses of radiation

165

from their close proximity to the Arcadian Project complex when the tactical warheads that destroyed Tripoli were deployed. Miraculously, Isabelle's dome shield had absorbed most of the blast—enough to keep them breathing anyway.

"No one recovers from this kind of trauma," said Travis. His one good eye shifted over to Aaron in the mirror. "But I guess that doesn't stop time from moving forward."

The days following the nuclear holocaust were a blur to Aaron. He'd been to hell and back, experiencing the worst pain of his life. The agony was unending as he drifted in and out of consciousness. Terrible visions of charred corpses filled his feverish dreams… bodies burning in the sweeping blasts… whole cities evaporating into shadow.

Ethan's espionage for the East Asian Coalition may have been the spark that set the world on fire, but none of the Arcadians were really innocent—Reblan Industries turned them into illegal super soldiers. Aaron joined the project for the money, just as Ethan probably sold the truth of their experiments for some massive payday. None of it was right.

As a doctor, Aaron knew that genetically modifying humans was an ethically slippery slope. He'd allowed himself to be altered anyway, but the power he was given was something for which the world was not ready. He felt deep shame in what had transpired. Power dynamics on the world stage could not tolerate what Aaron and the other Arcadians had become. The status-quo was thrown all out of whack—unleashing global thermal nuclear war with a few zero-day hacks piled on top to insure allied defenses like the HAMMER project couldn't stop the destruction. Ethan had been the lynchpin, but they'd all shamelessly destroyed the balance of mutually assured destruction. They'd been given too much power for mere fallible mortals. While they were an unprecedented threat to the geopolitical powers of the world, they were also the ultimate prize to be won.

The visions of the dead tormented Aaron—both in his dreams as well as every waking moment. The delirium and solitude of his radiation poisoning left him with nowhere to run. He couldn't get away from himself. He had no way of telling how long it had been since the blasts that destroyed the world. They'd had the computer memorize their bodies and minds because they'd expected to die…. Fate held other plans.

Travis's intrusion to his room was the first time anyone had spoken to Aaron since his arrival at the EAC facility. His only solace was that he could still feel Claire's presence in the back of his mind. She clung to life, trapped in a medically induced coma in a nearby room.

"Cl-Claire?" Aaron rasped. His throat ached from the intubation tube that had only recently been removed.

"They're waking her up later today, mate," said Travis. He knew what Aaron wanted to know. "Though, I don't think any of us will be getting out of here anytime soon." Travis sat down on the edge of Aaron's bed. "Do you reckon we made a mistake sending those copies of ourselves into the future?" he asked. "They won't know the truth about Ethan's betrayal. They won't know about any of this." He gestured broadly at the room around them.

Aaron grimaced.

"He's still alive too, by the way. They got him hooked up to a bunch of machines. Shoulda stomped him better. Bloody traitor."

"What do they want from us?" asked Aaron.

"The EAC? You'll have to ask them, mate," said Travis. "I don't know if being so special makes us lucky—these meds are rare buggers—or if we'd be better off dead with what's to come. I assume they'll want our help." He patted Aaron's ankle through the bedding. "I'll keep my ears open," he said. He leaned in closer and whispered: "They don't know my connection to Brooke allows me to understand Chinese." His one way connection to the multi-lingual woman was proving to be useful, though perhaps not worth the embolism that it had caused behind Travis's left eye.

Aaron rubbed his neck, but nothing eased his discomfort as he swallowed down a glob of thick spit.

Travis stood up, flashing his butt through the slit in his hospital gown. "I'll let you get some more rest," he said. He hobbled out of the room, leaving Aaron alone to mourn the loss of the world they'd once known.

Nothing could ever be the same again—not with so much death and destruction.

Aaron could feel the presence of the computer in his mind as well. He began to map out the facility in his head, following the flows of electric current through the walls. The process was draining, but he wanted to be prepared for whatever was to come.

CHAPTER
24

Relentless

The next morning after Orris Fen brought news of Elric's grandson's safety, Elric left Cormick the packhorses as a parting gift as he readied his own steed for his journey back to Erotos. Losing Elric's companionship was a hard hit to Cormick's morale.

Of course, he had not expected Elric to continue on their desperate quest once discovering that his grandson was alive and well, back in the Glowing City. Their goals were simply no longer aligned. It was a sad truth to contend with. Cormick was in it all alone now. Rylin was still depending on him.

The gypsies were kind enough to restock Cormick's food reserves. Pickled mackerel and herring were on the menu. Hailing from the coast, he was used to such briny delicacies, so his palate would not complain. He would have preferred a larger variety of flavors, not just the harsh, salty, pickled ones, but sustenance was sustenance and beggars could not be choosers. He had needed food that would not spoil. He was grateful for their charity.

When the blade-brother learned of Cormick's quest to find Sultrim, Cormick could tell he had piqued the man's interest. "It appears the Elensol boy was hiding more than a few details from me," said Orris. "He spoke of experimentations on students and of losing time, but not of a doorway to Sultrim. I see now why Elric traveled so far and wide, so quickly. He did not think Javic dead, merely lost."

Cormick asked about Rylin, but Orris knew nothing of his brother. The way Orris's eyes lit up when Cormick talked about the perilous journey ahead made him dare hope for a brief moment that perhaps he had found himself a new traveling companion in the blade-brother, but Orris made it clear that he had every intention of returning to Erotos alongside Elric.

Even a heart for adventure wasn't enough for Orris to join in on Cormick's fool's errand. Cormick was finding it difficult to stay positive.

They all shared one last meal together with the gypsies before they were set to head off in their separate directions.

Knowing he was about to be all alone, fending for himself on such an impossible task put a solid knot in Cormick's stomach. He was barely able to eat anything at all. Illiyna could feel his reservations and offered up an unhelpful bit of advice.

"Determination is very well and good, but there is a poem known along the Gulf of Nerim that feels relevant to your situation." She began to recite the poem verbatim:

"Quickly dipping, turning, flipping, scarcely skirting land and sky,

The kite gnaws at its string relentlessly, chafing fears both low and high.

Down the line and to the left, just past the piers ungainly mass,

The crashing waves of liquid jade churn forth a chill of winter glass.

A little boy of nine or ten is combing sand for rocks and shells,

He saves a few and casts the rest into the oceans midnight swells.

They call his name and search 'til dawn, through wave-swept coves and idle cracks,

Until the tide comes rolling in, forever blotting out his tracks."

Cormick felt heat rise in his face as the old gypsy woman beat him down with her words.

"You can spend your whole life relentlessly searching for what has been lost. I understand the value of family, but at some point you must be honest with yourself, or else your own life may end up forfeit in pursuit of a lost cause."

Cormick refused to admit defeat. His task may have been impossible, but he would not know for sure unless he went on the journey all the way to the end. He would search for Rylin until he knew he was dead, or until the Arid Hills took his own last breaths away. Rylin was tough—little, but determined. He couldn't give up on him now. His love was too great. He had to believe he could make it!

After their final lunch, Cormick watched as Illiyna imposed upon Elric one last unexpected request.

"Rose will not be safe with us forever," she said. "Would you be a dear and see that she makes it to Erotos? These lands are not welcoming to a young woman on her own. She needs to join her own kind in the Glowing City."

Elric hemmed and hawed, wishing to make haste in his travels, but ultimately agreed to the matriarch's request.

The girl was powerful—that much was clear from her shocking display the previous night. Cormick had only spent time around Ver'ati in Erotos. Rylin had only just started showing an aptitude for the Gift the summer before shipping off to the capital city. Magical abilities filled Cormick's mind with wonder. He couldn't help but feel jealous of all of Elric's skilled companions. Cormick was the oldest of five siblings. He wasn't used to being alone. The weight of the journey ahead felt suppressive on his lungs, but there was nothing to do but press onward.

As he bid Elric ado, they clasped each other in a tight hug. "If by some miracle you happen to find Rylin alive back in Erotos with your grandson, I hope it won't be too much of a bother to send someone out here to stop me from throwing myself up these mountains…." Cormick chuckled gravely.

"If that's the case, I will ride back myself," said Elric. "May Mast illuminate your path."

Cormick sighed to himself as he lashed the leads of the packhorses to his mount. There was nothing but the harshness of winter ahead. The rolling foothills extended for leagues before the real puzzle of the twisting mountain passes would begin. He had all of Professor Vanton's notes—an encyclopedia's worth of reading to contend with. As doubt crept in, he forced himself onward. One step at a time.

CHAPTER
25

Where the Lost Things Go

With the Great Device fully up to speed, its rings spun in a bright blur of silver. The spherical chamber was no longer accessible for Rylin and the bears to traverse. The beating heart of Sultrim pumped new life into the vast subterranean city. More lights turned on all throughout the ruins, growing from out of the depths with glowing tendrils of what Ma'freit referred to as *bioluminescence*. Large beacons reminiscent of the mirrored lighthouses on the coast shot light across the vast chamber of the hub and beyond. The hallways and tunnels of the ancient depths were illuminated for the first time in centuries. The glow looked like shimmering stars as Ma'freit flapped her powerful wings in their ascent.

Rylin was being lifted back up towards the surface tunnels. He clasped hard onto Ma'freit's thick fur as she bounced him around with each upward thrust. Kamila stayed at their side, wings churning twice as fast to keep up.

173

The suspension bridges that spanned the massive hub chamber were illuminated by strands of cord that stretched their lengths. The scale of the chamber was even grander than Rylin had imagined. Bridges far in the distance twinkled with atmospheric haze all contained within the confines of the hollow mountain range.

Ma'freit dipped suddenly to avoid an un-illuminated bridge nestled amongst the glowing ones—such was the state of the degradation.

When they reached Raljaska's den, Besel and Ashran were relieved to see Rylin and their sister. The three cubs frolicked into a cuddle pile while Kamila recounted her and Rylin's escape from Tanuk. Rylin eyed Raljaska warily. The mama bear had been bloodied by Tanuk's assault, but she was far from disabled. Her hair was bristled up, clearly agitated as she ambled towards Ma'freit.

Marred with superficial wounds from the tussle, the fur on the back of her neck stood up like a spooked cat where Tanuk's claws had torn into her flesh. Ma'freit helped pack the wounds with moss, gathered by the cubs—Raljaska rejected Rylin's offer to seam her skin shut with the Power.

Ma'freit and Raljaska insisted on conversing alone while Rylin waited with the cubs outside on one of the open-air stoops. The harsh winter air felt like a change of season compared to the heat beneath the mountain. Rylin gazed out across the snowcapped range as the moon began its rise. Being able to reach the Power did little to ease his anxiety. The bears were immune to direct attack with the Power, just like Ver'ati… and Goblikans. He anxiously bit his cuticles as he considered the many dangers lurking below the mountain.

The Goblikans were tunneling ever nearer. Ma'freit had not been able to elaborate much on that subject. Whunes labored away, clearing debris blasted by the Power. Raiding the treasure troves of Artifacts stored across the city was surely the Goblikans' objective. Rylin wondered if they might be after the same Artifact core Javic had already pilfered for Lieutenant General Cale Fisman.

To the bears, Tanuk was the least pressing concern at the moment. Their duty to protect the Artifacts was all that mattered to them. Rylin kept his head on a swivel for the murderous bear. He didn't want to be caught off-guard by the stalking behemoth. Tanuk's attack on Raljaska had been brief but vicious. While Raljaska was not too terribly maimed, the mother bear had been unable to prevent the hulking male from chasing after Rylin.

When Raljaska emerged after her conversation with Ma'freit, Rylin got his first look at her wounds in the daylight. She would have several new scars from the ordeal. Her left ear had a notch taken out of it. Her fur was matted with dark blood along the side of her head and all around her muzzle—she had clearly gotten a mouthful of Tanuk as well.

Ma'freit appeared behind Raljaska. The matriarch stepped out of the tunnel and launched herself off the mountainside without a word, soaring into the hazy sky.

"What's going to happen now?" asked Rylin.

Raljaska watched Ma'freit fly away until she disappeared over the next peak. "The hierarchy will meet to condemn Tanuk's assault on me," she said, "but until Tanuk shows his face again, there is little that can be done to punish his actions."

Rylin sighed.

"I am still your host," said Raljaska. "I will protect you with my life."

The bears were honor-bound creatures. Rylin knew Raljaska would keep her word.

"Come," said Raljaska. "We must prepare to defend ourselves." The great bear lumbered back into the tunnels.

Rylin followed alongside the cubs. He knew better than to ask any questions. The bears preferred to only speak when necessary. They marched down a branch of pathways Rylin had yet to explore, winding around behind Raljaska's den towards the mountain's summit.

Raljaska paused in a doorway and looked back. "This is where the lost things go," she said before entering the circular chamber ahead.

The ceiling arched up into a wide dome like a cathedral. It held a mechanical component—the roof could slide open. Windows high above let in natural light. Rylin put away his lightglove. The room was an armory with a take-off pad at its center for the bears to launch into the mountain air. Artifact knickknacks lined tall stacks of shelving that ran the perimeter of the structure—the clutter reminded Rylin of a flea market. Racks closer to the center of the room held long-handled halberds with thick rusted blades at their heads.

Crumbling Calvenite chains held aloft several suits of bear-sized armor. Raljaska approached a gleaming chest plate and stood on her hind-legs. She manipulated the chains aptly with her claws before sticking her thick limbs in through the holes. The armor settled snugly against her fur with a clang as the sheets of metal knocked together. She sat down on her haunch and used a hind-leg to cinch a strap tight around her middle. Next, she slid into a matching skullcap. When she was finished attaching the plate armor, she was transformed into a terrifying silver tank.

Raljaska bowed before Rylin. A wide saddle was attached into the grooves on her back. "Do you see this gem?" Raljaska asked. A glowing white orb that looked like a large iridescent pearl was entrenched at the top of her neck guard just in front of the saddle. "Go find its mate," she ordered. She raised her head and nodded towards an area of shelving.

Rylin approached the shelves hesitantly. This was the first time he'd been permitted to interact with any of the bears' treasures. A dozen talismans with gems of varying colors and sizes lined a shelf at eye level. Only one of the gems looked like Raljaska's pearl. Rylin retrieved it and walked back over to the bear.

"Put it on," she said. "Tuck it against your skin."

Rylin obliged. He clasped the cold chain behind his head and slid the gem against his chest. As soon as the gem touched his skin he could sense Raljaska's mind within his own. Her thoughts filled his head in an overwhelming jumble of inhuman logic and language.

I often think in what you refer to as the old tongue. Raljaska explained, projecting the words clearly into his mind. *We are now connected. Our thoughts pass freely.*

The gems must have been amplifying the bear's innate psychic abilities.

You can feel my intentions, as I can yours.

Rylin already knew what Raljaska wanted him to do next. He approached the old halberds. Most were rusted beyond use, but one still gleamed as if forged that very morning. Rylin knew it to be an Artifact—it was a weapon fit for a Guardian Rider. He wrapped his hands around the grip and hefted the heavy weapon into the air.

Kamila squealed. "You look like a Sul'rudonia!"

Sun Rider, Raljaska translated.

Rylin could barely lift the awkward weapon above his head. An anxious bubble formed in his gut at the thought of riding into battle. *Flying into battle!* "There's no way I can wield this—it's twice my height!" He didn't wish to see combat— atop a flying bear or otherwise!

There is no room for fear. "Climb upon me," Raljaska vocalized. *You have much to learn.*

CHAPTER
26

A Dangerous Game

Javic kept his eyes lowered to the polished floor. His reflection glowered back up at him. How pathetic that he couldn't even control his own abilities. Havorie had been distant with him since their accidental levitation atop the northwest tower. Already, rumors were circulating amongst the palace staff that Javic was the queen's paramour. Too many eyes had seen the mess he'd made of the breakfast buffet. Javic walked away doused in syrup and butter. It stayed oily on his skin, thick like his shame. While obviously unintentional, levitation was exceedingly dangerous.

His inadvertent use of the Power might have killed a lesser wizard on the spot, but Javic's capacity for the Power was remarkably high. He had been left with a splitting headache, but that was a far cry from the aneurysm that most wizards would have experienced attempting such a feat.

He knew better, and yet it still happened. After everything Shiara had taught him, he could hear her voice in his head:

You did WHAT?! She would have been enraged at his carelessness. Javic knuckled his forehead for the umpteenth time. He was horrified by his lack of control.

The fact that he'd traumatized Havorie by nearly forcing her to repeat her mother's unfortunate drop made him feel like the biggest asshole in Aragwey. He never would have hurt her intentionally, but it was too late to take back his reckless actions. When he reported for his next shift, Havorie wouldn't even look at him. Her lustful glances were all gone. Her emerald eyes held deep reservation. She was scared of him.

Javic was tasked with guarding the entrance to Havorie's chambers. Professor Vanton would have chastised him for allowing his emotional connection to the Power to take hold. He had relied on his feelings to control the Power too often—it had become second nature to him. Now he better understood the risks.

Footsteps approached. Javic stood up taller, trying to be the model guard. He didn't want to make any more mistakes. Ervia rounded the corner, on time for her meeting with the queen. She didn't look at Javic as she passed.

Not a good sign.

The women chatted in rushed whispers, just out of earshot. They kept sneaking glances back his way across the hall—the subject of their conversation was obvious. After the meeting, Ervia avoided Javic even more pointedly during her departure. She maintained a wide berth as she walked briskly from the chamber. Havorie continued tracking Javic from across the way as if he were some sort of dangerous animal.

Well, aren't I??

He couldn't blame her. He was supposed to be able to control himself. He'd acted worse than an immature child. His seventeenth birthday afforded him all the rights and responsibilities of an adult, but without the wherewithal to restrain his abilities he should never have been promoted out of initiate status by Lieutenant General Fisman. His inexperience was dangerous. And yet, the fact remained that he had been given the title of Ver'ati. It felt like an absurdity.

I nearly killed Queen Havorie....   Phandrol can't lose another queen in that same terrible way.

The thought of repeating that trauma upon the kingdom was too horrendous to consider.

At least I would have died too....

His own death would have been a mercy had he dropped Havorie over the side of the tower.

The queen didn't look up again, engrossed in more old ledgers as Javic was relieved from his duty by another one of Captain Sarvo's men. The disappointment Javic felt hurt physically in his chest. His heart thudded with hollow pangs. He'd messed everything up.

The one time anyone ever wants me romantically and I nearly drop her over the balcony.

His shame was immeasurable. He moved with a wilted posture, head slumped forward as he slinked back to the barracks to try to get some rest. His next shift was patrol duty. He would be up all night. Every guard had to take one late patrol a week. He would have to visit every chamber in the palace twice before dawn. If he finished too quickly, he'd be sent out for a third round.

The barracks was empty when he arrived. He was the only Queen's Guard trying to sleep midday. He reclined in his cot. It was set up in a recessed alcove like a coffin in a crypt. The cots were stacked three high upon the wall. He drew the curtain across the opening before beginning to massage his temples with his fingertips. The small circular motions alleviated his tension headache, albeit only momentarily. Still, some relief was better than none. He drifted off to sleep with a clenched jaw.

A rap upon the frame to his alcove roused him prematurely from his nap. He'd been dreaming about setting up gopher traps in a dense field of wildflowers. He could still smell a hint of lilac in the air as he struggled to pull himself back to reality.

"Javic? Are you in there?"

He recognized Mallory's melodic drawl as she knocked again with a quick series of bangs against the frame. Her sweet lilac perfume permeated the alcove.

It took Javic a moment to realize where he was. "What's happening?" he asked, sitting up as he vocalized the astute question. He banged his head at the top of his nook.

Mallory drew the curtain back upon hearing his voice. Javic pulled his sheet up reflexively. The vulnerability of his position washed over him. Mallory diverted her gaze. Her mouth pinched into a tight grimace. There were tears welling in her eyes.

"Mallory?" Javic asked, still confused. "What's wrong?"

She shook her head, unwilling to talk in front of a pair of guardsmen who had entered the barracks during Javic's nap. The concern etched on her brow stoked Javic's worries. The other guards grew silent as they observed the odd interaction. Mallory's chin began to quiver as more tears silently flowed down her cheeks.

"Can you guys clear the room for a moment?" Javic asked loudly. The other guards departed at a slow gait. Mallory refused to speak until they were completely gone and the door to the barracks had latched shut behind them.

Javic pulled his shirt back on over his head. "Tell me what's wrong," he ordered. Mallory's silence was making him anxious. His nerves were already so terribly frayed.

Mallory closed her eyes and let out a long exhale. "Professor Vanton was murdered," she said. Tears sprang out from under her eyelids as she squeezed them shut even tighter. When she opened them again, Javic recognized the fear bubbling behind her sadness.

Javic was shocked. Arius Vanton was a well-respected member of the Ver'konus. Javic knew him as a kind old man—quirky, but harmless. How anyone could hurt him was baffling…. Vanton had been more than a mentor to Javic— he'd been a true friend when Javic needed one most. He owed his life to the professor. Without his guidance, Javic knew he never would have survived his Dance of the Elements.

"Someone's been following me," said Mallory. "And I can't find Tyris. I'm afraid whoever killed Arius is after us both now."

"Whoa, whoa, back up," said Javic. "What did Professor Vanton drag you into?" As saddened as he was over Arius's death, he knew far too well the professor's propensity to rub certain authoritative folk the wrong way. Javic felt a flash of anger towards the deceased for daring to put Mallory in any danger—especially given her condition!

"Arius asked us to meet with one of his former students in the Archives. Tyris and I went, but Lyle—that's the guy's name—he wouldn't tell us anything—he only wanted to talk to Arius. And now the professor's dead!" Mallory was about to lose her composure again. She held her fists clenched at her sides. Her whole body was beginning to shake now.

Javic clutched her in a tight hug. She melted into his arms. Her emotions let loose as a torrent of sobs, wept into his shoulder. Javic's mind was still reeling. He caressed Mallory's head gently, stroking her soft hair with his fingertips as her unrelenting tears formed damp spots upon his shirt.

"They're trying to say he was killed by an Echo! Can you believe that? His whole office was firebombed!"

"What was this all about?" Javic asked.

Mallory shook her head with her face still pressed against him. She pulled away after another moment and craned her neck up to look in his face. "Lyle only said there was a conspiracy—that it involved the Crown. He didn't say anything more. I know from Arius that Lyle worked for Tannel Cresdale before he was transferred to the Archive Historians."

Javic felt his face grow hot with rage at the mention of Tannel. The leader of the Arcanum Council had been out to get Javic from the moment they met! Tannel wanted him dead ever since he'd returned through the doorway to Sultrim. Now

Tannel was killing his friends. Javic didn't have any evidence, but he knew Tannel was guilty—he felt it in his bones. Either the Council leader was even more hell-bent on hurting him than he ever anticipated, or Professor Vanton had stumbled upon something significantly damning.

"I can think of one conspiracy involving the Crown," said Javic. "If Tannel is behind it, no one is beyond his reach. I need to speak with the queen at once."

Javic tried to pull away from the hug, but Mallory gripped onto his hands all the tighter. She stared up into his eyes, her expression filled with desperation. "Please forgive me," she said.

Javic felt like he'd been punched right in the heart. He lingered there with his wrists held tight in her hands.

Mallory's gaze flicked back and forth between his eyes searchingly. "Forgive me—I didn't know," Mallory begged.

Javic continued to stare at her. Her tearful expression threatened to pull Javic down too. "What?" he asked. "What didn't you know? How dangerous this all is?"

Mallory froze, too choked up to speak. She gave a gentle shake of her head. She swallowed audibly against the lump in her throat. "I didn't know how much I was going to care about you." She was staring at his lips.

Javic was at a loss for words.

Mallory released Javic's wrists and put her hand over her subtly swelling stomach. Her eyes shifted downward as she spoke with a wavering tone. "I don't actually know that this is Arlin's child," she said.

Javic inhaled sharply, unable to mask his surprise.

"He has claimed it—he is so very commendable like that— but we both know what happened to me… what he saved me from. There is no way to be certain of the parentage. If it is not Arlin's child then I carry the bastard of a rapist. It will be but a babe in either regard, but it could go either way."

Mallory looked so small standing in front of Javic. He'd never realized the depths of the pain she was hiding. It was just behind her eyes. He felt like an even bigger fool. In retrospect, her sorrow had always been apparent. Arlin's physical standoffishness even made more sense. Javic felt considerably worse for having touched Mallory inappropriately the night of his return from Sultrim.

"I don't expect this to change anything," said Mallory. "I just thought you should know."

Javic didn't know what he should be feeling. He was overwhelmed by the vast range of all his despondent emotions hitting him at once. He quickly grew numb, blinking several times as he processed what he could to the limit of his capacity. "I'm not going to let anything happen to you," he said. He held her in his arms again, doing his best to comfort her despite his own unease. His mind spun in wild circles. They were all playing a very dangerous game—nothing less than their lives were at stake.

CHAPTER
27

Something Unexpected

Just when Havorie thought she had Javic all figured out he had to go and do something unexpected. The thrill of floating above the balcony felt like a dream turned nightmare as they came crashing back to earth, flattening out the breakfast buffet and sparking rumors of impropriety all across the palace in one fell swoop. It had been an unequivocal disaster. Her first time straddling a horny boy… feeling the swell in his pants against her thighs… it was intoxicating. Her mind had since wandered to Javic's surprising girth far too often. It was hard to concentrate on her duties! He stirred something within her. She'd had to scrub the evidence of her arousal out of her bloomers. She didn't need the maids thinking any more on the subject than they already did. And still, she couldn't help but wish to explore Javic's body further. To go from such

185

desperate arousal to screaming out in terror left her wary of her own feelings.

How easily my useless reign could come to an abrupt end....

She had so many aspirations yet unfulfilled. What a joke that she thought she could control Javic—the boy couldn't even control himself! His Power was great, but she had forgotten how much of a novice he still was.

She did not wish to speak with him again—not just yet. She didn't know what she wanted to say. With all the inappropriate thoughts bouncing around in her head, she was not sure it was safe to trust her feelings.

She knew Javic hadn't levitated with her on purpose, but that was entirely the point! His lack of control was a glaring liability to her goals! If Damian ever found out about the levitation, Javic would be banned from the palace grounds entirely. Accidents like that could not happen—they just couldn't!

Ervia had been particularly perturbed to hear about it from Havorie's own lips. The young maid did not like it one bit. She thought Javic should be sent away for everyone's safety. The Power was not something to be toyed with. Fortunately, Ervia knew her place. She would not say anything to Damian or anyone else. This was up to Havorie to decide. She wasn't ready to discard Javic.

Javic wasn't scheduled on the queen's guard detail again until the following day, but that didn't stop him from interrupting the tail end of her supper. Havorie waved off the other guardsmen as Javic entered her residence. She almost regretted letting him in when she realized he was not alone.

A young brunette stood in his shadow, hesitant to approach across the dining room. Javic bowed formally and continued his march to Havorie's side. Havorie knew who the girl was of course—Mallory, one of Javic's former traveling companions—Havorie had done her research prior to hiring Javic. She noted that something was off about the pair. A wild energy hastened Javic's footfalls while Mallory scowled fretfully across the chamber.

"What is the meaning of this interruption?" Havorie asked, her eyes darting like daggers between them.

"Forgive me, my queen," said Javic. "This is Mallory Worvon, a friend—"

"—Do not insult me," interrupted Havorie. "I had a dossier compiled of all your acquaintances before our first meeting. I know very well who you are Ms. Worvon. Approach me. I would like to get a better look at you."

Javic shot a glance back at Mallory. She curtsied shallowly before ambling over to join Javic at Havorie's side. Her short brown hair was disheveled. Her face was puffy; eyes red—it was clear that the young woman had recently been crying.

"Most humble apologies, my queen," said Mallory. "We bring grave news."

Havorie always strived to maintain control, but she did respect when it was time to listen. "Out with it," she said.

Javic stood at attention as Mallory told her story. She spoke of conspiracy and murder. Tannel Cresdale's former steward had been banished to the Archives. He knew something worth killing over. Havorie recognized the work of a sophisticated actor. There was no evidence—it was all being cleaned up faster than it could spill—they were grasping at straws.

"You say this conspiracy involves the Crown?" asked Havorie. "Well, I am the Crown, so how does this involve me?"

Mallory lowered her eyes. "I'm sorry, I cannot say," she said. "Lyle Stronghelm would only speak with the professor so I—"

"—So why hasn't anyone pressed this Stronghelm fellow harder?" asked Havorie. "You realize you've brought me absolutely nothing actionable."

"Mallory is in danger," interjected Javic. "Someone's been following her."

"And there's the dirty of it," said Havorie. "You seek my protection." She nodded solemnly. Her eyes turned to Javic. "What do you propose to offer in return?"

Javic grimaced. "Send me," he said. "I can go press this Stronghelm guy just like you suggested."

Havorie had her doubts. "What makes you think he will even talk now that the situation has grown so dire? Hell—what makes you think he's even still alive? This has 'cover-up' written all over it!"

"He's our only lead," said Javic, voice full of indignation. "We have to at least try! All we've been doing for weeks is digging up old statues and scurrying around in the dark! At least this is a solid lead."

Havorie leveled Javic with a steady glare.

"I know we're close to an answer," Javic continued. "Professor Vanton died because of what his former student wanted to tell him."

Havorie raised her hand above her head to usher silence. "Let me think," she said. It was indeed a delicate situation. The implication that Tannel was potentially responsible for her mother's death was troubling. She had no love for the man, but he had the full backing of the Arcanum. "You're being followed?" she asked Mallory.

Mallory nodded. "I noticed the same man three times today, always hanging back. He hasn't approached me, but I know I'm being watched."

Havorie nodded, weighing the risks. "That settles it. Whatever your informant might impart is surely no more than hearsay," she said. "Maybe he could still prove useful—Mr. Stronghelm is certainly worth pursuing—but he is *not* our only lead. We have another opportunity staring us in the face."

Javic's scowl deepened before she'd even finished. He understood at what she was hinting. Havorie recognized another well-tuned intuition when she saw one.

"I need you to go back out into the streets." Her instructions were for Mallory. "You are to be bait. If you are truly being followed than I daresay Javic can use his Queen's Guard status to arrest the goon. Confirming his employer could prove difficult. We need to really latch on here and squeeze until something more comes out of the woodwork. Go to Doctor Crane, I have it under good authority that he can give you access to a truth serum of sorts—he likes to brag about it at parties."

"Absolutely not!" cried Javic. "We're not risking Mallory! Your plan is far too dangerous! She's pregnant, for Mast's sake!"

Havorie raised an eyebrow. "I am your queen, need I remind you!?"

Javic diverted his eyes back to the floor.

"Are you not a powerful Ver'ati?" she continued to berate him. "You spit in Mast's eye—lifting us up into the sky in defiance of the laws of nature and man alike! I expect you will do whatever it takes to protect your *pregnant friend* while you ascertain the information we need." It was a statement of fact. She meant it as a dismissal. Havorie knew she was asking a great deal of Javic. In her mind, completing the task at hand seemed like a perfect way for him to prove himself still worthy of her favor.

"I won't do it," said Javic.

He used to be such a smitten puppy.

"There has got to be a better solution." Javic began to pace as he rambled on. "I'll go out searching for the answers myself—just leave it to me—there is no way Mallory is going to be bait for a firebombing psycho!—Do you even hear yourself? Professor Vanton was Ver'ati and he couldn't even protect himself! Mallory isn't Ver'ati! Mallory is just… well, she's just Mallory! And I'm not omnipotent! What if I don't see something in time!?"

Havorie put her hand up again. "Enough," she said. "I hear you. Perhaps the bait does not have to be Ms. Worvon—we only need the appearance of Ms. Worvon."

Javic narrowed his eyes.

"I dare say, she does share a similar stature with Ervia, don't you agree?" Havorie mused as she looked Mallory up and down. "Perhaps a bait-and-switch is in order."

CHAPTER 28

Bait and Switch

Javic fueled his connection to the Power with his anxiety. A jittery energy filled his limbs, leaving him feeling unsteady as he walked between the lines of pillars of the palace's long anteroom. He could sense a quickening of his blood. It coursed through his veins making his skin flush. He was a nervous wreck. The elevated confidence that consorting with the Power usually imparted upon him was overwhelmed by the stark reality of the situation. Ervia's life was in his hands.

As the doorman pushed open his charge against the wind, Javic's Ver'ati senses tingled. Awareness of a shifting pressure system high above in the clouds rang brightly in his inner ears. It sounded with a faint flutter against his hair follicles, reflecting the turbulence forming overhead as a high-pitched whir. The pressure was dropping—a storm brewing.

Javic was alert and ready for anything. Havorie wanted her answers. Javic was authorized to do whatever was necessary to uncover the truth. Ervia glanced back at him with wide eyes.

The lowly maid was just as displeased by Havorie's plan as Javic had expected.

"I was only hired to dust and change linens," she complained once more as she prepared to set out on her designated route across the central city.

"Yeah, well I'm supposed to be growing corn," Javic quipped back. He wasn't happy about the risks involved in their plan any more than she was. The mop of a wig he'd transformed to help disguise Ervia as Mallory had been grown out of an actual old mop. It was the right style, but it was only convincing in low light. The strands were far too thick, but as long as Ervia avoided standing directly under any of the lampposts it would be convincing enough. Once the hairpiece was covered by Mallory's shawl, Javic had to admit Ervia was the perfect stand-in for their deception.

Mallory had donned Ervia's maid uniform in turn, trading places for the evening like they were all a part of some sort of whimsical children's tale. Javic was relieved she would be safe in the palace while he attempted to lure her stalker out of the shadows. Somehow, Mallory even managed to make the drab maid's uniform appear provocative. A combination of her burgeoning baby-bump along with the slight mismatch in size between the two women made it a snug fit against her hips and buttocks.

Ervia turned back around once more to convey one final concern before stepping out from the safety of the palace: "I know you're supposed to hang back and all, but maybe just… don't stray too far," she said. "This is really scary for me."

"I understand," said Javic. "I'll keep my eyes peeled." He wished he could reassure her better. He couldn't blame her for having such reservations. Their plan relied upon him being able to catch the stalker by surprise. He was to identify the man, incapacitate him, and abduct him for interrogation. "For the queen," said Javic.

"For the queen," Ervia repeated as she wrapped Mallory's shawl more tightly around the sides of her face. She stepped out into the chilly night in earnest.

A Ver'ati battle in the streets of Erotos would be a disaster. Havorie had given Javic permission to do whatever was necessary, and while that tacitly included the possibility of such a clash, no one wanted to see such madness and destruction unfold. The magic and mayhem would be messy. Such deadly chaos was unpredictable. No—Javic needed to get the drop on Mallory's stalker.

It seemed unlikely anyone would make a move against Ervia while she was still in front of the palace. Javic didn't want anyone to notice him following her, so he waited several minutes before heading out. He hurried south along the Queen's Boulevard towards the market square at the head of the docks where he was to get his eyes back on Ervia. She was to maintain a slow pace so that Javic could catch up. He scanned his eyes across both sides of the wide boulevard as he stepped briskly against the wind. The streets were always populated in the Glowing City.

Mallory could only give a rough description of the man she'd noticed trailing her. "Tall, broad, cloaked, and dirty. He looked like he'd just crawled out of a hole somewhere. Just remarkably dirty…." She indicated that he was ugly as well—"with a big bulbous nose and goggles that covered his eyes."—He sounded exactly like the sort one would want to avoid in a dark alleyway or in broad daylight alike.

Javic assumed the goon would be a fellow Ver'ati, so attacking him directly with the Power would be out of the question. After some internal deliberation, he'd decided on performing a similar effect as Shiara's firestone earring. He would channel a vortex of energy out of the air around the enemy wizard, forming a positively charged void to drain him indirectly. He had grown increasingly familiar with energy manipulation from his practice with Belford's novel shielding material.

He was confident he could trigger a shock—he'd accidentally mildly electrocuted himself several times while working with light orbs, so he knew how painful even a small amount of energy could be.

Tiny freezing raindrops began to make their way down from the upper atmosphere. The icy misting stung against Javic's face as another big gust of wind whipped around him, sending the droplets horizontal. He pulled his cloak tight around his head and trudged onward.

He was becoming more worried the closer he got to the market without catching up to Ervia. He'd given her a bit too much of a lead despite her plea. At least he did not look out of the ordinary hustling down the street. Everyone was hurrying to their destinations to escape the rain.

The blotches of light from Lord Ethan's glowing orbs were more spread out the further away Javic moved from the palace. By the time he reached the market, he still had not come across Ervia. The market was mostly covered from the elements by a plethora of sheets, tied up to block out the sun during the daylight hours. The square was more populated than they'd anticipated when planning the route. Despite the late hour, people from all over the vicinity were taking shelter under the awnings from the sudden shift in the weather.

Javic's eyes shot back and forth as he scanned the crowd. He finally spotted Ervia standing halfway across the market, lingering beside a bakery stand. Relief washing over him upon seeing her still safe and well. He continued to scan the people around her, looking for any large, soiled men. On a first glance no one really met the description, but on a second pass he spotted a broad fellow in a dark cloak. The man was moving through the crowd straight towards Ervia, though he was still several dozen paces off.

There were far too many people present for Javic to be able to electrify any portion of the market without incapacitating at least a dozen innocent bystanders. Ervia needed to get somewhere less populated—and quick! The man had his back to Javic. He was closing in on Ervia with purpose. His shoulders were pointed straight at her. Javic bumbled his way through the crowd waving frantically at Ervia but she didn't glance in his direction. There was nothing he could do but watch as the man drew nearer to her.

With a raised arm he closed in, seemingly intent on snatching Ervia right out in front of everyone! She still hadn't even turned to look his way!

"Ervia!" Javic shouted across the market. His voice was eaten up by the wind. There was nothing else he could do to warn her. The man was already right upon her.

A frown crested Ervia's brow at the sound of her name on the wind. She turned her head in Javic's direction. The broad man was right there! Ervia's expression did not change. The man stepped right up to her… and then past her….

He grabbed a woman standing adjacent to Ervia playfully around the middle. It was the bakery stand attendant, working to pack up her goods as the rainfall steadily increased. The woman cried out, clearly startled by the man's surprise affection. She turned around and slapped him lightly against his chest before sharing another embrace.

Javic had read the situation all wrong. The cloaked man was not a threat. He wasn't the one he should have been paying attention to.

A pair of strong hands grabbed Javic from behind and yanked him into a narrow alleyway at his side. The surprise of being accosted led to Javic releasing the energy he'd been storing up for a quick attack. It shot out of him as a static field that prickled across his skin. It wasn't enough of a charge to electrocute anyone, but the man released Javic's shoulders at once, startled by the tiny shock. Javic spun around, immediately taking in the intimidating physique of his assailant.

The man was most definitely broad and tall. Javic was physically outmatched. The man was also extraordinarily filthy! Mallory hadn't been exaggerating! He was covered in soot from head to toe except for where he'd been wearing goggles. His skin shone through only around his eyes. Javic flinched as the man raised a blackened hand to remove the bulbous nose from his face. The odd prosthetic pulled away, revealing a perfectly sculpted nose underneath. "It's me, Tyris!" the man exclaimed, flashing a wide grin. "I'm in disguise!"

Javic held back the deadly burst of energy he'd instinctively whipped up. "What in the world…?" He had to focus on slowly releasing the charge in a more inert way. The energy soaked back into the Calvenite structures on either side of the alley until it was fully dissipated.

"I took a shift on a coal barge after Professor Vanton was killed," Tyris explained, "you know—just to keep a low profile. But then I had to come back to make sure Mallory was safe."

"I still can't believe it's you!" Javic exclaimed. Tyris looked like he'd just crawled out of a furnace. "You scared Mallory half to death!"

"I think I scared you half to death as well!" Tyris chuckled.

Javic let out a laugh of relief. He was just glad he hadn't been jumped by an actual enemy.

Ervia sprinted into the mouth of the alleyway and slammed into Tyris like a tiny bull. It was a full-body tackle. Javic hadn't a chance to stop her. Ervia was half Tyris's size, but he still went down to the ground. It was actually rather impressive. Javic couldn't help but laugh a little bit more as she beat at him with her balled-up fists.

"Stop! It's Tyris!" Javic chuckled as Ervia continued the pummeling.

Ervia paused her assault after another moment of comprehension. She looked up at Javic with her chest heaving. He reached out a hand to help pull her to her feet.

"What kind of freaky looking—? Why would you yank Javic into the alleyway like that—?!" Ervia exclaimed. "I could have torn a tendon running over here!"

Tyris climbed to his feet unaided and unharmed. If he felt embarrassment over what had just transpired, the coating of coal dust was certainly covering any blush his face may have held. "Hey… you're not Mallory," he said.

Javic felt a new respect for Ervia. She'd taken on a much larger man, knowing full-well he was probably capable of killing her with the Power with a single thought—such a heroically insane move just to give Javic a chance at fighting back. It had been an incredibly stupid thing to do, really, but Javic was still vastly appreciative. She had his back. He hadn't expected that from her. He didn't even feel like he deserved the heroism she'd displayed. They hadn't exactly been seeing eye-to-eye recently.

Ervia brushed the dirt off the hems of Mallory's dress. When she was finished she stood up tall and took several controlled, audible breaths—deep puffs in and out—an attempt to still her racing heart.

"We were hoping to catch and interrogate whoever was following Mallory," said Javic.

"That was my plan as well," said Tyris.

Javic cocked his head. "Mallory only saw you following her. Are you saying there's someone else?"

A silhouette fell across them as the light from the nearest glowing orb out in the market was blocked from shining down the alleyway by the body of another robed man. A short black rod in his hand had a tapered nozzle at its tip. The man lifted the rod to point straight down the alleyway.

Javic recognized the danger. He drew back in the energy he'd just released to the walls around him. The end of the man's rod began to glow white-hot. Flames ignited at once, expanding in the air, rolling forward to consume the entire opening of the alley.

Javic acted defensively. He ripped the wig from Ervia's head with the Power, repurposing the molecules of its weave to form the ultra-thin shielding material he'd learned to produce by watching Belford. The shield glowed blue as it strengthen with the flow of the energy he'd just stripped back out of the walls. Flames licked Ervia's face around the edges of the shield as it quickly stretched to block the brunt of the blast.

The shield shined brighter as it was bombarded by the fire. The more energy it received the stronger it held. The fire rebounded off the flat surface, ricocheting back towards its point of origin just as quickly as it had approached. When the flames finally died down, Javic located the bomber—already consumed by his own unnatural flame.

The market erupted into panic. Shrieks and screams filled the smoky air. Everyone fled at once.

Ervia's shawl was smoldering on her head. Her eyebrows had been singed to obscurity by the tremendous heat. She stood frozen, staring doe-eyed at the charred husk of the bomber. All his distinguishing features had been melted away.

"I guess we're not going to be getting any answers out of him," said Tyris with a deep grimace.

CHAPTER
29

A Devout Man

"Let's get out of here!" exclaimed Javic.

"Just one moment," insisted Tyris. "I want that fire rod." He darted over to the bomber's corpse and began to wrestle the thin rod out of its charred, crusty fingers.

Javic wasted no time. He grabbed Ervia by the elbow and tugged her down the alleyway beside him. Mayhem in the streets of Erotos was exactly what he'd hoped to avoid. A clap of thunder rang out overhead. Javic eyed the menacing sky as another flutter hit his eardrum. The storm was growing with a fast churn. Tyris caught up with them as they all popped back out onto the Queen's Boulevard just south of the palace. The dark south tower sat before them. Its spire lit up as a flash of lightning struck its pinnacle. The sky split in two for a moment before the bang reached their ears. It sounded with a deafening clap followed by a deep rumble that echoed through the streets below.

Javic glanced back at Tyris. He couldn't help but deliver a concerned frown. A trail of coal residue streamed from Tyris's body as the rain washed over him… a trail straight to a corpse.

Tyris caught the look. "No worries," he said. He shook his body like a wet dog as he repelled the filth from his skin and clothing. The majority of the grime fell away at once—enough to halt the trail with a pile of muck. He winked at Javic. "Same trick as staying dry. I hardly even need to bathe anymore!"

Ervia raised a judgmental eyebrow ridge. Her singed-off hairs made the expression nearly unreadable under the glow of the city lights.

"Did Mallory tell you about Lyle Stronghelm?" asked Tyris.

Javic nodded an affirmation.

"Good, well, I know where he lives now," said Tyris. "I followed him back to his apartment after his last shift—north of campus, over in the east city."

With the bomber dead, Lyle really was their only remaining lead. Rather than return to the palace with the shame of failure as his only news, Javic decided it was apt time to forge ahead. He knew what Havorie needed from him. "Do you already have a plan for Lyle?" he asked Tyris.

"Well, my gentle request certainly didn't work out so great," he said with a shrug.

It was time to pay Mr. Stronghelm a less friendly visit. Questioning Lyle was what Javic had proposed to do for Havorie to begin with. Her words kept repeating in his head—*What makes you think he'll talk?*

Tyris was still juggling the fire rod back and forth between his fingertips. The metal Artifact had absorbed heat from the rebound of its own blast and was yet to cool off.

The fire rod was an interesting device. It was certainly a useful tool for someone wishing to commit a murder that they could blame on an Echo. Its effect was far too explosive to be used for much else unless the magnitude of the fire could be tamped down in some way. Javic had little interest in playing with random Artifacts. It was too easy to turn oneself into a charred-up husk. One exception—he wished he had an Artifact that would help loosen Lyle's tongue for him a bit. Havorie had mentioned acquiring truth serum, but Javic wanted to avoid meeting with Doctor Crane. Something about that man had always felt a bit off to him for some reason. He couldn't quite put his finger on it. The doctor had been plenty polite and had even spoken encouragingly to him when he'd gone in to have his blood tested upon first becoming an initiate. Crane became chummy with him, but only after he'd seen how strongly Javic tested. The doctor's eyes just seemed kind of… empty—even when he was smiling.

Javic glanced back anxiously as they jogged through the rain. No one was following them. The street ahead was equally as clear. As they crossed over the Etwon Bridge into the east city, thoughts of Artifacts led Javic to a sudden realization. There was one Artifact that actually might be able to aid him with Lyle—one which he could use to harmlessly extract Lyle's deepest secrets. Lieutenant General Cale Fisman still held ownership over the brass spyglass. With it, Javic would be able to sneak into Lyle's dreams.

He hadn't spoken to Cale since joining the Queen's Guard. Last he heard the secretive man had used the spyglass to ascertain the location of the Artifact core, hidden by General Aldune. Cale had surely recovered it by now—Javic hoped he would keep it safe from Aldune and the other Ver'konus warmongers.

Cale had turned Javic into his co-conspirator against the rest of the Ver'konus leadership. He may have helped Javic out during his Dance of the Elements, but he'd also been the one who put Javic in danger in the first place by sending him through the Gateway to Sultrim.

The Officer Apartments were nearby. There was a good chance he would be able to find Cale there. He quickly told Tyris and Ervia his idea.

"That's amazing!   I've never heard of an Artifact with a property like that," said Tyris. "They truly can do anything!"

Ervia scowled deeply, perturbed by the concept. "That's so intrusive," she said. "I don't like that something like that even exists...."

"I've always been unsettled by it as well," said Javic. "At least if we control it, the enemy doesn't."

Upon reaching the Officer Apartments, Javic looked up the address for Cale's flat on the posted directory. He would be going on alone from here. New faces might put the lieutenant general on guard. The spyglass was the safest way for Javic to complete his mission. He didn't want Cale to be resistant. His relationship with the gangly man had been tumultuous. Cale asked for dangerous favors.   Javic had approached every request with poise and discretion. It was time for Cale to return the trust. Tyris and Ervia remained in the common area by the stairwell as Javic started up the stairs to Cale's flat.

Behind him Ervia leaned in close to view her reflection on the glass casing of the directory and immediately shrieked. "Oh, sweet Mast, how ghastly!" she cried out. "Why did no one tell me my eyebrows are gone!?"

Javic hastened his steps as Tyris began to mumble an apology of sorts.

Cale's residence was at the end of a long hall on the second story. Javic rapped his knuckles against the solid oak door. The knocks rang out as an urgent clamor. Worry that his luck had run dry arose within him when Cale did not answer. He wasn't certain Cale was home. He repeated his knocks, and then paused again for a moment to press his ear to the door. He employed his heightened senses to listen for any indication of a stir. He was about to give up when he picked up on an internal shuffling.

He waited as another minute passed. He'd nearly decided to knock again when several clicks finally sounded. Cale undid a series of locks before opening the door a mere crack. A chain caught its progress. Javic flared his nostrils as a pungent scent escaped through the crack.

Sickness.

Cale peeked out through the gap, fixing Javic with tired eyes. The apartment was completely dark inside. "Javic?" he asked. "Why are you here?"

"I have an urgent matter to discuss with you, sir," said Javic.

Cale closed the door again.

Javic blinked several times. He was surprised to catch the lieutenant general apparently sleeping. The moon was still up. No more sounds arose through the door. Cale was just standing there. Javic began to wonder if that was to be the end of the encounter. After a long pause, metal scraped against metal as Cale unhooked the final chain. The sweet stink of the apartment hit Javic in the face like a wet sock as the door swung open once more. He instinctively covered his nose with his hand and stepped back before he could stop himself. He scratched his nose, trying to play off his disgust as an itch. Cale eyed him with a raised upper lip.

The lieutenant general had looked unwell for quite some time now. However pale and greasy gray his skin had appeared the last time Javic saw him, his condition was severely worsened. He still had red blotches where the memory of the Paerto'sul inside the Dance of the Element's Blood Artifact had torn into him. The welts had become increasingly inflamed. Yellow pustules had formed across his face and neck.

"Are you alright?" Javic asked.

Cale grunted. His bloodshot eyes had dark bags beneath them that looked absolutely deathly when combined with his clammy skin.

"Have you seen an Ameliorator, sir?" Javic asked.

"I am a damn Ameliorator," Cale growled. He stepped aside, giving Javic space to enter his residence. "My body is purging," he said less harshly. "I will be fine."

Javic didn't really want to go inside anymore. The odor was downright foul! A trash bin topped with pus-covered bandages sat near the door. He wrinkled his nose in revulsion. It took all his strength not to retch. He breathed shallowly, trying not to intake the air too deeply into his lungs. He wished he could stop breathing altogether!

"What is so urgent that it could not wait until morning?" asked Cale. He flipped on a wall switch, suddenly bathing the small apartment in a harsh light from an overhead bulb.

Javic narrowed his eyes as he adjusted to the sudden change in lighting. Cale's living room was a cluttered mess. Soiled linens were heaped upon a solitary chair. Half-packed boxes of junk were strewn across the floor. A small dining table was stacked high with paperwork, layered into a dozen sloppy piles.

Javic swallowed a thick glob of saliva. "I need to requisition the brass spyglass," he said, jumping straight to the point. He had intended on some small-talk first, but his own scent aversion combined with Cale's impatience forced the issue.

Cale scoffed. "This is not the Archives," he said. "The spyglass is not up for grabs. It's not some toy to be trifled with! It will never reach public hands."

Javic was taken aback. Cale spoke as if the Archives were no better than a public library. Javic understood Cale's point though. The spyglass was quite powerful. It had a unique use case.

"*Requisition* wasn't the right word," said Javic. "I need to *borrow* the spyglass to extract some vital information from a reluctant source...." He chose his words carefully. The less he had to reveal about the nature of his mission the better.

Cale turned away. He poured himself a cloudy glass of water from a ceramic pitcher that he had perched upon a narrow shelf above what could only be described as a prayer mural of truly devout proportions. A grand depiction of Mast herself, naked and pregnant to signify her role as mother to all, was painted across the entryway wall.

Javic had not suspected the lieutenant general of being such a deeply religious man. It was quite the pious display! Mast was depicted traditionally—a great beauty with elongated limbs and deep curves. An angelic glow radiated out from the goddess, styled with bright colors and wide brush strokes. The whole painting was further surrounded with a boarder of wooden embellishments—disembodied teardrop-shaped breasts—each the size of a fist, delicately carved, lined up, and polished to a glisten.

Cale pressed his thumb firmly to his forehead while chugging down his entire glass of water. By the time he was finished with the last drop, a hint of color was starting to return to his cheeks. He still did not look well by any means, but the blood flow was a subtle improvement to his grim demeanor.

"There are challenges in this life that you have not even begun to consider," said Cale. "Things you won't discover for many years to come. You are still a boy—so young—I don't blame you for any of this. It is merely a fact that you are terribly inexperienced."

Javic spotted the brass spyglass. It was sitting atop a pile of clutter on a footstool beside the chair. The crusting of dried blood from the street urchin in North Galdren was still present upon its façade.

"Understand, I do not say this lightly," continued Cale. "You are too immature and ill prepared for the responsibility of wielding the spyglass."

Javic held his tongue, biting back some choice words he was really itching to spout back. He was filled with a flash of rage that flared hot inside of him. Cale was being infuriatingly condescending.

"It imparts an unseen toll," Cale said, clasping his hands together over his heart. "To see into another's mind is to truly experience a will beyond your own. It erodes one's sense of self."

Javic couldn't hold back any longer. "Suddenly you're worried about my wellbeing?" he asked with a sneer. He didn't care if Cale thought he was being rude. "You sent me through that Gateway to Sultrim knowing very well the risks involved." He shook his head in disgust, glaring at the lieutenant general. "And you sent Rylin there too! He was just a kid!"

"You know why I had to do that," said Cale. "It was a necessary evil to protect the world from the core's power."

Javic wasn't buying it this time. "Why not just destroy it then? Why keep something so dangerous around? If you are truly against using it to recharge the Orb of Parphim, why keep it at all?"

Cale locked eyes with Javic. "I couldn't destroy it if I tried! You don't understand anything! You are a teenager. Your brain is still developing. You take things so literally—black and white; right and wrong—morality is not so cut and dry in the real world. There is a greater good, though Mast knows walking the truest path can be a challenge. Your mother, Kali, was barely older than yourself when she set out to try to kill King Garrett. Such a waste! There are so many things you can't even comprehend! The way forward can become so clouded."

"You want to talk about my mother!?" Javic raised his voice. *The audacity of this man!* "If things are foggy for you, *old man*, I can clear them up really fast. You sent initiates to Sultrim to be eaten by flying bears just so you could get your hands on a lost relic that could have just as easily stayed lost forever! You don't get to tell me my brain isn't developed enough to appreciate the sensitivity of going into people's minds!"

Cale shook his head, his shoulders drooping at Javic's words.

Javic walked over and snatched the spyglass off the footstool. "I'm taking this," he said forcefully. "You can have it back when I'm done."

Cale crossed his arms in front of his chest. He scowled at Javic, a look of defeat in his tired eyes. "If you are truly insistent on walking this path, perhaps nothing will stop you," he said. "Remember who you are."

"I didn't come here for your advice," said Javic, starting back towards the door. "And just so you know, this place smells like shit! Crack a window or something!"

Cale did not attempt to stop him. "One courtesy," he said, "please return the device to Doctor Crane by first light. He actually does have a requisition that must be fulfilled. Do not forget you are still owned by the Ver'konus, even whilst you enjoy gallivanting around with the queen."

Javic paused briefly beside the mural of Mast as he reached for the door handle. He was surprised by Cale's request. He had always assumed the lieutenant general was keeping the spyglass for himself. Other members of the Ver'konus apparently knew of its existence.

Javic pulled open the door. His eyes slid across Mast's form one last time. A disturbing detail caught his attention before he turned to go. Tiny scorch marks sat atop the goddess's breasts, over where her nipples should have been. They were smoke stick burns—snuffed against the paint.

Whoever was responsible, the burns had surely not been left by a devout man.

CHAPTER
30

Dreamwalker

Javic had never personally used the brass spyglass before. He'd heard bits and pieces of Belford's tragic account of his attempt to free Kara's mind from the internal twisting's of Wilgoblikan's madness. Kara had not survived the ordeal, though the spyglass did its workings perfectly. Her body had simply been too worn out to continue living. Javic wasn't clear on the details of how the Artifact managed its wonders. Somehow, the viewport connected the spyglass holder to any sleeping mind locked within its focus. Kara hadn't exactly been asleep—her consciousness was fractured and trapped away inside. Regardless, the device showed the internal dreamscape of the subject to the viewer.

Javic hurried down the steps of Cale's apartment building.

"How'd it go?" asked Tyris as soon as Javic reached the lobby.

Javic's pent-up emotions from his talk with Cale clouded his thoughts. He was fairly certain he'd only gotten away with

208

taking the spyglass because the lieutenant general knew Javic could expose his theft of the Artifact core from General Aldune if he so desired.

He held up the spyglass and waggled it at Tyris before placing it back into the pocket of his robe. "How close are we to Lyle's apartment?" he asked.

"It's just around the corner," said Tyris.

The rain had lessened while they were inside. When they reached the street out front, Ervia paused at the end of the walkway. "I should head back to the palace," she said. "I don't feel like I'm really needed here. Besides, the queen deserves an update." She turned to go.

"Hey!" Javic called out to her. "I'm really sorry about your eyebrows."

Ervia glanced back over her shoulder. "You saved my life!" she exclaimed. "Don't worry at all! They'll regrow. Just go find our answers!"

Javic nodded to her. She'd played her part well. She curtsied respectfully before spinning back around and hurrying down the street. Javic and Tyris set out in the opposite direction.

Tyris took the lead. They rounded the corner, approaching another apartment building. "How close do you need to be to use that thing?" he asked.

"I'm not too sure," said Javic. "Show me to his door and I'll try to spy him from outside." His stomach fluttered nervously as the time to use the spyglass drew nearer. Cale's vague warning of an unseen toll circled his thoughts.

I could lose myself?

Artifacts were dangerous. That was nothing new. He'd come too far to stop now. He just hoped Lyle was asleep—his plan hinged on it.

The hallways in Lyle's building were narrow and lined with a dingy faded carpet. Half the light orbs recessed into the ceiling were burnt out, dark streaks marring their translucent casings. Tyris led Javic down a flight of stairs into the building's basement. One flight further and they'd be in the Erotos Underground altogether.

"The Arcanum really likes to keep this guy out of the way," said Tyris.

Javic sneered. "This is the same treatment Tannel wanted for me," he said. "Does anyone actually join the Historians of their own volition?"

"Not many," said Tyris. "You know something secret, don't you? Something you shouldn't? What'd you see on the other side of the Gateway?"

Javic grimaced. "There are too many conspiracies in this city."

"You know what? Never mind. Don't tell me. I don't even want to know," said Tyris.

Healthy choice.

Some knowledge was not worth the hassle. There was no reason to burden Tyris with anything about Sultrim or the Artifact core.

After several more twists and turns they finally arrived at their destination. The paint was peeling from the edges of Lyle's door. Tyris stood guard whilst Javic took a seat against the wall in the middle of the hallway. The spyglass was heavier than it looked. Javic held it up in his hands. Its dull brass casing was cold to the touch. The bloody handprint on its side was a stark reminder of the brutality of the Artifact's original owner. The Crimson Stalker was one horror Javic hoped to never cross paths with again.

He took a deep breath before lifting the viewport up to his eye. He wasn't sure what he had been expecting to see, but all he was met with was darkness. Something inside the tube was blocking the passage of light. He searched the area beyond the wall anyway, shifting the end of the tube back and forth as he adjusted the focus with a twist of the lens.

He began to worry that he wasn't close enough, but he kept scanning the length of the apartment until a flash of light briefly lit up the eyepiece. It happened so briefly that he had to question if it was just his imagination. He regressed his track until he caught the shine again. A spot the size of a pin prick gleamed against his eye. It was faint like a distant star. He gave the focal lens a gentle correction. The pinprick rapidly expanded to the size of a marble. It looked like a physical object hanging in the air, just an arm's length out in front of him. The sphere contained moving images, like some sort of projection, coming from within.

It was a dream in progress. He was viewing Lyle's internal experience. The shapes within the orb were warped. He felt like he had to squint to make any sense of it. He strained his neck forward, trying to lean in closer to the images.

He couldn't tell what he was seeing, though the shifting pictures were fairly crisp. He gave the focal lens a tiny turn more and immediately felt himself falling forward. The orb enveloped him as he crashed down upon it a moment later, slamming into something solid. A bookshelf rattled with the force of his collision. Several tomes tumbled to a fine tiled floor, landing with thuds.

"Watch where you're going!" spouted a young man seated behind a secretary desk at the other end of the room. "That's Councilman Cresdale's personal collection!"

Javic recognized Lyle from Mallory's description. His slightly sunken eyes had dark circles under them that reminded him a bit of Cale. Both men could have used a good night's rest and a hearty dose of sunshine.

Lyle rushed to Javic's side. He handled the fallen tomes with care as he worked at reorganizing the shelf. "Do you have a meeting with the councilman or are you just here to irritate me?" he asked, frustration clear in his voice.

Javic wasn't sure how to respond. He remembered how it felt having Cale in his dreams. The confusion caused by an external presence slid off easily. Shifting backdrops didn't even clue him in to the fact that he was asleep. Cale's line of questioning had transported his mind back to Sultrim—the immediacy of that dangerous situation thrust upon him once more in its entirety. His mind had rolled with the changes, showing Cale exactly what he wanted to see. Javic decided to use his words to stir the pot.

"I'm not here for Tannel," said Javic. "I'm here to meet you."

Lyle narrowed his eyes, a literal clouding of confusion swirling around him like a gray mist.

"I'm with Professor Vanton," Javic added. "He's just outside."

Lyle had been elsewhere in time—dreaming of his old job when he was still the councilman's steward. The room began to shift. Everything behind Lyle was the first to go. The bookshelf elongated, stretching inward to form the opening to a new passage. They were standing at the mouth of a long tunnel. Javic recognized the alcove openings of the Archives at once. The numbered nooks stretched on as far as the eye could see. Lyle's secretary desk was replaced by a long wooden counter and several turnstiles.

Everything swirled as Javic spun in place. He was mesmerized by the shifting backdrop. A hollow pang hit his heart as Professor Vanton shuffled in, hunched over slightly to avoid the low ceiling. Lyle's mind was filling in all the details.

"Professor!" exclaimed Lyle. "It's so good to see you!"

There was something peculiar about Lyle's version of Professor Vanton. He looked eerily off to Javic. Their old professor approached with a smile, but his eyes looked peculiarly flat. The light didn't reflect off of them correctly. His skin shimmered slightly as well, as if lit internally. The shine washed out his wrinkles, making him appear too smooth to Javic's eye. He was nothing more than a puppet of Lyle's subconscious.

Without a word, the professor whipped out his anti-eavesdropping crystal and tapped it with his tiny metal rod. The crystal stood up on its point in perfect balance on the counter. The dreamscape was blanketed by silence. Lyle was definitely familiar with Professor Vanton's security measures.

The effect was accurate to reality—all the auditory reverberations in the area were eaten up by the imaginary field generated by the equally imaginary crystal.

"What have you learned?" asked Vanton, his voice sharp but hollow.

There was something so very ironic about Lyle's own dream-character taking over lead in Javic's secret interrogation. The clandestine meeting was playing out exactly how Lyle imagined it should have gone. All Javic had to do was stand next to the professor and listen.

"Are you sure we can trust this one?" Lyle asked the professor, gesturing with his head towards Javic.

"He is my best pupil," Vanton said with confidence.

Javic kept a straight face. The professor could only say what Lyle's subconscious imagined for him. Javic was hardly Vanton's best student! He'd spent most of the professor's classes locked in the supply closet!

"I would not have brought him along if I could not trust him," Vanton gave Javic a little wink.

Javic smiled back meekly at the soulless illusion.

Lyle swayed back and forth with nervous energy. "Alright, as long as you vouch for him," he said. "I've actually known what I'm about to tell you for quite some time now. I'd dared hope if I kept Tannel's secret to myself he might see fit to bring me back up topside." His eyes shifted to Javic for a moment before sliding back to the professor. "I am no longer under such illusions." He exhaled slowly, holding on to the unspoken words for a moment longer. "I overheard a conversation that I wasn't supposed to hear—it's the reason I was banished down here to begin with." He shook his head, a deep frown pulling at the corners of his mouth.

The betrayal Lyle was experiencing settled like a fog over the chamber. The light orbs dimmed from all the despondent energy. Javic felt the emotion flow into him as if he were the one who had been damned to a shortened life amongst the Archive Historians. The walls behind the scorned Ver'ati slowly shifted their positions as Lyle's mind stopped focusing on their existence. The dream was becoming fragile. A heightened sense of urgency filled Javic. The dream would be coming to an end shortly. He focused his eyes on Lyle to stop the shifting walls from making him feel nauseous.

"I am too old to be kept waiting like this!" exclaimed Professor Vanton. "What is this conspiracy you keep dangling in front of me?"

Javic wondered how much his own emotions were affecting the dream world.

"My apologies professor," said Lyle. "It's just… I overheard this from Councilman Cresdale's mouth directly. I don't have any hard proof—"

"—Just spit it out already!" cried Javic.

Lyle shot a glare in his direction. "Many years ago, back before the death of Queen Nestra, Councilman Cresdale conspired with the Ver'konus—specifically Lord Ethan—to have the baby princess injected with Inhibitor."

Javic's jaw dropped open. He snapped it back shut. This was not the conspiracy he thought he was unraveling! He shared a confused look with the imaginary Professor Vanton.

"Whether or not Queen Havorie has the ability to channel, I cannot say," said Lyle. "Inhibitor would mask her connection to the Power if she was destined to wield it. Tannel and Ethan didn't want Havorie to ever grow to challenge their supremacy. They weren't willing to take the chance that she would inherit her mother's abilities."

A cascade of ramifications crashed through Javic's mind. "The antidote…?"

Lyle nodded. "The antiserum could prove my words true. If the queen can't reach the Power, it won't do a thing, but if she can, any innate abilities would soon manifest in full."

The string of lights spanning the infinitely long tunnel behind Lyle began to flicker out incrementally. The darkness was closing in on them. Soon, the whole passageway melted away, slipping out of existence, lost to a dark void. It was just another poorly lit corner of the room now. Lyle was barely clinging to sleep. Javic suspected if the man turned around too quickly he'd find himself staring at the backs of his eyelids.

"Who has the antiserum?" he asked.

"Only Doctor Crane has access to that," said Lyle. "He's the one who engineered Inhibitor for Lord Ethan in the first place. Again, I have no proof, but Queen Havorie may have been the first to receive a dose…."

"They tested it on a baby?!" Javic shook his head in disgust. "Was Doctor Crane involved?"

Lyle's face pinched up. "It was Doctor Crane I overheard all of this from in the first place—he was speaking with the councilman. After I'd heard everything they realized I was still in the adjacent chamber. I was reassigned to the Historians the next day—the bastards!"

Javic had heard enough. His feet lifted up from the floor. He was floating with the power of intention. Rather than bumping into the ceiling he continued his rise through it effortlessly. Lyle looked up at him with a confused scowl as he floated away. The distance between them grew quickly until Javic was once again immersed in darkness, staring off at Lyle's dream-marble. He became aware of his hands holding the spyglass and immediately lowered the lens from his eye.

It felt like coming out of a trance. Javic's head spun with vertigo. He couldn't climb to his feet fast enough. Tyris hurried over to lend him a steadying hand. The hallway felt like it was moving beneath his feet. Tyris gripped him by the shoulders and stared into his face as he wobbled sideways.

"Are you feeling well?" he asked with a concerned frown. "You're looking a bit pale…."

Lyle's revelation spurred Javic into motion. "Havorie's been Inhibited!" the words exploded out of his mouth. He shoved past Tyris, wishing to make haste with the earth shattering news towards the palace. He immediately regretted his decision. Within two steps his equilibrium went sideways on him. He stumbled face-first down the hallway, his feet churning beneath him desperately until he ran out of carpet and smashed the crown of his head directly into the wall. The world spun as colors flashed before his eyes. Tyris cried out. His voice sounded like it was echoing from off in the distance. Javic's blood pressure spiked. Darkness closed in all around him as he slipped from consciousness.

* * *

A distant howl roused Javic's senses. He awoke lying on his back on a cot. He tried to sit up but several pairs of hands shot out and held him in place. "Where…?" Javic gasped before he recognized Tyris's face staring down at him.

"You took a pretty hard spill," said Doctor Crane, the owner of the other pair of hands. "Earned yourself a concussion."

Javic's eyes wandered across his surroundings. He was in Doctor Crane's underground infirmary near Candeer fountain. He spotted the brass spyglass sitting atop a surgical equipment tray at his side.

Doctor Crane followed his eyes. "Thank you for delivering that," he said. "You are one of very few people who know of its capabilities."

Javic internally panicked as he realized what had just transpired.

Did we just hand a baby-drugging monster the ability to see into everyone's dreams?!

His pulse quickened again. He had to keep his head on straight. He couldn't let on that he knew anything of consequence. "Of course, doctor," he said. "You wouldn't want something like that getting lost." He ran a hand up to his head, expecting to find a sore spot, but was surprised by the lack of any pain as he felt around.

"You're lucky you got to me before moondown," said Doctor Crane.

Only now did Javic realize his connection to the Power was gone. He sat up slowly. No one tried to stop him this time.

"Your buddy here carried you in like a champ!" laughed Doctor Crane. "You're all fixed up now. You can leave whenever your feet are steady."

"Thank you so much, doc," said Tyris. "Truly outstanding work! Quite the contusion you fixed there!" He helped Javic to his feet.

"Thanks, doc," repeated Javic.

Doctor Crane grunted dismissively as he reached into his lab coat and pulled out a pack of smoke sticks along with a lighter. He lit up as Tyris led Javic by the elbow out of the infirmary. They'd only gotten a few paces down the hall before Javic pulled back on Tyris, attempting to direct him over to the side of the walkway. Tyris resisted him, dragging Javic onward another couple of steps against his will.

"Wait," Javic whispered sharply. "We need to get our hands on some…" Javic trailed off as Tyris flashed him a quick look of consternation. Tyris stretched open his pocket, showing Javic a leather pouch he had tucked away inside of it. "Is that the antiserum?" he asked.

Tyris nodded. "A whole kit," he said. "Now let's get the hell out of here before he notices it's missing!"

Javic continued on behind Tyris once more, heading for the stairs that would take them back up to the surface.

Another muffled howl rang out from afar, quieter this time from down the long hallway. Javic stopped in his tracks. The cry came from a Whune—the tone was unmistakable. He wasn't frightened, but it stirred something inside of him. He knew some of Wilgoblikan's Whunes had been captured in the Underground a few months ago when he'd first arrived at the Glowing City. He'd heard the same bloodcurdling roars the last time he walked these halls as well—back on the night he first learned Mallory was pregnant. He was surprised the monsters had been kept alive for so long.

An image of Salvine's face gazing back at him leapt across his mind—her lips tightly pursed, unbridled curiosity, the way she always looked at him. It was like she was trying to read his thoughts. Admittedly, he hadn't thought about her in quite some time. The desperate roars reminded Javic of when Belford was transforming Kara back into her human body. The howls sounded like cries for help. They filled him with such sorrow. Kara's transformation had briefly given him hope that Salvine and the other Whunes might be able to be saved. He knew the chance of finding Salvine amongst Wilgoblikan's horde was slim to none, especially with most of the dark wizard's Whunes already long dead by now, but the wiry cries still gripped him frozen.

"Now what?!" asked Tyris. He was getting fed up with Javic's lingering.

Despite the urgency of Javic's mission, he felt himself being drawn back. "Do you hear that?" he asked.

"The roars?" asked Tyris. "That's a Whune...."

He knew Tyris wouldn't understand. He just needed to see the creature for himself. Heading back was probably the last thing he should be doing under the circumstances. He couldn't quite explain it but he felt impelled to go see the last of Wilgoblikan's creations. "This will just take me a minute," he insisted.

Tyris shook his head. "I'm not letting you go by yourself," he said.

Javic nodded in gratitude of Tyris's companionship. He didn't understand why Javic needed to go back, but he followed along without further complaint. With the moon down, the fire rod in Tyris's pocket made him just about the best backup Javic could imagine.

They followed the ruckus of the monster's cries, shuffling back past the little infirmary. Doctor Crane was preoccupied inside. The howls stopped the moment Javic reached a sliding metal door. The beast was within. It had already sensed his presence.

He slid open the door. It squealed quietly. The room inside was encased in darkness. It remained deathly silent as he peered around.

Tyris reached past Javic and flipped a switch on the wall. The room was flooded with a bright white light that chased away all the shadows. It was a surgical room. An oversized examination bench was fit with thick leather restraints at the center of the chamber. Javic's eyes immediately went to the two Whunes present, standing propped upright in body-tight cages.

Both Whunes remained completely still as Javic entered the chamber. He crept forward cautiously. The beasts' eyes followed him as he stepped closer to them. The stink from their pores filled his sinuses. He wrinkled his nose, fighting his disgust to move closer still.

He didn't know what he was looking for. It wasn't like he could distinguish who a Whune once was from looking at their tumorous flesh. One was male and one was female. That was the only human characteristic that remained after Wilgoblikan's terrible work. He focused in on the female Whune.

He recalled seeing a wedding band on a Whune's finger once. His eyes traveled down the scrawny Whune's arm to its wrist. He'd given Salvine a foolhardy trinket the last time he'd seen her back home in Darrenfield—a silver bracelet with the emblem of a dove. His heart began to race as he spotted a glint of silver gleaming up from the beast's wrist. A thin reflective chain flashed under the intense lighting. The dainty band was dug in tight to the Whune's flesh. Javic knew that shine. It reflected white—fine Tarisian silver.

Salvine? Could it truly be…?

He was afraid to get his hopes up. He stepped as close to the beast as he dared move. The Whune puffed out a breath of hot air from its wide nostrils. Javic gazed up into its bulging yellow eyes. It slowly rotated its arm, offering Javic an unobstructed view of the dove charm embedded into its forearm.

Tears stung at Javic's eyes as he stood aghast. He stumbled backwards into Tyris, knees weakened by the shock. Tyris helped hold him up. Javic clutched his hands together over his heart. "I—I…" he stammered. "I know her… I know who this is!"

Tyris remained rigid as he eyed Javic with a wary regard.

"I… I can't leave," said Javic. He stared into Salvine's vicious, inhuman eyes.

She's really in there….

He knew she would tear him to pieces if she wasn't locked away in her cage. Even so, he couldn't abandon her—especially not to the care of Doctor Crane! Javic already knew the spyglass was the key to restoring her mind. If her prematurely aged body could also be restored, Salvine stood a real chance!

Lord Ethan was brought back from his decrepitude—why not Salvine?

Javic turned back towards Tyris. "I'm going to need you to deliver the antiserum to the queen without me," he said. "Tell her Lyle believes Tannel Cresdale, Lord Ethan, and Doctor Crane all conspired against her when she was a baby!"

Tyris's glower darkened further with each name Javic added to the list. "Sure, I will get this to Queen Havorie for you, but first, who is this?" Tyris asked, his eyes shifting back over to the Whune.

"Tyris, meet Salvine," said Javic, "a girl from back home!"

CHAPTER
31

No Man's Land

There was a railway—a secret, underground, Goblikan railway—smack-dab in the middle of the Torus Desert. And that was how they were going to return to Erotos. Belford could not bring himself to believe Wilgoblikan's words. Their group wouldn't be taking the road south. Instead, they were to march straight off into the desert carrying only enough provisions to make it halfway across. It sounded absolutely insane!

An underground railway—really?

The desert was full of wild, masterless Whunes, apparently. It was the last place they should be trekking, especially not on the word of perhaps the most terrible man Belford had ever had the displeasure of ever interacting with in his entire life!

Belford was so utterly convinced Wilgoblikan was making the whole thing up that he dosed him with the final remnants of truth spores that Livian had cooked up for him before departing from the Rosa Marsa the final time. Ethan, not one to be left out, led the questioning. Amazingly, Wilgoblikan's answers did not waver. He was telling the truth. There really was a secret railway. It was indeed underground, smack-dab in the middle of the desert, and it was the fastest way back to Erotos. They were to set out towards the heart of the wasteland—no man's land.

"How do you think I got my Whunes south so quickly while you were fleeing from me?" Wilgoblikan asked Belford, reveling in his superior knowledge.

A vision of Kara—so inquisitive and innocent before Wilgoblikan twisted her into a Whune—flashed across Belford's mind, stoking his hatred for the evil man.

"The railway leads straight to the Erotos Underground."

Ethan scoffed. "Garrett really managed to dig out a mega-project right under my nose? He was a sneaky bastard—I'll give him that!" He chuckled amusedly to himself. Ethan had a nostalgic look in his eyes. Garrett had been a nemesis to him since ages past. Belford felt a vast sense of disappointment emanating off of him, though surely he would never admit to missing his rival.

Satisfied with Wilgoblikan's answers, Ethan went on to oversee the purchase of all the necessary supplies for their journey. He bought it all with a satchel of gold he'd created with the Power just before reaching the desert's Powerless zone. He'd transmuted the precious metal despite Arcanum law. No one made any comment on the cardinal rule break. Of course Ethan didn't care about inflating Aragwey's gold supply. "Rules for thee, not for me," he joked as he traded the coin and their horses for ten healthy camels, plus enough food and potable water to last the approximate three-day journey through the dunes that lay ahead—ten large casks, after some quick math.

The water alone nearly filled the back compartment of the coach they'd rolled in on. They hired a fabricator in town to help remove the wheels and install sled tracks for the off-road journey. Shiara and Vera rode up front on the driver's bench with only Ader joining the water casks in the back. He was still recovering from an overdosing of Livian's mist. The four largest camels hauled the coach. The other six carried the rest of the travelers. Gord's camel was also necessarily quite large. No one wanted him riding another animal to death.

Whatever distaste Belford had for riding horses, he felt doubly so for camels. The ornery creatures bellowed loudly, grunting and moaning at one another as they walked. Their jarring steps lurched and swayed the occupants of their saddles terribly. Belford had to hold on extra tight so as not to be thrown from their tall backs—not to mention how difficult it was to get up between their awkward humps in the first place. Belford's camel tried to bite off one of his ears for simply standing too close while the herd owner was explaining where to grab the saddle in order to climb up. It was a comedy of errors every moment he was around the foul mounts.

Gross, slobbering, fart machines.

The caravan set out at first light the morning after the alterations to the coach were finished. Belford tied a white cloth around his brow to protect his head from the intense rays of the sun. Soon, though, he had a mighty dehydration headache pinching at his temples. It didn't seem to matter how much water he drank. He'd already sweated out all his salt. Dehydration had its ups and downs. It meant less pee breaks, so at least he didn't have to climb in and out of his camel's saddle all that much. Unfortunately, his butt, back, and arms all became so terribly sore that by the end of the first day out from Vermholt, he could barely even move when he finally stepped down from his mount.

He was grateful to get to sleep atop a stilted cot as they set up camp for the night. The sunset radiated a magnificent orange haze that stretched across the whole sky as the low rays reflected upon the dunes. Dazzling stars soon filled the wide heavens, illuminating the rolling sand with a pale blue glow as the temperature dropped. Belford was glad not to be in agony on the cold, compact ground with the state his battered muscles were in. The lofted cot kept the sand flees away—mostly. The bites he did receive itched incessantly.

Arlin helped Vera rewrap the hilt of her Talus Shard while their campfire roared. He used the olive green sash of her dress as a replacement for the bloodstained yellow wrappings. Earlier in the day Vera had stripped off the dress's gray outer layer. She looked very much like a bride on her wedding day now, wearing only the frilly white slip that had been underneath as she began to spar with Arlin.

Belford knew the sword gave her all its combat knowledge, but her display of shifting stances and strikes was still impressive to see. He sat with Shiara and Ader, watching in silence as the steel rang together.

Arlin showed Vera another secret of the blades—he tapped the glowing gems together, attuning the swords. They could now sense one another's intentions as they continued their practice. They swung their blades fast and with precision, like some choreographed dance.

"The Talus Shard is a memory crystal," said Arlin. "The blades are learning from each other."

Vera and Arlin, it seemed, were mostly just along for the ride. Belford recognized some of the moves he'd used against the Crimson Stalker repeated in Arlin's strikes. Vera responded in turn, twisting fluidly to deflect the attacks. Belford cheered on the exciting display, but soon caught Ader staring at him instead of watching the spectacle of the Talus Shards. "I would like to pledge to you, my fealty," he said slowly and clearly, holding Belford within his glossy gaze. "It is what Mikel would have want. For me. For you. Together."

Belford was taken aback. He had always been fond of the Naffeim brothers. "I don't understand why you'd want to do that," he said. "It's dangerous around me."

"Don't insult the man," Shiara said harshly.

"Is alright," said Ader. "My brother… we discuss many time. I serve you. You make change to this world." There was no room for Belford to decline.

"It's the same reason we all follow you," said Shiara upon seeing his reservations. "Not everyone is in a position to make change. And most who are don't wish to." She eyed Ethan darkly across the camp. He was busy vigorously picking sand from his nostrils.

"Thank you," said Belford, "but I'm not so sure any of you are putting your faith in the right person."

"Mikel die for you," said Ader, "to try to save the ship, to help you escape. Now, I fight for you. You make change— you understand?"

Shiara raised her eyebrow as Ader became more forceful with his words. Belford wouldn't be shirking out of this one. Ader wasn't going to let Mikel's sacrifice be in vain.

"Of course I'll do what I can," said Belford. "But that doesn't mean I know what I'm doing here."

Ader's face relaxed. He reached out and placed a hand on Belford's shoulder. "We help you," he said.

"Just don't get yourself killed for me," said Belford. "Too many already have."

"You are good man," said Ader. "We do it together, for Mikel."

Belford's lips pinched up into a frown. "For Mikel," he finally agreed.

Shiara nodded to him in approval before turning her gaze back upon the dancing blades.

On the second day of their journey there was no shift to the scenery. The dunes all looked the same. Belford hadn't seen a living thing apart from a few stubby cacti since setting out. His mind wandered as he hummed songs written by long dead musicians.

Vera overheard his musings and wouldn't stop pestering him until he agreed to sing the tune in earnest.

"*There is a house down in New Orleans,*" sang Belford.

"Where's that?" asked Grine.

Vera shushed him.

"*They call the Rising Sun,*

And it's been the ruin of a many poor boy,
And me, oh god, for one."

Belford began to blush from embarrassment upon seeing the way Shiara and Vera both fawned after him. Shiara tried to hide it, but Belford caught a hint of a smile on her lips when he glanced back over at the women between verses. Vera was grinning at him unabashedly with fluttering eyelashes. Belford's voice wavered slightly.

When he finished the song everyone but Wilgoblikan applauded his performance. The old Goblikan was up in front of the caravan, leading the way with a compass.

"You got some of the words wrong," said Ethan, needlessly bringing Belford down and making sure everyone knew he hadn't written the song himself.

"That was brilliant!" cooed Vera.

"Everyone quiet!" ordered Wilgoblikan.

All eyes shot forward at the Goblikan's serious tone. A low rumble in the distance carried on the breeze. The vibration grew louder as a plume of sand lifted into the air above one of the distant dunes.

"What is that?" asked Ethan. "It sounds large…."

"It's a Whune," said Wilgoblikan. "Everyone spread out! It already smells us!" He kicked his camel hard, dashing off to the left of the group.

"Protect the coach," ordered Ethan. "We need that water! I'll go bring that idiot back." He took off after Wilgoblikan.

Gord tossed the bo staff Artifact out in front of his camel. It hung in superposition, twirling in the air in front of him and his mount as he rode off in the opposite direction as Ethan and Wilgoblikan. Belford assumed Gord was abandoning them at first, but he was glad to see the staff raised up a screen of sand, obscuring the coach from the approaching threat.

"What do we do?" asked Belford, eyes wide with concern.

So many Powerless Ver'ati….

Arlin rode up alongside the coach and silently extended his hand to Vera. She drew her Talus Shard, steadying her emotions before hopping onto the back of Arlin's camel. They rode up the nearby dune together to get a better look. Belford joined them as Shiara took over steering the coach. Ader climbed up onto the front bench with her.

The approaching sand cloud was being kicked up by something big alright. It wasn't just big, it was huge… monstrously so! And it was closing in on them fast! It looked like a plump grub, blown up to the size of a city bus. Its eerily humanoid face was crowned with two curved horns. The most prominent feature of its flat face was its wide mouth, turned up into a terrifyingly joyous grin. A jagged display of long spiky teeth protruded from its jaws—it had several layers of the evil chompers like a shark.

It was unlike any Whune Belford had ever seen before. Its sheer size alone filled him with dread. It moved with a wriggle, snakelike, swaying in a serpentine pattern as it closed in on them across the sand.

Gord reigned in his camel alongside Belford and Arlin. "Desert vermin," he spat.

The fight was coming their way faster than the camels could run. Belford had no idea how any of them could possibly survive such a beast. The wormy Whune's mouth was as wide as the coach!

Arlin and Vera tapped the gems in their hilts together again, retuning their affinity to one another. "Hang back," Vera ordered Belford as Arlin set their camel bounding down the dune towards the freakishly large grub.

Belford had never felt more useless in his life.

Gord stormed ahead a moment later, charging the beast head on. His swirling bo staff looked like a twig in comparison to the Whune's teeth.

The creature was closing the distance quickly.

Arlin's camel balked upon sensing the approaching danger. It reared up, kicking and flailing, until it managed to toss both Arlin and Vera to the sand. The cowardly camel cantered away, not looking back as it fled into the distance.

Gord's camel was better trained. The Goblikan reached the slithering beast first, whipping up a tornado of sand in its face with the bo staff Artifact. The giant worm suddenly twisted like an alligator in a death spiral, bashing into Gord and his camel with its massive girth. Man and mount were both sent tumbling to the sand. The bo staff was knocked from its superposition—it went flying like a tomahawk back towards Belford before crashing into the base of the dune.

Arlin and Vera were back on their feet, sprinting light-footed across the sand with their blades held high. They split up, flanking the Whune on either side as it wriggled its mouth over to feed on Gord's downed camel. With a chomp that filled its gaping mouth with sand, the beast tore the camel in two.

Gord punched the monster in the neck with his spiked fists, but as large and strong as the Goblikan was, his attack was as ineffective as a fly pestering a horse. The giant beast chewed the lifeless camel with a satisfied smirk on its creepy face, unperturbed by Gord's bashing.

Arlin and Vera struck next, slicing at it in unison. The horrible beast did take notice of their attack as they ran down its length, slashing at its hardened skin on either side. Their blades glanced off its thick underbelly, but sunk in deeper above its formidable calluses.

Gord leapt up and clung to one of the creature's horns. It immediately twisted its head up, snapping at the Goblikan with its powerful jaws. Belford had no idea how Gord managed to hold on. The Goblikan kicked his boot into one of the monster's large eyes repeatedly, annoying it more than anything else. No one had caused any real damage to the creature.

The beast slithered forward in response to the attacks, knocking Arlin and Vera out of its way as it proceeded forward towards the rest of the party. Gord deftly continued kicking it in the eye.

"They can't stop it!" Belford shouted down the dune to the others—Shiara, Ader, and Grine. Sharith Grine wobbled in his saddle as he steered his camel alongside the coach. Belford could see the fear in the young Ameliorator's eyes even from the distance. Belford turned back towards the crazed Whune as it continued charging closer.

The beast smashed its face into the sand, attempting to knock Gord loose from its horn. He held on through several slams before the forces became too great to resist. The creature lifted its head to slam into the dune again, but Gord was already dislodged, sprawled out in the sand. The worm's right eye was a gouged out mass of blood, but like the other Whunes Belford had encountered in the past, it showed no indication of pain or slowing from the damage. Dazed in the sand, Gord could do nothing to protect himself as the monster gnashed at him, tearing him to pieces within its mighty jaws.

Belford turned away from the gruesome display. His camel had also had enough. The mount reared up and sent Belford tumbling to his back at the top of the dune. The camel bellowed in terror as it fled the scene. Belford landed poorly, compressing his diaphragm and knocking the wind out of him. He wheezed pathetically on the sand as he attempted to draw in a breath. He rolled over onto his knees, sputtering for only a moment more before tossing himself down the dune towards the fallen bo staff Artifact. It seemed like a logical action, though the tumble disoriented him terribly.

Vera and Arlin hadn't yet caught up to the beast. It finished off Gord and slithered away again, up the last dune before the coach.

Belford's tumble took him right where he had intended, though not very elegantly. He spit out a mouthful of sand as he grasped onto the Artifact's grip and used it to climb back to his feet. He chased behind Arlin and Vera back up the dune as panicked cries arose from the coach.

Nothing remained of Gord but a bloody smear and a severed arm as Belford shambled along within the Whune's trail. He didn't think there was really anything he could do, but he couldn't run away like his camel, so he kept after the beast.

When he reached the top of the dune again, the coach was already smashed to pieces, lying on its side. The camels were all loose, dead, or dying, and all the water was spilling out and disappearing into the sand.

The ripples of Shiara's firestone earring looked like a shimmering mirage. The Whune charged into the energy-sapping cloud headlong, crying out with a deep howl as the Artifact began to drain its life force.

Arlin and Vera both ran up the creature's languid backside again, taking advantage of its pause to slice the monster lengthwise as they went. Belford knew Shiara's earring had a limited capacity. The beast was stunned, but not incapacitated.

Vera grunted as she drove her blade into the folds around the creature's neck. Arlin joined her, hacking away at its thick skin. Its blood began to seep out—dark globs, already coagulating as they fell.

Ader was nearby, crouched over Grine who had been thrown violently from his camel. Belford scanned his eyes across the crashed coach searching desperately for Shiara. He found her trapped beneath one of the sled tracks. She was attempting to dig herself out, but the Whune's facilities were quickly recovering.

Vera and Arlin—still hacking away at the back of the monstrosity's neck—looked to have nicked an artery. They were thrown off once more as the beast shook its grotesque head like a wet dog. Blood rained down all around the Whune as it twisted wildly. By the time it finished shaking, the sand was soaked. The monster refocused in on the overturned coach. It bit into the side of the wagon, its teeth crunching straight through the wooden frame and into the remaining water casks with ease. The casks popped like melons in its wide mouth. The creature threw its head back, projecting another geyser of its own blood into the air as it destroyed the last of their water supply.

Shiara cried out in pain as the Whune pushed down on the coach with its fat neck.

Belford rushed around to the far side of the coach. The monster's remaining eye followed Belford as he ran past it to where Shiara was pinned. It turned its jaws, tossing the remnants of a water cask as it went to take a chomp out of the camels still hitched at the overturned coach's front. Its teeth shredded the helpless animals with ease.

"Come on!" Belford cried as he tugged Shiara free of the wreckage.

The camels' panicked bellows ceased. The Whune's giant lips curled up around its toothy maw as it crunched their bones.

It's smiling!

The monster swallowed before opening its mouth again. A low voice rumbled up from deep in its throat. "I SEE YOU, BOY!" the beast boomed.

The realization that the Whune was intelligent enough to speak was horrifying to Belford. Wilgoblikan's Whunes had started out as people, but he'd not assumed the same of this great worm of an abomination.

Shiara was back on her feet. Belford ran with her arm-in-arm, fleeing from the terrible monster. It already had them locked in its sight. The creature flopped across the coach, crushing the remnants beneath its hefty mass as it pursued them.

Belford tossed the bo staff into the air, hoping to obscure their path from the beast. Sand did start to whip up into the air, but the Whune was upon them far too quickly. Belford turned to face the gaping mouth, prepared to be devoured like Gord and the camels. The bo staff twirled into the monster's wide maw as the beast bit at Belford. A gargle of a choke sounded as it snapped its teeth shut again, just shy of reaching Belford and Shiara.

It opened and closed its jaws repeatedly; wriggling its whole body in an attempt to dislodge the bo staff from the awkward position the stick had taken up in its throat.

Somehow, Arlin and Vera both managed to maintain their balance while climbing back up the beast's spine despite its violent motions. They resumed hacking at the exposed artery in its neck. Belford and Shiara dashed for safety. Vera wedged her blade up underneath the nicked artery. She sliced upward, severing it with a violent movement.

With every wriggle of the Whune's bulbous body, a spray of dark blood gushed out from its neck. It tried to shake Vera and Arlin off again, but the loss of blood left it weakened beyond recovery. They continued to chop away, not stopping until the creature finally bowed over, falling lifeless.

Wilgoblikan and Ethan began riding back. The two men had been watching the madness unfold from over the next dune. Wilgoblikan was particularly pleased with the outcome despite all their losses. He laughed and clapped for Vera and Arlin. "What an incredible display!" he exclaimed.

"What the hell is wrong with you?" Belford shouted at him. "How can you be so happy right now?! Gord is dead… and most of the camels… and the whole bloody coach is destroyed, along with all our food and water! We're all dead!"

Wilgoblikan ignored him entirely. "Keep cutting," he ordered. "We must bring the head as an offering! Oh, how perfect!" He approached the dead beast and climbed up its face to its forehead where a clear crystal shard Belford hadn't noticed before was protruding from the creature's skin. "Help me—cut here," he said up to Arlin.

Arlin stabbed his sword against the crystal and helped Wilgoblikan wedge the shard free. It was surprisingly long, looking like a thick root coming up from the center of the creature's forehead. Wilgoblikan clutched it to his chest as he climbed down.

"What the heck is that thing?" Belford asked.

"A memory crystal," Wilgoblikan answered nonchalantly.

"So, what does it do—hold memories?"

"I just said it's a memory crystal, didn't I?"

"But, like, whose memories are on it… or in it or whatever?" Belford insisted.

"It holds the Whune's memories, of course, you nitwit. It works exactly like those Talus Shards—you're not simple are you? I assume you're aware of Power Artifacts."

Belford scowled at him. "Yes, I'm aware of Power Artifacts."

"It's not a difficult concept. The crystal is trained by the experiences of the beast—so we can't just have all that training going to waste, now can we?"

Belford stared back at him blankly.

"We can't," Wilgoblikan answered his own question. He placed the long crystal into his pocket. It still protruded out from the top a little bit.

"We don't have any more water," said Belford, speaking slowly and enunciating every word to show his irritation of Wilgoblikan's chipper attitude. "And Gord just got eaten!"

"Oh, I'm sorry," said Wilgoblikan, "was Gord your best friend all of a sudden? Thank you, Gord, for your sacrifice. There, may we move on now? We are close enough to walk to the Graveyard from here, and this head will buy us all passage. It's a good fortune, indeed!"

"Get to cutting," Ethan ordered up to Arlin and Vera who were both still silently watching the exchange.

Belford felt like he'd left Aragwey and entered Crazyville. He wondered if the sun had rotted everyone's brains out as the Talus Shards eventually managed to hack through the great beast's thick neck, severing the head entirely. They tied the "offering" to the broken coach's metal sled tracks to make it easier for the remaining camels to tow the giant head through the sand, and then they continued on like lunatics, wandering the desert afoot.

CHAPTER
32

A Train to Crazyville

The ruins of Eversted were close enough to reach on foot... but certainly not before nightfall. With no water, and only a giant severed head as company, delirium soon set in for Belford and the other desert travelers. They did not stop, continuing to trek on throughout the night hours.

The giant Whune head began to turn purple, its massive swelling tongue lulling out of its mouth as it dragged across the sand. The smell was rancid beyond reason. Belford wasn't sure how all the flies swarming around it managed to find their ways to the rotting flesh within the vastness of the mostly lifeless desert, but here they were nonetheless, buzzing around the open neck hole where the Talus Shards had done their butchery.

Belford trudged onward with the rest of his companions, hoping that each dune would be the last in their grueling journey. He was disappointed every time when the sands seemed to stretch on forever ahead of them.

234

He may as well have been dragging his own tongue across the sand for how dry his mouth felt. He'd finished what was left of his canteen hours before sunset and he was pretty sure he'd already sweated every drop back out. The cool night air had him shivering. His legs and feet kept cramping up on him—a symptom of his chronic dehydration. He wasn't feeling like himself. He would have even accepted a canteen full of horse blood right about now had Gord been alive to offer out such an absurdity to him again.

I'm going to die, wandering this desert, following Wilgoblikan....

His organs hurt. His head was pounding. There was nothing to do but take another dizzying step forward—and another—endlessly across the sand.

By the time the sun began its rise, the smell wafting up from the bloating head had become so terribly rank that he found himself repeatedly gagging at the stench. He tried to stay upwind, but the air was too stagnant. The foul stink was impossible to escape.

His delirium had advanced to the point that he was having hallucinations. There were the usual withered corpses at the corners of his vision of which he'd grown fairly accustom to by now—remnants of the nuclear holocaust that destroyed his world. But his mind kept conjuring up additional glowing forms in the mirage of heat along the horizon as well. As the sun rose higher, he could have sworn he saw a hand the size of a mountain stretching high out of the haze into the bright sky.

It wasn't until they got closer and the statue solidified further rather than disappearing into the rising heat that Belford realized it was not a figment of his imagination after all. More half-buried statues protruded from the sand as the group ambled on.

"I told you we were close!" rasped Wilgoblikan through a dry throat.

The sight of the Graveyard reinvigorated the travelers' fortitude to continue on. Their proximity to the ruins of Eversted drew nigh.

"This is where the last battle of the Cleansing took place," said Ethan. "Where Garrett's Goblikan army was destroyed."

"That was before our time," said Wilgoblikan. "You'll find the sands very much alive today."

A company of slender, spindly-legged creatures was already galloping towards the travelers, descending from the high vantage points of the various statues and other ruined structures. They ran on all fours, kicking up a dust cloud behind them.

"A welcoming party?" asked Grine, squinting in the direction of the cloud.

"Not quite," said Wilgoblikan. "Those are Sentinels." He did not elaborate further.

As the gangly creatures drew nearer, Belford realized they were larger than he'd initially thought. Even hunched over as they were, they clearly stood at least as tall as camels. There was nothing but sand to compare their size to, so it was difficult to tell just how big they actually were until they were almost right on top of them.

They bounded across the dunes, fast as race horses. A bad feeling settled in Belford's withering gut. The half a dozen approaching Sentinels meant to pick a fight—that much was clear. Arlin and Vera drew their blades preemptively. Belford wished he still had the bo staff Artifact, but the giant Whune's powerful jaws had crunched it into splinters.

"Prepare the offering," Wilgoblikan ordered. "And hamstring the camels so they can't run."

Arlin and Vera looked at each other and then back at Wilgoblikan.

"They'll love the brain matter," said Wilgoblikan. "The camels are a bonus."

"I'm not cutting up the camels," said Vera.

Wilgoblikan frowned. "Have it your way," he said. "I suppose they'll enjoy the sport more this way anyway."

The camels eyes rolled nervously as the Sentinels descended the dunes around them. The pale wrappings on the creatures' faces split open, parting grossly along with their unusual vertical jaws as they hissed at the gleaming Talus Shards before them. They halted their advance, forming a blockade between the travelers and their destination.

The camels tried to follow the party as everyone huddled together, abandoning the poor beasts of burden to the whims of the Sentinels. The gawky predators accepted the offering. They surrounded the giant head and camels at once. The Sentinels used their pointy arms like spears, pouncing on the severed head and gouging repeatedly into the thick skull.

The camels attempted to flee, but a singular poke brought one of them down to the sand. The remaining camel wasn't strong enough to pull forward without help. There was simply too much dead weight on the other end of its harness. Belford grimaced as the Sentinels slowly picked the poor animals apart, hooting and chuckling like a band of chittering monkeys all the while. He had come to terms with the fact that nature was cruel—however, the Whunes were anything but natural. They were a perversion. Their cruelty held no bounds. They repeatedly stabbed at the camels' groins and underbellies while the helpless creatures bellowed for mercy. Their amusement sickened Belford. He turned away, disgusted. The Sentinels allowed the party to continue on unhindered as they feasted upon the giant head's rotting innards.

"Foul, aren't they?" Wilgoblikan asked rhetorically. "I told you you'd be glad for hauling that head along with us."

Belford thought his *I-told-you-so's* were getting old. He didn't envy Javic, being related to the smug, psychotic bastard. *What was he to Javic again? His uncle? No, great uncle.* He'd forgotten exactly what Elric had said about the Goblikan all those months ago in Felington. *Wil was Elric's dead wife's brother,* he recalled. Wil was Javic's family. He wondered if Elric had told Javic the whole truth about his great uncle yet.

By now Javic should have passed his proficiency exam and been allowed to leave the academy grounds. Belford couldn't really envision Javic wanting to stay with the Ver'konus. Returning to his grandfather was the only path he could see for the thoughtful boy despite what he'd said about wanting to help push Belford to the top. Javic was not a military dog at heart. Belford hoped he was doing well.

Their remaining march into the ruins of Eversted went unopposed. They did spot more Sentinels lurking above as they passed between dilapidated structures, but the crouched figures did not come down to harass them. Not all the Whunes in the Torus Desert were masterless.

They crested one more dune and found themselves on a steep downgrade, approaching a grand pit at the center of the old city. The pit was as wide and deep as the largest industrial quarries Belford was aware of existing back in his time. A long procession of more traditional hulking-beast Whunes hefted huge buckets of broken bedrock chunks and sand out of the pit. They wound their way up a path, spiraling the outside of the pit. All the way down at the bottom, they looked like ants carrying crumbs.

An old shirtless man with a long white beard approached the group, venturing out alone from the base of a narrow tower that overlooked the pit. Wilgoblikan's face pinched up in annoyance before the bug-eyed man even reached them. Belford took the reaction to mean the old man's presence was an insult. He cared not whether sending the toasted-skinned, senile-looking fellow was a jab at Wilgoblikan's station or at Wilgoblikan personally, because the sun-soaked angel was carrying a bucket of water equipped with a handy ladle.

"Hey, I know you!" exclaimed the old pit warden, pointing at Wilgoblikan as he handed the bucket over to Ethan.

Ethan ignored the ladle, instead tipping the entire bucket to his lips as he drank deeply. Arlin had to snatch it from his hands when he didn't stop after several seconds and began sloshing the precious water down the front of his shirt. Arlin took over serving everyone more fairly—pouring a mouthful in between each traveler's desperately parched lips before allowing Ethan to go back for seconds.

"We wish to go south," said Wilgoblikan.

"Another train south? You're definitely not on the schedule," said the pit warden.

Wilgoblikan glowered at him darkly. "I have this," he said, withdrawing from his pocket the memory crystal he'd pulled from the giant Whune's forehead.

The pit warden took the crystal from his outstretched hands and stuffed it under his sweaty armpit. "A train can be arranged," he said, "once your guests finish drinking the rest of the drugs."

Belford spit out his third ladleful.

"Relax," said Wilgoblikan, holding up his hand. "This was expected. The concoction will only disorient you. This is the only way forward."

"We can't have you lot remembering everything you see!" exclaimed the old pit warden. "This is Goblikan business!"

"Don't worry, it should be a pleasurable experience," said Wilgoblikan, addressing the grumbling concerns of the group.

Belford stared out into the vast empty space above the pit, his eyes becoming unfocused. He was contemplating his own stupidity for accepting a drink from the shriveled-up raisin of a man. He already felt like there was something off with his perception. It wasn't just the heat or his advanced dehydration—the world looked like it was bubbling up all around him, like a slowly boiling pot. It was subtle, but he could see it more clearly the closer in distance he focused his vision. The back of his own hand rippled softly as if formed from a sheet of fine silk. The slow churn was mesmerizing to watch.

The drugs were coming on fast.

CHAPTER
33

Euphoria

Ethan was freaking out. He immediately took off his shirt and panted like a dog as he poked at his own muscles. He appeared to be lost in some sort of existential crisis, awkwardly flexing as he pinched his skin. He kept shrieking for some reason. Whatever the drugs were doing to them all, Belford had never experienced anything like it in his life. He was grateful he hadn't consumed as much as Ethan—the selfish prick had gotten way more than his fair share of the dosed water.

With a blessing from the crusty pit warden, Wilgoblikan led the group down the winding walkway. The laboring Whunes took no notice of them, tirelessly hauling their buckets to the surface. A wave of vertigo hit Belford as he peered over the edge of the walkway. The pit was several dozen stories deep— a super structure in itself! He felt like he was circling a drain as they slowly descended counterclockwise into the earth.

By the time they reached the bottom they were masked in deep shadow by the high walls all around them. The constant downgrade wore blisters into the sides of Belford's big toes where they were rubbing against the fronts of his shoes. The wavering effect of the drugs only grew stronger as he felt his blood pressure spike. He glanced up at a patch of daylight shinning high above on the pit wall, trying to steady his racing heart. The glare hurt his eyes. He touched his hand to his forehead. He was burning up! Wilgoblikan insisted they were quite safe—that the drugs were harmless—but the nagging thought that his heart might explode wouldn't leave Belford's mind. His pulse continued to pound beneath his clammy skin. He wished he could sit at the bottom of a cold shower and just lap up the spray until the sensations stopped.

A tunnel at the depths of the pit was lit by blue glowing rocks—he wasn't sure if it was his imagination making the rocks glow or if some sort of bioluminescence had been manufactured and brought to the location. The walls of the tunnel were lined with the glowing stone, providing just enough light to avoid stumbling over the uneven ground.

The tunnel looked fake to Belford, like painted styrofoam on an old film set. He couldn't get over just how unreal everything looked. The stone certainly felt real beneath his fingertips, though—hyper-real! A sensation like cold water running across his skin seeped up from the stone as he ran his hand along the wall. He touched one of the glowing stones next—it felt slimy against his skin in comparison, but the luminous property didn't transfer to his hand.

"Don't touch that," Wilgoblikan ordered.

Belford wiped his fingers on his pants.

The tunnel widened into a vast cavern as they marched on. A cold draft blew against them; the earth was breathing. A dozen iron rail tracks lined the cavern along with several vacant trains. The various tracks converged and split numerous times before diverging off into separate tunnels—a massive train station, fit with platforms and all.

Open cars loaded with dirt and debris filled an approaching train. It rolled up slowly with a deep rumble towards the terminus. Whunes returning from the surface with empty buckets made for the new haul and began parting it out.

The travelers stopped and waited while Wilgoblikan chatted with the train's conductor. Belford sat along the wall, watching the Whunes work as his wavering head filled him with nausea. The effects of the drugs were steadily rising. His skin was beginning to tingle ever so softly with an internal buzz. His breaths swelled in his lungs, filling him with a euphoric sensation that made him shiver. Each breath brought a new wave of endorphins rolling through him like a lapping tide.

He ran his hand up his own chest, setting off waves of pleasure that danced across his skin as if he'd done the same motion thrice over. The tingling waves made him gasp. The ghostly vibrations from the touch diminished after several peaks in sensation. Each breath he took added to his sensitivity.

Shiara, beside him, shook his leg as Wilgoblikan approached once more. Her touch felt even better than his own. All the hairs on his body stood up at once, reaching out to her in hopes that she might merely nudge him again.

"We've got a train," said Wilgoblikan. "Follow me."

Arlin tried to drag Ethan along—he'd stripped to his underwear and was lying flat on his stomach on the platform, refusing to use his legs. Wilgoblikan ended up having to help Arlin. He picked up Ethan's discarded pants before taking up half his weight upon himself. They carried him like the lump he was over to an awaiting passenger car. Ethan's screeches were disturbing to everyone. The sound of his unintelligible wails filled Belford with anxiety.

The train car they were led to appeared to have been meant for cattle rather than people. It had narrow slits for windows and iron hitches all along the walls. Belford assumed its passengers were usually mindless Whunes. The thought that the tunnels ran the length of Aragwey gave him a claustrophobic feeling. He didn't like the idea of being trapped so far underground once they got going. He wondered how the Goblikans kept the air fresh so deep beneath the surface—whether there were escape hatches or any other safety precautions in place in case of emergencies.

A particularly fat Whune with a tumorous lumpy back carried in a crate of provisions to their car. It contained dried meat and several loaves of stale bread along with what was hopefully a clean cask of water. Everyone drank slowly, hoping they weren't dosing themselves any further.

Wilgoblikan tossed Ethan's pants into the train car along with an empty bucket. "You can piss in this," he said. "I'll be back tomorrow to refill your lanterns." He slammed the squeaky metal door shut and latched it from the outside.

"I don't like this at all," said Grine. The warped scowl on his face made him appear to be made of clay. His skin was too lumpy—though that was probably just Belford's perception. The drugs were coursing through them all. Flashes of color sparked across Belford's vision, dark purples and greens flowing in a grid pattern that overlapped with the wiggling lines of his slowly boiling reality.

Ethan shrieked again. Belford covered his ears as the wiry cry echoed terribly throughout the tin can of a train. Ethan was being obnoxious, jumping back and forth trying to grab Vera's Talus Shard blade out of its sheath. A noticeable bulge was forming in his underwear. He looked to be enjoying the dance with Vera despite the piercing howls that escaped him.

"Get off me!" Vera cried, kicking Ethan away like an unruly dog.

Arlin hastily snatched Ethan's discarded pants up off the floor and used the garment as a restraint. He hooked the crotch around Ethan's neck and yanked the fool backwards. Ethan choked and sputtered in a terrified panic, but Arlin didn't stop pulling until he had Ethan against a post at the center of the train car. No one batted an eye. Everyone was sick of Ethan's shit. The de facto leader of the group flailed violently, grabbing above his head at Arlin's face. Arlin twisted the pants around the post and back around again to encircle Ethan's wrists. It worked to stop him from lashing out with his hands, but he continued to kick at everyone in front of him. Arlin unbuttoned his shirt and used it as an additional ligature to bind Ethan more securely to the post. Ethan wasn't done—it became clear his thrashing would not be subdued quite so easily.

"More bindings!" exclaimed Belford as he undid his own shirt to add to Ethan's restraints.

Grine and Ader followed suit, stripping down to prevent Ethan's bad trip from hurting anybody.

Splat.

A thick glob of Ethan's spit hit Belford directly in the face.

A smug look flashed across the asshole's dehydrated lips. Belford snapped. Ethan had pushed him too far this time—*The disrespect!* Belford knew Ethan wasn't in his right mind, but he no longer cared. He curled his fist up into a ball and socked Ethan straight in the jaw with a hard right hook.

The strike rippled up Belford's arm, sending the counterforce stinging into his bones. He'd landed a solid blow. Ethan responded by spiting a spray of blood at Belford, laughing manically all the while.

"There's no winning with someone like him," said Vera.

She stepped up to Ethan from behind and gagged him with a piece of cloth around his head. Ethan eyed Vera sideways. His blocked mouth curled up into an infuriating grin. When Belford realized Vera had used her underwear as the gag it only made him more furious. Ethan knew what Vera had done, and he was clearly pleased with the outcome. He slumped forward against the makeshift restraints but continued to wriggle his legs together as he sucked on her underwear.

Belford wanted to kick Ethan in the crotch when he noticed the man was fully erect and nearly bursting from his own under garment. Before he could act, Vera latched onto him and wiped the blood and spit from his brow with the sleeve of her dress. She brushed him tenderly, cleaning him up despite his scowl. Vera leaned in and kissed him on the mouth.

The kiss came as quite the surprise! It pulled the anger from him in an instant, replacing it with a sensual explosion of tactile fireworks. He leaned into her, reciprocating aggressively. The drugs had him feeling like they were melting together. The velvet softness of Vera's lips set off flashes of light in his brain—a cacophony of synesthesia that overtook his senses.

Vera pulled away slightly and whispering into his mouth: "You stood up for me." She planted another slow kiss on his lips. His teeth buzzed with the desperate energy.

The drugs chose that moment to take a particularly *unusual* turn. Belford felt like he was tumbling sideways into a hole— the train was moving, but it was more than that—his consciousness splintered away, dissolving into a more basic state. He and Vera continued to kiss, but he wasn't really aware of his body anymore. At first it was as if he were watching from outside of himself as the tears streamed down Vera's cheeks and moistened her plump lips. He could taste the saltiness as the droplets flowed down to the corners of her mouth and intermingled with their kiss. The physical sensations oozed through him with a lingering buzz, fanning the flames of lust and desire within.

He didn't feel like a person anymore—Belford was gone. He was an undefined blob of cells. It all came on so fast! He was pure Freudian id wrapped in a naked-monkey-meat-creature suit, and as unromantic as that notion sounded, his deepest yearning was to occupy the same space as another naked monkey meat creature. Their tongues met as their hands wandered across one another. It was a deeply instinctual exchange.

He was overtaken by the pleasure of touch as they swapped groping caresses. He was lost to it all, his thoughts spiraling into a choppy ocean of passion. The waves were orgasmic, tingling from the tips of his hairs to the ends of his toes. He was but a tiny boat attempting to weather a vast storm, sailing towards an endless dawn.

Vera moaned into Belford's mouth as Shiara appeared over her shoulder, kissing her neck from behind. Belford and Vera weren't the only ones lost to the throes of euphoria. Whatever shame or reason would have normally restrained their movements was washed away by the Goblikan drugs stoking their internal tempests.

Vera slipped her white dress from her shoulders and let it fall in a heap at her feet, unabashed by her nakedness. It felt to Belford like the most natural thing. She turned towards Shiara and returned her kiss passionately. Their eyes were the size of saucers in the lamplight. They pulled away from one another. Shiara disrobed next, an animalistic hunger in her movements. There were no inhibitions left to restrain any of them. Everyone else ceased to exist to Belford as the two women turned their attentions back on him simultaneously.

They pressed their bodies together in a tangled embrace, sliding over him like jigsaw pieces. Belford kicked his pants from his body. There was nothing separating them now as he felt the warmth of their skin seep into his own. He wasn't sure where one body ended and another began. The softness of their forms enveloped him. Shiara sucked on his fingers while Vera straddled him on the cold floor. It was all so visceral—primal!

He held Shiara's jaw in his palm, pushing his thumb between her pouty lips to feel her tongue. She nipped at him slightly before redirecting his hand lower. Much lower. She slid rhythmically against his moistened thumb.

Vera bucked against him, consuming him whole with unexpected swiftness. His excitement grew quickly as she gyrated in desperation. He thrust his hips, matching her rhythm. Their sounds were lustful growls of bliss, quickly rising in timbre towards a euphoric peek. But before Belford could arrive at that destination, Grine appeared over Vera's other shoulder, stroking her hair and kissing on her exposed neck. She shuddered at his touch, craning her head back as she squeezed Belford between her thighs. After a few more joyous seconds she lifted herself off of him and got down on her knees and forearms in front of Grine instead.

Vera stared directly at Ethan as she stretched her back like a jungle cat. Ethan was still hard and twitching against his leg.

Grine gripped onto Vera from behind. Ethan watched with wide, unblinking eyes as Vera moaned breathlessly under Grine's touch. He held onto her hips as she bumped back into him fervently.

While Belford was preoccupied with a twinge of jealously that he hadn't the mental capacity to even begin to unravel in his current state, Shiara withdrew from his hand and was suddenly in Arlin's arms. Belford's heart pounded as his unsatisfied loins fluttered with angst. Shiara matched Vera's pose, presenting herself for Arlin. Animal lust buzzed through the air. The chorus of moans was contagious as everyone writhed together in their deep drug-fueled stupors.

Vera pulled away from Grine, crawling towards Ethan with a wild look in her eyes. She was on the prowl.

Arlin held Shiara up by her shoulders and neck as Ader joined the fray. The typically reserved man kissed Shiara through her moans.

As bizarre of a sight as all of that was, Belford's attention was drawn back towards Vera. She was crouched over Ethan's lap, hands reaching into his underwear.

It's all wrong!

A part of Belford felt a deep discomfort in what he was watching. His mental capacity may have been reduced to a state of clouded confusion, but he still knew Ethan didn't deserve to feel Vera's warm embrace—not in the slightest! He'd abused her.

Grine caressed Belford's knee—the unexpected touch distracted him momentarily. He pulled away from Grine, refocusing his attention back on Vera.

She had disrobed Ethan entirely and withdrawn his aroused shaft. She held the foreskin pinched between her index finger and thumb like a stinky dead fish as she reached for her Talus Shard. Neither Ethan nor Belford realized her intentions until she started slicing. Just a quick cut and it was done in an instant. Ethan's castrated genitals flopped to the floor. He let loose a bloodcurdling scream through his gag.

Only now did everyone else take notice of what had just transpired. Vera sat back on her feet, fixing Ethan with a steady gaze as he wriggled back and forth. A pool of blood expanded quickly beneath him. He continued to writhe until he eventually fell still. His eyes glossed over but remained open, staring into Vera's face with a horrified glimmer of understanding that slowly faded away as he bled out on the cold metal floor.

CHAPTER
34

The New Truth

The EAC doctors that visited Aaron wore hazmat suits whenever they entered his room. He was still radioactive. The ominous clicks of their Geiger counter frightened him absolutely shitless. A multitude of tiny pops came fast—it was the scariest sound Aaron had ever heard in his life! He knew what radiation could do to a person. Melting from the inside out, writhing in continuous, nerve-rending agony was about the worst way he could imagine going out of this world.

If it wasn't for the specialized course of nanobots hard at work inside of him corralling the remaining high-energy particles in his blood, his skin would have already began to slough off, along with his fingernails and teeth. Without the high-tech intervention, his insides would be soup.

Along with the nanobots, a simple treatment of potassium iodide was also administered to help protect his thyroid. The pills were worth more than their weight in gold. Most of the world's remaining population would be exposed to the fallout to some degree. Aaron and the other Arcadians were receiving better medical treatment than money was capable of purchasing. He was grateful the EAC wanted him alive, but he already knew the inevitable survivor's guilt coming his way would be horrendous.

First, he would have to survive.

He slept while he waited for Claire to be roused from her medically induced coma.

A bang at his door brought him out of a nightmare—the scorched shadows of the evaporated dead lingered as mere blotches across his vision. He blinked the sleep from his restless eyes.

Standing before him was another ghost, but this one was made of flesh.

Yosef Reblan—aged Israeli CEO and founder of the Arcadian Project—scowled down upon Aaron. Yosef had woken him from his nap by letting the door slam into its stopper as he entered. Aaron had assumed Yosef was killed by the blast that leveled Echo Facility.

Of course the EAC got him too….

Yosef didn't have radiation burns like Aaron.

He must have been extracted by the helicopter that came before the warheads struck.

"Hello," said Yosef.

Aaron glared up at him.

"Your radiation levels have been adequately reduced. In light of this, our hosts would like for me to stress that you are not a prisoner here. They also wish for you to understand that if you do leave the facility prematurely, the radiation outside will most definitely kill you."

Aaron swallowed hard. His throat still hurt from his recent intubation. "Where are we?" he asked.

"This is just some black site," Yosef said waving his hand dismissively. "I really can't say. It doesn't matter, regardless. This facility is a temporary measure until all of you *Arcadians* recover enough to be of service."

Aaron scoffed. "Why would I ever help you again?"

"The service is not for me, boy!" Yosef retorted. "Nor is it for the EAC. What we all must do is quite obvious—can you not see?"

Aaron didn't feel like playing games. He fixed Yosef with a flat stare.

"I thought you were supposed to be a good problem solver," said Yosef. He paced across the room to the mirror where he sneered at his own reflection, checking between his teeth for remnants of food before speaking again. "There is only one technology that can possibly clean up the mess of fallout that is circling the globe. That is to say, my technology—you Arcadians. You can control the power of the atom with your mind—you can break down the radioactive material faster than the thousands of years it would otherwise take to degrade naturally. It is dangerous, but doable."

Aaron scoffed again. "You want me to clean up your mess?"

"I don't care what you do," spat Yosef. "I'm just delivering their message. You know how the EAC loves their social credit. The choice is up to you. With or without your help, billions will die—it's just a matter of degree. You and me? We can save some. That's worth something to the EAC. I suggest you leverage their goodwill. They are the only superpower left on the planet. We will all have to work very hard to salvage what we can of the world. Would you be able to live with yourself if you didn't?"

Aaron grimaced. "Where's Claire?" he asked. "I heard they were waking her up today." He could still feel her nearby in the back of his mind, but she had not responded to any of his attempts at communication. The silence was making him anxious.

"She's awake," said Yosef. "You can go see her as soon as you can stand up and walk, but be warned, she is not in a good way. Just follow the red tape—it leads to every room that we are allowed to access on this floor—she's just down the hall."

Aaron's stomach sank at Yosef's words. The thought of Claire in distress tugged at him urgently. He knew what he needed to do, but he wasn't sure his body was ready. He hadn't attempted to get out of bed yet. He was still attached to both a catheter and an intravenous drip. Yosef's invitation was enough motivation for him to remove the tubes himself. He knew what he was doing; he'd administered his fair share of catheters as a medical resident. He waited for Yosef to depart before unhooking himself from everything. He grimaced as he slowly tugged the catheter tube free.

Swinging his feet over the side of the bed drew a grunt out of him—a strain to his muscles. His legs had grown weak with atrophy after spending an unknown number of days reclined. He hobbled through the door. Just as Yosef said, red masking tape formed an arrow pointing back at him. A line continued on down the hall with additional arrows off-shooting towards most of the doors.

The hallway swayed before him as a wave of nausea sloshed across his gut—he had to slow down. He steadied himself against the wall, trying to hold back his empty stomach from dry heaving. He could feel Claire. She was straight ahead. He forced himself to continue forward despite his unsteadiness.

The worry that drew him onward could not have been more founded. He was unprepared for what lay at the end of that red line.

Claire's room was a mirror image of his own. Her distant eyes did not brighten when she recognized Aaron. He made for her bedside. He knew something was wrong—he still couldn't reach her across their bond. "Are you stopping me on purpose?" he asked, choosing his words carefully in case anyone was secretly listening in. Their bond was not something Aaron wished to share with the EAC.

Claire didn't move. Her eyes shifted slightly, but she still wasn't looking at him. Her hands remained folded neatly over her stomach atop the blanket. Aaron could tell she'd been crying. Her face was puffy, especially around the eyes. "I reinforced the wall," she said calmly, voice void of emotion.

He knew she was referring to the mental walls that they'd developed jointly to stop their ever-waking thoughts and recollections from spilling over into one another's minds. She'd restricted him before when she wanted to hide her emotions from him. "Please, talk to me!" he implored. A sense of dread filled him as Claire still refused to meet his eyes. The worry pressed firmly on his chest. It manifested as tightness, his breath hanging in the balance.

"I can't let you feel this," she whispered.

Aaron gripped her interlocked hands between his own. "You're scaring me," he said.

Claire squeezed her eyes shut, unable to speak the words for a moment. "She's gone," she said, "I lost her—a miscarriage." Emotion struck her as the devastating words escaped her lips. Tears burst silently through her lashes. Her chin scrunched up, a slight quiver shaking her voice. "I could f-feel her… she was there, and then just…." *Our baby is gone.*

The pain of acknowledging the new truth tore her apart.

The wall inside her shattered in an instant, brittle shards exploding outward. Aaron was struck by her anguish even before full comprehension set in.

Their baby had barely existed, but already Aaron and Claire were forever changed. Aaron hadn't dared to envision their future amongst the desolation of the world, but all he could do now was imagine what their daughter's face might have looked like had things gone differently—had she been allowed to be born.

It was like a fogged mirror—her tenuous form too hazy to make out—a future that would never come to pass. He could almost see it. He wished to live inside the fantasy. He labored to imagine her more clearly. The harder he held on, the more the illusion crumbled under the pressure. His mind clung desperately to the pieces until they turned to dust and slipped from his grasp entirely.

Claire sobbed as Aaron sank to his knees beside her. They squeezed each other's hands, clinging desperately together.

Aaron reached out with his mind, hopelessly probing with his extra-sensory abilities into Claire's womb. He did not doubt her earnestness. He simply had to see for himself.

The radiation had shredded her insides. Millions of cellular discrepancies littered her body. Nanobots were fixing what they could, but the corruption was widespread. The fetus was gone. He shifted his mind to her ovaries.

Claire sensed the bodily intrusion. She pushed Aaron back out again, locking him from both her body and mind simultaneously. She cut off his access to the matter markers inside of her—the supercomputer gave privileged access to one's own cells—but Aaron had already seen the extent of the damage before the wall came crashing back down.

It wasn't just the fetus—all of Claire's eggs were destroyed.

Aaron turned his attention on his own body. In all his worry over Claire, he was yet to assess himself. He found he was just as damaged as Claire—corrupt genetics and cancerous cells abound. They were both sterile, without any doubt. Their insides had been fried. There was no solace to be had. Aaron would never be a father, nor Claire a mother.

Their connection had made Aaron believe Claire was a part of him—that they were a part of each other—but deep down he knew it was an illusion. They were intertwined, but they were still alone. Even with her mental wall up, simply looking at Claire filled Aaron with grief. He built up his own wall, keeping the torrent of negative emotions to himself. Shared feelings too often formed feedback loops. There was already too much to mourn.

Out of mercy, they each sealed in their loss, pulling away from one another. The distance brought its own numb pain, like a throbbing limb, drained of blood.

Aaron felt his capacity for processing emotion quickly waning, shutting down under the relentless torment. The numbness felt like depression—his old friend. He clung to it like a board at sea. To feel nothing was more palatable than the immensity of his loss.

CHAPTER 35

House of Horrors

Livian stepped gingerly through the empty promenade that separated the Free Goblikans' headquarters from the pyramid. She'd been strapped to Nal Viershin's chest the last time she passed through, flying in the opposite direction. She was finally being allowed to return to the comfort of the pyramid, albeit only temporarily while she completed an important task for Nal. The metal egg that could recall the dastardly beads nestled against her arteries was no longer in Nal's sizable hands.

The Power Artifact that ensured her obedience had been passed off and was now dangling from a chain around Sir Kierington's armored neck. He walked beside her with a steady stride, fingers clutched firmly around the dimpled egg.

Livian was glad she still made him so terribly nervous. She could work with that.

She still considered Nal to be the bigger obstacle to her freedom. He was domineering. Fortunately or not, he hadn't the time to manage Livian any longer—not after Lord Ethan's miraculous escape left most of the Goblikan commanders deceased.

Since that night, Sir Kierington had been sticking to her side like a greasy stain she just couldn't wash off. What they lacked was trust. Nothing a few spores couldn't fix. She just needed to find a way of slipping them to him without him noticing. His mind would become hers—simpler said than done. Livian had a vial of love spores reserved for Sir Kierington, just waiting in case she found her elusive opportunity to strike. Over the course of the week since Lord Ethan's escape, Sir Kierington had overseen her throughout her duties. She'd dosed several dozen more unruly Goblikans with her spores. The number of *crazies* brought in by the Free Goblikans dwindled as Nal maintained his stranglehold over the region. The deaths of the other commanders only served to consolidate his power.

In some ways Livian's predicament had become simplified by the reduction of leadership—she only needed to worry about pleasing Nal now, and not the dozen other psychopaths formerly at the top of the command structure. Not to mention the relief she felt to never have to see Ives Redbone ever again. He had disturbed her deeply. And yet still, she remained as trapped as ever by the egg Artifact and Sir Kierington's untrusting disposition. She was grateful to retain her ability to channel, even if it was only when given permission. Sir Kierington could feel her intentions when she connected to the Power. He could prematurely end her life with the press of a button.

Livian had been doing her job well. Nal was pleased, Sir Kierington relayed that much to her. Every Goblikan Livian dosed had been transformed into a model recruit for her makeshift regiment. The rest of the Goblikans still called them the Crazies. The group unanimously embraced the moniker—it garnered wariness and fear. Tavallon needed an army to fend off the ever-encroaching barbarian horde. Forward reports warned a first wave of attackers, mounted on horse-sized lizards, was not long from seizing the coast. They pressed closer to Tavallon by the day. Preparations to defend the city were already underway. The Crazies would play their part.

At the pyramid, Dhron greeted Livian with a scowl. The wide entrance to the grand structure swallowed them up as they continued in, walking side by side. Dhron spoke in a dry rasp: "They tell me I am to forge forward with my monster-master work. I insisted, not without eyes-on approval from you first."

Before being whisked away by Nal, Livian had taken control of much of the staff and guards at the pyramid with her spores. Now, her people were no longer in command of any stations. Nal didn't trust her any more than Sir Kierington did. Additional Goblikans had seized control of the grounds. Livian eyed the new faces lining the entry hall—twice as many men as she had sunk her spores into. It was superiority through sheer numbers, exactly as Nal intended.

The Goblikans were trained in physical combat as well as with the Power. They stood at attention, forming a row of sharpened spears. Any further uprising would have to be paid for in blood, no matter the position of the moon. They appeared to be coexisting peacefully with her people for the moment—she expected nothing less; it was a matter of survival—everyone knew what was coming. They all had a fair grasp of the common good: Protect the city. There were not enough soldiers in Tavallon for them to begin turning on one another. Without cooperation, all would perish under the forthcoming barbarian assault.

Livian pursed her lips. "I'm not exactly in a position to say 'no' to Nal, but it is certainly nice to be back under this pointed roof."

Sir Kierington followed behind them in escort as they entered the labyrinth that was the ground floor of the pyramid.

"You won't like my projects," said Dhron. "I know your opinion of brutality."

Livian grimaced.

"Of course you can't refuse Nal," said Dhron. "But at least for now you are safer, here with me." He'd leveraged his life to bring her back to the pyramid. He loved her so very much. It was fortunate how much Nal needed them both!

Dhron led the way to a dead end. A bare wall stood before them in the narrow passage. Dhron reached out and pressed his hand against a worn stone. The stone slid inward—a secret button that unhinged a chunk of the wall. Cool air blasted against them from out of the hole. The opening revealed a long set of dark stairs, leading deep beneath the surface.

Dhron flipped a switch on the wall, igniting a line of gas torches that illuminated the depths of the secret passageway. He strode ahead, leading Livian and Sir Kierington down to his house of horrors.

A roar echoed up the stairwell. They moved slowly across the narrow steps. Livian recognized the deep howl—it sounded like the terrible lizard that had consumed Lieutenant Canbel whole during their initial assault on the pyramid. At the bottom of the stairs, Dhron continued forward with a spring in his step. He was excited to show off his toys, even knowing Livian's distaste.

Dhron's lab was lit sporadically by gas flame. It was a sprawling natural craven expanded even farther by workings of the Power. A wide walkway led up to a long, shallow ramp that carried all the way back up to the surface. It ended at a massive metal hatch at the top of the cavern. The hatch was attached to a track. It could be rolled free, drawn by wide gears visible in the ceiling.

Behind Livian, opposite the ramp, thick Calvenite bars stretched floor to ceiling, walling off Dhron's creations from the rest of the cavern. There were several distinct enclosures as well as a series of smaller cells carved directly into the wall at the back of the cave. None of the cages were illuminated much by the gas flames. The lighting was mostly located on the far wall from them. Livian could not see into the shadows with her ill-adjusted eyes.

Dhron approached a curved mirror at the center of the cavern in front of the cages. It stood on a hinged base, twice Dhron's height. He pushed the base firmly, rotating it to reflect the glow of the flames—a spotlight into the nearest tall enclosure. "I would like for you to meet Stomper, m'lady," said Dhron. "You killed his brother."

The light fell across a great lizard just like the one Livian barely managed to choke to death with her black mist. The monster's dark hide rippled with thick muscles. A pair of useless nubby arms was tucked against its chest beneath a wide toothy maw big enough to crunch a horse.

"Lovely," Livian said coldly. She stepped nearer the cage. The monstrous lizard lowered his huge head, fixing her with one of its giant slit-shaped eyes. "Listen up, Stomper," she projected, "be a good boy or I'll melt your insides like I did your brother.... What was his name?" she asked Dhron.

"Chomper," he replied.

"How apt," said Livian. "I'll melt you like I melted Chomper!" she yelled out to the monstrosity.

"Apologies, m'lady," said Dhron, "there's no use talking to him." The Goblikan stooped his pasty bald head. "He is not a Whune. He's more of a masterless eating machine—an animal. He does not understand language—hold no worry of a grudge. Stomper has terribly low intelligence—untrainable—I grew him from a chicken embryo, you see. His brain is hardly the larger."

Livian couldn't take her eyes off the enormous beast. "So this is one of the projects Nal told you to restart?" she asked.

Dhron nodded an affirmative.

"What good is a beast like this in the streets of Tavallon?" Livian scoffed. "He would eat our own army!"

Sir Kierington stepped up beside her. "The barbarians are said to ride lizard-mounts that can run straight up walls.

Fortifications are useless to fend them off. They put their wizards into the hearts of the cities they take."

Livian eyes lingered upon Stomper's teeth.

"Their tactic is to dominate and control the physical space, which means once they enter, we all die, or else they do."

Livian felt Sir Kierington's eyes on her. His hands were relaxed at his sides for perhaps the first time since he'd received the egg Artifact from Nal. "I see," she said. "And so Nal aims to fill our walls with even bigger lizards?" She shifted her gaze towards Kierington. "So that the barbarians might not like what they find once they get inside?"

The corners of Sir Kierington's mouth twitched up into an amused smirk. "Bigger lizards with Goblikans riding on their backs," he said. "I think you know a few Goblikans who might be *crazy* enough for the task."

Livian sighed. She wished Kierington wouldn't take such joy in her misfortune. It was becoming a tad gratuitous. "A preposterous plan," she said. "How could we possibly even control them? You heard Dhron—untrainable!"

"That leads to project number two," said Dhron. He shifted the mirror to aim at one of the smaller cages at the back of the chamber.

"Nal wishes to use Whunes to lure the great lizards around the city," said Sir Kierington.

Under the shine of the mirror, dozens of eyes reflected back. That was just one cell. More dark figures huddled together in every cage all along the wall. Only now did Livian realize there were even more cells stacked vertically, filling the whole wall of the tall cavern. The shackled, naked bodies of Tavallon's poorest were huddled before her, staring back at her with broken, vacant expressions.

"This is our Whune-stock," said Dhron. "I know what you're thinking—yes, they are all rather thin. Unfortunately, we had poor crop yields this past year and that has taken a heavy toll on the herd. I grew false calories for them to feed on but one can only stomach so much of that conjured mush."

The Arcanum knew from their spies that all the poor had gone missing from the streets of Tavallon about two years ago. Livian's acquired assumption had always been that Garrett was stockpiling Whunes for an imminent offensive. With Whunes only living for a few years before expiring, tensions had grown within Erotos, rising higher with every passing month that a new wave of the monsters did not appear along the war front. Now Livian knew why.

There must have been thousands of them… all the missing civilians—what remained of them. Dhron shifted the mirror across the wall, allowing the sheer magnitude of the prison to sink in. The light slid back and forth, drawing more individuals to the fronts of their cages. A wall of gaunt prisoners gazed down upon Livian through the dark bars, all hope already drained from their hollowed eyes.

<h1 style="text-align:center">CHAPTER
36</h1>

Sun Rider

Rylin's legs barely reached the foot stirrups on Raljaska's saddle. Even so, once he was hooked in place, he felt unstoppable. The halberd Artifact had a special nook on the saddle beside his right foot where the base of the handle was able to rest. He could pivot the long blade around in a wide arc whilst keeping it braced. He clutched the saddle horn firmly within the knuckles of his left hand. His weapon was held steady by his right. There were no reigns for steering—the Paerto'sul did not accept human direction.

Rylin relied on his feet to keep him anchored in place while Raljaska pulled aerial maneuvers. She had been holding back with him before when he'd just been clasping at her fur. With the pearly gems connecting their minds, he knew her moves the moment she conceived of them. He flexed his feet against the rings of the stirrups—their intuitions synchronized—the bear executed an effortless barrel-roll. Rylin kept his chin up as the bright blue sky swirled into a downward view of the treetops. The steep mountainside whizzed by.

Feel the freedom of the wind. Raljaska's thoughts permeated his mind. *Steady your heart.*

They'd been training together like this for a week now, ever since the Guardians all donned their ancestral armor at Ma'freit's warning. The bears were under high alert, readying themselves for the imminent Goblikan invasion. Deep passageways abandoned for years were once again under the watchful eyes of the Paerto'sul. They patrolled tirelessly, awaiting the Goblikan breach.

After meeting with the rest of the hierarchy, Ma'freit returned to the depths to keep her psychic abilities aimed upon the Goblikans' advance. Word amongst the bears was that the intruders' tunneling was slow but methodical—a host of Whunes worked like ants, scraping diligently through the bedrock both night and day. When the moon was present in the sky, the Goblikans aided their slave-beasts by blasting new caverns into the dense stone. The Whunes carried the debris back down the long tunnel, out of range of Ma'freit's mental probing. The earthquakes continued with alarming frequency as the contingent drew near.

As we invert—this time, activate the halberd.

Rylin embraced the butterflies in his stomach. The halberd Artifact was no simple melee weapon. When the moon was present, Rylin could channel his intentions down the length of the pole. A tightly woven coil hidden within the shaft sucked up the ambient energy of the surrounding air and subsequently redirected it as a beam of electrical current. A persistent lightning arc traveled out from the tip of the blade, melting and sparking indiscriminately wherever he pointed.

Aim for the outcropping.

Rylin held his breath as the wind whipped across his face. The air chilled as the halberd charged up for a blast. Raljaska tucked her wings briefly, rotating upside down again. Rylin released the weapon's energy, aiming the halberd with a wobbly hand. A swath of rocks on the mountainside blasted skyward as the beam's arc ripped across them.

Raljaska righted herself before swooping down for a hard landing upon the outcropping. She took several jarring steps before coming to a halt. She turned around slowly, allowing Rylin to gaze up the slope at the smoldering trail he'd just etched. He'd missed the outcropping by several dozen paces. Aiming the halberd was difficult enough while stationary!

Raljaska made no comment as she turned once more to gaze downhill. A fire was burning just within the tree line at the end of the blackened trail. Rylin quelled the flames quickly with a heaping of snow brought down from the branches above with a little coaxing from the Power.

Raljaska continued to stare down the mountainside. "Do you see that goat?" she asked.

The Paerto'sul had impeccable vision.

Rylin narrowed his eyes, scanning the trees below. He finally spotted the brown mountain goat slinking away from them down a crag.

"Hit it with the lightning and we shall feast upon its flesh."

Rylin slowed his breath, focusing on aiming the halberd true. Unlike an arrow, there would be no drop to its arc. With his thoughts, the Artifact powered up again—it only took a moment to reach capacity. The arc of lightning flashed out, glowing white hot. A metallic scent lingered upon the wind. The arc crackled and popped as it scorched a dark path across the rocks.

The goat leapt deftly, narrowly avoiding the beam. Rylin tried to adjust his aim but nearly lost his grip on the pole in the process. Raljaska lowered her ears. The goat shimmied deeper into the crag, slipping out of sight.

Rylin could tell that Raljaska was disappointed. He could feel the bristly emotion as it seeped through the bond of their shimmering pearls.

Not one to give up, Raljaska spread her wings wide and lifted Rylin back into the sky. They soared down the slope, quickly closing the distance to the crag. Rylin was overwhelmed by Raljaska's animalistic urge to hunt and devour. The narrowed focus dripped across into his own mind. One singular objective fueled their joint actions. The goat was theirs. They wanted it, and ineptitude was not about to stand in their way. The loose rocks of the crag were still shifting from Rylin's blast. They tumbled down the crack in the mountainside where the goat was hiding.

Rylin felt Raljaska's intentions. He was to shoot again—another inversion was already underway. As Raljaska twisted upside down above the crack, Rylin released another blast against the rocks. Raljaska's killer instinct across their bond helped Rylin fix his aim with increased confidence, only floundering as he spotted a dense shadow on a direct collision course with their own.

Sensing Rylin's unease, Raljaska completed the roll and craned her neck up just in time to spot Tanuk in a free fall above them. His wings were tucked at his sides, diving in a steep descent.

A sneak attack!

Their shared awareness responded. Raljaska changed course with the flap of a wing, spiraling off to the right. Tanuk whizzed past like a dart, bouncing hard off the crag and leaping back into the air in continuous pursuit.

Rylin's body slipped between tingling weightlessness and the intense downward force of Raljaska's upward wing flaps. Rylin pointed his toes in his boots, clutching to the saddle with every bit of his strength. Raljaska spun nimbly, twisting through a series of harrowing defensive maneuvers. She flapped her powerful wings with vigor, attempting to gain altitude. They were still too far out from the summit for there to be any hope of the other Guardians rendering assistance. Tanuk gained on them steadily.

Rylin shot a glance back over his shoulder as Tanuk edged closer. The bear had donned his own armor—a jet black set, shiny like obsidian. The bear's dark eyes were locked on

Rylin. All Rylin could do was hold on as Raljaska's wings beat to a frantic tempo.

Rylin shot a desperate arc of energy from the halberd between Raljaska's beating wings. Tanuk dodged the beam, staying on them like a shark on blood. Raljaska knew Tanuk was closing in. She spun in the air, shifting Rylin away from Tanuk's claws.

The bears collided.

Claws scraped against metal plating, squealing sharply as the two beasts tumbled together back towards the mountainside.

The death spiral ended just in time. Both bears kicked away from one another and spread their wings. Rylin barely managed to maintain his grip on the halberd as his ankles fought the strain of keeping him in the saddle.

Despite Raljaska's size advantage, nothing was certain when it came to combat between such deadly titans. Raljaska's wings fought the wind, trying to gain enough distance for Rylin to attack again with the halberd. Rylin blasted energy out behind them repeatedly, unable to aim effectively over his shoulder.

Tanuk shifted about, easily evading the blasts. He was still gaining on them. A sense of pure panic flowed between bear and rider, compounding across their conjoined minds. Tanuk stayed in Rylin's blindspot over his left shoulder. Rylin twisted in his seat, attempting to capture Tanuk within his sight once more, but there was no time to take another shot at him. Tanuk made his move, reaching out and slashing Raljaska across her left wing. She tumbled like a hamstrung horse. The wind roared in Rylin's ears as they plummeted out of control towards the cliffs below. Blood spurted into the sky is a spiral flurry from out of the deep gash in Raljaska's veiny wing. Crimson droplets rained across the rugged landscape.

The world spun in a swirl of sky and rocks as they spiraled out of control. Rylin cried out just as Raljaska slammed into the side of the mountain. Dust and darkness immediately enveloped his senses. They smashed through the rock face and into a hidden chamber beyond.

Rylin tumbled from the saddle. A mound of Calvenite flakes broke his fall. He landed with a painful smack, sprawled out on his back. His head spun as the breath rushed from his lungs. Lying upside down, he peered deeper into the wide chamber all around him. The darkness had come on so abruptly, it left him disoriented. The dense shadow was all-encompassing. The hollow space he found himself in was filled with eroded pillars. He couldn't see far, but the echoing crash of their entry bounced back at him at varying intervals, hinting at a vast chamber. A streak of sunlight shined in through their entry hole, illuminating Rylin's immediate surroundings. The chamber appeared to be part of some sort of ancient aqueduct system—thankfully dry at the moment. He coughed out a mouthful of dust as he rolled over onto his knees. He'd been thrown nearly twenty paces beyond where Raljaska skidded to a halt against one of the thick pillars. He could no longer sense her thoughts in his mind. She remained motionless, crumpled in a heap of bloodied fur and twisted wings.

Rylin could see the halberd glinting just ahead of him, deeper in the cavernous chamber.

Tanuk landed within the narrow opening to the outside world and roared into the darkness. "I will purge you from these halls, filthy human!"

Rylin forced himself to climb to his feet, fighting the burn in his legs and back. He scampered for the halberd as Tanuk swooped down gingerly to the stone floor and began to lumber towards him. Rylin snagged the weapon off the dusty floor as he staggered past. His head was still spinning in a dizzying twirl, eyes rolling with his lost equilibrium. He dipped between pillars, putting as many obstacles as he could between himself and the bloodthirsty bear.

Tanuk slowed down as he entered the rows of pillars. The gaps between columns were plenty wide for the bear to pass, but the zigzagging path Rylin took was difficult for Tanuk to duplicate. A rain of Calvenite flakes fell down from the high ceiling as the bear scraped against the pillars in his haste to reach Rylin.

There was no plan. Rylin nearly lost himself in the darkness as he fought to pull ahead of Tanuk. He dipped behind one of the pillars, breathing hard as he tightened his grip on the halberd. With the weapon in hand, it was time to make his stand.

Tanuk slowed down when Rylin's footsteps ceased. "Where are you hiding, little human? You will not escape me again!"

Rylin scooted silently around the side of the pillar at his back, keeping out of Tanuk's sight as the bear searched the vicinity.

"I can smell your stink!" Tanuk roared.

Rylin steadied his breath. He focused on drawing energy into the halberd's hidden coil. The tips of his fingers ached from the cold as the coil hungered for energy. The blade began to glow, casting a pale light across the crumbling columns. Shadows formed throughout the chamber. Tanuk growled angrily as he closed in on the light source. The pounding of the bear's paws against the dusty stone rattled Rylin's teeth as the bear drew near.

Rylin could sense Tanuk's location from the vibrations. He hopped away from the pillar at his back, intentionally revealing his position. He swung the halberd in front of him like he was casting a fishing lure and unleashed its energy in a wide sweeping motion.

The arc of lightning sprang forth, crumbling every pillar it crossed. Tanuk roared out once more as the ceiling began to collapse on top of him. Dust arose as debris smashed into the ground. A column beside Tanuk struck the bear across the back. The guardian was instantly pinned to the floor. He disappeared, consumed by the dust plume.

Rylin didn't linger. The whole mountain rumbled—a deep, bone shaking rattle. The chamber was on the verge of collapse!

"Rylin!" Raljaska's deep voice boomed from off in the distance. Their pearly gems were too far apart for the mind sharing to function.

Rylin dashed in the direction of the entry hole. More pillars began to tumble all around him—huge portions of the ceiling coming down with echoing crashes in the darkness. Tanuk may have been buried, but Rylin was not out of danger by any means. He'd started a chain reaction. His feet slid in the dust as he changed directions to avoid a crashing column. He could see Raljaska ahead of him now. She was backing up slowly towards the hole as she took in the runaway destruction of Rylin's attack.

"Hurry to me!" she yelled as her sharp eyes spotted his mad dash through the dark.

Rylin carried on as fast as his legs could manage. Raljaska bowed down as he approached, aiding his climb into her saddle. Dust and chunks of stone rained down all around them as she lifted him into the stale air. She had to strain her injured wing to attain liftoff.

A piece of debris struck Rylin in the back of the head. The corners of his vision darkened momentarily. His pulse was pounding. A roar at his back informed him that Tanuk was still alive and on the move again.

The entry hole in the wall above them was narrow and had already partially closed back up with crumbling decay.

Hold close, Raljaska warned.

Rylin pressed his body up against the saddle—there was no room for error. He sucked in one last breath of clear air and held it as the plume of dust enveloped them. Rylin's vision became obscured.

Raljaska's armored belly scraped against the rocks as she clawed forward into the crisp mountain air. They burst forth from the mountain.

"Yah-hooo!" Rylin cried out as they escaped the plume. He re-angled the halberd back up into a more comfortable position. He was finally able to breathe a sigh of relief. The air felt electric in his lungs.

The celebration was premature.

With a second poof of Calvenite flakes, Tanuk burst into the open air behind them.

Raljaska spun about, turning sharply to face Tanuk. She held a steady position, giving Rylin the best chance at a shot she could as she let out a deafening roar. Rylin aimed the halberd true and unleashed its fury.

Tanuk's helmet split in two—his flesh frying the moment the arc took him between the eyes. His wings stalled out and twitched at his sides. He tumbled from the sky, crashing down into a river far below.

Raljaska dove after him, following Tanuk's body until the river carried him over a cliff and down another long drop. Raljaska perched along the edge of the waterfall. She and Rylin tracked Tanuk's descent with their eyes. He didn't flap a wing as he fell through the misting waters. He splashed down into the white rapids far below.

They watched the churning pool in silence for several minutes.

Tanuk did not resurface.

Raljaska huffed a breath of hot air out from her furry muzzle. Her bloodied wing was mostly congealed already with dark clots. She turned in a slow circle, searching back up the mountainside. "Now, where did that goat get off to?"

CHAPTER 37

More Questions Than Answers

Elric's days of gallivanting about protecting young wizards with his sword should have been long behind him. Traveling with Rose and Orris was giving him flashbacks to his time working for Ethan and the Ver'konus. Elric was no longer such a young man. The weight of the road wore on him more heavily in his ripened age. Sleeping on the coarse ground left him with aches and pains that never fully faded—little injuries that added up as the journey dragged onward. The stiffness in his joints made him feel like a pair of rusty sheers trying to walk when he got out of the saddle. He was half the fighter he once was—but that was not to say he wasn't still capable of wielding his blade.

At night when the party made camp, Elric and Orris shared stories from their pasts. They'd experienced many similar hardships in life, losing friends and loved ones along the way. Elric remembered well his own years training amongst the Paerto'radam. It had been an intense experience. The swordsmen's guild only kept the best. Elric eventually washed out like the vast majority of participants. He was never a fully-fledged blade-brother like Orris Fen. The younger Phandolian swordsman had gone far down that path, continuing to live off the guild's stipend to this day. Elric was glad to be traveling with such an honorable and skilled man.

Rose stayed quiet as a mouse. Orris and Elric kept a lively discourse, but Rose never once talked about herself. She only spoke when presented with direct questions—and even then she mostly stuck to giving single word replies. It had been that way all throughout Antara as they traveled back towards the Phandolian border on horseback. Elric was curious about Rose, but he was not one to pry into the business of others. She clearly did not wish to open up to him.

To Elric, Rose looked like a young woman barely out of her teens, but when it came to wizards, appearances could be deceiving. Still, he felt her youth to be earnest. She carried herself like a doe in the woods, eyes always shifting, watching the road from under her hooded brow. She kept her dyed hair wrapped at all times. Her head stayed down whenever any other travelers crossed their path.

As they approached the border between Antara and Phandrol, Elric could see Rose's riding posture shrink at the sight of the Phandolian border agents in the distance. Security was always a grave concern for Phandrol. Ver'ati were surely amongst the guardsmen. They weren't about to let any Goblikans sneak in under their watchful gaze. Leaving Phandrol, Elric had passed through the same station. Getting out was easy. Returning would bring more scrutiny. Rose would be forced to converse.

"Are you worried, dear?" Elric asked.

Rose bundled her cloak more tightly around herself. "This is the border?" she asked. "I assumed it would be… grander."

To her point, the solitary nondescript building along the side of the dirt road was not much to look at. The real eye catcher sat another quarter league onward: An impassibly wide and deep gorge—gouged out of the earth by Ver'ati builders more than a century before to separate the queendom from Antara. It remained hidden by the landscape until one was right upon it. For many leagues it spanned, north and south, funneling all travelers in the region to the solitary bridge that spanned the impressive gap. First, though, they needed to make it past the nondescript building before them.

"Illiyna told me I might want to go off road from here—avoid the border guards entirely," said Rose. It was the most words she'd spoken all week!

Elric's eyes shifted to Orris. The blade-brother was already staring back at him with a wary scowl to match Elric's own. Rose saw the exchange and shot Elric her own frown when he turned back towards her. Elric wished to let her down gently. "I'm afraid that's not really possible," he said. "The only way into Phandrol is across the bridge that lies just ahead of us down this road. There's a very deep gorge, you see. It's not climbable for any of us—least of all an old man such as me."

"Illiyna suggested I use the Power to bridge the gap," said Rose.

Orris burst with laughter. "Are you going to bomb your way past the gates of Erotos when we get there too?"

"You have little to fear from the border agents," said Elric, trying to soften the news after Orris's mockery. "Young wizards come to Phandrol all the time seeking sanctuary from persecution."

Rose drew back on her reins and crossed her arms over her chest. Her horse came to an immediate halt. "I do not wish to be inspected—not by them—not by anyone!"

Elric stopped beside her.

Orris turned his mount around to face Rose. "Even if the climb were possible, walking to Erotos from the other side would take weeks."

"It really is out of the question," said Elric.

"I didn't suggest we climb," said Rose. "I suggested I *bridge the gap.*"

"You best start preparing your answers, hun," said Orris. He had been fed up with Rose's secrecy for days now. "You'd have to be one impossibly powerful witch to span this vast gorge! It took two teams of Ver'ati Builders working in tandem on either side of the chasm to form the path ahead. The gorge is too deep for support structures, so they had to manifest it all at once to prevent gravity from tearing it apart."

"Do not fret," said Elric. "You'll just receive all the usual queries, like—"

"—Who are you and what is your business within Phandrol?" interrupted Orris. "And don't even begin to look nervous, for Mast's sake, lest they hold us up all afternoon!"

Rose leveled Orris with a steady glare. All the meekness of her usual demeanor vanished in an instant. "That is all very easy for you to say—you can answer those questions without raising more suspicions!"

Orris turned his horse back around. "I've had enough of this," he said. "The longer we stand here yapping, the longer it will take us to reach Erotos." He kicked his heels in, leaving Eric and Rose behind as he rode off down the road. A trail of dust stretched out behind him.

Elric shook his head. Orris may have been honorable, but he was not patient. "I am sorry, my dear," said Elric. "I'm sure Illiyna meant well with her advice, but it is not practical. Besides, it is too late to divert. We've surely already alerted the outpost of our presence by now." He gestured towards the dust cloud. "They would only send a party out to apprehend us if we rode for the gorge without checking in."

Rose stubbornly remained in place, still glaring after Orris.

"Come on," said Elric. "I'll just say you're my niece. Let me do the talking. You may be able to use the Power, but that doesn't mean you have to admit it."

Rose studied Elric's face for a long moment. Her lips remaining pursed. She eventually gave a tiny nod of approval. They continued on behind Orris with a semblance more trust between them than they'd started out the day with. By the time they caught up with Orris, he was already conversing with one of the border agents.

Most of the guards within eyesight were Phandolian, distinguished by their cream-colored shirts and white sashes. Several Antaran agents were present as well, dressed in darker uniforms. The Antarans were seated beneath a large tent in the cool air. They didn't look up as Elric and Rose rode past, too engrossed in a game of Crowns to care about the travelers departing from their lands.

Elric recognized the Phandolian agent standing with Orris. He was the same man who had processed Elric and Cormick's departure from Phandrol several weeks earlier. He ordered them all to dismount from their horses. Another guard hitched their reins to a post as they were ushered towards the lone building.

"We're under heightened security. All entry into Phandrol requires approval from the magistrate," explained the guard.

"Has something happened?" asked Elric. Under normal circumstances, a few quick questions about imports and intentions were all that was required.

The guard shook his head. "It's just new protocol. Magistrate Jeroum recently took command of this outpost."

An Arcanum Magistrate controlling entry into Phandrol....

It was unusual. The Phandolian Guard had always maintained jurisdiction at the border before. As they entered the building, a pair of black-robed Ver'ati fell silent. The men eyed them warily from across the entry room.

"The magistrate's office is just through here," said the guard, hanging back at the door. "One at a time, please."

Orris strode inside without hesitation. A nervous bubble formed within Elric's gut. He hadn't been expecting an interrogation. They hadn't gotten their stories straight pertaining to Rose.

"Do hurry," Elric called after Orris. "My niece needs to use the latrines."

Orris flashed him a less-than enthusiastic grimace before closing the door behind him.

Rose's wide-eyed expression was not helping. Elric sat down between her and the guard on a bench just outside of the office. The two Ver'ati across the room restarted their hushed conversation. Their eyes continuously strayed over to Rose as they talked. That in of itself wasn't worrying—Rose was an attractive young woman—but Elric could only imagine the pressure inside of her to remain calm under their stares. After several agonizing minutes, Orris finally reappeared in the magistrate's doorway.

"You're next, Elric," said the guard.

Elric was mildly surprised the man remembered his name. He could not say the same about the guard. Elric had always been better with faces than names. He arose from the bench, eying Orris for any hint of concern. The swordsman's face was a perfect mask of neutrality as he palmed the hilt of his Talus Shard blade.

Orris whispered quickly to Elric as they passed each other. "Don't lie."

Elric swallowed sharply against a lump in his throat. Despite having done nothing wrong, he felt an uneasiness growing inside of him. He entered the make-shift office to find Magistrate Jeroum seated behind a cheaply constructed desk. Several crates sat beside him—his personal belongings, yet unpacked.

"Tea?" Jeroum asked. The Arcanum official channeled energy into a kettle, warming the contents before refreshing his own cup.

"No, thank you," said Elric, though his throat could have used the moisture.

The magistrate poured a second cup despite Elric's protest. He slid the ceramic vessel across the desk. "Sit," he ordered.

Elric stepped up to the desk and placed himself onto the plain wooden stool that was available to him.

Before asking any other questions, the magistrate retrieved a small box from one of his crates and undid a clasp at its front. He tipped out its contents into the palm of his hand—a clear puck. It looked like glass. Jeroum kept his eyes on the smooth object as he began his queries. "Let's start simple. What is your name?" he asked.

"Elric Elensol," answered Elric.

The puck filled with a milky white color, becoming slightly opaque.

"And what is your business within Phandrol?"

Elric took a sip of the tea. It was a soothing mint-honey brew. "I'm heading to Erotos with my niece to meet with my grandson—he's a member of the Ver'konus."

The puck's transparency faded entirely and its hue yellowed, giving it the appearance of carved ivory.

Jeroum scribbled down a quick note on a pad of paper sitting in front of him. "And how did you become acquainted with Orris Fen?"

"Well, that's a rather long story," said Elric. "We actually once trained together long ago at the Ek'radam Monastery."

The color within the puck swirled internally, yellowing further. It was obviously some sort of Power Artifact. Elric stopped looking at it. Its mysterious ever-shifting nature filled him with undo anxiety.

"You are a blade-brother as well?"

"Oh, no," said Elric. "But I did train with the brothers for some time. I was a swordsman for the Ver'konus in my youth."

Jeroum nodded as he penned another note. "That was not such a long story," he said.

"I suppose our re-acquaintance is the longer portion of that tale," said Elric.

Jeroum placed his pen down and looked up at Elric with his full attention for the first time. "I'm all ears," he said.

Elric forced a smile. Jeroum did not match his energy, too focused on studying Elric's face. Elric took another sip of the tea. "This actually is quite tasty," he said. Jeroum's flat stare did not change. "Right, so yes, there had been some confusion. I was under the assumption that my grandson had traveled to Antara in his duties, but I was mistaken. He was actually in Erotos, and so he sent Orris Fen to retrieve me."

"And who exactly is your grandson?" asked Jeroum.

"His name is Javic—Javic Elensol," said Elric.

Jeroum leaned over and retrieved a ledger from out of a crate. He did not say a word as he flipped through the leather tome. The handwriting within its pages was inked in a tiny script. Elric sipped at his tea to fill the silence. The magistrate continued his questioning after another moment. "And what is your association with one Cormick Gansly? I see here he was with you when you came through the border last month."

Elric nodded. "We believed his brother was with my grandson at the time—again, we were mistaken."

Jeroum wrote down one more note. "Alright," he said, "you may go. Please send in your *niece.*"

Elric swallowed one last mouthful of tea with a big gulp before placing the teacup back down on the desk. He stood up and headed for the door. He hoped Rose had been paying attention when he was talking about his life. She needed to play her role as his niece convincingly.

Rose eyed him with a concerned frown when he stepped out of the office. He gestured with his head for her to go in next. No one was conversing anymore in the waiting area. The Ver'ati across the room watched as Elric traded places with Rose.

The way the magistrate's puck shifted colors when he'd fibbed about traveling with his niece filled him with worry. He hadn't the faintest clue how it could have possibly known of his slight deception, or even if that was what it was really doing. He knew some Artifacts held powerful mental properties. He'd never seen a truth detector before, but he'd heard of stranger phenomenon from Power Artifacts before— like that spyglass that could see into dreams.

Rose entered the office and was gone for less than a minute when an explosion wracked the building. The magistrate's door flew from its hinges. The bang was deafening. Elric's ears rang with a high-pitch whine that shocked his senses. Black smoke poured into the waiting area.

Orris was on his feet in an instant, his blade already in his hand.

Rose burst from the smoke surrounded by an aura of wild energy. She shouted something indiscernible—Elric couldn't make out her words over the ringing in his ears. Orris's muffled voice arose next, murmuring a frantic response to the girl. Rose gestured with a sweeping motion and a wall of blue light shot up from the floor, bisecting the room. The floorboards disintegrated as Rose reused the matter to form a transparent film.

The two watchful Ver'ati were on the other side of the divide. They'd been caught off-guard by the explosion just as much as Elric. Rose gestured again and flames flashed on the other side of the film. Their screams were snuffed out by the hiss of the fire. All the oxygen beyond the film was eaten up by the unnatural blaze in an instant. Elric hadn't the time to process what was happening. A vacuum effect sounded in a loud whoosh as the flames formed a backdraft. The main door of the building blew outward under the immense pressure, forming another deafening bang.

The blue glowing film flashed bright white as the explosion absorbed into the material. Elric had only seen such a display once before: Belford's protective dome on the top deck of the Rosa Marsa during their escape from the harbor in North Galdren.

The guard that was seated beside Orris finally made it to his feet. He pulled a knife from his belt and lunged towards Rose. Orris moved faster. The Talus Shard blade made quick work of the border agent. He cut the man down to his knees in less than a second. The horrified expression on his face melted away as another slice ended his life.

The shield-wall dripped into a pile of goo as Rose tore it down. She ran through the charred remains of the Ver'ati and exited the building. Orris reached out a hand and pulled Elric to his feet. He was still dazed by the blasts.

"Come on!" cried Orris. His voice sounded hollow in Elric's ears. Orris could see the confusion clear on his face. "She said the whole outpost has been Compelled—they're all Goblikans!"

The chaos left Elric's head spinning as he followed Orris and Rose outside. Rose began frantically unhitched their horses from the post. The other border agents nearby looked over in bewilderment. Rose's attack on the outpost was so unimaginable to them that they didn't even try to stop her as she finished freeing the beasts and climbed into her saddle. Elric and Orris followed in turn. Their poor horses' eyes rolled in fear as they galloped onward towards the bridge to Phandrol.

Behind them, the chaos was only beginning to unfold. The other guardsmen were finally putting the pieces together. The clomp of more hooves sounded at their backs as the border agents mounted up and galloped after them.

"Goblikans?" Elric asked. "How can you be certain?" He realized it was a bit late to be questioning their moral standing. Four men were already dead, three of which were wizards. If they weren't Goblikans, the Arcanum would not be forgiving.

"The magistrate was here for me," said Rose. "Only a Goblikan could have known I was coming!"

A ball of fire whizzed over their heads. More wizards were in pursuit—whether they were Goblikans or Ver'ati, Elric didn't care to guess. Either way, distance was their friend. Thoughts could kill with aim or close enough range.

Rose gestured behind her at the road. The ground lurched and cracked, filling the pathway with debris. It would slow their pursuers down, if only for a moment.

Ahead, they crested a hill and the land dropped away, revealing the grand gorge and spanning bridge that was their only escape route. The bridge was built from Calvenite—no other material could possibly hold its form over such a distance without additional support. The bottom of the gorge was out of sight, masked in shadow far below. Massive fittings grown out of the earth held the hanging structure to the cliffside. They pushed their mounts faster in the downgrade. The beating of the hooves changed to clangs as the metal horseshoes struck against the Calvenite walkway in the lead up to the bridge.

The platform was just wide enough for the three of them to ride abreast. It was narrow for how far it stretched. Elric could feel a slight give to the walkway as their combined weight bounded across it.

Another fireball whooshed past on their left. It struck the far side of the gorge where it stuck like tar, burning against the sheer rock wall. Their pursuers had crested the hill behind them.

As they passed the halfway point of the bridge, Rose slowed her mare. Orris and Elric soon overtook her. Elric puffed out his cheeks, staying low in his saddle as several more balls of fire zipped by, too close for comfort. One of the fireballs struck the bridge surface ahead of them, spooking the horses with its dancing flames. Elric whipped his reins hard, driving onward. They all leapt through the fire.

A sharp groan sounded from the structure behind him. Elric didn't look back until he'd burst from the other side of the bridge and out onto the hard soil. Orris was still by his side. Rose was trailing behind, burning a coarse matte streak in the sheen of the Calvenite beneath her horse's hooves as she went. She was converting the wizardly material back into regular stone.

The bridge lost its integrity as it transformed, buckling beneath her—the weight of the structure snapped the weakened slate in multiple positions across the expanse. Rose surged from the edge of the bridge as it crumbled into the gorge behind her. On the far side, several of their pursuers plummeted along with it into the chasm. Most of the men had yet to reach the bridge. Their horses pranced about along the edge of the drop.

Rose rejoined Elric and Orris in formation. They galloped onward into Phandrol. Elric counted his blessings. Rose was full of surprises. Their sudden flight left Elric with more questions than answers. Rose pushed the pace faster. He wanted to trust her…. The alternative was admitting that he might be traveling with a murderous fugitive.

**CHAPTER
38**

Rift

The Earth was poisoned—torn asunder. Far from the blast zones, the nuclear fallout of the EAC's preemptive strikes would still cause birth defects and cancer for generations to come. There would be starvation across the globe. It was too late to change any of that.

Radiation rained down upon the narrow band of latitudes where crops once thrived, now rendered inedible. Major cities were rubble—their populations wiped away along with every wrinkle of the land. As powerful as the Arcadians had become, they couldn't turn back time. Their unprecedented abilities were simultaneously the most powerful and the most limited resource on the planet. There were only thirteen Arcadians, counting Yosef. The computer needed their eyes and intentions to alter the world around them.

The EAC kept them all working around the clock, racing the winds to burn the radiation from the skies and soil before it could spread to every corner of the globe. It was difficult not to feel like their impact was insignificant. Aaron barely got enough rest between shifts to keep him sane… somewhat sane anyway. His nights had been wracked with terrible nightmares of burned bodies with blackened eyes. Sometimes he didn't even need to be asleep to see them. They twisted at the corners of his vision, writhing in pain and locking Aaron with their accusatory stares. Still, he preferred to stay awake. The nightmares were always worse than the waking visions. He knew it was all a manifestation of PTSD—all the Arcadians had it—the whole world had it! The corpses haunted him more mercilessly when he became exhausted from his duties.

The Arcadians had been separated into three teams. Each group was sent to purge a different sector of fallout across the globe. Aaron's team consisted of Claire, Wes, Isabelle, and Michelle. With Ethan's lies exposed, Michelle begged to be separated from her husband—Ethan had betrayed her more than anyone. She sat up front in the Chinook duel-blade helicopter, releasing the excess energy in the airborne irradiative particles ahead of them. The radiation diffused as heat into the atmosphere, forming a hazy orange glow that stretched out as far as the eye could see. The burning sky may as well have been the biblical end-times—they were living through an apocalypse.

Instead of centuries of high-velocity particle release, all the excess energy in the atoms within their zone was boiled out into the air all at once. Their EAC pilot held back as the fog of fallout ignited into a firestorm that spanned the horizon. It was easy to keep their distance. They needed only to be in eyesight to enact their will. The sky shined like a golden aurora borealis as the flames swirled on the wind.

The pattering churn of the helicopter's blades drowned out conversation. Aaron and Claire didn't need to talk to work together with precision. Through a wordless exchange they imparted the same process as Michelle, burning up the irradiative particles that had settled to the ground on their side of the helicopter. Everywhere they could see, they targeted, sweeping flames across the land. The radiation flashed into intense heat. The rolling hills and farmland below were bathed in a raging inferno that matched the original devastation of the EAC's blasts. The ground melted—sand and dirt turned to molten glass within the intensity of the flames. The conditions below briefly mimicked the surface of the sun.

The nukes had aimed to choke the planet, starving anyone who managed to survive the blasts. All the military targets and major population centers had been eradicated. Little remained of the world they once knew.

Firebombing the countryside, Aaron knew Claire was lost in her memories—the mental wall she'd constructed around her private thoughts was intact, but he knew her well enough to read her without having to resort to probing her mind. She was thinking about her lost family. Aaron wouldn't have been surprised if the Dublin Riots of her youth were at the forefront of her thoughts as well. Her expression remained distant as she worked on unleashing the flames below. The Dublin Riots were nowhere near the scale of devastation being raining down upon the land now, but Claire's childhood trauma was inevitably triggered by the glow of the fire. She was losing her whole world all over again. They all were.

No one would survive in the valleys below. Although the EAC pilots didn't speak a lick of English, the communications the Arcadians received on wrist-worn devices were clear. Their orders came directly from the top brass of the EAC military, still operating at near-full scale and capacity despite retaliatory strikes against the Asian continent. The words of their handlers were only reassuring before they started their grueling work: *No one within your zone can possibly survive the present level of radiation. Burn it all.*

The inferno they produced was a mercy. Death by radiation would have been far more painful than the flash of flame. That's what Aaron told himself. It was certainly true, but it still tore at his heart to conjure the flames knowing that he was raining down death upon so many poor souls.

The Arcadians' proximity to the fallout meant that their nanobots were having to work overtime to fix the accumulating damage to their bodies. Cancer could be stalled with technology, but the corruption to their genetics left them riddled with more holes than Swiss cheese. Aaron was coming to terms with his sterility—he couldn't imagine bringing a child into this hell-scape anyway. There was no hope left; no joy. Claire matched his mindset. As far as he could discern from the occasional snippet of emotion that still slipped through their bond every now and again, she too felt like death incarnate.

Seeing a faint trial of smoke rising from a secluded farmhouse's chimney shook Aaron's resolution. If they didn't cleanse the farmland, the planet would starve. All the death and destruction weighted so heavily upon him. He had to keep reminding himself that he was cauterizing the world's wounds as the countryside burned. Anyone still alive beneath them wouldn't be for long. There weren't enough healing nanobots for everyone.

Aaron didn't know exactly where he was on any given day. The countryside all looked relatively the same. Their escorts led them around blindly. They weren't supposed to ask questions—just burn the radiation away as efficiently as possible. It was always the same view: Endless sprawling farmland. The sky burned, the land burned. It was literal hell on Earth. Despite their efficiency, the process of clearing the radiation would take years to complete.

Continuous famine for a decade was all but inevitable. Eventually, once the fires burned out, the land would be reset. It would once again be safe for life, though it would remain barren until crops could be re-sewn. They were playing a long game. It was all humanity could do at this point to stave-off extinction.

Aaron's team was always too tired to socialize by the end of their long days. He wanted to spend his time with Claire, but he could tell his presence only dampened her mood. The looks she's give him made his chest ache.

After months of the same grueling schedule, Aaron awoke to a new message on his wrist-worn device: They were being recalled.

Aaron rubbed the sleep from his eyes as he sat up in his cot and read the message over again. "Wake up, guys," he said, rousing the rest of the team from their slumbers. They were all sharing a room within a bunker the EAC had prepared for them. "They're calling everyone back together again—a new mission…."

Wes yawned as he crawled out from his sleeping bag. He read a couple snippets of the message aloud. "A critical mission… time sensitive…. What is this? What could possibly be more critical than clearing the fallout?"

"Beats me," said Aaron. "But we leave in an hour…."

"Dibs on the shower," said Isabelle, bolting from the room before anyone could object.

Michelle sat up with a scowl. She clearly wasn't thrilled at the prospect of seeing Ethan again.

Claire rolled over, resting a little bit longer while everyone else began to pack up around her. Aaron briefly recalled a shared dream they'd slipped into. They'd been walking together across the fields of glass—nothing but the steady crunch of their steps to break the silence within the purified void….

A supersonic jet awaited them on the tarmac when they got outside. After a quick two hour flight they found themselves at another airstrip—this one nestled in a mountainous nook. The plane shook as strong winds shifted them side-to-side in their descent. When they landed, Ethan, Travis, Brooke, and Yosef were already present, waiting on the tarmac. The two groups approached one another, all with the same tired expressions on their faces. Michelle refused to look at Ethan. Ethan did not break the tension.

"Where are the others?" Wes asked after greeting Travis.

"You'll be told more once we get out of this incessant wind," said Yosef.

The remaining Arcadians—John, Garrett, Hannah, and Emily—remained absent as EAC escorts led everyone across the airstrip to a communications building. A giant satellite dish on the roof rotated slowly. Michelle continued to avoid Ethan's gaze as they entered the instillation. He kept looking over at her longingly. The unsaid words between them were palpable. Michelle wanted none of it.

Travis fell to the back of the pack with Wes and Aaron. "Ethan came up with some sort of plan to save the world," he said. "Apparently, the EAC thinks it's legit."

They entered a conference room and were immediately joined by the remaining Arcadians via video chat. The video was low quality. They were clearly aboard a jet somewhere. Their faces appeared on a screen high on the conference room wall.

"Now that we are all connected, I shall begin," said Yosef. "This operation has already been approved by the EAC. This meeting is your briefing." He looked up at the screen. "Your plane is en route to Central America where a critical mission will soon commence. Your group was the closest to the region, which is why you didn't meet us here in Nepal, but rest assured, all of us will be joining you on this critical mission shortly."

"What about clearing the radiation?" asked Wes. "It's kind of important, don't you think?"

"This is not time for questions," snapped Yosef. "Your previous mission, while important, is less critical."

Everyone listened with concerned scowls.

"Unfortunately, neutralizing the radiation has proven to be a very slow process—we always knew it would take years, but at the rate we have been progressing it could take a decade or more. The vast majority of humanity will have starved by then, but now, thanks to Ethan, we have a faster solution to work with. Our new primary objective is to generate additional arable farmland at more central latitudes."

"What does Central America have to do with this?" asked Garrett, sticking his face up close to the camera as he interjected. "Are you going to have us growing corn in Panama or something?"

"Not at all, Mr. Rames," said Yosef. "Not at all. Our mission is to sink Central America into the ocean."

Everyone continued to stare at Yosef in stunned silence.

"I think you got garbled there," said Hannah. "It sounded like you said we were going to sink Central America."

"That is what I said," said Yosef. "We are going to sink it into the ocean."

"Sink what?" asked Travis, narrowing his eyes.

"Sink all of Central America—do try to keep up please," said Yosef. "We need to adjust the world's currents in order to change global rainfall distribution so that we can terraform the less-radioactive central latitudes that are currently desert into arable farmland."

"I still don't follow," said Travis.

"That doesn't surprise me," said Yosef, "but I'll humor you. Before continental drift combined North and South America millions of years ago, places like the Saharan Desert were lush rainforests. To feed humanity we must bring back those conditions as quickly as possible. We must sink Central America and connect the Pacific and Atlantic Oceans on a grand scale."

"Could that even work?" asked Brooke.

"Yes," said Yosef, "they believe so. The EAC has had their top scientists running endless simulations. No other option makes for a quicker resolution to the famine. Each year that passes before new crops yield will mean a further decimation of humanity. We need to do this and we need to do it immediately."

"What about the people in Central America?" asked Claire.

"I would like to hear on that as well," said Hannah. "That region was spared from direct nuclear ordinance strikes—it is still heavily populated—hundreds of millions of people…."

"You're not understanding the gravity of the situation," interjected Ethan. "If we don't change the currents, billions more will die.'"

"You're asking us to kill millions—"

"—To save billions," said Ethan. "That's billions with a 'B.' It's ultimately a giant trolley problem. Simple analysis. We choose the lesser evil. The deserts of Africa can become the Cradle of Humanity once more."

"Wasn't the Middle-East the Cradle of Humanity?" Travis asked.

"The Middle-East was the Cradle of Civilization," corrected Brooke.

"That's arguable," said Garrett. His large face filled the screen once more. "There actually is compelling evidence of ancient civilizations predating the last ice age—"

Yosef muted the screen, cutting Garrett off mid-sentence. "We board the supersonic jets again once they finish refueling. Departure is in one hour. We can do this from the air with several teams eroding the land in swaths."

"No," said Claire. "I won't have any part in this. I'm not killing millions of people—that's psychotic!"

"Psychotic would be letting everyone in the world starve when we can actually do something about it," said Ethan. "We all have to come to terms with the fact that we are capable of anything! We need to start using our abilities more intelligently. We can fix the world—reform it better than before!"

"I'm with Claire-bear," said Travis. "Everyone has always been capable of anything on the inside. It's the choices that make the man."

"What sort of nonsense…?" asked Ethan, waving his hand dismissively. "It's a simple equation. If we don't act, we doom the world."

"Look around!" Claire exclaimed. "The world is already destroyed!"

Ethan scoffed. "Your defeatist attitude isn't going to help anyone. We don't need you—either of you!" He gestured sharply at Travis.

Michelle stood up and walked out of the room without a word. Claire and Travis joined her, expressions of distain on each of their faces.

Aaron felt Claire's anger bristle across their bond when he didn't get up and join her in her exit. Killing millions of people was a terrible choice, but the numbers were undeniable. He needed to do the moral thing. It felt wrong, but it wasn't a real choice. Too many lives were on the line. If he didn't help, it would take the other Arcadians longer to complete the mission. He knew it was happening with or without him. If he could prevent more people from having to starve to death, he had to try.

I'll do what has to be done—so that you don't have to.

Aaron reached out with the words to Claire through their bond, but her reinforced mental wall no longer held any cracks. He banged at the metaphorical door, antsy to explain his reasoning, but it was like her curtains were already drawn and loud music was blaring inside. She didn't want to hear anything he had to say.

Ethan lowered his voice as he continued on. "Three of us per plane should be sufficient for cutting our lines. We fly high and shave the land back and forth until the job is done."

Wes and Isabelle were both watching Aaron, concern in their wide eyes. Aaron got the impression that they were still undecided, but that they were following his lead.

Claire and the other walk-outs didn't join them as they re-boarded the jets. Aaron felt dead inside as they achieved liftoff. The Hippocratic Oath he'd sworn when becoming a doctor kept tugging at his thoughts. The nagging feeling was invalid. Ethan was right. They had to take the least harmful path. Their power was that of gods. The natural course would bring an end to humanity. It wasn't a real choice. They had to act.

CHAPTER
39

Windows to the Soul

Shiara's head pounded as if she'd been out for a long night of drinking. The Goblikan train continued its steady chug through the darkness. There was nothing to see beyond the train car as the tight tunnel whizzed by. Everyone sat on one side of the car, avoiding Ethan and the puddle of blood that had escaped him. The sight was sobering, but the lingering hallucinogenic properties of the Goblikan drugs were taking a long while to subside.

Ethan's pale corpse faced away from them. No one wanted to look at him, Vera least of all. She sat at the far end of the group beside Shiara, staring at the wall. Sweat dripped down her brow, her body slowly expunging the remainder of the drugs from her system.

In the far corner, Ader had been snoring for the better part of the last hour. He was finally showing signs of rousing from his drug-induced nap. They had all become uninhibited animals, and then digressed into language-less, inanimate objects,

293

before finally being allowed to return to the land of the living—sans Lord Ethan—but only after their bodies had shut down and reset with a long, slumbering rest. Ader sat up, smacking his lips together as he joined the remaining passengers at the side of the train car.

"We can't tell anyone about this," said Belford.

"The murder or the orgy?" asked Grine.

"Any of it!" Belford exclaimed.

"What were you thinking?!" Grine turned on Vera.

The girl sat with a somber expression on her face. Her eyes remained focused on the wall. Shiara expected her to try to play dumb—act like she hadn't been thinking at all—but Vera's true response surprised her: "The desert took away his Powers," she said. "I saw him sitting there and I just... I just couldn't stand the thought of him ever getting them back."

Everyone sat with that for a long moment. Shiara reflected on her life choices leading up to the present. She'd joined the Ver'konus on staunch moral grounds. Coming from a wealthy family, it wasn't like she needed the military stipend or anything. She always believed she knew where she stood as far as her duty to the organization and to the people of Aragwey. As Ver'ati, she felt she had a responsibility to humanity. As a member of the Ver'konus, she considered herself to be a shepherd of sorts. The organization wasn't perfect, but it was the best there was. She'd joined the resistance to save people from monsters like King Garrett and his Goblikans.

Ethan had been her commander for most of her life, though she hadn't actually met the man personally until the start of their mission together. Admittedly, his persona certainly had left a lot to be desired, but when it came down to it, Ethan had put his life on the line to help end Garrett's terrible reign, just like everyone else who had gone on the mission.

Now with King Garrett finally out of the way, the path forward had been cleared for Ethan to unify Aragwey to its former glory—a united nation, the likes of which had not been seen for a thousand years since the days of John Graven!

And now Ethan was dead.

"Forgive me, Ms. Nighfield," said Ader as he gathered his scattered memories. "I shame myself deeply."

Shiara felt her face grow warm. "You guys really need to get over this already," she said, glancing back and forth between Belford, Arlin, and Ader.

"Get over what?" asked Belford. "I remember nothing." He was clearly lying to protect her from his ill-conceived notion of her shame.

Shiara scoffed. "Stop being such prudes! It's just sex." She leaned over to Vera and kissed her once more—a gentle peck on the cheek. "It's perfectly natural for people to appreciate one another," she said.

Ader withdrew meekly back into the far corner of the train car. His embarrassment was contagious. It was clear by all their red faces that the men were ashamed of their promiscuous behavior. Vera, on the other hand, was filled with a very different emotion. She almost looked content.

"As for Ethan," Shiara added. "None of you liked him. If I can admit he deserved what he got, the rest of you damn well can too." She wasn't sure how much she believed her own words, but no one argued with her. Shiara turned back to Vera and spoke quietly for her ears only. "Are you alright, hun?" she asked. "That's the second time I've seen you do that."

Vera grimaced. "Somebody had to," she said.

Shiara narrowed her eyes.

"Now Belford can take over the Ver'konus and actually do some good in this world," said Vera.

"I hope it's really that easy," Shiara responded.

Vera's eyes shifted to her suddenly. "Have I done a bad thing?" she asked. "I know he wasn't as evil as the Goblikans, but he wasn't a good man."

"I don't know," Shiara said honestly. "I don't know what he did to you, just as I don't know what his death will mean. Aragwey is a mess. *He was our commander....*"

Vera's expression darkened with every word.

"I won't tell anyone you did this," Shiara added. "Pushing Belford to the top is the right move now."

Belford looked up briefly, frowning. His ears were burning, but he tried not to make it obvious that he was listening in.

"We don't need Ethan," said Vera. "No one ever needs people like him. All he ever did was sit in the palace and lord his power over everyone. He hurt innocent women, just because they reminded him of his dead wife—simply for not being her." Vera stared Shiara down. "My eyes weren't right."

Shiara shied away from her steady gaze. Her prior defense of Ethan suddenly filled her with a far worse shame than any that consumed the men. Her heart wept for Vera.

There was nothing more to be said. Vera turned back to face the wall. She placed her hand on the hilt of her sword before closing her eyes and taking several deep breaths.

Shiara glanced over at Belford. His eyes were clouded over with tears. Shiara knew he was a powerful wizard—the most powerful!—he had the Mark of Kings on his arm. What he lacked was experience as a leader. He was a bumbling fool in the world of politics. That had always been obvious to her. If he was Aragwey's only hope of salvation, Shiara wasn't sure she liked their chances. She'd always believed in Belford's potential, but his transition to ruling the Ver'konus was supposed to be a slow and steady process—a passing of the torch some years in the future when the time was right, not now when he was still so ill-prepared.

Everything was on the precipice of total chaos. Ethan's absence would leave a power gap like no other. Right and wrong became hazy when so many lives were at stake.

Vera nudged Shiara with her elbow. Shiara looked back over at her. Vera placed the Talus Shard down between them. She kept ahold of it, but allowed Shiara to join her in partaking in the blade's masking effect. Shiara laid her pinky alongside Vera's. The Talus Shard immediately soothed her temperament, draining her fears and doubts away.

CHAPTER 40

Deadly Truths

While waiting for Javic's return, Mallory heard a rising commotion within the palace's anteroom. Shouts rang out from down the long hall. She entered the pillar-lined chamber at a side door. A grubby bum was crying her name over and over again. The guards were preparing to restrain him, but none of them wanted to be the first to touch the soot-stained man.

Ervia had returned to the palace earlier in the night with news of her and Javic's encounter with Tyris. He was the one calling out for Mallory now. She recognized his voice. She also realized that it was he who had been trailing her in disguise the whole previous day. Learning of the subsequent attack by an assassin using the same firebombing Artifact that killed Professor Vanton made Mallory's breath catch in her chest. Seeing Tyris now without Javic left her feeling lost— like a useless ball of nerves being thrown about by fate.

Javic's plan to use the brass spyglass to see into Lyle Stronghelm's dreams was inspired, but Mallory didn't like the idea of him running around the city by himself. There was a conspiracy out there worth killing over. Javic was powerful, but he was also youthfully reckless. There were too many unknowns—too many deadly truths that desired to remain hidden.

Mallory ran across the anteroom, hoping to diffuse the quickly escalating situation between Tyris and the guardsmen before anyone got hurt. Swords had already been drawn and Tyris was threatening everyone with a short metal rod.

"It's alright!" Mallory cried out as she swept through the room. "He's with me!"

Tyris calmed visibly at the sight of Mallory, but all the guards remained on edge. It didn't help that none of the guardsmen knew who Mallory was in the slightest.

"Filthy beggars are not allowed in the palace," said the man in command.

"Where's Javic?" Mallory asked Tyris, needing to ease her fears.

The commanding guard turned to study Mallory's face when Javic's name escaped her lips. "Javic Elensol should be on night patrol duty right now," he said.

"And who might you be?" Tyris asked indignantly.

Another guard responded for his commander. "That's Captain Sarvo, you grubby bastard—show some respect!"

"Answer the lady's question," insisted the captain. "Where is young Javic?"

Tyris narrowed his eyes at the captain. "I'm not his keeper."

"Certainly not," said Captain Sarvo. "That would be me. Why am I not surprised to hear he is out shirking his duties?"

"I don't care about any of that," said Tyris. "I already told you, I'm here with an urgent message for the queen!"

Captain Sarvo chuckled. "I don't care if you were sent here by Mast herself, you're not passing through this anteroom. Not with your life."

"Eat shit!" Tyris growled. He pointed his little metal rod into the captain's face once more.

"That's enough from you," said Captain Sarvo. His eyes held an eerie calmness. "Leave here now or be cut down." He didn't even raise his voice. He didn't have to. He withdrew the blade on his hip just one finger's width.

"Are the two of you done measuring your sticks yet?" asked Mallory, attempting to return a hint of levity to the situation. Really, she was pleading. She placed herself between them, smiling widely. "There's no need to resort to such viciousness." The men continued to eye one another with distain. Tyris's uncharacteristic aggression was not going to end well. "Mast almighty, there's no reason to get so worked up!" She gave a fake laugh.

Tyris's expression softened upon taking in Mallory's obvious concern. "Alright," he said, finally backing down. "That's fine. I'll leave. But I will speak with Mallory first."

Captain Sarvo studied Tyris's rod with a wary regard. "Not a step further," he warned.

Mallory stood her ground between them. The captain finally backed away after another moment. Despite his strong words, it was clear he preferred a peaceful resolution to the situation.

"Make it fast, then be on your way," he ordered.

Mallory led Tyris to the tall entry doors, still anxious for an update on Javic's situation. "Are you insane?" She smacked Tyris on the shoulder. "You're going to get yourself jailed or worse! Now please tell me already—where's Javic?"

Tyris waved off her concern. "I have a lot to say and very little time, so just listen."

Mallory frowned.

"Javic interrogated Lyle in his dream. The man believes Doctor Crane, Tannel Cresdale, and Lord Ethan all conspired together to have the queen injected with Inhibitor when she was a baby."

Mallory's jaw dropped open.

Tyris pulled a leather pouch out of his pocket and pressed it firmly into Mallory's hands. "This is an Inhibitor Kit. Inside you'll find the antiserum. Get it to the queen at once. If Lyle's information is genuine, she'll be able to channel!"

"I don't know what to say," said Mallory. "Why isn't Javic here telling the queen this himself?"

Tyris grimaced. "Javic is with Doctor Crane."

Mallory cocked her head. "But you just named him as a co-conspirator...."

"Aye," said Tyris. "We went to Crane for the antiserum, but then we came across a pair of Whunes in his lab.... Javic knows one of them."

"Wait... what?" Mallory didn't understand. "He knows one of the Whunes?"

Tyris nodded. "Some girl from his hometown—he called her Salvine. He was kind of freaking out. I really should get back to him...."

Mallory knew of Salvine—of Javic's infatuation with her before her disappearance. Elric was a big talker. She'd learned more about Javic from his grandfather than he probably would have liked her to know.

"Just take that kit to the queen," said Tyris. "She has to know the truth!"

Mallory's heart was racing. Tyris departed from the palace as abruptly as he'd arrived. Mallory hid the kit in her dress and made her way back down the long hall. She attempted to use the side door she'd entered from but the handle was locked on the anteroom's side.

"Go back past the Charisms," said Captain Sarvo.

"But I was just in there!" Mallory complained.

The captain did not repeat himself.

Mallory sighed. She stepped quickly back around the pillars, passing the captain on her way towards the Charisms chamber.

Captain Sarvo called out to her again as she stepped through the doorway. "If you see Javic before I do, let him know he should find new employment."

Mallory didn't give him the satisfaction of looking back. If Tyris was right, she was about to change everyone's fates! She entered the Charisms chamber.

"Place your hands on the altar," said one of the guardsmen posted within.

She hurried to the central dais where the three Charism orbs were held in place by leather harnesses within a wooden box. They remained translucent, confirming once again to the guards on the night shift that Mallory could not channel, was not currently channeling, and had no Power Artifacts on her person. They let her through.

As soon as she was out of the security chamber she burst into a full-on sprint. She couldn't imagine how Queen Havorie was going to react to her news. To learn that she'd been violated as a child by the most powerful men in the state…. It was a horrible thing to have to tell anyone, let alone the queen. But then, Mallory also offered the antidote to Havorie's affliction….

Havorie was awake and pacing her chambers when Mallory arrived. The queen's eyes darted to the doorway as Mallory entered. Mallory paused with her hands on her knees, chest heaving to catch her breath. A harsh expression filled Havorie's face.

Mallory bowed her head as she handed the leather pouch over to the queen. Havorie opened the flap straightaway, looking quizzically at the syringes held within. Once Mallory had caught her breath she repeated Tyris's words verbatim. She watched Havorie's expression shift from horror to rage. Once Mallory told her of the significance of the syringes in her hands, Havorie turned away entirely to face the far wall, but not before Mallory had seen a flash of the whites of her eyes. Havorie was terrified. The story the young queen had believed about herself forever—that she was a regular, non-magical girl, not special like her mother—was immediately turned on its head.

"All you have to do is inject yourself with the antiserum and you'll know if the conspiracy is true," said Mallory.

Havorie turned back around, eyelids drooping with exhaustion. It had been a terribly long night for everyone waiting on the outcome to Javic's mission. "They've conspired against me my whole life," Havorie said quietly. "All these powerful men." She breathed a heavy sigh. "They have hamstrung me so that I could not stand up against their control. I don't know how I could have ever expected anything different from any of them." Tears began to well up in her eyes. She made an exasperated groan. "Treacherous swine!"

The emotional outburst was warranted. Mallory stood back as Havorie began to pace her chambers. The young queen looked like a caged animal. Mallory sensed the pent up energy inside of her, begging for release—she had a whole life of lies to rewrite.

Havorie stopped her pacing suddenly. Her head swiveled back around to lock Mallory in her sight. "Where's Javic?" she asked.

The worry in her eyes hardly seemed fair given that she was the one who sent him out into the streets to gather her answers in the first place. Havorie had risked Javic's life knowingly. Part of Mallory didn't want to tell her out of spite, but the queen's furrowed brow was the only selfless expression Mallory had seen her make. She could tell she cared.

"When he went to retrieve that antiserum, he discovered one of Doctor Crane's caged Whunes is Salvine." Mallory studied Havorie's face. Her blank look spoke volumes. "She's a girl he thought he lost, from back home."

Havorie's eyes became slightly unfocused. She gave a slow nod of understanding. "I don't know that I ever truly had him, but how strange—right now, I feel like I've lost him."

Mallory felt her lip quiver. Salvine's survival was incredible news for Javic. Mallory wanted to be happy for him. She should have been praying for Salvine's recovery. Instead, an unavoidable heaviness had settled upon her chest. At the same time, she felt so terribly empty—as empty as a pregnant woman could feel, anyway! Emotionally, she was hollowed out. She knew exactly how Havorie was feeling. Neither one of them had ever truly had Javic Elensol.

Havorie caught the look of consternation in Mallory's eyes. The queen breathed out her own heavy sigh. "He really could have been quite useful to me," she said.

Mallory screwed up her face.

Havorie carried the Inhibitor Kit across her chamber to a wide wardrobe and tucked the pouch away inside.

"You aren't going to use the antiserum now?" asked Mallory.

The corner of Havorie's mouth twitched up for a brief moment. "I'm going to get some much needed rest," she said. "You may remain here at the palace as my guest. Go see Ervia for accommodations—she'll know where to set you up." It was a blunt dismissal.

It seemed odd to Mallory that the queen would delay taking the antidote. Perhaps a good night's sleep would make things more clear for her in the morning. In Mallory's mind there was only one path forward. It was inevitable: Havorie needed to become the all-powerful queen she was always meant to be.

CHAPTER
41

Mortal Wounds

"Whunes have an extremely high cell turnover rate," said Doctor Crane as he stretched his back against the bench in his exam room. "It allows them to heal from otherwise mortal wounds, but it also prematurely ages the flesh."

Javic understood the conundrum at hand. Whunes lives were accelerated, only lasting for a few years at most. When Belford turned Kara back into a human girl, her cells had already accumulated so much damage that her body gave out from the strain of attempting to free her mind. Kara was a Whune for less than a month. Salvine had been suffering for much longer. If they transformed her back without undoing the cellular damage, she wouldn't survive the process.

"I will say, you are correct in your assessment, though," the doctor continued. "I've already determined that the hosts' original DNA still resides within—do you know what DNA is, boy?—it means their bodies can be mended like you desire. But every cell has to be purified and reset in one procedure to

305

prevent cancers and other ills from propagating. And then of course there is always the risk of schisms."

There was nothing but risks. No one had ever successfully restored a Whune's humanity.

"I've determined that the physical Whune-traits are generated though bio-electric expression. The muscles and tumors can be melted away in the same manner—by directing precise electrical charges into the hosts' cells. It is not a simple procedure, but it is a doable one, technically speaking. The stumbling block for me has always been the mind—but now with this…." Doctor Crane twirled the brass spyglass in his fingertips. "The consciousness can be accessed and perhaps… coaxed out."

Javic knew it was possible. Belford swore Kara's mind had been freed before her passing. Javic had no choice but to succeed where Belford had failed. Salvine needed him. Perhaps it was possible in theory… but the pressure he felt was borderline debilitating. His final moment with Salvine back in Darrenfield replayed in his head.

…The attempted kiss she'd denied.

He'd been filled with such chagrin. In the days that followed, he replayed the moment ad nauseam, wishing fretfully that he could take the romantic gesture back. Later, when he learned of her fate and believed her lost forever, he tortured himself by playing out detailed alternative scenarios— *Could I have convinced her to stay if I was more suave?*—If only he could have delayed her… any amount of time could have possibly made some difference—just enough to change her fate so that she would no longer cross paths with Wilgoblikan Whune. It was all hopeless fantasy. It had eaten him up for so long—consumed his idle thoughts—until one day… it just stopped. At some point he accepted that she was gone, never to return….

Only now she had.

None of his mental self-flagellation mattered anymore— Salvine was here! She was still alive. He needed to focus on the one thing that mattered. This time, he would do whatever it took to save her from her terrible fate.

Doctor Crane had already sent an assistant to retrieve Cale to aid him with the medical procedure. Turning a Whune back into a human was a similar procedure to de-aging. Javic knew from Havorie all about Cale and Crane being part of the team of Ameliorators that reset Ethan's cells. Belford had laid the groundwork for all of it to be possible. Crane managed to solve the puzzle of how King Garrett kept himself young for a century.

With that knowledge on their side, Salvine stood a real chance, but it was not without its risks. Javic didn't dare let hope cloud his judgment. Salvine needed him to be cautious. The reality was that they would be making a medical breakthrough if she survived.

Crane grimaced at the old bloody handprint on the tube of the spyglass. He wiped it clean on the sleeve of his lab coat before placing the Power Artifact back down next to a pair of forceps on his equipment tray.

"If you really want to do this, I'm willing to give it a try," said Doctor Crane.

Javic had no trust for the doctor after everything he'd learned, but he knew he was a competent Ver'ati. Crane's medical knowledge and experience was unsurpassed by any other Ameliorator in Erotos. If anyone could give Salvine her body back, it was Doctor Crane. "You fix her body, and I'll fix her mind," said Javic.

Crane had been understandably vexed by Javic snooping in his lab, but when he found out Javic knew the human behind one of his captured Whunes, he took pity on him.

"Did you know it takes a Ver'ati with superb strength to control that Artifact?" Doctor Crane asked.

Javic shook his head.

"Don't worry—I've seen your blood," said Crane. "You won't have any problem at all. You're more powerful than even your mother was. I don't say this lightly. You are the strongest in decades—behind our newest bearer of the Mark of Kings, of course. You can thank your grandmother for the potential you possess."

If Javic wasn't so focused on Salvine he would have been less caught off guard by Crane's comments. He scowled at the doctor.

"You can thank her for that bump on the ridge if your nose as well," said Crane.

Javic narrowed his eyes. The bump had always labeled him as an outlander to the other children in Darrenfield. His grandma Teresa was a local…. "Did you know my grandmother?"

Doctor Crane chuckled wryly. "No, of course not, silly boy! It's all written in your blood!"

"I always thought the bump was from my mother's side," said Javic.

"Nope," said Crane. "Definitely from your father's mother. You're an interesting kid. If you're equally as compelling as an assistant I might just have a job for you if this whole thing with the queen doesn't work out." The words felt sinister coming out of the good doctor's mouth. He slapped his knee. "These last two Whunes have had a rough ride," he said changing the subject back to the matter at hand. "The research I've done—the rest did not survive, but I have gleaned invaluable insight that will be of much use." Crane gestured for Javic to follow him from the examination room to the lab where Salvine was caged. "Be a dear and carry that tray," he said.

Javic picked up the silver equipment tray that held the brass spyglass and hustled after the doctor.

"I've been probing their minds for months," the doctor continued. "The intellect behind our girl is impressive. I've never seen anything like it!"

Javic didn't like him referring to Salvine as 'our girl' but he wasn't about to argue with the doctor while he was being so amiable to his cause.

"The rest were pure brutes, mind you, so when the little dove used her wits to escape her cage I was quite pleased."

They reached the sliding metal door to the lab.

"She got out?" Javic asked.

"Sure did," said Crane. "Smashed my old assistant's skull into pieces in the process. Don't underestimate her. My tinkering has already returned much of her facilities. This will be an interesting final test—*can they be reverted?*"

When they entered the lab, Salvine's yellow eyes were full of crust. It almost looked like she'd been crying. Her Whune-body showed no other hint of emotion as she followed his strides across the chamber.

"What do you say we practice with this one first?" asked Crane, prodding at the other Whune with a thin wire rod he'd retrieved from atop a cabinet. He shoved the wire between the bars, stirring up a response from the previously silent beast. The Whune could hardly move in its tight confinement, but it shook with rage at being prodded.

"The beast knows it's doomed," said Doctor Crane. "Only room for one in there." He stabbed the wire into the creature's forehead. It howled out in vicious retort. "These electrodes will help with the physical transformation."

The wire stabbed beneath the creature's flesh. Doctor Crane used the Power to turn the tip molten for a brief moment, fusing it in place. The Whune shook, but the electrode did not detach. The doctor retrieved several more wires and speared each of the Whune's limbs one at a time. He drove the electrodes deep into the flesh.

Javic was disturbed by the whole setup, but he would accept anything that gave Salvine a better chance at survival. A rap at the metal slider brought his attention around to Cale. The Ver'ati must have left in a hurry from his apartment for him to have gotten to the lab so quickly. The lieutenant general looked as sickly as ever, but he smiled at Javic as he entered the chamber.

"Thank you for coming on such short notice," said Doctor Crane.

Cale shrugged. "I couldn't say no," he said. "Not after all the help Javic has been to me."

Crane pulled up three rolling stools and placed them one-by-one in front of the prepared Whune. "Well then, let's get slicing," he said. "We're starting with the male as practice before moving on to our little dove. I've been calling this one Grunter, because he grunts a lot—Don't worry Grunter, you're in excellent hands!—You see all these tumors around the neck there? They're compressing on the windpipe. Hence the grunting. I will go in solo to clear that area first to mitigate risk of suffocation. Then you begin, Cale."

Cale breathed deeply. "I'm ready," he said.

Javic could feel a shift of the energy in the air as the lieutenant general accessed the Power. The electric tingle intensified further as Doctor Crane embraced his abilities alongside Cale.

"Javic—just watch for now," said the doctor. "Feel what I do with the energy and you just may learn something here. You'll know when it's your turn—by then he'll appear as a man once more."

Javic nodded. He picked up the brass spyglass and held it tight in his fist as he settled into his stool. He wasn't particularly pleased to be observing the transformation. The nostrils on Doctor Crane's hooked nose flared as he directed the first charge through the electrode that ran into the Whune's forehead. The creature's whole body went rigged. A deep wet growl arose—a gurgle in its throat. Javic could sense the change of energy as it flowed from Doctor Crane's fingertips and down the long wire into the Whune's body. Javic inhaled sharply.

He's using his own internal energy!

Shiara had drilled it into his head to never attempt such a dangerous act.

"Yes," said Doctor Crane, responding to Javic's shock. "This practice is not usually taught to one so young as you—it is easy to drain oneself without care—but this is the only way to be precise enough to impress biological change. You'll notice very subtle shifts in the energy if you probe with your thoughts."

Another ripple of current flowed down the electrode and into the Whune's body. Its howls grew in intensity. Javic had been through this before with Belford and Kara. Memories of Kara's screams still haunted Javic's dreams on occasion. He knew the cries would only grow more desperate.

The Whune's bulging neck began to shrink back into its body. The creature screeched out in agony—already, its vocal cords had shifted. It sounded more like a man than a beast. A sobering thought crossed Javic's mind: He'd taught himself to dehumanize Whunes when he thought they couldn't be saved. It had been easier to consider them monsters—to pronounce the human inside dead. Javic realized he needed to start seeing Whunes as the enslaved people they truly were.

The reframing of his perspective brought a dose of empathy that gnawed at his insides. The poor man screamed and shrieked all the louder as Cale joined in with the complicated procedure. He sent a subtle vibration down the electrode attached to the transforming man's left arm. His inflated muscles shrank, leaving over-stretched dangly skin behind that drooped low over his bone. His skin held the consistency of a tanned hide—somehow even more grotesque on the smaller human frame. Cale shifted his focus once the muscles and tumors adequately retracted. A sharp kinetic charge streaked across the man's stained skin—it split open and then detached entirely, sloughed off into a heap at the bottom of the cage. Fresh pink skin with youthful elasticity emerged from within as if bursting from a cocoon.

Doctor Crane worked on the man's right side while Cale continued on down his left. Javic could feel all the charges the two men used. The range of current was so slight that Javic could hardly discern the differences. He may have been given the title of Ver'ati, but his new senses would take time to develop. He needed to train his heightened awareness to a much deeper degree to be able to truly understand what Doctor Crane and Cale were doing.

When they'd finished their detailed work, an ugly, naked mole rat of a hairless man slouched at the bottom of the cage. A pile of blubbery flesh and tanned skin thrice his mass lay beneath him. The mess spilled out between the bars. He was as scrawny as a mouse—not a bit of extra fat or muscle on his bones.

His face twisted into a crazed expression. With bared teeth, he growled a primal bellow that sent saliva spraying into the air. His arms were skinny enough to fit in between the bars. He lunged forward and reached at Doctor Crane. The doctor didn't flinch. He turned towards Javic with a wide grin. "It's time to use the Artifact," he said.

Javic swallowed down his doubts. There was no room for that now. He lifted the brass spyglass to his eye. He took one last look at the smooth, pink skin of the man's face. His feral expression was a contortion of rage. Javic closed one eye and focused all his attention on the light coming at him through the viewport. Unlike before when he'd had to search for Lyle's dream, the shine of the transformed man's mental orb lit up with a dark shimmer. He couldn't make out any images, just a wavering velvet curtain. It was the size of a large melon, floating before him. The orb shifted about erratically in front of Javic's eyes—its position corresponded with the location of the man's head as he thrashed about within his cage. Javic twisted the focal lens, attempting to lock on to the bouncing ball like he'd done with Lyle's dream, but the man's motion was too severe for him to achieve a proper aim.

"Can you restrain his head?" Javic asked Doctor Crane.

The doctor gestured sharply, smashing the man to the side of his cage with an unseen force. The man's body continued to writhe around but his head and neck were steadily pinned.

Javic focused back in on the shimmering blob. He twisted the focal lens again, trying to dive in like he'd done with Lyle. He felt a dense resistance. It was as if he were bouncing off the shimmering curtain. The orb wavered violently as Javic beat against it with his attempts to pierce through. The effects of his probing appeared to be cumulative. The surface rippled wildly as he continued to press into it. With a final twist, he struck the weakened veil, and this time it absorbed him. It was like falling into a tar-covered ocean. He sank in slowly, feeling a tightness envelope his chest and lungs. The black ripples reflected a dark face staring menacingly back at him. He fell through the conscious curves, consumed by the expanding abyss.

The jagged treetops of a dark forest filled his vision, stretching across an endless horizon. He drifted through the thick atmosphere, sinking to the surface. There was no breeze—no rustling leaves or any animal sounds either. It all felt so static, like a painting of a forest rather than the real deal. The trees rose up all around him until he found himself standing upon an empty roadway of dirt and mud.

Javic drifted along the path, not really running, though his legs did churn beneath him. He was floating just above the ground. The trees shifted by until a solitary stagecoach appeared before him from out of the darkness. He slowed down, approaching more cautiously. The whimpers of a canine broke the silence of the dark dream, escaping from within the coach's back compartment. He pulled the doors open. Inside he found a dozen thin wire cages, double-stacked in the dim space.

A dog stared back at him with shining eyes. Javic formed a ball of light in the palm of his hand, using the power of intention. The glow chased away the shadows, igniting the entirety of the compartment with its brilliant shine. The dog recoiled from the glow, pressing itself up to the back corner of its cage.

A groan escaped a lump at the bottom of another one of the cages. A dirty tattered cloak stretched across the mound—it was a man, shriveled and scrawny. The man turned his face up at the disturbance. Javic recognized him as an older and even more skeletal version of the man Doctor Crane and Cale had just carved out of the Whune.

"I'm here to save you," said Javic.

The man groaned, exhausted eyes rolling up into his head at the harsh light.

Javic turned down the brightness of his orb with another thought. "What's your name?" he asked.

The man rolled over, turning to press his face against the meshing of wire. His wrinkled skin held an expression of pure terror. "There's no savin' me, boy," said the man, a thick Antaran accent on his lips. "And he's gunna get'cha too."

"Get me?" asked Javic. Before the man could elaborate the crack of a whip pierced the air. Javic felt a sting arise on his cheekbone. Warm blood trickled out from a gash just beneath his left eye. He cried out in shock as he spun around.

A rotund behemoth of a man stood behind him, holding a wicked riding crop in his hand. The large man raised the crop and struck again, lashing Javic on the shoulder this time. Javic crashed back against the cages. The yellow dog bit at his backside through the chicken wire. A very real pain flayed his nerve endings, sending ice running through Javic's veins. The strikes hurt as bad as if they were real. He hadn't been expecting such visceral sensations inside the dream.

The man's bearded jaw jutted out as he sneered at Javic. He raised his crop again, but Javic was already running. He darted away, off the road into the trees.

"He's gunna get'cha!" the yell of the caged man rang out behind Javic. Manic laughter escaped the back compartment— whaling cries of insanity that shook Javic's resolve. The clomp of the fat man's footfalls chased after him into the woods.

This is ridiculous, thought Javic. *I have to get a grip!*

He was breathing like he was actually running. He had to remind himself that he was just in a dream! He could do anything he set his mind to. The lumbering stride of the fat man's footfalls continued to chase after him, but Javic wasn't willing to play by his rules anymore. He kicked off the ground and floated into the air, rising up above the treetops with ease. The fat man shouted wordlessly, cracking his riding crop in anger as Javic floated farther away.

Javic turned in the air, flying back towards the coach as quickly as he could, determined to see his task through. He directed himself back to the dirt road as the fat man chased after him below. He wouldn't have a lot of time once he reached the coach. He landed hard beside the imprisoned man and immediately gripped ahold of the wire at the front of his cage. Javic's hands worked better than knives as he yanked the chicken wire away.

"Come on!" he cried. "We haven't much time!"

The lump of a man snarled at him. "The only way I'm leaving here is with him dead!"

Javic reached in and tried to pull the man out by force, but he bit him on the hand!

"He'll beat me if I even think of leaving!" the man hissed.

The hulking captor burst from the tree line. Javic was out of time. He looked at the poor shriveled man before him with disgust. "I'm not sticking around!" cried Javic. "Save yourself or be trapped here forever!" He reached into his belt and willed a long blade into existence from an invisible sheath. He dropped the sword within the pathetic man's reach before jumping back into the air. The menacing captor swiped at his feet, but Javic was too fast. The cuts on his cheek and shoulder still stung as he retreated back up into the clouds.

He couldn't save the man if he wasn't willing to save himself.... He clawed his way back through the veil. Once he was far enough away from the dream he was finally able to pull the spyglass away from his eye. He sighed, disappointed with his performance. He hadn't expected such resistance, nor the physical pain. He felt his cheek. A raised welt met his fingertips.

Doctor Crane and Cale were no longer in front of him. They'd moved on to Salvine while he was preoccupied. He twisted around to look at the Calvenite cage to his right— Doctor Crane was putting the final touches on Salvine's new body. Her repaired skin was pink and raw. Her hair was non-existent.   Her scrawny body was lankier than Javic remembered. She was reclined atop a pile of blubber that the Ameliorators had just finished slicing off of her.

"Thank you," rasped a harsh voice to his left. It was the caged man—miraculously, he was back in control of his body!

Javic was pleasantly surprised by his success. "What happened…? Did you…?"

"I slit his throat when he came at me," said the man, eyes still rolling as he came out of his haze. "He was me… a shadow of me." The man began to sob. "I killed myself."

Doctor Crane and Cale looked over at the sound of the emotional breakdown. "You did it!" exclaimed Cale.

"Did you doubt me?" asked Javic.

"Not for a moment!" Cale laughed.

Doctor Crane gave an approving nod.

Javic's eyes strayed back towards Salvine. She was sitting eerily motionless atop her old flesh with her legs crossed. If he hadn't known better, he would have thought she was already back in control of her body as well. She was still a Whune. She wore Salvine's flesh as a disguise. It was strange that the beast wasted no energy shaking the bars of her cage.

"Whatever you just did, it's time to do it again," said Doctor Crane.

Salvine's gray eyes remained locked on Javic as he rolled his stool over in front of her cage. The dove charm dangled loosely from her emaciated wrist now. Her calmness was somehow even more disturbing to him than had she been flailing violently. There was no need for anyone to restrain her as Javic raised the spyglass to his eye once more and focused in on her shimmering curtain.

CHAPTER
42

Spire to Heaven

Stranded along the desolate beach of her subconscious, Salvine was trapped in near solitude. It was a mental prison of torturous design. After being recaptured, more meddling by Doctor Crane forced her mind back inside of itself—just as Wilgoblikan had done to her many moons ago when he first turned her into a Whune. Her alter-ego, Ash, had free reign of their shared body now. While Whunes did not normally sleep, Doctor Crane had returned that functionality to her. Ash visited Salvine when slumber overtook their twisted body. In her suppressed state, Ash's companionship was the only thing keeping Salvine somewhat sane.

An endless storm raged overhead in the un-waking nightmare. It blackened the long coastline as far as the eye could see. Rolling whitecaps crashed like thunder against the rocks. The wind was biting—a continuous spray of salt and sand that stung like needles. Salvine had grown numb to the sting it imparted upon her flesh.

There was nowhere to go. Nothing to see. A useless attempt to wander inland ended with a single glance behind—the beach still lapped at her heels no matter how far she ran. The crashing waves were frigid beyond reason. More than once Salvine attempted to drown herself of her sorrows in the terrible tide. She found her misery did not end so easily—the sea wasn't real. She felt the icy sting of the crashing froth. Her mind told her she was out of air, and she suffered the panic-inducing pressure in her lungs, and yet she remained conscious indefinitely, undying.

Ash watched from the beach with sad eyes as Salvine wallowed in the waves. She intentionally inhaled the sea water into her lungs, hoping beyond reason it might end her misery. She arose after several agonizing minutes of convulsing without breath. Her white dress clung to her skin. She shivered, her heart filled with despair as she waded back through the lapping waters. The breathless cold felt real enough. She dragged herself free of the current and sat down beside Ash on a large driftwood log.

"Why do you do that?" asked Ash.

Salvine rolled her eyes. "I would do anything to escape this hell." Her teeth chattered together as she spoke. She wished she could simply tell herself she wasn't really freezing, but the mental prison didn't afford her the ability to make changes. "Do you think the doctor might finally kill us today?" she asked, though she dared not hope.

Ash shook her head. Her long black hair whipped sideways with the wind. "He is content to tinker with us further."

Salvine breathed a heavy sigh of disappointment.

"Would you like to build another sandcastle together?" asked Ash.

The passage of time was difficult to gauge with the consistency of the gray sky overhead, but during their first week together on the beach they had attempted to construct a sandcastle out of the wet sand. The tide rolled in, destroying it, but it was still the only fun Salvine had had so far on the awful beach.

Salvine grimaced as her stomach churned. She leaned forward and retched up some seawater between her feet. "I'm not really in the mood," she said once she was finished expunging the briny fluid.

Ash huffed out a wordless sigh.

Salvine knew Ash was just trying to help. Sadly, there was nothing she could say that would make her feel any better about her situation. Salvine rolled off the log and buried her face in the sand, if only for the change of scenery. Ash was gone when she looked back up. It was like that with her sometimes—coming and going at random. Salvine wished she could leave this wretched place alongside her.

A peculiar sound fell across Salvine's ears over the din of the howling winds. She turned at once and was surprised to find Ash still present, standing shoulder deep in an immaculately carved-out pit.

"How'd you do that so quickly?" asked Salvine.

Ash stood up, only her eyes peeking out over the top of the hole. Salvine could tell she was frowning without even seeing the rest of her face. "I just thought about it," she said.

Salvine stepped across the coarse sand, over to the side of the hole. Seawater was seeping in through the walls of the pit. One glance from Ash and all the holes were patched and the puddle hardened into a crystalline floor. Salvine hopped down to join her. The relief from the stinging sands was immediate. The wind gusted just overhead. Ash's ability to manipulate the dreamscape was the spark of hope Salvine so desperately needed.

"Can you carve tunnels?" asked Salvine, her voice small against the roaring storm.

"I thought you didn't want to play," said Ash. Her stringy hair suddenly bounced up into a mop of tight curls. She didn't appear to be conscious of the change.

"Building a tiny sandcastle doesn't interest me…" said Salvine, "but a big one…" she raised an eyebrow.

"Somewhere else to go, other than this beach," mused Ash. She glanced at the inland wall of the pit and gestured like a wizard. The pit elongated in an instant, turning into a long trench. When the trench reached the embankment it burrowed into it, forming a perfectly round tunnel in the sand. Ash lifted her hands into the air—a great geyser of earth exploded into the sky in the distance. It was raining sand, but every grain landed with precise form, settling into compressed blocks of stone that culminated in the erection of an immaculate spire, piercing the clouds with its grandeur.

"Th-that's amazing!" exclaimed Salvine. "Does this tunnel lead…?" She gestured up at the spire.

"I made stairs right to the top," said Ash. "Would you like to see what's above the clouds?"

Salvine laughed as she grabbed Ash's hand in her own and tugged her down the freshly carved tunnel. Salvine's excitement was contagious. Soon, it washed over Ash, sweeping away her prickly demeanor. Ash giggled alongside her as they skipped hand-in-hand down the path. The walls exuded a soft luminance to guide their way. Only when they reached the foot of the spire did Salvine appreciate the truly massive scale of Ash's creation.

"This is enormous!" exclaimed Salvine. A wide spiral staircase corkscrewed into oblivion above their heads.

"I've never created anything before," said Ash, glancing down at her feet in chagrin. "I needed to make it large to withstand the storm."

"I wasn't critiquing," said Salvine. "It's perfect! I'll race you to the top!"

A competitive spark lit Ash's eyes as the girls clamored up the stairs together. Their legs grew tired before they'd gone more than a few rotations around the wide spire. They climbed on with growing anticipation of the view at the pinnacle. The climb was long and laborious, but anything was better than standing on the frigid beach. A bright glow at the top of the spire drew them onward.

When they finally reached the top, Salvine was not disappointed. A small viewing platform sat just above the quickly flowing cloud layer. The billowing froth churned in waves to match the tempest of the sea hidden far below. She felt like she was on a rock in the middle of a mystical ocean as it flowed beneath and around her. The violent shape of the clouds did not shake her resolve to get closer to the edge. They were above the winds. The storm stretched as far as she could see to the horizon in every direction. Above, a hazy sky shined glorious warmth down upon Salvine's face. She had been devoid of heat for so very long. Her lips tingled with relief from the numbness that had settled within them. The radiance soaked into her skin.

"I'm really glad you're here," said Salvine, gazing over at Ash.

Ash turned and gave a nonchalant head nod. She didn't understand the immensity of the gift she had just given her.

They stayed to watch the sunset, sitting like madwomen at the edge of the platform with their legs dangling into the perfect carpet of cloud. Salvine felt a cool condensation form on her toes—beads of water that ran down and dripped from the bottoms of her soles. Her legs captured a fine misting as well. They gleamed in the golden light when she lifted them back up to the platform. The sun turned blood red as it descended into the clouds. A deep orange hue lit the atmosphere. Salvine and Ash didn't speak. They just basked in the evanescence of it all as the light shifted and danced its final rays across the sky before dipping into the layer of gray. When night fell in earnest another glorious display awaited them: A million flickering stars that stretched all across the wide heavens. The moon arose to sit upon the clouds to the east, throwing its milky rays onto the hollow waves of the rolling storm.

Salvine was in awe of the display. Her eyes wandered over to Ash as the moon climbed higher. "Thank you for this," she said.

"I think, perhaps, I'd like to create some more things," said Ash. "Perhaps a whole city up here above the clouds."

"I'd like that very much," said Salvine.

The months of Salvine's internal imprisonment continued to roll by, but Ash returned to Salvine every time she slept and followed through on her design. She added new structures for Salvine to traverse each day. The architecturally dubious towers stretched high above even the spire, connecting to each other with arching bridges and long precarious walkways. Salvine didn't care about the lack of safety. She loved exploring all the twisting routes and high overhangs. The thrill of standing on the edge was her greatest entertainment. She nearly fell on several occasions, but she knew she couldn't die here, and while she did still suffer from loneliness, at least she had Ash to keep her company some of the time.

To Salvine, Ash's presence was warming. Admittedly, she was not much of a conversationalist. Salvine was beginning to recognize Ash for what she really was: A lost and segmented part of her own psyche. Ash was childlike in her unknowing of the real world, but she was not unintelligent. She was constantly learning and growing in ways that never ceased to garner surprise.

One day while awaiting Ash's return, Salvine amused herself sliding back and forth along a zip-line wire route that Ash had installed between several of the towers. The sky split open with a tear that splayed the heavens asunder. Salvine stared wide-eyed, mouth agape at the hole in the atmosphere. She landed hard back on her feet at the end of the zip-line run. A man floated through the air far in the distance, high above the clouds. He descended rapidly from the broken sky with his arms spread wide like wings.

With a breathless rasp, Ash called out from behind Salvine, nearly scaring her off the ledge. "He's found us!" she cried. "Just like you always said he would!"

Salvine turned to face Ash, a mask of confusion wrinkling her brow.

Ash's skin was pale and sickly in appearance—a great exhaustion ravaged her demeanor, though her expression was one of much jubilation. "Our body has been transformed back into its original form," she said with a strain. "Now, Javic has come to free your mind from this place."

Salvine was dumbfounded. She'd abandoned her fantasies of being rescued by Javic long ago. It hardly seemed possible he was here! She rubbed her eyes and then strained to observe the floating newcomer once more. He was much too far away to call out to. Salvine stood perched at the edge of the tower, watching as he descended into the choppy storm clouds below.

"He found us," Ash repeated. "He really found us!"

CHAPTER
43

City above the Clouds

Javic fell through the spyglass into Salvine's cloudy world. He dropped as if through water. The gravity he experienced was more of a suggestion than a law, but try as he might, he could not control his descent. Before him, piercing through the charcoal-dark storm clouds, a series of mega-structures drew his focus. They were impossibly tall with crude structural elements reminiscent of blocks a child might erect—only they were each the size of a mountain. Bridges and towers broke the sharp lines of the constructs with a webbing of impractical pathways and catwalks. With no visible railings or other safety features, a single misplaced foot would bring a fall into oblivion.

He attempted to drift closer to the towers, but the further he sank, the faster his rate of decline became. The storm at his feet was his inevitable destination. For a moment, before the weather obscured his vision entirely, he spotted a pair of girls perched precariously on the side of one of the high catwalks.

The city vanished as Javic sank into the gray. By the time he emerged below the cloud cover, he was soaked to the bone and shivering from the cold. This was the most visceral dream he had ever experienced, through the spyglass or otherwise. A ragged sea churned a terrible ruckus beneath him. The waves bashed the shore, driven by the high winds. Javic sank fast towards a beach that spanned to the horizon in either direction.

The footings of the enormous structures he'd witnessed above the clouds sat just beyond the sandy coast. He knew he needed to get back up to the city above the clouds—to where he'd seen the girls—but unlike the other dreams he'd injected himself into, he was unable to float back up off the ground once he collided with the sand. He attempted to will a sword into existence in case he came across anything dangerous, but found his ability to manifest changes was absent entirely as well. He wasn't in control here. He shook off the self-doubt that arose within him as best as he could, trudging forward on foot with the wind at his back in search of a way into the sky.

There was no possibility of traversing the tower footings. The scaffolding of the mega structures was nowhere near human scalable with their enormous fittings. Javic came across a tunnel at the edge of the beach that angled towards the nearest structure—a great spire. He proceeded down the tunnel for lack of a better path forward. He was glad to leave the stinging sands behind as he headed beneath the dunes.

He kept his eyes wide, searching for any hint of threats as he pushed onward. The vast scale of the dreamscape was much larger than he'd anticipated after the quick in-and-out of his last experience.

When he reached the inside of the spire he knew he'd come the right direction. He was met with a spiraling set of stairs that looked to continue on forever upward. He sighed to himself before beginning the monotonous climb. He was resolved to reach the city above. He kept climbing until his legs grew tired of the constant churn, only stopping to catch his breath when a terribly realistic cramp gripped his thigh and forced him to pause and ponder his limited progress. It felt like he had been at it for at least an hour… and yet he was still far from the top of the massive spire!

Time in dreams didn't always pass at the same rate as time in the waking world—he knew that from his own dreams. If he'd truly been inside Salvine's head for so long, he assumed Doctor Crane and Cale would have attempted to pull him back out by now.

What if they tried to rouse me but it didn't work? What if I'm stuck in here?

They were concerning thoughts. This dream did feel more suppressing than the others he'd previously walked. His mind was becoming increasingly cloudy. Several times already he'd forgotten for a brief moment that he was in a dream at all! Even with his lucidity at risk, he marched on—it was all he could do.

Inward and upward, he hugged the outer wall as it spiraled around. Each stair took him two strides to cross and a third step to rise to the next level. The inside edge was open to the hollow core of the spire. Javic didn't dare get too close, feeling the distance he'd climbed so far in his shaky legs.

He tried to keep his focus, but it was difficult to stay sharp with the monotony of the climb. His thoughts wandered to the unknown. He was clueless about the workings of the spyglass. His face still stung where he'd been whipped by the torturer in the previous dream. Reality mixed with the imaginary inside the Power Artifact in ways he could not even begin to fathom.

He forced his cramping legs to work overtime. Slowly but surely, he could tell he was making progress—a distant glow at the top of the spire drew ever nearer as he wound his way up the daunting stairwell. It only became obvious that the glow was sunlight when the shine began to fade—night was falling inside the dream world at long last.

As he got closer to the top, leaning towards the middle of the spire brought him a view of the stars directly overhead.

I'm almost there!

But with only a few revolutions left to go he came across an eerie figure poised in the shadows—a gangly girl, crouched awkwardly like a toad. Her legs were spread wide, arms limp at her sides. Her white dress was tattered at the hems, with a long slit torn to just above the knees, freeing up her legs for quick movement. Still, the dark-haired girl stayed motionless. She did not greet Javic as he approached. He eyed her warily as he stepped slowly up several more stairs. She remained crouched against the wall, unperturbed.

"Who are you?" Javic asked.

The girl maintained a shameless stare. "You may call me Ash," she said.

Javic found her unblinking expression profoundly unsettling. He felt an animalistic presence within her. "I know what you are," he said. "You're the entity within Salvine that serves Wilgoblikan, aren't you?"

Ash cocked her head slightly. "I am," she said, her eyes fierce. "But I am not the same naïve beast I once was. Your doctor friend unraveled me piece-by-piece and put me back together anew. I'll tell you straight away, I no longer feel the need to kill without reason."

"That's comforting," said Javic.

"We would not be having this conversation otherwise," she quipped.

Javic grimaced. "Answer me this: Do you still serve Wilgoblikan?" There was no use dancing around the subject.

Ash's fingers wriggled against the step. In Javic's mind he likened it to a cat flicking its tail. Ash maintained her flat stare. "He no longer owns me," she said. "But… in good faith, I will admit, I do feel him drawing steadily nearer every day."

So she does have a connection with that monster!

Javic's stance was unwavering. He would do whatever it took to save Salvine from Wilgoblikan's twistings. "Where is Salvine?" he asked, eying the final revolutions of the stairway above them.

Ash arose swiftly from her squatted position. "She's waiting for you at the top." She gestured for Javic to pass her by. "I just wanted to get a good look at you first."

Javic didn't delay. He scooted past, watching Ash closely for any sign of aggression as he did so. The odd girl didn't move a muscle—just continued to stare blankly at him. When Javic was several steps beyond her position she spoke out to him once more.

"You should know," said Ash, "Salvine doesn't need you anymore. I protect her now. She's not the same girl you once knew—she is much more."

"It's you keeping her here, isn't it," said Javic.

"I keep her safe," said Ash.

She admits it!

Javic had nothing else to say. He kept climbing. Ash didn't move from her step for as long as Javic watched. He kept his eyes locked on her for as long as he could, until the stairs curved back around on top of themselves and she was lost from view. Javic's heart was pounding against his ribs. He bolted up the final steps, racing to the top. When he arrived, the full moon was there to greet him. Hanging low on the horizon, it cast its hollow glow across the sprawling cloud tops.

Salvine was there, waiting for him, just as Ash promised. She was seated on the edge of the pinnacle platform, gazing out at the moon. Her back was to him. Javic didn't remember her fair hair being so very long. The tips dangled upon the platform behind her in a neat pile. She was humming a melodic tune that Javic didn't recognize.

Just below the platform, the dense clouds of the storm churned to form a perfect edge. Salvine kicked her feet through the mist as it rolled around the spire. She ceased her humming as Javic stepped closer. She didn't turn around as she spoke to him:

"The clouds always hang right here," she said. "It looks almost like an ocean, doesn't it?"

The beauty of the view was not lost on Javic, but it was hardly his focus or concern. He crouched down in place, still several paces back from the edge. He didn't want to get too close to the side. "I thought I'd never see you again," he said.

Salvine turned on her wrists to halfway face him—her legs still dangling over the ledge. Her gray eyes flashed in the moonlight. "I waited so long for you… I started to think you'd never come," she said. "Are you really here this time? You're not just a figment of my imagination?" Her lips quivered, eyes falling unfocused against Javic.

Her expression tugged at his heart.

"I met your shadow," said Javic. "She called herself your protector, but she was created by twisted minds probing inside your head."

Salvine narrowed her eyes at him.

"She's a monster—no better than a parasite," said Javic, shaking his head in disgust. "What I've learned… the only way I know to get you out of here is for you to kill your shadow. She's the one keeping you here. Ash must die."

Salvine recoiled towards the edge of the platform so hard that Javic feared she might slip right over the side. Her eyebrows arched together, visibly wounded by his words. "I know what Ash is," she said, "what these men put inside of me—"

"—Then you understand—"

"—but she's not like that anymore. She's changed. She wouldn't keep me here. Ash is not a monster… anymore… not to me." Tears were welling in Salvine's eyes.

Javic reached out a hand, trying to coax her back from the edge. He was disappointed by her resistance, but after meeting Ash, he was not entirely surprised. The Whune had its tendrils deep in Salvine, twisting away at her empathy whilst keeping her trapped inside herself. The only way he knew to bring Salvine out of this nightmare was with Ash's destruction. "I don't know if I can do it for you, or if it has to be you that kills her," he said.

The tears burst from Salvine's large eyes and streamed down her cheeks. The revelation of her true captor must have been tough to process. Javic clung to the hope that she would know his words to be true. "You need to call her up here and then push her over the edge. Your mind will be released from this hell at once," he gestured to the harsh lines of the structures rising up on either side of them.

"She's a part of me," said Salvine, her voice sounding in a whisper. Her tears continued to fall silently.

Javic shook his head. "You can't think like that," he said. "She.... *It*—was placed in your head by a madman. You need to fight. It's time for you to take your body back!"

Salvine pulled her feet back up over the edge of the platform. Javic was finally able to take a breath as she scooted back from the edge. She wiped the tears from her cheeks with the back of her hand.

"We can do it together," suggested Javic, "if that will help."

Salvine shook her head. "I think it has to be me," she whispered.

Javic nodded.

"He's telling the truth," said Ash, slinking up the opening to the staircase. There was no telling how long she'd been listening in.

Salvine met Ash with a breathless stare.

"I didn't know I was keeping you here at first," said Ash, "but I knew it true when I realized the extent of my abilities here."

Javic climbed off his butt and got into a low balanced stance in case Ash rushed at them.

"You really are trapping me?" Salvine asked, voice trembling with emotion.

"It's better here than in the doctor's cage," said Ash.

"It's the same thing," snapped Salvine. "A prison."

Ash stopped advancing at the top of the steps. "But I built you this sanctuary," said Ash.

Javic shifted his body to place himself between Salvine and Ash. "Salvine's body is human again," he said. "There's no room for you—for a Whune."

Ash backed away, skirting the hole of the stairwell as she moved to the far side of the platform. "I think, perhaps, he is right," said Ash. "I don't know how to be human." She edged closer to the relentless storm. "If there can be only one of us, it should be you."

"What are you doing?" asked Salvine, panic quickly rising in her voice.

"The only thing I know will release you," said Ash.

"—Wait!" cried Salvine. "Not like this!"

"Thank you. You've taught me so much," Ash said calmly. "It's been a better life than I dare say most Whunes get to lead—being here in this place with you."

"Please!" Salvine begged.

Javic was only just getting a glimpse at the relationship that had blossomed between Salvine and Ash. Seeing Salvine's reaction to the prospect of losing Ash made his heart twinge with sorrow for her loss. It must have been so very confusing for her.

"Don't ever let them put you in a cage again," said Ash. She flashed Salvine a solitary strained smile before stepping backwards over the side of the platform and plummeting out of sight.

Salvine screamed in anguish as Ash was consumed by the dense storm clouds. She clung to Javic, sobbing beyond consolation.

"This was the only way," he said, rubbing the back of her head with his fingertips. Salvine felt so very frail in his arms. "It had to be like this."

After only a moment more, the gravity in the dream world shifted. Javic felt himself growing lighter by the second until his feet refused to remain on the surface of the platform altogether. Salvine clung onto him all the tighter as they lifted up together into the air. They were floating, completely weightless. They drifted above the mega structures, back towards the waking world, locked in each other's tight embrace.

CHAPTER 44

Raising Mountains

Aaron felt dead inside. The mission to change the world's tides by sinking Central America into the ocean was by any physical metric a smashing success. Emotionally, however, the toll of all the millions of deaths weighed upon Aaron with a crushing pressure that wouldn't relent. He could see the same dead-eyed expressions on the faces of all the other Arcadians who had taken part in the mission. Wes never smiled anymore. The detachment they all were experiencing was a coping mechanism—Aaron knew it—but it was also the only thing that held back the onslaught of anguish. The numbness was a reprise in that regard. It imparted the side-effect of stifling his drive to continue forward in his duties. It all felt pointless.

This whole thing is a joke.

Life is a joke.

He had become a murderer out of necessity. He told himself he was only acting as a tool for humanity's greater survival—he'd done what he had to in order to save the greatest number of lives from starvation, but that did not relieve him of the guilt

334

that gripped his chest like ice in his veins anytime he allowed himself to think about the suffering he had caused to the innocent people down below.

When will this be over?

How much is enough?

When he closed his eyes he could still see the images of the rolling dust clouds. The earth had been blasted skyward by their pointed thoughts—huge swaths of land eroded and dispersed into the coastal waters. The dust formed billowing structures many miles wide as their supersonic jet flew back and forth across the narrow landmass. Wes whipped up a monstrous storm to blow the dust clouds out over the ocean so that their solemn work could continue as efficiently as possible.

Their jet stayed at a high altitude. The process felt less personal from afar, but somehow that disconnect only made it worse. They were too high to see the cities they obliterated in much detail. Aaron's imagination had to fill in the faces and stories of the poor people who never had a chance—never even knew they should have evacuated the region. There wasn't any time to give a warning. Aaron and company rained death upon them—complete indiscriminate carnage.

Eventually the oceans on either side of the narrow continent flowed together. The water was a murky brown all around in every direction; a choppy churning of mud and debris. Tides the whole world across were shifted permanently from the change in circulation. The Central African plains and low-latitude desert regions of the world would receive much more rainfall as the jet-streams overhead matched the new flow of the water below.

Claire had ignored all of Aaron's attempts at communication. She must have hated him. She judged him for what he'd decided to do just as he judged her for doing nothing at all. He understood her resistance to partaking in the destruction—no one deserved such a terrible responsibility. He was glad Claire wasn't needed. She was spared the trauma. Ultimately, he had saved her from it by doing the deed himself. He just wished she could at least appreciate that it was a dirty job that needed doing. *How can she not understand the necessity?!*

Claire was too far away for Aaron to sense her through their mental bond. They were on opposite sides of the globe. After enough time went by, Aaron began to feel that it was best that way. He didn't want to feel her scorn. He feared what seeing the disapproval in her eyes might do. The job had been difficult enough without feelings of self-loathing completely tearing him apart. As it was, the tumultuous feelings bubbled just below the surface. He was already finding it so very difficult to continue on every morning.

Finally, today, the mission was complete. Aaron expected to be tasked back to radiation removal like Claire and the other dissenters to the Central American mission, but his watch popped in with a new directive from EAC command.

"They want us to build mountains?" asked Isabelle in disbelief.

"Forming a new 'bread bowl' right in the middle of the Saharan Desert," said Wes. "It's smart."

The task was to raise the Earth's crust along the western coast of the African continent as well as across the southern edge of the Saharan Desert so that rain would fall and be funneled into rivers that would form new arable land. It was the fastest way to terraform the region. The EAC wasn't messing around!

Fixing the planet felt like an impossible task, but changing the waterways to foster greater food production in a less-radioactive region was certainly a good start. There was so much yet to do! Each Arcadian could only do one thing at a time. Aaron wondered what John, Garrett, Ethan and Yosef were up to. The foursome had been pulled from the Central American team the week prior for some task of which Aaron was not privy. Aaron's team was the largest group of Arcadians, consisting of himself, Isabelle, Wes, Emily, Hannah, and Brooke. They splintered further, Aaron going with Wes and Isabelle to start the coastal mountain chain while the others worked on the southern range.

"I guess we'll meet you in the middle," said Hannah as the group split in two.

It wasn't until they got started that they realized it would take careful placement of more than a thousand individual peaks at varying elevations encompassing the entirety of Western Africa before the rain-shadow effect could be counteracted. The westward side of the range caused the rain to release as the air was forced upward by the mountains. The hard part was catching the runoff and sloping it inland, between the harsh peeks at the coast so that the rivers would run in a counter-intuitive manner, streaming towards the desert they meant to transform instead of back out into the Atlantic.

They weren't forming mountains at random. Detailed schematics were delivered to them. They donned augmented reality spectacles to see the necessary shapes they needed to mold in order to create the desired effect. They weren't able to capture all the rainfall—the coast would become a jagged rainforest—but they did manage to funnel dozens of sizable offshoots together into one massive river easily the length of the Nile, running west to east across the continent.

The augmented reality schematics took the guesswork out of the task, but the region was still massive enough to require several months of ground-shaking shiftings of the earth. The locals fled inland as Aaron's team dragged the impassible range into existence.

One evening, after finally having spotted the edge of the southern range in the distance converging on their position, Wes interrupted mealtime to read an unexpected message he'd received, encoded from Ethan.

"It's tagged: Mega Breaking News," said Wes. "*The EAC is working on their own version of the Arcadian technology—they are preparing to release a whole new set of matter markers, controllable by their own super computer.*"

"Ethan sent this?" asked Aaron through a mouthful of rehydrated potatoes.

"It came from Ethan, but it's also signed by Garrett, John and Yosef—their whole group," said Wes.

Isabelle spat on the floor at the mention of her despised uncle Yosef—she was as compulsive with it as a nun crossing her chest at the devil. Wes ignored the outburst—it was just what she did.

"I set up a secure channel to stay in touch with the other teams when they started splitting us up—Travis and Hannah are in on this message too—all the Arcadians will see it."

"If Ethan and Garrett are in agreement, they must be certain," said Isabelle.

"The EAC won't need any of us anymore if they figure out how to make their own Arcadians..." said Wes. He kept his voice low and covered the microphone of his wrist-worn device with his palm. They all held the same posture. There was no evidence they were being monitored, but they always acted as if the EAC was listening in—it was just safer that way. "Ethan is spearheading this. He wants us to form a *rebellion...*" he only mouthed the last word. "You know, while we still have the technological advantage. He's asking us all to unite with him—he says it's our only chance to survive what they have planned."

"I don't want to abandon what we are doing here," said Aaron. "The world is going to need the food that this mountain range will help grow."

Wes and Isabelle both nodded in agreement.

"He's not asking us to stop," said Wes. "He aims for us to take the continent as a sovereign state. If we control all the food, we control the whole world."

After contemplating the proposed course of action for several hours, messages from both Hannah and Travis appeared alongside Ethan's. Both of the other groups were onboard to take back control of their destinies as long as all the Arcadians were in agreement.

Wes typed out a simple response and transmitted it out to the other teams. "We're in."

Isabelle and Wes embraced—a fortified will forming between them through their mental bond. Watching them, Aaron ached for his connection to Claire. He felt like he was missing half his heart. He grew a bit giddy at the prospect of working alongside her again. They would be forming something good—something that would feed what was left of humanity. With all the Arcadians banding together, they could do anything they set their minds to. They all had a lot of healing to do after the terrible tasks they'd completed under the guidance of the EAC.

Aaron sat with a slew of new emotions prickling his insides. He'd grown so accustom to being steeped in numbness. He turned in for the night, but he didn't sleep. They were camped in a mobile habitat, plopped down for them by a helicopter as high up their newest peak as it could fly before the atmosphere got too thin. It was best to stay at high elevations for their work so they could see the constantly changing lay of the land. Aaron contemplated the challenges that were to come. Rebellion would not be bloodless. It would not be easy. He hoped preventing the EAC from securing control over the world might bring some inkling of redemption to his wary soul. The EAC dared to destroy the world—they didn't deserve to get to rule it! He hoped the new direction would help ease his conscience. He didn't know if it would work, but he figured it was worth a shot. The weight on his shoulders had grown so terribly heavy.

CHAPTER
45

Reckless Abandon

Queen Havorie awoke the next morning after her meeting with Mallory, locked in a petrified stupor. She pulled her sheets up over her head, blocking the sun from her eyes. The hour was late, but she didn't care to start her day. She didn't want to think about her duties. She'd never felt so lost and dejected. The whole city had conspired against her. All the top officials in the Ver'konus and the Arcanum probably knew she's been unjustly Inhibited—a crime against a baby! They'd prematurely minimized her potential threat to their vile existence. Mallory presented her with the antidote to her affliction, as if a simple injection could fix all that was wrong. Havorie had a lifetime of betrayal to process.

The thought that she could be made whole again made her heart beat rapidly in her chest—a nervous flutter that twisted her stomach up in knots. She didn't even know what it meant

340

to be whole. She had never even considered that she might be able to reach the Power. The Charisms didn't react to her. The Inhibitor masked her potential from her personal Detector as well. The dials danced for Lord Ethan and the other Ver'ati, but not for her. She'd been so blind! She had no idea the extent of the manipulation going on around her. Her whole life was a lie!

A rap at her chamber door forced her to respond. "I do not wish to be interrupted," she yelled out.

"It's me, Ervia, my queen," said her loyal maid. "You've got your monthly meeting with General Aldune scheduled first thing this morning."

Havorie exhaled an exasperated breath. "Must I really endure such wretched punishment? Can we not push seeing the oaf back to later this afternoon?" she asked. General Aldune hadn't explicitly been named in the conspiracy to undermine her, but Havorie couldn't imagine Ethan's top general not being in the know. Aldune had always been one of her least favorite individuals.

"You scheduled it specifically for the morning because the moon is currently down—you didn't want him to abuse the Power to bully you or the staff," reminded Ervia.

Havorie sighed. Ervia was right. It would be best to get it over with before moonrise. Ervia entered the chamber when Havorie didn't offer a counter argument.

The young maid rushed to the bedside and pulled back the drapery. "You're not even out of bed yet!" she exclaimed. Her eyebrows didn't match her tone, drawn on flatly after her real ones had been singed away by the would-be assassin in the market. Ervia immediately grabbed the hairbrush from Havorie's side table and began to accost her golden locks with reckless abandon. "I don't think I can fix this in time," she said, a disgruntled scowl lingering across her lips.

Ervia was becoming more and more like Madam Jusair now that she had taken over all of her former personal maid's duties. Worrying constantly about Havorie's oft disheveled appearance was the bulk of Ervia's job now.   The disappearance of Madam Jusair still irked Havorie deeply—the way everyone moved on without so much as a word. The kind woman had been Havorie's wet nurse when she was but a babe.   She'd been a lifelong member of the palace staff. Madam Jusair had practically been a surrogate mother to her in Nestra's absence. She hated Damian for making the woman disappear—all because Havorie had been poking her nose around places he felt it didn't belong. So much had been taken from her.

Ervia pulled back Havorie's sheets the rest of the way, coaxing her out of bed and over to her wardrobe.

"What about the blue one?" asked Ervia.

Havorie shrugged.

"It's my favorite on you," said Ervia. She drew out the frilly gown. It was quite formal given the lack of occasion. Havorie donned it anyway.   It cupped her breasts tightly, with a swooping neckline that would distract Aldune should he drift towards his typical drunken rage.   She did enjoy its extravagance. Havorie always found that the older the man, the more unabashedly he stared.

Havorie gazed upon Ervia in the mirror. The young maid was busy cinching up the back of her dress. Havorie hadn't told her about being Inhibited yet. She wasn't ready to tell anyone. She hadn't injected the antiserum. The kit Mallory brought her was still sitting on a small shelf within her wardrobe. She wasn't sure when she would be ready to use it. She just knew she wanted to keep it close. She grabbed the leather pouch and slipped it into her pocket before heading over to the vanity where Ervia was preparing the makeup brushes.

"There's only time for a basic look," said Ervia, frantically dabbing at foundation.

Havorie was already late for the meeting. She worried Ervia would make her look like a clown at the speed she was brandishing the brushes. When she was finished, though,

Havorie had to admit she looked an image of perfection—much better than she was feeling inside, anyway. She hiked up her dress and sprinted from her chamber down the long corridor. Ervia kept pace, adjusting Havorie's hair as she ran, attempting to hide some additional tangles she'd missed while brushing. She half-expected Aldune to have given up and left by the time she made it to the meeting chamber, but the general was still present when she arrived.

General Aldune glanced up with a bored expression on his face when Havorie entered the room. His gaze immediately landed within her cleavage. He did not comment on her tardiness—all was forgiven based on the stupid grin that arose upon his lips. Havorie was pleasantly surprised to find the general to be sober. She made a mental note: Morning meetings were definitely the way to go with Aldune.

"What news does the Ver'konus offer today?" asked Havorie.

Aldune's eyes shifted slowly up to her face. "Recruitment numbers are down again, month over month," he said. "Everyone knows war is coming. Parents are hiding children with the Gift from our recruiters. It's a story as old as time."

Havorie couldn't blame anyone for wanting to hide from the Ver'konus.

"There is some good news, though," he continued. "Doctor Crane has devised a new blood test that can determine the likelihood a set of parents will have a child who can access the Power. The potential to breed a new generation of Ver'ati is close at hand. It won't help the current war efforts, but by combining genes from the right folks we just might be able to solve our generational decline issue."

"A breeding program?" scoffed Havorie. "We're talking about people here, general, not cattle."

Aldune cocked his head. "Recruitment will be easy if we offer enough gold. We'll need Councilman Cresdale to rubber-stamp the transmutation of more coin for the treasury's coffers, of course, but the breeding will be purely consensual with a high enough offer—if that's your concern. We need to reverse the downtrend before we lose our blood quantum advantage. I'm not even talking about the Goblikans here." He held up his hand when Havorie opened her mouth to interject. "The barbarians are the new threat. They've been breeding like rabbits up on their glass plains! A generation of wizards, just for this invasion! Meanwhile, we've been culling our numbers every month sparring against the Goblikans. What we need is a new school filled with proven candidates, born to be Ver'ati soldiers. And no, I am not volunteering to run that program, though I can think of an old cod or two who could do the job well enough."

"Any word yet from the north?" Havorie asked, alluding to Lord Ethan's mission.

Aldune's lips pinched up tight for a moment. "I've heard mixed reports. The barbarians are slicing through the countryside as easy as hot butter. No resistance. The Goblikans don't have the numbers. Their forces are pathetically thin now at our border, marching all they can spare north to Tavallon. As for our secret mission… well, it was a success. King Garrett is dead." He didn't sound overly enthused. "An Arcanum agent replaced him, as planned. Ambassadors are en route to us, bearing a ceasefire proposal. That'll be next week's news, officially."

"Why do you sound so grim?" Havorie asked.

Aldune glanced up from staring at her chest once more. "A Free Goblikan Alliance has claimed Tavallon. Our assets failed to obtain control. The Goblikans all knew Garrett was dead the minute his heart stopped pumping—we always knew there was a risk of that happening. It's a messy situation. The Goblikans haven't called the Ambassadors back, which may be a good sign. They also haven't denounced the fake Garrett. All our eyes and ears know for certain is some brute named Nal Viershen is currently in charge of the Goblikan contingent."

"You really buried the lead talking about recruitment numbers," said Havorie.

General Aldune smiled through his teeth. "I wasn't exactly planning on telling you all of this, not today, anyway—seeing as the Ambassadors aren't yet out of Kovani territory."

"Well, I do appreciate the candor," said Havorie. The meeting was going more cordially than she'd anticipated. "What of Lord Ethan?"

Aldune shook his head. "You've heard all I've got for you," he said. "I've no word from Lord Ethan directly. He disappeared after the assassination." The general clapped his hands together as he arose from his seat, signaling an end to the meeting.

Though Aldune's news was heavy, Havorie was pleased with the overall jovial tone of the meeting. The general didn't usually show her so much respect—he'd almost treated her like an equal! The only thing still eating at Havorie was not knowing whether Aldune was part of the conspiracy to Inhibit her or not. On a reckless whim she pulled the leather kit out from her pocket and placed it squarely on the table in front of her.

Aldune paused as he eyed the pouch with curiosity.

"Do you know what this is?" Havorie asked.

Aldune continued to stare as Havorie opened the pouch and filled an empty syringe from the clear vial of antiserum. Havorie watched his reaction closely. There was definitely a glimmer of understanding in his eyes, though he kept his composure.

"What are you going to do with that?" he asked.

Havorie was being impulsive, goading him to see if he would let anything slip as to his knowledge of her condition. "I'm going to see how much I've been lied to my whole life," she said.

Aldune's lips cracked open into a subtle smile as Havorie moved the prepared syringe to the nook of her arm. "You know what? You should do it," he said. He laughed with a deep chuckle that rocked his whole body. The glee on his face made her second-guess her resolve.

She injected the antiserum anyway.

"Give 'em all hell, kid," he said, chuckling again as he made for the door. "You've got my blessing."

Havorie immediately felt foolish for showing all her cards. A rush of anxiety overtook her. Aldune's reaction was not what she had expected. *He sounded almost proud!* It was also clear he already knew the truth before her.

Aldune sauntered out of the meeting hall, leaving Havorie to herself. She needed a moment to gather her thoughts.

I really just did that!

She pressed her thumb over the injection spot. She didn't feel any different… perhaps a bit woozy from the needle prick. She wondered how long it would take for the antiserum to take ahold. Her mother had been a tremendously powerful Ver'ati. For the first time in her life, Havorie got to wonder at the limits of her own potential. She was descended from the great Emily Fox, after all! Whatever Power she held within her blood would soon emerge whether she was ready or not.

A glow from under the sleeve of her gown brought her attention to her wrist worn Detector. She immediately knew something was amiss—what her eyes saw didn't make any sense.

Firstly, the hand that detected one's strength in the Power— of which she'd grown so accustom to always pointing in Javic's direction—was now unwaveringly aimed back upon herself. She stared at the glowing dial in silent disbelief. The glow was so bright it burned into her vision as a purple blotch that floated across her focus.

Normally, she oriented her reading of the Artifact's dials by the permanent twelve-o'clock position of its broken fourth hand.

That dial no longer held a fixed position.

The *broken* hand floated free along with the rest of the dials. The long, thin needle was dancing—just the inklings of life—

some distant signal, picked up for the first time in Havorie's memory.

She had no idea what the fourth hand was even attuned to detect!

A sudden chill flowed across her skin. It was more than just a draft through the chamber—her body was tingling; becoming more sensitive. It was her senses—they were expanding—exploding outward with incredible detail! She knew about Ver'ati senses, but she'd never imagined how it might feel to be aware of so much all at once. It was overwhelming! She immediately knew impossible things that stretched far beyond the confines of her body. The world around her was bathed in an entirely new light. She could feel the environment with her mind as surely as reaching out and touching it. The moon wasn't even up yet! As the time to moonrise drew nigh, she became aware of the whole palace—and then the whole city—and the Rivers Etto beyond, coursing across the land with a constant churn. She knew the flow as surely as the blood in her veins. The land was alive. It was part of her, and she it—there was no distinction.

A strange wonderment flashed within her and then slowly faded away, leaving behind an unsettling clarity in its wake. She became unnerved by how vulnerable she suddenly felt. She was just a girl, hidden behind her magically fortified walls. She felt like something was coming after her. She dared hope that undue paranoia might be a side-effect of the antiserum, but the more she sat with the feeling, the more she felt inclined to believe her instinctual dread was very much founded in reality.

Something was coming.

Something malevolent.

It was just a feeling—but she couldn't ignore it.

CHAPTER
46

The Secret in the Tunnels

Belford couldn't shake the feeling that the train should have been free from the dead-zone of the desert by now. He had no idea of the position of the moon, but since recovering from the Goblikan drugs he was yet to feel the comforting embrace of his connection to the Power. It wasn't just that he was cut off—he couldn't sense any matter markers present in the earth around the train at all, nor in the train itself—his amplified senses were gone. He didn't want to jump to any conclusions just yet, but the absence was becoming increasingly worrying. He feared that they had all been Inhibited by the Goblikan drugs.

They were still at the mercy of Wilgoblikan. His deal had been made with Ethan—to return the lord to Erotos in exchange for the antidote to his psychic castration. Eventually, Wilgoblikan would return to the train car, and when he did, he would find Ethan literally castrated, and no longer amongst the living. Whatever his reaction, Belford and company were no longer interested in the status quo. When he arrived, they would make the first move—escape, and retake control.

A plan was hatched.

When the train screeched to a crawling stop, Vera and Arlin crouched on either side of the locked door and waited while Belford, Ader, and Grine all stood to block Ethan's corpse from view with their bodies.

A key turned in the lock. The rusty door squealed opened. "We've got a cave-in ahead," announced Wilgoblikan. "I've brought some corn-feed and a jug of water to tide you all over while we wait for the Whunes to clear the track." He held up a worn burlap sack filled with the corn-feed, more suited for cattle than humans, as he made a sweeping glance across the blank faces before him. A hefty jug of water sat against the tunnel wall at his back. "It shouldn't take too long, the tunnel is intact, only part of the track is covered—a couple days' delay at most." He stepped further into the compartment, holding up the sack, searching for anyone eager enough to relieve him of it. His eyes drifted down to the bloody mess at their feet. Arlin and Vera made their moves. It was too late for Wilgoblikan to retreat. He grunted as they grabbed him from behind. Arlin hooked in around his neck, securing him in a chokehold so that Vera could relieve him of his keys.

Once Wilgoblikan ceased his struggles, Vera peeked her head out of the train car. "It's clear, for now," she said. The sounds of Whunes shifting through rubble could be heard ahead in the darkness.

Wilgoblikan's eyes slid back and forth between Ethan's corpse and Belford in quiet resignation. "The Whunes are not of my making," he said. "They will not stand down. I very much doubt any of you will survive against them without the Power."

Belford narrowed his eyes. "Did the drugs Inhibit us?" he asked pointedly.

"It's disconcerting, isn't it—being Powerless?" asked Wilgoblikan. His infuriating grin made Belford want to slap him. Arlin flexed his arm, choking him more tightly for a moment. "No, it's not the drugs," he grunted. "There are strange shiftings of the Power at these depths—it has become inaccessible—a recent phenomenon, currently under investigation. Returning to the surface should clear you right up."

It didn't make any sense to Belford. He knew from his memories of the distant past that the expansion of the matter markers could be controlled by the Virus Replication Protocol, but the technology to interface with the protocol should have died with the end of his era.

A dead-zone like the desert, but only at an arbitrary depth in the Earth's crust....

It was a mystery Belford hadn't the time to unravel.

"How many Whunes are out there?" asked Grine.

Wilgoblikan ignored the question. "We can make the same deal," he said to Belford. "It doesn't have to end like this. I care not who grants me back my abilities, just so long as my capacity is returned."

Belford stared into Wilgoblikan's yellow eyes. "I can strike that deal," he said. "I will be the new commander of the Ver'konus, after all." He gestured to the floor, doing his best to not show any emotion as he spoke. He didn't expect Wilgoblikan to be afraid of him, but he hoped the evil bastard might respect him more if he thought he'd killed Ethan to usurp him.

Wilgoblikan returned a callus, calculating gaze.

"I'll level with you," said Belford. "We *really* don't want to be locked in this compartment any longer. I think we can all agree, the sooner we get to Erotos the better."

Wilgoblikan nodded slowly.

"We must be getting close by now. Exactly how far out would you say we are?"

Wilgoblikan wrung his hands together. "Not far. A day or two on foot to the final station."

"The same as the delay," said Belford.

Wilgoblikan's gaze shifted down to Belford's hands for a moment. "If you swear to the deal, I will lead you around the Whunes. There is a side-passage we can take." He cocked his head, measuring Belford's eagerness.

Belford felt like he was in the middle of a staring contest. "I will see that you receive the antidote to your Inhibitor, just so long as the Power truly does return to us when we get out of this damn tunnel," he said. "I swear to it."

Wilgoblikan's eyes wandered away from Belford, sliding across each of the travelers in turn before finally settling upon Vera for a long moment. He exhaled sharply through his nostrils before looking back over at Belford. "Then I will be your guide," he said. "We can bypass this section entirely. The side-tunnel is several leagues back—that's our best bet."

Belford nodded in agreement of the plan.

"Will you let go of my neck already?" Wilgoblikan complained to Arlin.

Belford nodded.

Arlin grunted in distaste before releasing his grip.

The old Goblikan got in line with the rest of the travelers as they exited the compartment. Vera used Wilgoblikan's key to re-lock the door behind them. She had a distant look in her eyes.

Belford paused beside her. He took her hand in his own. "Everything's going to be alright," he said.

She met his eyes but maintained her stoic expression. She still had the hilt of her Talus Shard clasped in her left palm, allowing her to hide away inside. "I know that," she said, brushing off his words of reassurance. She pulled her hand away from him, but not before he noticed a dark crusting of dried blood around several of her cuticles.

Belford cringed. Wilgoblikan was very perceptive. He must have notice the blood as well. He knew who really killed Ethan.

They continued on in silence, slinking away with everyone else past the row of train cars. The group picked up their pace once they were clear of the caboose, moving briskly down the dark tunnel until the train was out of sight, lost to the dense gloom. Ader and Grine each had one hand on the water jug, hoisting the vital resource up between them as they shuffled along. Belford and Wilgoblikan carried lanterns at the lead. They kept the flames dialed down low to avoid any undue attention as they hurried back in the direction from which the train had come. Everyone's shadows were cast long on the tunnel wall. The sounds of the Whunes laboring away in the distance continued to ring out down the long tube as hollow echoes that diminished as their distance from the train grew. The scrapes and clangs of the Whunes' tools persisted until they reached the side-passage of which Wilgoblikan had spoken.

The branching tunnel didn't have a train track running through it like the main passage did. It was extremely tight, at times forcing the entourage to walk single file. Belford got the impression that they were in a natural cavern system—he couldn't imagine the purpose of such a tight passage otherwise. Its direction was meandering, leaving blind curves and dark corners. The terrain was rugged with many inclines and declines that slowed their progress. A claustrophobic waist-high stretch brought everyone to their knees. Belford shifted the lantern ahead of him before shimmying along behind it through the tightest point.

"It gets wider ahead," assured Wilgoblikan. "We are approaching the cause of the restriction in the Power—an ancient Artifact from a bygone era."

After everyone was through the crawling section, the cave did indeed widen. Talk of an Artifact settled Belford's internal questions about the missing matter markers. As the cavern expanded, a faint glow lit their path forward. An audible hum vibrated through the rock beneath their feet. The Goblikans had excavated the area, their Whunes chipping away at the cavern wall with pickaxes. Evidence of their venture littered the cave floor. Through a chiseled-out hole, a glowing relic shined like a giant iridescent pearl—a perfect sphere, white like the full moon, just about the width of a train car.

"What *is* that?" asked Belford.

"The ancients placed these devices all across Aragwey," said Wilgoblikan. "We discovered this one here years ago. There's many like it buried deep in the earth all across the nation. They were dark until recently. The real question is *why are they all turning on?*"

In the short time they spent staring at the glowing Artifact Belford could have sworn the shine grew slightly in intensity. The energy field disabling the matter markers was becoming stronger.

They left the jumbo-sized Artifact behind them, continuing on through the cave as it looped back around towards the main tunnel. Artifacts cutting off the Power beneath Aragwey was exactly the sort of thing Belford didn't want to have to worry over. He wasn't the commander of the Ver'konus yet, but the path ahead was obvious. If the Power went out across Aragwey, the whole nation would become vulnerable. They'd be plunged into chaos. He doubted the existing institutions would be able to maintain their stranglehold on the land without the Power to back them up. Even the Mark of Kings on his arm would be useless if he was no more than an ordinary man.

When they reached the main tunnel on the other side of the collapse, Belford pushed the group onward as fast as their feet would allow. Without the presence of the matter markers, his mind was silent for the first time in ages. He was free of all the extra-sensory detail that the Power usually afforded him. Unfortunately, it felt more like being blind than being free. He'd grown so accustom to feeling his surroundings with his abilities. He couldn't shake the lingering feeling that their time was running short. He just wanted the journey to be over.

CHAPTER
47

Luraru's Bite

Rylin sat low in Raljaska's saddle. Many of the tunnels in the depths of Sultrim were too tight for him to ride in comfort. He had to press himself against the prickly fur on the back of Raljaska's neck to stop from scraping his head along the ceiling as the bear lumbered ahead on her patrol. Her three cubs—Kamila, Besel, and Ashran—frolicked behind her. Raljaska had opted to keep her cubs close at paw as the threat of the Goblikans drew ever nearer.

Their patrol route was to end down at the Endless Spring. The electrically charged underground lake was already at full capacity. The rapidly spinning rings of the Great Device had filled the basin to the brim with invisible energy. The charge overflowed into the air. Rylin could feel the buzz of the current even at a distance—a static tingle that flowed across his skin. The effect was all encompassing within Sultrim's depths. When the moon was up, Rylin could sense the vast pool of energy like a beacon calling out to him, just begging to be

354

touched. Fortunately, he knew better than to mess around with something so powerful. The energy store was too vast for him to have any hope of controlling it. Pure potential, spiraling in chaos.

Ma'freit was still down at the spring, continuing to track the Goblikans' positions with her telepathic abilities. Somehow the pool helped her reach farther with her mind. The Goblikans had come close to breaching the city across multiple sectors, stopping just shy each time. Their tunneling was erratic. Whether they were lost or simply toying with the psychic bear was a matter of debate. Rylin assumed the Goblikans were waiting until moonrise to begin their assault.

Ma'freit commanded the Paerto'sul's defense of the lowest levels, sending out timed patrols to the most likely points of ingress. The bears made their rounds and came back to the matriarch in a constant churn. Any breach would be reported in quick order. Ma'freit was ready to respond with the full might of the Guardians' forces. A contingent of bears rested along the shore of the Endless Spring basin, awaiting her word. Their fur stood on end from the static charge in the air, making them all look like giant balls of fluff.

Every bear knew their duty to Sultrim. The Guardians of the Sun had stockpiled meat along the wall of the basin—elk, goat, and numerous scrawny hare carcasses—all piled together. There would be no need to hunt while they waited for the Goblikans to arrive. Every bear, young and old, had a role to play.

Raljaska paused at a split in the tunnel and listened for any hint of intruders. Rylin was fairly certain the small opening at their side was the same tunnel he'd used to escaped Tanuk while fleeing with Kamila—the one that spiraled down to the Great Device with its massive spinning rings. He ran his hand along the deep gouge marks within the opening where the bloodthirsty bear had attempted to snag them as they ducked through.

Ashran and Besel stomped about playfully at Rylin's side, biting at each other's ears.

Raljaska growled at the cubs.

The young bears ceased their tussling at once.

Rylin could feel the vibrations of the Great Device rising up through the earth.

"The passage is too narrow for me," said Raljaska. "Climb down and check the integrity of the tunnel." She chose to vocalize the command rather than project the words into Rylin's head through the pearly gems that connected their minds.

Rylin shared a look of concern with Kamila. He threw his leg over the saddle horn and slid down to the tunnel floor. The halberd Artifact was heavy, but he wasn't about to leave the weapon behind. He hefted it free from its nook before proceeding.

"May I go with Rylin?" asked Kamila. "I can help carry *Lu-rar-u*." The young bear growled the guttural name she had given Rylin's halberd—the throaty roar sounded to her like the Artifact's crackling lightning as it echoed up the mountainside, distorted by the wind.

Raljaska huffed out a wordless affirmation. She knew Kamila was competent.

The talisman around Rylin's neck lost its connection to Raljaska as he stepped away from the great bear. Kamila pushed her backside up against the halberd pole, helping Rylin lift it into the air. They started down the narrow tunnel together.

"When you reach the human halls, follow the corridor away from the Great Device," said Raljaska. "We shall meet you where the path allows for my size."

Rylin was glad to have the weapon. As heavy as Luraru was, knowing it could release a powerful blast of lightning even with the moon down gave Rylin a sense of security that fueled his bravery. He didn't enjoy the close confines of the tunnel, but he had traversed it before and knew where he was going.

The heat from the Great Device brought sweat to his brow. It was laborious towing Luraru along even with Kamila's help. They kept the tip pointed forward and ready to attack, though the tunnel was exactly as it had appeared the last time they came through during their escape from Tanuk. The heightened vibrations of the Great Device made Rylin's teeth rattle as they drew nearer to the contraption.

At the end of the chute-like tunnel the hallways of the human-sized sanctuary opened up around them. The Great Device was just down the hall—its spinning silver rings blocked the shortest path to the Endless Spring basin. Rylin and Kamila followed the main hallway as Raljaska had instructed. They were in the lowest halls of Sultrim. It wasn't until they passed the final chamber and scooted into another narrow tunnel that Rylin's worst fear came true.

The earth began to shake.

He was certain the ceiling was going to come down on top of him.

A grinding sound grew louder as the ground rumbled in a violent timbre. It was clear that this quake was not caused by an Echo. Kamila yelped in terror as the tunnel split wide open above them. A dark chasm cracked the compressed Calvenite flakes that formed the plaster of the tunnel. At their backs in the final chamber, the floor fell away—a sinkhole into the Goblikan tunnels.

A jagged mining bit whirred, protruding into the cavity of the chamber from out of the hole in the floor. The large drill blasted a thick cloud of Calvenite dust into the air. Rylin braced himself against the side of the tunnel as the stale wind hit him in the face. As soon as the shifting motion ceased, he whipped Luraru around to face the heavy machinery. The metal teeth of the drill stopped churning as an unseen operator realized they'd hit a pocket of air. The equipment rolled back beneath the floor. The machinery fell completely silent, leaving the constant vibration of the Great Device as the only remaining sound.

Rylin could feel his heart pounding against his rib cage. He tried to steady himself, but fear gripped his chest. "Run on ahead," he whispered into Kamila's fuzzy ear, "you have to warn everyone!"

Kamila didn't argue with him. She bolted onward through the cracked tunnel as fast as her furry feet would carry her. Rylin stayed still, waiting anxiously as a sour stink began to waft up from the hole. It was the foul odor of Whunes, lurking just below in the darkness. A series of cackling hoots rang out—to Rylin's ear they sounded almost like a pack of weird dogs. A grating screech was followed by chuckling laughter. A spindly stick of an arm reached up through the hole, towing a gangly body cautiously through the cloud of dust.

Rylin had never seen a Whune before, but this was not at all how he'd imagined them. Judging from Javic's stories, the Whunes he'd encountered were an entirely different sort. Rylin held off his attack, waiting for the spider-like creature to emerge fully into view. The beast was a tall target, but it was not a wide one. Rylin began to draw energy into Luraru. The creature sensed the danger. Its head immediately swiveled to face him, fixing him with its beady yellow eyes. An earsplitting shriek escaped a toothy maw—the terrible creature's unusual head split open vertically from the bottom, its jaws unhinging and spreading wide to form a grotesque gullet.

Its insectoid appearance filled Rylin with a jittery, instinctual terror that tainted his aim. The Whune's jaws snapped shut again as Rylin unleashed Luraru's built-up energy. The streak missed low between the creature's legs. The Whune sprang up and speared its pointed limbs into the rotted ceiling. It didn't stop moving, scampering upside-down across the ceiling towards Rylin with deadly speed. The vertical slit of its jaw stretched open again; another deafening shriek rattled Rylin's brain. He reignited Luraru's arc, sweeping it back and forth across the tunnel. The Whune continued straight up the crack and out of sight within the narrow gap above his head.

That's not good....

Rylin got a glimpse of the creepy bugger as it wriggled nearer to him across the rugged ceiling chasm. He attempted to pivot Luraru higher, but he couldn't quite get the halberd into the steep angle he needed in order for it to be effective. Realizing Rylin's disadvantage, the Whune stayed up high, just out of reach of Luraru's tip, cackling menacingly all the while.

One of the creature's pointy arms came jabbing down at Rylin's face. He thought it missed him at first, but then a sting settled into his flesh, burning the length of his cheekbone. A thin trickle of blood dribbled out and ran down his chin. Luraru wasn't long enough to fend off the gangly monster!

Rylin ducked down as low as he possibly could, crouching over his ankles. Two more spindly Whunes arose from the hole in the floor. Only now did Rylin realize just how perilous his situation actually was. He swept the beam of the halberd back towards the hole, burning through the legs of one of the incoming Whunes. Its limbless torso plopped to the floor. It continued to writhe about as its partner dove from the chamber entirely, fleeing the attack in the opposite direction.

In the quick moment Rylin took his eyes off the Whune above him, the thin creature made its move. Rylin tried to bring Luraru back up again, but the beam dissipated before he could fix his aim. The glowing tip of the blade went dark as the last of the ambient energy in the vicinity was expelled through the Artifact's point.

It was Rylin's turn to shriek as the Whune lunged down at him. A glorious ball of dark fur darted over his head from behind, smashing into the side of the Whune and taking it to the tunnel floor just in front of Rylin.

Kamila!

She chomped down on the Whune's arm and wrenched her jaws viciously from side to side. The thin limb severed entirely within her grip, tearing free at the creature's shoulder joint. Kamila pulled away from the Whune, spitting out the detached arm like the foul prize it was.

The creature cackled again in response, stabbing at Kamila with all of its remaining limbs at once. One unlucky poke pierced her left wing. Kamila roared out, recoiling in pain from the jab.

Rylin whipped Luraru back down. He couldn't send out another blast of energy, but the weapon still had a sharp point. He drove the blade forward, sending the tip straight into the Whune's skull. It didn't cease its struggles until he'd pushed concernedly deep into its brain.

"I thought I told you to run!" cried Rylin. He wasn't really complaining.

"Mama's just ahead," said Kamila. "Let's go!"

Rylin didn't waste time looking back. He could already hear more Whunes clawing their way up through the breach. A painful numbness in Rylin's hands helped him realize he'd frozen the tips of his fingers to Luraru's grip. He could barely feel his hands at all! His fingers wouldn't unclench from the icy handle. Kamila got back under the halberd pole and dragged Rylin and Luraru up the final curves of the tunnel.

The Artifact's hungering consumption did not combine well with the enclosed space of the tunnel. Luraru had a bite to her. Rylin gritted his teeth. The sting in his hands focused his mind. He needed to reach Raljaska. Mama bear's jaws were five times larger than her baby's.

Kamila slowed, leaving Rylin to drag Luraru onward unaided. She swiped at the first Whune to catch up with them. The young bear roared out, the cry echoing through the tunnel.

"Keep going!" she insisted.

Rylin focused on maintaining his footing across the uneven surface. When he rounded the final bend, he was greeted by Raljaska's muzzle peering down at him from the end of the tunnel. He felt an extra burst of energy in his muscles as he made eye contact with the hyper focused bear. A thought appeared in his mind.

Lead them straight into my mouth.

Raljaska stepped to the side of the opening, vanishing from Rylin's sight.

Kamila caught back up behind him. She nudged him onward, propelling him through his final steps before Raljaska's ambush position. Raljaska was waiting with mouth agape, ready to deliver a deadly chomp. Kamila trotted out behind Rylin, finally free from the tight confines. They both turned to watch as the closest Whune stuck its head out of the opening only to have it promptly bitten off by the giant bear. Raljaska crushed its skull like a ripe melon.

Rylin wished he hadn't watched. The sight and sound would stick with him.

Now that they were away from the pocket of depleted energy, he was able to fire Luraru's lightning again. His fingers ached worse as the energy-hungry Artifact unleashed a devastating bolt down the narrow tunnel. No more Whunes emerged from the opening when he was finished.

"Can you fly?" Raljaska asked Kamila upon noticing her cub's injured wing.

The veiny membrane spurted with blood as the little bear flapped hard enough to lift herself into the air. "I can do it," she grunted.

"Go," said Raljaska. "Find your brothers. They await on a high perch."

Kamila took the dismissal in stride, staying aloft as she darted down the hallway in the direction of the nearby hub chamber.

Rylin struggled to free his hands from Luraru's grip. He hoped he hadn't done any permanent damage to himself. He climbed into Raljaska's saddle, ignoring his discomfort as he latched onto the saddle horn with his frozen fingers.

A nearby roar indicated there were more bears nearby. Raljaska turned to face the sound. "We must go," she growled. "There are many breaches."

Rylin sank deep into Raljaska's fur. His nose filled with the scent of her musk as he clenched his fingers amongst her oily bristles. Her warmth sank into his fingertips. The ache began to tingle. The sensation grew more painful as the bear's body heat revitalized his nerves.

Hold on tight. Raljaska's words permeated his mind.

He squeezed Luraru to his side within the nook of his elbow. His frosty fingers clenched deep into Raljaska's neck as the bear staggered forward. Her lumbering strides shook the corridor. She took towards the hub chamber at full speed.

Aim true.

The massive hub chamber sparkled with a million distant lights. The city was fully roused with the energy of the Great Device. The lights along the bridges overhead looked like constellations upon a night sky.

More spindly Whunes—this time with fleshy wings attached at their backs—darted through the hollow mountain. The air was abuzz with the awkward creatures. A swarm in the distance looked like mosquitoes with their limbs dangling beneath them. They were ferrying stolen Power Artifacts back to the floor of the depths. Raljaska extended her wings and leapt from the Calvenite-flake dunes. She was already fixed on one of the flying Whunes.

Rylin breathed deeply in through his nose. He needed to steady his heart. He felt Raljaska's intentions. As the bear tucked her head, Rylin unleashed Luraru's rage. The Whune fell out of the air, its body fried by the arc. The creature was already dead. Its dangling legs went rigid as it spiraled down to the dunes.

Raljaska twisted through the air, searching for their next target. Rylin's eyes swept across the floor of the depths. Several fires burned. More drills had burrowed through the compressed Calvenite floor. A steady stream of stout and muscled Whunes rushed out from the Goblikan tunnels and into the teeth and claws of more than a dozen Guardians.

The bears tore at the fleshy brutes. It was the same across all of the incursion sites. The Whunes were armed with pickaxes and sledgehammers—hardly the best weapons against the armored bears. It looked like a feast more than a battle.

The stick-bug Whunes with their stolen Artifacts were quick, but they had nowhere to go. The Guardians stood strong, astutely blocking all the exits. Rylin blasted several more of the awkward creatures out of the air from afar.

Down below, the muscled Whunes just kept marching out. The Paerto'sul could hardly keep up with the flow. Ma'freit's mate, Corshen, was positioned directly above the nearest tunnel, swatting at the Whunes like fish in a barrel. Rylin recognized him from his gleaming armor—it appeared almost blue as it reflected back the pale bioluminescence of the hub chamber. A flying Whune shot through the gap, barely evading Corshen's claws as it darted up into the hub. Raljaska tucked her wings, dropping like a hawk towards her prey. Rylin didn't have a chance to attack with Luraru. Raljaska struck the Whune against her armored chest. Rylin was jarred by the force of the disgusting splat. The bear spread her wings wide just in time to catch their descent. She landed with a thud beside Corshen.

Raljaska roared out an impassioned greeting to the other bears before thrashing the nearest Whune with her sharp claws. The Guardians had all the Whunes corralled again in quick succession. Rylin's efforts weren't needed, though he did manage to spear one Whune on Luraru's point before the slaughter abruptly ended. They'd barely gotten started when the influx of Whunes ceased—not a single beast more emerged from the tunnel's orifice. Across the hub, other fights still raged on.

Corshen huffed out a breathy snarl. "I can see more waiting below." He poked his head deeper into the hole. "What are you waiting for? Come up and die!" The opening was too tight for any of the bears to enter. Corshen shoved one of his massive paws down as deep as he could reach, batting at the Whunes. He yelped, withdrawing a bloodied paw. The elder bear backed away from the opening as a bulbous figure shuffled up through the pass. It was a blubbery lump of a Whune strapped with a suit of dark metal spikes. Its whole body was covered head-to-toe with the wicked prongs, like some sort of deranged porcupine.

Corshen batted at the suit, testing the strength of the dark metal. The spikes held firm, not bending under the force of Corshen's paw. The Whune twisted defiantly, pricking the old bear with one of its sharp points. Other bears made attempts as well, prodding desperately at the spiny foe. None managed to lay a paw on the Whune's body before being pricked. The Whune shuffled around with heavy, deliberate steps. It reached down into the tunnel opening and retrieved a spear from one of its cohorts waiting below. The Whune shifted to face Corshen again, forcing the Paerto'sul back with repeated jabs from the weapon.

Unarmored Whune's flooded the opening once again. With the bears' line broken, the tide of battle shifted rapidly. More flying Whunes darted from the hole, streaking up towards the Artifact troves.

Ignore them—you must stop the fat one.

Rylin didn't need to be told twice. Raljaska knelt down low on her front paws giving Rylin the depth of angle he needed to strike the rotund beast with Luraru's lightning. He didn't even have to aim. The brilliant flash that burst forth was drawn to the metal suit. Rylin unleashed the full electrical flow at his disposal. A blinding spire lit up the entire hub. Rylin diverted his eyes to save his vision. The ceiling of the vast chamber was visible to him for a brief moment for the first time—a distant gray haze. There were more bridges than he'd ever imagined. He continued to feed Luraru's rage, not relenting until the troublesome Whune was nothing more than a blackened husk. The metal suit fell into a spiky pile as the body crumbled away.

"Good human!" Corshen exclaimed. "Now go stop those buzzards from stealing the treasures!"

Rylin's fingers twitched at the cold. They were numb again. He knew he'd be hurting later. There was no time to worry about that now. Raljaska leapt into the air, chasing after the pack of flying Whunes.

Rylin released a blast from Luraru too early. The pack scattered as the miss streaked across the hub. Rylin grimaced at the sting in his hand. He clung onto Raljaska's saddle as the bear began to maneuver after the nearest Whune.

They all continued to climb, whizzing by a series of dark bridges. Raljaska got in close, ducking her head at the proper moment for Rylin to blast their target out of the air. The Whune's body crumpled against Raljaska's chest as she flew through the tumbling corpse. She swerved towards the next closest Whune. Just as Rylin was about release his shot, a series of tiny roars pierced the chamber. Raljaska's ears wiggled. She knew the cries of her babies. The mama bear twisted away from the pack of Artifact thieves to focus on her cubs.

Rylin's eyes weren't good enough to locate them in the gloom of the cavern. Raljaska was fixated. She burst forth with frantic flaps of her wings, letting out a monstrous roar of her own. A froth of saliva burst from her jaws, splattering against Rylin's cheek as he clung desperately to her saddle. Once they got closer to the cubs, Rylin finally spotted the three young bears perched upon a dimly lit platform at the side of the hub. The babies were attempting to stop more flying Whunes from exiting a passageway with arms already filled with Artifacts. The cubs meant well, but they were severely outnumbered and already surrounded. The gangly Whunes pranced around the small bears, stabbing at them with their devilishly pointed arms.

Rylin couldn't strike with Luraru without risking hitting the cubs, but in a moment of divine fortune the entire breadth of the Power's offerings became available to him. Beyond the confines of the hollow mountain the moon began its rise above the distant horizon. Rylin knew it in an instant as his senses sharpened to a fine point.

His instincts drove his attack. He whipped up a fierce wind that turned the Whunes' focus away from the cubs. He struck out at them one at a time, calcifying their internal fluids to end their existence. The bodies went rigid—literally cast in stone. It was the quickest way Rylin could think to dispatch them.

Ashran bit onto a petrified Whune's arm. "Ouch! My teeth!" he grumbled, releasing the rock hard limb from his jaws.

In mere moments, Rylin had managed to turn every Whune present into grotesque statues. Kamila erupted with a jubilant squeal.

Good Rider. The whisper of a thought caught him by surprise. *Your heart is brave and merciless, just like a Paerto'sul's.*

Rylin felt a twist of embarrassment at Raljaska's praise. He could feel her gratitude flowing across their connection. He'd only done what was necessary to save the cubs.

That is exactly the point. You are one of us now.

Rylin sensed a familial pride behind her words—such a simple declaration. Their bond bloomed as their mutual trust reached new heights. It was a comforting feeling.

Raljaska craned her neck, gazing down into the depths. There was more work to be done. The Whunes' attack showed no sign of relenting. Now that Rylin could use the Power, the Whunes didn't stand a chance. He wondered how long it would take the Goblikans to join the fray of battle now that the moon had risen....

The risks were plentiful, but the Power's draw made him feel unstoppable. He shook off his knowledge that delusions of grandeur were perhaps the most common side-effect of consorting with the Power. Only a hair of self-doubt remained within him as Raljaska tucked her wings, diving back towards the dusty dunes below.

CHAPTER
48

Vexed

The merry misfits under Livian's command were the very definition of expendable. In lieu of executions, the Crazies were tasked with fending off the impending barbarian siege forces. Operation: Wizards on Lizards was afoot. The eclectic band was soon to be tested—their mettle tempered by combat. Livian's most competent converts were to ride within iron baskets attached to harnesses atop the backs of Dhron's terrible bipedal lizards. The thunderous beasts with their nubby arms were still hidden away beneath the pyramid's promenade within Dhron's secret prison lair. They were positioned for a quick release into the streets of Tavallon.

Whune runners, grown from prisoners, had been draped with shimmering fabrics. When the time was right, they would be sent sprinting across the city with the giant beasts in tow. Wherever the barbarians chose to concentrate their smaller, wall-hopping lizard mounts, Dhron's abominations would soon be deployed. The best part: Thanks to a set of spherical Power

367

Artifacts plucked from Dhron's special collection, the great beasts were effectively immune from direct manipulation with the Power. They could only be slain by physical assault or environmental attacks once the moon rose and added the Power to the scope of the battlefield. Their Goblikan riders were present to counter such possibilities.

Dhron managed to grow five more beasts in the time it took the barbarians to arrive upon their stoop. No one knew if it would be enough. The beasts were all slightly smaller than Stomper—still an impressive transformation from the mere chickens they had been just days before. Dhron's understanding of genetics had been refined through experimentation. His creations were as magnificent as they were terrible. Livian had to admit his scientific knowledge outpaced her own, even with her vast understanding of fungi and their varied effects on the chemistry of mammalian brains.

Dhron combined his work with the wits of civilizations past when he fed each lizard a Power-stopping Artifact sphere. Livian did not envy the team tasked with tracking down, collecting, and sieving through the heaping mounds of droppings left behind by the monstrous creations in order to retrieve the devices.

The enemy was knocking at Tavallon's walls. The barbarians stood beyond the city limits to the north. Their rhythmic chants were meant to psychologically disturb. It was clear they were waiting for the moon to rise before properly beginning their siege. The enemy was operating under the presumption that the Power would bolster an advantage to their forces. Nal disagreed. Dhron's abominations were merely the first surprise that was in store. The Night Hawks stood by at the edge of the pyramid's pinnacle balcony, waiting to base-jump and glide across the city in order to provide reinforcements as needed. If all else failed, Livian's spores stood as their last line of defense—Nal gave her permission to use them again to subdue the entire region, but only as an act of last resort. She'd spent the greater part of the previous week producing endless canisters of her lovely creations.

Sir Kierington had been given charge over the detonator. A long strand of canisters lined the pyramid's steep outer walls. With the press of a plunger, the knight could blanket the city with Livian's mind-controlling mist. Only those prepared with oxygen tanks and masks would be able to resist her will.

"You won't need to channel at all," said Nal as he adjusted the heavy tank on his back.

Livian rolled her eyes. "Are you sure you will be able to maintain lift with all that extra weight on you?"

"I flew carrying you, didn't I?"

Livian crossed her arms, unamused.

"I'm serious, though," said Nal. "Standing orders are to pop your beads if you channel without permission."

"Don't worry," said Livian, "I'll just wave these signs at any barbarians if they get too close." Livian was to be the director of the Whune runners. She had a dozen wooden placards with symbols representing the different sectors of the city painted upon them.

Nal ignored her sarcasm as he made for a table of refreshments placed out by the kitchen staff.

Livian gazed across the dusty city. The streets could have used a good rain. To the north, somewhere beneath the wide promenade, the tongueless Klain and Terrible Tora—Livian's squad leaders—were standing by. Despite their histories, they were the most reliable of her converts. Tora kept host of Merrick Firefist and a newer recruit named Harlock who had been banished to the Crazies after failing to secure the Governor's mansion on the night most of the Goblikan command had been poisoned. Meanwhile, Klain kept watch over the wolf twins. Altogether, they would be riding the five freshly grown giant lizards plus Stomper. The rest of her checkered crew was staggered across the city with spyglasses locked on her position atop the pyramid. At her signal they would release the Whune runners and direct them wherever she signaled.

Their strategy was sound and their forces prepared and ready. They needed only wait for the barbarians to make the first move so that they could counter. Tavallon would not be easily occupied.

As steadfast as Livian tried to portray herself, she was a knot of nerves within. It felt like she was back on her first day at the Academy. In combat, victory was never certain. In the final minutes before moonrise, she found herself too anxious to take her seat by the painted placards. She didn't know how Nal could eat at time like this! The big galoot had a plate full of lamb shanks and a bucket of clams at his side. He kept slamming the suckers back like he hadn't eaten in a week! The fact that he was wearing his winged suit—fully prepared to be going airborne at a moment's notice—was a level of audacity that repulsed Livian.

To hurtle through the air with a belly full of clams!

Her stomach hurt just watching him!

"You can't eat either?" asked Sir Kierington, cupping the egg-shaped Artifact that could end her life in the palm of his hand like some sort of meaningless knickknack to fidget with.

"We may as well start calling him Seagull-man Nal," she muttered under her breath.

Sir Kierington chuckled, sloshing his goblet of wine as he shook with the sudden laughter. The blood-red swill splashed to the tile floor, barely missing their feet. "He really is eating those like there's no tomorrow, isn't he? Though, there is no guarantee of tomorrow, I do suppose."

"Some men like to pack in the protein before a battle, whilst others just seek to numb themselves with alcohol, *I do suppose*," mocked Livian.

Sir Kierington's lips pinched up at the jab. "Do you know why King Garrett kept me around? It's the same reason the Goblikans entrust me to watch over you. I'm not a wizard. I can't melt faces with my thoughts."

"Is it your charming personality?" asked Livian.

The fool smiled back at her sass. "It's because when the moment calls for it, everyone knows I will do exactly what is necessary—no matter if that's pressing this button to eviscerate your body, or arming that plunger over there to blanket the whole city in another abominable mist. At the end of the day, I'm reliable."

Livian turned her back on Sir Kierington and signaled a servant over. "Could you bring me a cup of chamomile tea, please?" She needed something to ease her stomach.

"You know, I can feel your pulse through this," said Sir Kierington. He was right behind her, practically breathing down her neck! "I can feel more than just your intentions. I know your every impulse. Your emotions betray you."

Livian turned slowly to face him, not willing to let him fluster her composure. Sir Kierington held the dimpled egg in his hand, gently caressing it. He always had to shove that thing in her face—showing her who was in control. "My impulses?" she spat. "What exactly is it that you want from me? Do you truly take such joy in this antagonization? Do you have nothing better to be doing with your time?" she asked, maintaining eye contact sharp enough to spook a flock of geese.

"You like to play games, don't you?"

She threw her hands up. "Those beads are plugged inside of me deeper than any man should ever hold domain over a woman. I know you don't agree with my views on the world, but despite the contempt I hold for you and everything you believe to be right and just that I know to actually be wretched and rotten—despite it all!—I have not disobeyed. I have taken every command, done every deed, filled every canister. So do tell me, how have my impulses betrayed me? I'm dying to know, really! Do you think I cannot see the lay of the land from so high in the clouds? I know why the Goblikans keep me around too."

Sir Kierington's jaw hung agape.

"I cannot speak towards your *reliability*, but I am here because I can do things no one else can—things no one else has ever even imagined possible!"

A smile slowly crept across Sir Kierington's lips as she continued to berate him.

"With enough time, I will control the hearts and minds of everyone. And I mean everyone! I can make the world love me. Don't think that I don't see straight through that smug look on your face! Deep down you're just a frightened little boy lost in the deep dark woods."

"Oh, yeah? What does that make you then?"

"I'm the wolf stalking your shadow in the moonlight. You fear me—and rightfully so! You keep me muzzled like a dog because you know what I would do if you ever let go of that leash. You—a man whose first name I've never bothered to learn! *Sir Kierington, knight of some dead king's court, thou who 'gets shit done so well that everyone relies on him.'* How does it feel to be the one person standing between me and my final judgment over all of this wretchedness?"

The knight reached out and clasped her hand in his own. He bent at the waist, drawing her fingers up to his lips where he planted a small kiss. "Arimond," he said. "My name's Arimond—Ari for short."

Livian stared back at him quizzically.

"I can feel everything you're feeling. You needn't worry so much over the barbarians. Tavallon will not fall. If any get too close, be comforted to know I am quite adept with my sword."

Livian glanced down briefly.

"That wasn't a euphemism!" he chuckled. "I trained at the Elswani Monastery for years. I've lived in your lands, seen the truest values of your people."

Livian wasn't falling for his steely blue eyes.

"I admit I did judge you harshly for your crimes against my kinsmen—Compulsion is even a crime to your Arcanum! Now, though, that I can see inside of you, wolf or not, I know how much you constantly deflect. Only one of us is really a scared child hiding inside."

Livian swallowed at a lump in her throat—oh, how he vexed her! The servant she'd asked for tea returned. He handed her a cup and had her hold it as he poured from a kettle with a long spout. The soothing scent of the chamomile wafted up into the stale evening air.

The Power called out to her suddenly as the moon began its rise. Denying its song was the hardest thing she had to do every day when the moon first crested the distant hills. Even the threat of the embedded beads was barely enough to suppress her urge to latch on and take it for all it was worth. She missed that embrace when it was gone. She wished she could take an intoxicating dip in the Power's ravishing waters.

"Oh, look over there," said Sir Kierington, "the moon's finally risen." He thought he was so suave.

For someone so *reliable*, Livian wished *Ari* was a little more predictable. Every time she thought she had him pegged, he had to go and act in such a terribly unexpected manner. It was enough to cause confusion within a poor woman!

CHAPTER 49

Meat Grinder

Across the depths of Sultrim, the Paerto'sul vehemently battled the intruders under their mountain. With the Power heightening Rylin's senses he was able to observe the battlefield in precise detail during Raljaska's descent. More spike-covered Whunes had emerged whilst they were up high. Rylin knew he should be tending to his frostbitten fingers, but pressure from Raljaska across their bond kept him focused on the greater needs of the city. Numbness had returned to his digits… at least that made the pain easy to ignore. Too many flying Whunes had already successfully pilfered entire sacks of Power Artifacts despite the best efforts of the bears. The guardians grew more frustrated with every additional treasure that slipped from their collective grasp. They fought desperately to contain their losses.

Rylin knew the spike-covered brutes in their metal suits would be easy to fry with Luraru, but his fingers ached at the thought of firing up the energy-sapping Artifact even one more time. With the full range of the Power at his disposal, he figured he could find a more expedient resolution to the problem—one that wouldn't hurt his fingers quite so much. He could see all the brutes from his vantage point perched atop Raljaska. The duo soared beside one of the lower bridges in the central sector of the hub chamber while Rylin prepared himself mentally to attack with the Power. Unlike the Paerto'sul, the Whunes were not immune to direct manipulation. Rylin could end them now from a distance, before anymore Artifacts slipped through the cracks in the compressed plaster dunes below. He just needed to figure out how he wanted to do it....

He'd calcified the waspy Whunes that had been threatening Raljaska's cubs. It was perhaps an odd choice of attack, but it had certainly proved to be effective. He went with his instincts, beginning the calcification process on the first of the troublesome brutes below. There were eight spike-covered Whunes in total, spread out across the breach sites. One by one, Rylin turned them into statues. It was simple once he put his mind to it. He had impeccably accurate senses through his connection with Raljaska. In effect, he was seeing through her superior eyesight. With their combined senses he reached into the bodies of the Whunes and expanded their skeletons, converting muscle, fat, and ultimately flesh into more bone. The process shrunk them in stature. None remained standing. They all crumpled over before fully solidifying, hardening in place as lumps on the ground rather than the more statuesque poses Rylin had envisioned when he first started out with his experiment. In the end, it mattered not. Each of the spiny fellows now resembled giant sea-urchins, dried out on a beach.

Once all the Whunes were dispatched, Rylin heaped mounds of Calvenite flakes from the nearby dunes into each of the breach holes. He sealed them off, converting the degraded material back into a pristine condition. He imagined he was molding giant corks out of sand. He'd never shifted such large volumes of material with the Power before. Manipulation on such a scale took deep concentration, but also felt exhilarating to achieve. Back in Erotos, initiates were never allowed to partake in such large transmutations. He understood the draw to become a Ver'ati Builder—getting to form grand structures out of the earth. The act of creation gave its own buzz separate from the high of convening with the Power. When he was finished capping the holes, nothing short of the Power itself would be able to break through again. The Goblikan mining equipment wouldn't make so much as a scratch without wizardly intervention.

Whether or not the invaders had gotten what they came for, Rylin hadn't a clue, but he met no Goblikan resistance as he sealed up the holes. The breach sites remained capped and undisturbed as Raljaska completed a lap around the vast chamber.

He'd sealed every breach he was aware of existing apart from one: The hole in the human halls near the Great Device. His concern passed through to Raljaska across their bond. Raljaska swooped back around, gliding towards Corshen. A contingent of bears stood guard beside the first hole Rylin capped, listening for any indication of further digging or magical mayhem below. Corshen laid down flat on his belly beside the Calvenite cork. Several other bears were already similarly collapsed. Rylin assumed they were feeling for vibrations, but after Raljaska landed they were met with a rude truth: The spikes of the brutes had all been coated with poison. Every guardian who had so much as been pricked by a spine was already dead or dying. Frothy saliva dripped from their mouths, soaking into the dry ground. It was already too late. There was nothing Rylin could do to save any of them. Corshen huffed out a final phlegmy breath as he succumbed to the fast acting poison.

Raljaska roared out a pained lament—a cry that was joined by many other guardians all across the depths. The roars echoed throughout the hub chamber in a chorus of thunder as the bears mourned their dead.

I have to seal the last breach alone.... Rylin pushed the thought across to Raljaska.

He sensed hesitancy within the great bear.

Do you doubt me? I can do it!

He had no choice. He was the only one who could fit down the passage.

Raljaska's words boomed across his mind. *It is not your determination I doubt—rather your size. It is difficult to trust such a large task to someone so small. The Great Device must be protected at all costs. You mustn't let the intruders tinker with it!*

The bears were very touchy about their solemn duty to the city.

Despite Raljaska's appreciation of Rylin, she couldn't help but see him as one of her cubs. Rylin felt the protective energy radiating off the great bear through their bond. Raljaska called Kamila down to support him in clearing out the remaining invaders from the human passageways. Rather than seeing it as a vote of no confidence, Rylin was simply glad to have a companion for the dangerous task at hand. The eldest cub soared down from her high perch. Her wing had fully clotted by now and was no longer spraying blood when she flapped it. Fortunately, there was no sign of any Whunes having exited the passage when they arrived at the narrow crack in the wall. The lightning-fried bodies of half a dozen spindly Whunes lined the tunnel beyond where Raljaska dropped him off—the final attack he'd made against them with Luraru had been amply effective. He didn't take Luraru this time. After everything he'd done out in the hub chamber, he was feeling very confident in his abilities with the Power and didn't wish to be weighted down.

They crept quietly through the cracked passageway. Rylin used his connection to the Power to feel ahead for any hints of life. It wasn't until he reached the drill site that he encountered anything living. There were no brutes, only more stickbugs. This time they were much easier to dispatch. Rylin froze them in place with his calcifying attack. He went about sealing off the last hole as soon as they were neutralized. Kamila stood at his side like a loyal hound—her teeth and claws were unnecessary but it was still reassuring to have her along. There was plenty of debris present from the shattered ceiling to use in filling in the hole. He tossed everything down the chute until it piled to the level of the floor—Whune bodies included—and then melted it all down before transmuting and solidifying the material into slate. Finally, he converted the stone into Calvenite, and just like that, all the breaches were capped. There was nothing stopping any Goblikan from tearing it all apart again of course, but Rylin reckoned perhaps coming across a fellow Power-user might make them take pause. They'd been prepared to battle the Paerto'sul, but they weren't expecting a wizard.

He didn't dare think they were gone for good, but he hoped beyond reason that they might take until the spring to regroup before making another attack. By then he would be well on his way down the mountain, or so he hoped. He had empathy for the bears' plight, but ultimately everyone knew this was not his fight—not once the thaw arrived.

Rylin glanced back up the cracked tunnel to where he knew Raljaska was anxiously awaiting their return. He'd been connected to the Power long enough that his over-confidence was fading.

"Mama said to clear all the halls," said Kamila, sensing his reluctance.

Rylin nodded sheepishly. He didn't want Kamila to think him a coward. His concern was his suspicion that the Whunes had pierced precisely into the human halls on purpose. If intentional, it meant they knew the strategic significance of the area. Rylin was only beginning to understand the importance of the Great Device. The rumblings of the spinning machinery drowned out his thoughts as he and Kamila trotted towards it down the long empty hallway. As they got closer to the epicenter, Rylin's skin tingled all over from the flow of charged particles. His hair stood on end. He glanced over at Kamila. She was a ball of pure fluff. They were both awash in the invisible currents.

The silver blur of the device's spinning rings blocked their progression down the main passage. Kamila led him on another way—up a spiraling ramp that encircled the Great Device and led to more human-sized halls above. The sound of voices escaped a central chamber located just above the Great Device. Rylin ducked down in front of the entryway and glanced over at Kamila with wide eyes. She could hear them as well. Several men were talking, but the rumbling vibrations were too loud for Rylin to distinguish their words even with the Power improving his senses.

Kamila suddenly tucked her nubby tail and rolled her eyes sideways at Rylin. "Did you hear what they said?" she murmured.

Rylin shook his head.

"They said they're gunna raise a demon!"

Rylin narrowed his eyes. "A demon?" he asked. "Is that worse than the Whunes?"

Kamila balked at the question. "They are talking about needing blood. Lots of blood." There was great fear in her voice—for a bear, anyway.

The Paerto'sul rarely spoke with much inflection, so Kamila's sharp tone made Rylin take caution. He peered around the corner slowly, attempting to ascertain the layout of the chamber without the Goblikans inside noticing him. There were just two of them, both men, dressed all in black with thick hide cloaks to keep them warm. The walls of the chamber were covered in odd dusty glass panels. Many were cracked—a few were shattered entirely—but some were undamaged, their displays aglow with flashing images and numbers. Most of the symbols were unfamiliar to Rylin. He'd never seen anything like it in his life! The two Goblikans stood in front of one of the rectangular panels. They were arguing as they tapped upon it repeatedly, shifting the displayed information with each press of a finger.

"We must kill them," grumbled Kamila. "But don't damage the controls."

At the center of the chamber a thin railing surrounded a hole in the floor. The blur of the Great Device's rings flashed across the opening. Rylin avoided the hole as he moved into the room. He already knew exactly how he wanted to dispatch the Goblikans. He knew he would be unable to attack them with the Power directly, so he did the next best thing: He ignited their cloaks with a concentrated blast of ambient energy stripped right out of the charged particles in the air. They didn't realize they were on fire at first. The sizzle started small and then expanded rapidly in a flash of flames that enveloped them as wholly as if their cloaks had been doused in alcohol. The two men howled out in surprise as the fire crawled across their pasty skin.

Kamila rushed in simultaneously, leaping on the nearest Goblikan and biting at his flaming face without hesitation. Rylin was worried her fur might ignite, but she managed to pin the man down and tear out his throat without the flames transferring to her. His gurgling cries soon ceased. The other Goblikan, in an act of desperation, tossed his flaming cloak at Rylin before dropping to the floor and rolling about wildly. The hiss of steam suddenly filled the chamber. Rylin's eyes burned as the Goblikan managed to quell the rest of the flames and fill the air with a smokescreen at the same time.

Rylin covered his face as the steam stung his flesh. A hot blast of wind sent him hurtling backwards. He struck his head against the side of the railing, nearly falling into the hole in the floor. The spinning rings hummed their constant churn a mere pace from where he'd landed.

Kamila snarled aggressively. The dark wizard surely had more experience battling with the Power than Rylin, but against Kamila's claws he was just another pin cushion. As he attempted to flee the room, Kamila pounced on him, striking him in the back and knocking him into Rylin. The Goblikan tripped and tumbled headfirst over the railing. The rings of the Great Device devoured him in an instant, turning the hapless Goblikan into a fine red mist. The spray splattered Rylin directly in the face like a wet sneeze.

Kamila rushed to his side, staring down at the bloody smear. The Great Device had become a meat grinder. "You got him!" she exclaimed.

Rylin felt like he was going to be sick. The air had a metallic scent to it now. He didn't want to breathe it in, but it was already in his sinuses.

Beep! Beep! Beep!

A series of loud chirps suddenly sounded from one of the wall displays. Rylin covered his ears with his hands as he looked over at it.

The vibrations coming up from the floor were growing in intensity. The rings of the Great Device began to spin even faster than before. Kamila tucked her tail and scooted from the room in short order. Just as Rylin turned to follow her, he felt like the air had been knocked from his lungs. He fell to his knees once more as he experienced a sickening moment of nausea. It happened abruptly, as fast as water flowing through loose fingers. All his heightened facilities left him all at once. The Power was gone—snatched from his grasp—he knew it was missing without even having to reach out to it.

It was clear from the wall displays that some sort of process had just begun. The result was that the Power was gone. Rylin tried to steady his mind, searching for any inkling of his lost connection, but it was completely absent, as surely as if the moon were missing from the sky. Its departure left a hollow feeling in his gut.

CHAPTER 50

The Crazies

The low-pitched blare of a horn signaled the beginning of the barbarian siege on Tavallon. The horse-sized lizards described in early reports from the coast as "huge geckos" were more like oversized monitor lizards by Livian's gauge as she observed them through her spyglass from atop the pyramid's pinnacle balcony. Still, their thick arms and long necks were nothing to scoff at. The agile creatures were up and over the outer wall and already beginning to devour the frontline of defending soldiers before the rumble of the starting horn finished echoing through the streets.

No amount of soldiers could have protected against the breakneck speed of the incursion. Nal was keeping his Goblikans out of the mix for the moment. They were spread out across various rooftops waiting for the Crazies to have a go at the enemy first before revealing their positions.

With the outer wall overrun, the barbarian wizards drove their reptilian mounts onward towards their primary target:

The most protected location in all of Tavallon—exactly where Livian stood watching the chaos unfold.

The riders were decorated in polished plate armor that gleamed in the daylight. Atop their heads sat horned helmets that gave them ghoulish appearances. As intimidating as they looked, to the battlefield they were nothing more than terrain-agnostic heavy cavalry. The barbarian army had plenty of traditional units as well, but they couldn't climb walls. The rest of the enemy forces were all still dawdling about at range outside the city's fortifications. The Kovani military with their spearmen and archers held strong at the outer doors—the lizards had taken the path of least resistance by scaling the walls.

Livian imagined the gecko riders typically did most of the work for this army, going straight for the head of the city as per their recycled strategy. It was unnerving to watch the strange mounts scamper over buildings and down alleyways as fast as darts. There were several dozen of them inbound all at once. It was difficult to tell the exact count with them popping in and out of sight along their unconventional route. Their speed outpaced even her most exuberant estimates going into the battle.

"Do it now," ordered Nal, standing beside her with his own scope, observing the action.

Livian held a placard inked with a red pyramid high above her head—a signal to Terrible Tora's squad to emerge and protect the grand structure. A metal hatch on the north side of the pyramid shifted open, unseen gears rattling and grinding away beneath the ground. It was not the speediest of processes. Some of the gecko riders were already nearing the halfway point in their rush towards the pyramid by the time the hatch was fully open. Only a few blocks separated them from the northern promenade. Precious time continued ticking away with no movement from down below. Worry set in for Livian when the first gecko reached the edge of the long walkway, and still not so much as a roar had escaped from Dhron's lair.

A long exhale was made in unison by all the viewers on the pinnacle balcony when a lone Whune finally dashed up the subterranean ramp, a scarf of shimmering fabric flapping behind it. Stomper's toothy mug emerged from the hole in quick pursuit. Harlock was in position as the beast's rider. The iron basket on Stomper's back had narrow bars that were bent into oblong ovals around Harlock. The Goblikan looked like he was encased in a colossal kitchen whisk. The iron bars had a dual purpose. Apart from being physically strong, they would also help thwart environmental attacks with the Power from propagating into Harlock's space. Iron was known to disrupt channeling when in high enough concentration if a wizard did not compensate for its presence.

A chase was underway—one which the Whune did not want to lose. The two-story tall behemoth at its back towered over the trees and various planter boxes that were scattered across the wide promenade. The Whune ran straight for the incoming gecko. Everything was progressing perfectly to plan.

And then the runner slipped.

It was a stupid mistake. The ground was dry. It shouldn't have been a problem, and yet....

The dusty gravel kicked up beneath the Whune's feet, and down it went with a tumble most ungraceful. It didn't catch itself in the slightest. The Whune's face slammed roughly into the stone walkway. Everyone viewing the maneuver from atop the pyramid gasped.

Stomper was out for blood. He didn't slow his stride one bit as he careened straight over the downed Whune. It was a vicious trampling. The giant lizard went back for seconds. He stood in place over the poor Whune and churned his feet until there was nothing left beneath him but a mass of bloody pulp. Only then did Stomper go in with his jaws, nipping off chunks of flesh from the twitching lump and tossing them to the back of his throat.

With no control over the monstrous lizard, Harlock was helplessly along for the ride. Livian could hear his screams from the distance as Stomper's motion sent him bouncing violently against the sides of his iron cage.

Stomper stopped eating suddenly and turned in a tight circle, searching for the source of the cries. Perhaps the beast wasn't as unintelligent as Dhron believed…. The oversized lizard suddenly stood up tall and intentionally fell straight backwards onto his back. The iron basket warped under the beast's weight. Harlock screamed all the louder for it. Stomper rolled on his back like a wallowing pig, dragging Harlock's cage through the smashed corpse of the Whune until Harlock and the bars were both draped with a disgusting mess of twisted up entrails. Stomper got back on his feet. The reptile stood up tall again and repeated the same maneuver once more. This time, the cage broke free from its harness and skittered loosely across the ground.

Harlock still couldn't manage to shut up.

Stomper waddled forward on his massive legs, approaching the detached cage. He was like a fox fixated on a rabbit's den. He craned his bulbous head down and wedged his jaws between the bent bars, separating them out even wider. The cage shot off Stomper's snout as if it were spring loaded. It tumbled across the walkway once more. The terrible lizard chased after the bouncing cage, having the time of his chicken-brained life. There was nowhere for Harlock to go. He tried to slip out through the malformed bars, but Stomper was on top of him again far too quickly for him to escape. The enormous lizard slurped Harlock straight out of the side of his cage faster than Nal working on his clams.

Livian glanced towards the Goblikan Commander. He stood with his hands on his hips. His disappointment was palpable. Livian wondered how his stomach was feeling right about now.

Down at the hatch, Tora and Merrick's lizards were finally making their way up the long ramp. A second Whune runner led the procession. This one gave Stomper a wide berth and managed to keep its footing as it sprinted across the promenade.

The first gecko on the scene was well trained and did not divert its path at the sight of the larger beasts standing in its way. It sidestepped the sprinting Whune and attempted to thread the needle between Tora and Merrick's lizards. By the time the barbarian rider realized he was unable to attack Dhron's beasts directly with the Power, Tora Combusted his mount and sent him tumbling to the stone path. The gecko crumbled away as ash in the wind. Merrick's lizard went in for a snack. The barbarian's armor shredded as easily as his bones in the jaws of the giant beast.

A dozen more geckos entered the promenade straightaway. Tora continued gesturing silently from her cage, Combusting every enemy mount that got close enough for her to target.

Merrick joined in on the slaughter. He used the Whune runner to form a living bomb—living for a moment anyway…. The explosion ignited the air with its impressive magnitude. A fiery plume formed, obscuring Livian's view of the battle. Several barbarians were sent flying from their saddles. That was as close to the pyramid as they were going to get. The giant reptiles feasted on the wizards, scattering their ravaged bodies across the promenade. Livian knew their terror but she held no pity for the invading forces. Aragwey had enough problems without barbarians trying to raze the nation's population.

The air above the promenade popped and sizzled as the barbarians and Goblikans traded attacks. They piled environmental effects on top of one another. A whirlwind rushed across the promenade—a storm of swirling ice that was met with a tornado of flames. The resulting steaming mist put a haze over the battlefield. Bits of molten rock and other debris struck across the area indiscriminately. The giant lizards' flesh was too thick for them to take any damage, but the dazzling display did confuse them momentarily.

The barbarians who still had intact rides knew they were outclassed. Rather than lingering to trade shots with the Goblikans, three of them successfully broke away from the pack and managed to slip by the larger lizards to resume their rush on the pyramid.

Stomper, still crunching on Harlock's remains, was attracted by all the commotion. He finally made Dhron a proud papa by moving to intercept the breakaway geckos like the true predator he was. Stomper didn't need Harlock's help to best the barbarians. The killer lizard used its tail to whip one of the geckos straight into the dirt before trampling over the top of it. Never before had there been a more aptly named monstrosity! Stomper smashed the barbarian rider straight through his mount's spine.

The remaining pair of geckos scampered up the great lizard's side, biting all over as they climbed. Stomper cried out a deafening roar. They were just making him angry. The geckos may have had sharp teeth, but their jaws were too small to cause more than superficial wounds across Stomper's backside. The giant lizard spun wildly, unable to dislodge the smaller creatures.

Stomper stood up tall.

Livian knew what was coming next.

The beast jumped back, smashing geckos and riders alike beneath his hearty mass.

The promenade was cleared of invaders. Livian scanned her spyglass north across the city. There were dozens more geckos still missing from the ones she'd watched climbing over the outer wall. They should have all entered the promenade by now if that was where they'd been headed. The misty air obscured Livian's vision. It took a moment before she was able to locate the missing geckos. To the west, just north of the Governor's Mansion, a large grouping of riders had amassed. Livian suspected they aimed to rush the pyramid from the west to avoid the killing field in the north promenade.

Livian glanced over at Nal. He nodded an affirmation. Livian was already prepared with the next placard. She held up a painting of a simple blue house. Klain and the wolf twins sprang into action. Another Whune runner zoomed up the ramp, sprinting due west towards the Governor's Mansion. The three new giant lizards moved as a pack as they shuffled after the runner.

With Klain's tongueless situation and the wolf twins' nonverbal disposition, the trio had been working on a system of novel hand gestures to signal their moves to one another. It was heartwarming to watch them learn to communicate again. Livian had no clue what they were saying when they flashed their signs, but conversing with one another had visibly improved their demeanors over the past weeks. Klain passed her a note one evening while they were training, informing her of the wolf twins' preferred names—Sid and Wyatt.

The barbarian riders couldn't see that they were about to be headed-off by the pack. They kept to their doomed route.

Klain was in the lead. As the pack neared the tall dividing wall at the edge of the promenade, the barbarians reached the mansion and turned east as anticipated. They were rushing straight for one another. Klain stuck his head out the top of his cage, getting a better view. His large body could barely be contained by the iron bars. His hand shot up beside his face. He was gesturing for the twins. The pair nodded back at him. Klain's hand withdrew into his cage and then reemerged with a sheet of fabric which he carefully unfolded and then tossed over the eyes of his lizard.

The Whune runner continued on, pursued by the wolf twins' mounts while Klain's beast thrashed its head back and forth attempting to dislodge the blinder. Klain kept ahold of the fabric, completely stopping the giant lizard in its tracks. Eventually his mount stopped fighting and became docile. The twins continued on around the wall without him. Klain had positioned himself as a final line of defense.

The barbarians engaged with the twins. The wall partially blocked Livian's view of the battle as it unfolded but she could see the barbarian formation scatter as the massive lizards went into a feeding frenzy. Brilliant flashes of light were followed by shouts and a series of quick explosions. The twins were severely outnumbered by the barbarian wizards, but the enemies attacks were absorbed by their iron cages.

A few geckos began to crest the wall. Klain held steady, his lizard's eyes still draped with cloth as he waited for the geckos to descend.

One of the twins—Livian couldn't tell which from the distance—nearly went down as six or seven geckos swarmed over the top of him all at once. The twins were being overwhelmed by sheer mass despite the ineffectiveness of the enemies' attacks. It would be a death of a thousand cuts if someone didn't change the numbers.

Livian began thumbing through her signal placards. She wished to send Tora and Merrick in as backup.

"No," said Nal, watching her closely from the side. "Not yet. It's too early. If you combine the groups we'll never be able to split them apart again."

Livian was the only one who even really cared about the Crazies. They were just numbers to Nal. Livian continued searching her placards for a red house that would signal a runner to lead Tora and Merrick towards the Governor's Mansion. Nal glanced over at Sir Kierington expectantly. It was his duty to stop her. Rather than threaten Livian with the dimpled egg Artifact, Arimond stepped up behind her and clasped her around the waist, physically dragging her back from the stack of signs just as she'd found the one she was looking for.

"You need to learn to listen, woman!" spat Nal. He stepped over to the stack of signs, picked up the one with the red house on it, and then broke it in half over his knee. He tossed it over the side of the balcony for good measure.

Livian stopped struggling against Sir Kierington's strong hands. He released her as soon as the fight left her body. She turned towards Nal, unable to stop tears of frustration from welling up in her eyes. "Why would you do that, you stupid pest! You've sentenced them to death!"

Nal stepped up to her with his hands behind his back as she was speaking. He didn't flinch from the spittle that flew from her mouth as she raged. "They were always going to die," he said with callous disregard. "If any of the Crazies survive— now *that* would be a bigger problem."

Livian had failed her troops. The rooftop Goblikans were still holding back. Livian realized now that they were waiting for one side to eradicate the other with the intent of mopping up the survivors. Livian couldn't help but feel responsible for their demise despite having been tricked as well. The Crazies weren't bad people—not anymore. They didn't deserve such foul treatment… to be used and immediately destroyed.

A warning horn blared from south of the pyramid, drawing Nal to the edge of the balcony. A fresh contingent of barbarians was attempting a sneak attack. They'd managed to evade detection by being submerged in the river harbor until they were already within the city. The geckos were adept swimmers—twenty or so of the speedy creatures scaled the harbor walls all at once.

"Night Hawks! On me!" shouted Nal. He dove over the railing with arms spread wide. A burst of unnatural wind sent him skyward the next moment. If anyone should have been called crazy, it was Nal. One by one, his Night Hawks followed in his place, shooting high into the sky off the steep walls of the pyramid before soaring on their winged suits towards the surprise threat.

A worried clamor arose from the various staff and officials remaining on the pinnacle balcony. Sir Kierington's voice rose above the clatter. "Everyone remain calm!" he pleaded. "We always knew they might pull some sort of stunt. That's why the Night Hawks were standing by to begin with."

Livian stepped up beside Sir Kierington and casually relieved him of his goblet of red wine. He let her take it from him, perhaps assuming she meant to refresh the beverage.

Livian had other plans.

She walked back over to the placard with the blue house on it, raised it above her head, and then quickly sloshed it with the red wine. She hoped the meaning obvious to the Whune handlers keeping watch down below.

Arimond's face drooped like she'd just stomped his puppy.

A Whune runner shot up the ramp and buzzed past Tora and Merrick before curving around the northwest corner of the pyramid towards Klain's position.

"It was the right move and you know it!" Livian defended herself before Sir Kierington had a chance to say anything. She sipped the remaining drops of wine out of the bottom of his goblet before handing it back to him.

"Nal would make me pop your beads," he said.

"Well then I guess it's a good thing he's not here," she snapped back.

Arimond was all talk.

Livian lifted her spyglass back up to her eye. Down below, Klain's situation had become dire. He'd removed the blind from his lizard's eyes and was presently engaged with the barbarian forces. Many of the geckos that had been attacking the wolf twins had moved on and were now concentrating their efforts on overwhelming Klain. He was completely overrun. His lizard had a gecko clamped in its jaws, but it didn't matter. There were simply too many of them.

Livian bit her own lip too hard, drawing the taste of blood as Klain's lizard collapsed to the ground. The geckos chomped mercilessly at the giant reptile's underbelly. It was like watching a ball of ants devour a wasp.

An unnatural cloud began to form above the tragedy. Dark drops, thick as oil rained down on the undulating ball of geckos. The goopy globs stuck to the top layer of attackers like pitch. A flash of fire roared to life, blanketing the pile. The geckos scattered, unable to shake the flames.

Merrick Firefist was the mad artist behind the blaze. He and Tora worked together to time the oily drops—just enough to separate the geckos from Klain's lizard. The giant reptile flailed about, caught up in the flames slightly itself. It shook like a wet dog, sending burning droplets flying everywhere.

Klain was still alive. He used the Power to help strip the remaining fire from his mount. The tar increased in viscosity, helping the beast shake it all away.

The Crazies had everything back under control. Nal and the Night Hawks, on the other hand, were finding flight difficult amongst the barbarian onslaught. Balls of ice fell like boulders from the sky to the southwest of the pyramid. A talented Aerologist must have been amongst the attackers. The ice chunks formed high in the atmosphere and streamed down silently around the Night Hawks. An intense wind sent ice and wizards alike careening sideways through the air. All the manipulations of the Power stacked on top of each other, forming an unpredictable gale of a storm.

Livian watched as several Night Hawks were knocked to the ground, dead on impact. "We're losing too many! We must use my spores!" she pleaded with Sir Kierington. The look on his face told her everything she needed to know.

"Such extreme measures shan't likely be necessary," he said. His posture was tense, despite his words.

They stood beside one another, watching the Night Hawks fight, each internally calculating the chances of success with every additional fallen warrior. Livian had to admit, the Night Hawks weren't entirely useless. The daredevils swooped down like a flock of crimson-stalkers dining behind a fishing net. They eviscerated invaders with every pass.

Several geckos inevitably dashed through the madness unscathed, continuing their rush on the pyramid.

Livian counted four units, but then one exploded suddenly into a bloody mist—a final swoop by a Night Hawk before the geckos got out of range. The three remaining lizards sprinted on unimpeded. Livian no longer needed her spyglass to track them, they were getting so close! They entered the promenade unchecked. Everyone watching from the balcony realized in gasping horror that it was already too late to stop the barbarians from reaching their location. There were no defenders between the barbarians and the viewing party. The first of the three geckos reached the steep incline of the pyramid's outer wall and bounded up it without missing a step.

Livian grabbed Sir Kierington's arm. "Will you not let me use my spores even with this fight upon us? These are wizards—have you no sense?"

Arimond shook her off. He retrieved a silver marble from his pocket, popped it into his mouth and quickly swallowed it down. Livian recognized it as one of the Power-stopping Artifacts the great lizards had been fed. Sir Kierington withdrew his long sword and brandished it deftly. "I already told you—you won't be needing to channel."

His confidence was infuriating. Livian prepared herself to use the Power anyway, steadying her heart and mind with her envisioned success of one day creating a reunified Aragwey. If Arimond's time to expire was upon him, at least he wouldn't be holding her back any longer. Livian stepped away from the edge. The first of the geckos was upon them. Up close, the scaly beast was ugly. Old scars covered its chest and gristly arms. It hefted itself and the barbarian wizard on its back up and over the railing. Dark beady eyes shifted across the horrified onlookers. The gecko flopped to the balcony, its belly slapping against the tile. Its forked tongue flicked from its mouth, tasting the air as everyone scattered for their lives.

Livian should have run for cover as well, but instead she stood behind Sir Kierington, curious to see him in action. The cocky knight ran headlong at the muscular creature. The barbarian wizard tried to destroy him with the Power, but the Artifact in his belly did its job. The gecko's jaws snapped at him, but he dipped to the side and hacked at its exposed neck hard enough to get his sword lodged in the creature's dense muscle.

The gecko swiped at him, in shock as blood gushed from the wound. It was already dead—it just didn't know it yet. Dark red blood flowed down its head and into its eyes. It stumbled to the side and dumped its rider from its back.

Arimond jumped on top of the creature, kneeling down on its face momentarily while he retrieved his stuck blade. The creature hissed as it flailed beneath him. Ari made for the rider without delay, leaping over the still thrashing gecko to reach the man. The barbarian climbed to his feet just in time to be ran through with Ari's sword. The blade pierced him under the arm at a thin gap in his armor's coverage. Ari tossed him back over the side of the pyramid. The barbarian's body left a streak as it slid down the façade.

A second gecko slapped to the balcony's tile behind Sir Kierington. Ari turned and lunged at it before it could get its footing. He cut it, but it was far from disabled. He danced with the reptile, searching for another opening to strike.

The third gecko's claws scrapped against the railing beside him, already halfway over the barrier. The creature was about to flop down on top of Arimond!

"Watch out!" Livian shouted the warning.

The knight fell backwards as the lizard came down. The barbarians did not squander the opportunity to strike back. One of them attempted to melt Sir Kierington's chest plate to his body. The armor began to glow, becoming more malleable as its temperature climbed. Fortunately for Arimond, the iron alloy in his armor's blend resisted the brunt of the attack. Ari still cried out as the chest plate scorched him through his padding, but the damage could have been much worse.

Livian had half a mind to let him be devoured—it would serve him right for having such an ego—but she also knew it would be a waste of his talents. She reached out with her mind and transformed one of the placards at her side into a metallic disk. It shrank in size as the molecules pulled together into a much more compact material. She sharped its edge with another thought and then sent it flying. The makeshift saw blade shaved past Sir Kierington and then sliced cleanly through the necks of both lizards as they went in for the kill.

The barbarians slipped from their decapitated mounts. Arimond hopped back to his feet unscathed. He hefted his sword with all his strength, ruthlessly hacking the fallen wizards apart against the hard tile.

Only after he was completely finished did Livian approach him. The ferocity faded from his expression as she stepped up to his side. The heat of battle was replaced by genuine gratitude to still be amongst the living. Livian continued past him, peering out with her spyglass to see how many more geckos had managed to slip by the Night Hawks.

As she gazed across the city, a jarring thud pounded within her chest—a knock, straight in the heart. She felt the Power slip from her grasp as if she'd been attempting to channel while the moon set. She turned to check, but of course the bright orb was still low on the horizon, continuing its climb… it didn't make any sense! To the southwest, the savage ice storm evaporated in an instant. The Night Hawks plummeted from the sky. The men screamed as they fell quickly to the ground with no Power to stir the winds.

Livian's first thought was to panic over the unknown—*Could the barbarians have restricted all of us at once?*—but the invaders weren't channeling anymore either.

The Power was gone from everyone.

Whatever the cause, neither side was prepared for such an occurrence.

Livian slipped a vial out from her pocket—love spores she'd been saving for Sir Kierington. They didn't need the Power to enact their changes. She uncorked the vial and huffed the fumes into her mouth. They wouldn't do anything to her. She already had all the memories they would impart. She turned back towards the knight, a sultry look in her eyes. The frantic expression on Ari's face turned from concern to confusion. Livian leaned in, kissing him full on the lips while she gently blew her spores deep into his lungs.

When she pulled away, his eyes were already beginning to gloss over. He did not fight her as she removed the dimpled egg out from around his neck and placed the chain over her own head instead.

The Power may have abandoned Tavallon, but there was still a battle to be won. Livian marched over to the placards and held up drawings of both a red and a blue boat to send the Crazies towards the remaining invaders at the harbor. Next, she began hooking up the detonator that would shower the city with the contents of her prepared spore canisters.

A solitary tear slid from the corner of Sir Kierington's eye.

"Do you see it now?" she asked him. "All that must be done?"

The foolhardy knight bowed his head before her. "I am yours," he said.

She knew he was deeply repentant for having stood in her way for so long. He walked back over to her side and helped her finish arming the detonator.

"Would you like to do the honors?" she asked.

Sir Kierington didn't waste any time. He pushed down on the plunger, sending an electric spark through the series of wires at his feet. The charge carried instantly to all the canisters on the sides of the pyramid. A chorus of hisses sounded as they began to release their fine mist. The pyramid was soon floating once more atop a cloud just like the first day Livian arrived in Tavallon.

This time, when the streets cleared, there would be no one left who wished to challenge her supremacy over the Goblikan stronghold.

CHAPTER
51

Lady Nighfield

Less than a league west of Erotos, Rose nearly fell from her saddle when the Power abruptly vanished from the lands. She cried out in shock as her facilities left her in a flash. Elric thought she'd been stung by a bee by the way she hooted out. They soon realized the absence was shared by all wizards. The gates of the Glowing City were sealed by the Queen's Guard when they arrived. The officials feared an attack. To be barred entry from the city at the last moment of their journey was an unfortunate and unexpected final hurdle. Everyone was on edge as rumors spread that the interruption to the Power might have been caused be an active Echo in the vicinity. Many of the travelers trapped outside the gates decided to caravan west for the evening, hoping to wait out the event. No one wanted to be caught in a major Echo.

Elric wasn't about to turn around now. Rose and Orris stood in agreement. They'd all come so far. Their horses were near exhaustion. News of the incident at the border remained behind them… for now, at least. Elric and Rose took the horses over to the extended-stay pasture while Orris kept their spot in line at the locked gates.

When they returned from the pasture, Orris was chatting up an old woman dressed in a fine silk dress. The powdery blue fabric matched a tiny hat pinned to her white hair, styled in an up-do. She'd just arrived at the doors with a basket full of produce from a poorly timed shopping trip.

"I can hardly believe you're back!" she exclaimed. "I was beginning to think I'd drop dead of old age before you returned."

"Has it really been that harsh of a winter?" asked Orris with a grin.

"You've no idea. This city is about ready to pull itself apart from all the cracks that have formed—and I'm not just talking about the earthquakes! There's terror in the streets now, haven't you heard? Some say bombs, others say Echoes." She put her hand up to her mouth and spoke more quietly. "It was firebombs. Take it from me. When you live as long as I have you learn to tell the difference—Echoes hit indiscriminately, you see. These were assassinations." She waved her hands dismissively at Orris's worried scowl. "You know the jackals in this city. They've grown so restless waiting for the war with the Goblikans to boil over that they've started consuming each other! It's sad to see, truly."

Elric caught Orris's eye. The swordsman put his hand on the woman's shoulder and turned her around to face Elric and Rose. "These are my travel companions, Rose and Elric Elensol," he said. "And this is Ennis Nighfield, a friend of the Order."

"Nighfield?" questioned Elric. "I know a Shiara Nighfield."

Ennis nodded. "That's my daughter, when she's not too busy forgetting I exist."

"Well, I for one owe her my life," said Elric.

Ennis eyed Elric queerly, taking in his features more deeply for a moment. "Elric Elensol. So you're the boy's grandfather. I met your grandson, Javic, back before Orris set out to find you. Lovely lad you've got there." She smiled at Elric, a pinch of color rising in her cheeks.

"Have you any word of Javic?" Orris asked. "We discussed a fee on deliverance." He turned towards Elric. "I do expect to be compensated for my journey, by the way, lest that wasn't clear."

Elric nodded curtly. He hadn't a bit of coin to his name at the moment—but Orris didn't need to know that....

"I actually did receive a letter from the boy early last month," said Ennis. "He requests you meet him at the palace."

Elric and Orris both raised eyebrows at her words.

"The palace?" Orris scoffed.

"You must be mistaken," said Elric. "My grandson, Javic Elensol—he's an initiate at the academy."

"Aye," said Ennis. "I know what I'm saying. I've still got my mind about me!" She pursed her lips defensively before explaining further. "He was raised as Ver'ati this last Dance of the Elements. He works for the queen now."

Elric shouldn't have been so surprised. He knew better than anyone the dangers of the Glowing City—its tendrils tended to strangle.

"From the sound of it, he awaits anxiously for your return. Why don't you follow me in?" suggested Ennis, grabbing Elric's hand with her free arm and leading him down the line of travelers waiting for the gates to reopen.

"But they aren't letting anyone in..." said Rose.

"Don't worry, my dear," said Ennis, not breaking her stride. "The House of Nighfield still garners some respect around here."

Orris gestured with his head for Rose to follow after Elric and Ennis. Ennis's hand clasped onto Elric's elbow as they walked.

"How was Shiara doing the last time you saw her?" asked Ennis. "She hasn't braved an appearance home in years. Is she still biting her nails?"

"Not that I recall," said Elric. "She was doing well—healthy. The Ver'konus has her working very hard."

"You don't need to make excuses for her," said Ennis. "She's always had such important things to do."

Elric caught a hint of an eye roll from the old woman as they continued walking.

The guardsmen at the gates saw Ennis coming from the distance. They stood up taller and straighter as she approached.

"Open on up," she said.

The guardsmen shared a look. "We had to seal the gates because the Power stopped working, Lady Nighfield," said one of the men.

"You're not leaving me and my guests out in the cold," she said. "It's starting to rain!"

"This is official policy, m'lady," said the guard. "In case this is some kind of attack."

"Oh, come on now," she said sternly. "It's probably just an Echo. It's not like I'm asking you to let any of these other poor saps in." The guards balked at first, but Ennis stood firm. She placed her hands on her hips and tilted her head down slightly in an expression of annoyance.

"I suppose an exception could be made."

Elric was beginning to see the family resemblance now.

Ennis beamed a bright smile at the glowering guardsmen. "Thank you, dears." She rolled her eyes again after they finished letting them through the gates. She bid Elric farewell with a sly wink and a nod once they were inside. Ennis headed off to her manor while Elric, Rose, and Orris started towards the Queen's Palace to find Javic.

CHAPTER
52

The Fourth Hand

Following Havorie's briefing with General Aldune, the mysterious fourth hand of her Detector had only grown more active—something was definitely drawing nearer to the palace.

Tick.

The thin needle twitched again.

Havorie kept to her schedule, taking meetings in the formal meeting hall from atop her throne. The throne room was a judicial space, and unlike the informal meeting hall it did little to express the grandeur of Havorie's station. Still, little embellishments like her finely carved oak gavel embossed with the form of a fox, along with the royal crest—encased in resin into the speaker podium at her front—did serve to remind visitors of the weight behind her rulings. A line of prominent citizens came before her, airing various grievances she couldn't have cared less about—property disputes; unmet contractual obligations; personal slights—all the regular things. She was a glorified judge. It was all mind numbing. Her rulings stood as justice to the lords and ladies of the land. She kept her Detector hidden on her, high up her sleeve to block the shine emitted by its dials.

Tick.

Between meetings she convened with the device. She'd seen the same sweeping motion before from the 'Strength in the Power' detecting hand whenever Javic happened across the Etwon Bridge from the east city. That hand was permanently fixed back upon herself now and still glowing brightly. Without knowing what the fourth hand was attuned to detect, she didn't know if she should be concerned by the curious wanderings of the needle. She doubted it could possibly be anything good….

When is it ever a good surprise?

The source moved at approximately walking speed as it traversed the Glowing City. She watched the hand slide, shifting from pointing towards the northeast to aiming straight north of the palace.

Tick.

And then the Power slipped from her reach.

Havorie had yet to even grasp ahold of the Power in earnest, but she knew it was gone from her influence when her awareness of the energetic currents around her evaporated back into obscurity. The loss of her heightened senses coincided with an unceremonious knock in her chest. It felt like a physical part of herself had been ripped away as her sensations retreated. She was once again blocked, just as she had been her whole life with the Inhibitor restraining her destiny.

She thought she was the only one at first—that the antiserum had failed—but then Captain Sarvo's voice projected out of the nearby voice box as he made an announcement: "Queen's Guard heed caution. The Power has been suppressed within the vicinity—it's potentially just an Echo, but keep all eyes open until further notice."

She snuck a peek at her Detector as her guards cleared the throne room. Echo or not, the palace was immediately closed to the public. She folded back her sleeve to find that the forth hand had stopped moving.

A terrible sense of foreboding gnawed at Havorie's insides. She had the sudden urge to get up and run. She gave in to the feeling. She didn't tell anyone where she was going. She hiked up her dress and slipped out the back door of the hall before scurrying back down the long passageway towards her private chambers. She dashed down the final hallway before her rooms, leaving several startled guardsmen in her wake.

Suddenly, the earth began to shake. She quickened her pace. As soon as the doors were within her reach she burst through into her entry room. The safety she usually felt in her private chambers eluded her. The quake only grew in intensity. Gazing out the windows, she could see that all the traffic had stopped on the boulevard beyond. People were out of their carriages, gawking and pointing back at the palace. It was only then that she realized the rest of the city wasn't shaking—only the palace was.

Havorie stumbled back to her bedchamber. She made her way over to her wardrobe where she retrieved the silver scroll that allowed her to see through walls. She tested it quickly on the wardrobe door. The Artifact still worked even with the Power missing—*Thank Mast!*

She took the device with her as she headed back out to the entrance room. She pressed the Artifact's translucent film against the wall beside the doors, forming a window into the hallway outside her chambers.

The guardsmen on duty didn't include Javic. He was still off watching over Salvine at Doctor Crane's facility. With the Power gone, Havorie wasn't sure Javic's presence would have provided her with much comfort anyway. The guards who were present had all moved away from the windows and were sheltering in place.

Havorie checked her Detector again. The fourth hand was still holding steady. The shaking intensified even further. When the crescendo finally hit, she thought the whole palace might actually rumble apart despite being made from Calvenite! Not in all her years had she experienced a tremor quite so bone-rattling! All across the palace, glass windows began to shatter. The inner sanctum exploded with a noisy ruckus as the wall of windows smashed apart and tumbled down into the gardens. Every pane blew out under the intense vibrations.

And then, just as suddenly as it began, the shaking stopped.

Havorie's eyes returned to the Detector.

...

...

...

Tick.

The fourth hand jerked back to life with a twitching motion.

Out in the hallway, the guards picked themselves up off the floor, brushing shards of glass out of their hair and uniforms. Nervous laughter escaped their mouths—the sound didn't travel through the wall, but from their body language it was clear they were shaking out their jitters.

The perceived danger had passed.

The palace was still standing.

A distant scream carried in through the open holes where the entry room windows once resided. The cry ended with a sickening thud. The guards in the hallway heard it as well. Their expressions darkened as they unsheathed their weapons.

A moment later, an older man Havorie did not recognize entered in through the doorway at the far end of the hall. He was dressed in a guardsman's uniform. Havorie could have perhaps mistaken him for another one of Captain Sarvo's new hires, but his nonchalant walk was far too calm given all the madness in the air.

Havorie immediately consorted with her dials once more. The fourth hand ticked with every step the gray-haired man took. Havorie's breath caught in her chest. The fake guard gestured once at each of her men. They exploded into a red mist that hung in the air, obscuring her view through the one-way film. Havorie had to stifle her own cry. The shocking display of violence happened so suddenly! The hallway dripped with pieces of her guards' entrails, no chunk larger than a thimble. They'd been splattered out of existence in an instant.

The assassin channeled again, drawing the liquefied remains of the men out from a narrow strip before him. He continued his stroll down the unsoiled swath of hallway towards Havorie's unprotected chambers.

The Power was still unreachable. Somehow the assassin was immune to the outage. Javic's story of a man he called the Crimson Stalker using the Power in North Galdren when the moon was down flashed across Havorie's mind. She'd doubted the truth of the anomalous tale when she first heard it. Now, she only wished she'd taken the warning more seriously. The assassin was coming straight for her, and there wasn't a thing she could do to stop him.

CHAPTER
53

Heart of Darkness

The long steady incline up the Goblikan tunnel to the final railway station was more grueling than Belford had anticipated when first setting out on foot. His calves kept cramping up on him. He really could have used a banana, if only for the potassium. After so many days beneath the ground eating nothing but corn-feed, his nutrition was suffering. His muscle mass had done nothing but diminish since arriving in Aragwey. Protein had been scarce on the road. With no end in sight, fighting fatigue was a constant battle.

Maintaining sanity in the darkness was a separate and even more daunting struggle.

He still hadn't grown used to the suffocating depths of the void. When the group finally broke from their march to make camp for a few hours of rest, they turned down the gas lanterns to a dim hiss. Belford found himself staring into the encroaching shadows instead of closing his eyes. The backs of his eyelids looked so similar to the endless tunnel that he almost couldn't tell the difference. His vision played tricks on him. He saw shapes in the shadows—creeping silhouettes poised in the thick air. The figures drew nearer ever so slowly. He couldn't help but fixate on the figments. His eyes wandered back to them repeatedly, unable to find rest.

Their forms were imposing. He sensed malevolence all around him. He knew it was just a reflection of his inner turmoil—his doubts, fears, and traumas all turning out at once to haunt him. His awareness of his condition did nothing to make him any less unsettled by the experience. The fear was real. The moment he turned a lantern towards his demons they evaporated into the light. The trouble was, as soon as the light shifted away, the shapes settled right back in again.

They were always watching him.

What are you waiting for?

It was just the incessant darkness… being away from the sun for so long was not natural! He'd hardly felt normal in days—weeks, if he was being honest with himself. The ego death he'd experienced on the Goblikan drugs was just the cherry on top of the mental corruption he'd endured! Livian's mist had left him with as many holes as additions to his memories of recent events. It was utterly confusing! He felt estranged from his own experiences, almost like his memories were all just stories told to him rather than experiences he'd truly lived. Anticipation for the end of their dreary journey was all that kept his frayed nervous system from boiling over into a panic, equal parts existential and physical.

It wasn't just him—everyone else was going a bit batty as well, constantly checking over their shoulders as they walked. The darkness brought out the paranoia. They would be able to hear anything approaching down the echoey tunnel from a vast distance. During their last break, Shiara snapped at him when he came sneaking back after relieving himself downhill from the group. He hadn't meant to frighten her. He'd been gone for a while, squatting in the dark. The silver marble Power Artifact he'd cut from Arlin's stomach and then subsequently swallowed into his own digestive tract was still somewhere inside of him. It had protected him from the Power being used on him when Garrett's scepter made him otherwise vulnerable to such attacks. Searching his stool in hopes of recovering the device took time. He hoped he wouldn't need the same surgery he'd performed on Arlin to get it back out again....

"Mast almighty!" spat Shiara, her voice sounding in a hoarse hiss. "I thought you were up front!" She must have believed him a Whune, come to rip her asunder. The corners of her eyes welled up with moisture. Even Shiara had her limits. Belford was surprised he'd caught her dozing. She hadn't been sleeping much these past days either. She punched him squarely on the shoulder as he passed her. "Don't sneak off like that again!"

"Would you rather I went uphill?" he snarked back.

"I mean it!" She scowled at him as she raised her fist to repeat the strike.

"Alright, already! Sheesh! Calm down," Belford grumbled back.

Vera sat up beside Shiara. Her eyes shined, reflecting the dim lamplight.

"And zip up your pants," said Shiara.

Belford fumbled with his zipper before slipping back in beside Vera. He found his spot once more, spooning up against her backside until it was time to set out again.

Tensions remained high as the group continued their hike. The approach to the final train station held a steeper incline the nearer they drew. A deep rumble began to flow through the earth. The low vibration sounded almost like the hum of an engine in the distance. Belford's first thought was that the Goblikan train was coming in behind them, but then the rattle grew into violent convulsions.

"An Echo!" exclaimed Shiara.

"Home sweet home!" hooted Grine.

Worries that the Whunes had finished clearing the track fast enough to catch up proved unfounded. The steady shine of electric light bulbs soon reached their eyes, signaling the end of the tunnel. The station was within reach. Everyone's spirits were reinvigorated as they marched onward. Inversely, the continued absence of the Power fueled a general unease. The feeling grew stronger the higher they climbed. Belford missed the security of his abilities.

The tunnel opened into a wide cavern that contained many branching tracks. A dozen trains could have sat side by side. The sprawling space was reinforced with a Calvenite ceiling. The Goblikans had wired the secret station directly into the Glowing City's power grid. A string of lights ran the length of the platform, filling the air with an electric buzz. The shine washed out the lamplight as they drew nearer. There were no trains currently residing at the station. Only one single-board rail vehicle sat at the end of one of the long runs of otherwise empty track. A melted and re-hardened puddle of metal lay where the engine should have been. It was unsettling to think Garrett had built all this right under Ethan's nose. An army could have shown up in the middle of the Erotos Underground at any time if Garrett had willed it so.

Wilgoblikan stepped up onto the empty platform, leading the way ahead.

Belford peered through a doorway into an overturned office. "It looks like everyone left in a hurry," he said.

"Why is it abandoned?" asked Shiara.

"How should I know what's happened?" asked Wilgoblikan. "This place was bustling with activity the last time I came through."

When they followed the path forward, the answers to all their questions resolved in the form of a misplaced, dilapidated building. The Calvenite structure bridged between two sides of a deep chasm with sheer, unclimbable walls. It sat cockeyed right where the entrance to the Underground should have been. The top portion of the building was encased in stone—the hole the structure came down through was capped off from above.

The rock had been converted from running water. There were still ripples and splashes across the transmutation's surface.

"Is that Laudry hall?!" exclaimed Shiara.

"I can see my old office…" said Grine, pointing up at a crooked second-story window.

"What's it doing down here?" asked Wilgoblikan.

The sinkhole that had consumed the lecture hall the previous autumn had been partially carved out by Goblikan hands. The chasm below stretched down into a dense heart of darkness. The tomb of a building was twisted and compressed under its own weight into a warped version of its once regal self.

Vera clung to Belford's arm. "It sank the night Lord Ethan became young again," she said softly. "I preferred him bedridden."

Belford squeezed her hand back.

"A bunch of people died here that day…" said Grine.

"Is there another path forward?" asked Shiara.

Wilgoblikan gestured ahead vaguely. "This was the only passage that connected to the sewer system."

"Any chance it's passable?" Shiara asked Grine.

The young captain held up his hand in front of his face, rotating his wrist until his palm matched the off-kilter orientation of the building. "There's an exit at the back," he said, "maybe we get lucky and it lines up with the tunnel?"

"This whole cliff looks unstable," Wilgoblikan chimed in.

The ground was still rumbling from the Echo as Belford hopped onto the first step in a set of crooked Calvenite stairs that attached to the building's entrance. There was only one way to find out if they could get through to the other side. Going back certainly wasn't an option. They would starve before they reached another exit point down the sprawling railway. The stairs were bent back so far that Belford ended up walking on the pointed tips of their edges. He maintained his balance to the top of the short flight, only to stumble on the very last step before the broken outer doors.

Arlin's hand caught Belford's shoulder from behind, helping steady his footing.

"Gunna break your fool neck," said Shiara as she passed them both.

The entry hallway twisted downward like some sort of county fair haunted house from a bygone era. The group moved slowly, climbing across the rubble of broken plaster and buckled tiles. Only the Calvenite outer shell of the structure still held its form, albeit warped. The inner walls and other finishes had been rendered to bits by the malformation of the more flexible outer material. Splintered desks and chairs cluttered the opening to the main lecture hall. Exposed wiring dangled from the ceiling into the faces of the travelers.

The rumbling earthquake picked that moment to grow in intensity. Laudry Hall shook and wobbled around them. Broken furniture tumbled down the hallway like rocks from a cliff, smashing into the pile at the end.

"This Echo is sinking us more!" cried Shiara.

"We're shifting too low!" exclaimed Wilgoblikan as they all watched the hallway grow significantly steeper. "It's going to drop us right into the hole! We should turn back!"

Grine suddenly pushed past Belford. "I've got an idea!" he shouted. "Follow me!" He ducked through an opening to a flight of stairs.

Arlin, still at Belford's side, gestured for Belford to go on ahead of him. He had his eyes aimed up the long hallway watching for more tumbling debris. Belford could barely stand with the magnitude of the sheering motion around him. Erotos was known for its quakes, but this Echo was stronger than the usual tremors. His teeth rattled together while his legs turned to jelly beneath him.

When he finally found enough of a footing to get through into the stairwell, the decomposing body of a Ver'ati greeted him at the bottom of the steps. The corpse jostled around in a crumpled pile within a black cloak. Ahead, Grine ignored the open-eyed stare of the dead man. He headed up the stairs to the second story on hands and knees. Belford remained at the bottom to help the others through behind him. The corpse was mummified—the process that turned the water flooding the top floors into stone had also sapped the body of its fluid, hardening the flesh.

Vera and Shiara crawled through the opening, each startled in turn by the body. They both clung onto Belford, forming a human chain to pull themselves up the stairs behind Grine.

Ader made a detour over to the dead Ver'ati. He attempted to close the man's eyes with his fingertips even as the tremor bounced them about. He soon gave up—the skin proved too hardened to manipulate. He settled for a quick prayer in the old tongue. "*Fortano umpendium eliqueth. Evenroth cortonus bri denderum.*"

The sweet flowing words were the same Ader had spoken during Kara's eulogy. Mikel had translated his brother's prayer for everyone in attendance—it was something about the soul finding peace in the afterlife—Belford wished he could remember it more exactly; he'd been quite distraught at the time. His fingers reached into his pocket and squeezed onto Kara's broken butterfly pendant. He'd carried it with him all this way. The delicate golden wings flexed under the pressure of his thumb and index finger. The memories stung more than the sharp metal. He'd stayed behind on the Rosa Marsa while everyone else lit Kara's body on the pyre. Too devastated, he fixed his heightened hearing on the funeral, listening in from the distance. His eyes stayed pointed down into the murky red waters of the Great Minthune as it rushed beneath the anchored steamer. It felt like it had been just the other day.

Ader wrapped the dead man's head within his cloak before proceeding onward.

Wilgoblikan eyed the exchange with apathy as he bumbled by. Respect for the dead was not a trait he possessed. Belford saw his true form—Wil was more akin to a dangerously intelligent wolf than a human being. He was a psychopath, prone to brutality. He could only be counted upon to be self-serving.

Grine continued to lead the way up and around the corner of the second story to a window opening large enough for them to pass through. Their path forward resided below. Laudry Hall was indeed sinking deeper into the chasm. The cliffside beyond looked like it was rising up to meet them. Grine handed Belford his lantern before crawling out and jumping to the crumbling walkway. Belford passed the light source back down to him once he regained his footing. The building was sliding fast. One by one the travelers jumped from the window like rats from a sinking ship. Arlin held off until last, leaping through without a moment to spare as the building made a sudden drop. Huge chunks of rock tumbled down from above, crashing into the deep chasm as the hall slipped free from its stone cap. The building disappeared into the abyss.

Laudry Hall crashed noisily below in the darkness, only settling fully after the ground stopped shaking. With haste engrained in their steps, the travelers counted their blessings only briefly before trudging forward into the Erotos Underground.

CHAPTER 54

By Any Other Name

The divine radiance of the sun was too bright for Vera's dark eyes as she climbed up the ladder from the sewers with the rest of the tired travelers. The fresh air felt crisp in her lungs. It was a relief to be home after everything she'd been through. She was finally free! Lord Ethan would never hurt her again. She'd taken control of her destiny—right by the balls—and she wasn't sorry!

Belford was the key to everyone's salvation—she knew it in her bones! *Beautiful Belford!* He didn't talk much about his past, and she knew he had his demons, but Vera had no doubt he was a good man. Anything he did for Aragwey would be better than Lord Ethan's exploitative buggery. Just being above the surface raised Vera's spirits vastly. The bright sky above eased the weight on her shoulders. Their journey was finally over. Bathed in the brilliant sunlight, the warming rays caressed her grateful skin, filling her with all the hope of a glorious fresh start. For the first time in forever she could envision a happy future for herself. She hadn't spoken to Belford about it yet, but she wished to be his personal swordsman going forward. It was an important job, keeping the next leader of the Ver'konus safe. With her Talus Shard blade, she was up to the task.

She extended her hand and helped Belford up through the open hatch and into the street. After navigating the Underground they'd finally emerged right beside the Etwon Bridge in the east city. The towers of the Queen's Palace loomed above the Arcanum Cathedral across the bridge. A slow wobble was still visible at their crowns—residual motion from the savage earthquake.

No one batted an eye as their party, filthy and dazed, dragged themselves out of the hole and across the bridge. They joined a throng of people out in front of the palace when they arrived. The Power was still missing from the Ver'ati. Vera didn't know what any of it meant, but she overheard from the crowd of gawking onlookers that the Echo had originated at the palace.

On approach to the entrance, Shiara was the first to spot Elric Elensol stepping past them in the opposite direction.

"Elric?" she cooed. "Do my eyes deceive me?"

Vera had never been formally introduced to the man, but she was aware of him. She knew he had been one of Lord Ethan's swordsmen long before her time. Ethan had respected him, which probably meant he was a piece of crap and to be avoided. Despite her reservations, half the party—Shiara, Belford, Arlin, and Ader—all went up to him, greeting the sun-touched elder with joyous hugs.

The mood shifted when Elric spotted Wilgoblikan standing beside Captain Grine.

Elric stared the old Goblikan down. "What's he doing here?" he asked Shiara.

"A prisoner, well used," she said. "Our mission was a success, though we should be telling that to the queen first."

"Nice to see you too," said Wilgoblikan.

Elric turned away from Wil, ignoring him pointedly with a puckered scowl as if he were a pile of stinking rubbish. "You really got the bastard?" he asked.

"Cold and dead," said Shiara. "But not without its price."

Elric's eyes searched across each of their faces again, counting the absences. His hand went to his heart. "Ethan… and, no! Not Thorin!" His forehead creased into a thousand wrinkles as his eyebrows rose in commiseration of the loss. "He was truly the best of us! Oh, how dreadful. I'm so sorry my dear." He embraced Shiara again. She let him hold her to his chest for a long moment, neither one of them wanting to let go.

The somber hug ended with more than a few sniffles. Elric wiped his eyes free of moisture after Shiara stepped back. "You've all done a wonderful thing for Aragwey," he said. "Never doubt that."

Shiara let out a heavy sigh. "So what are you doing here? You look like you just fell down a hill."

Elric wiped his dirt-stained brow with the sleeve of his shirt. "The road is a harsh mistress," he said. "We've just arrived back to the city as well. I've been in Antara for the past several months."

"What on Mast's green tit were you doing in Antara?" Shiara asked.

"That is a bit of a long story," said Elric. "I can tell it later, but I was just trying to enter the palace to find Javic—he works for the queen now—but something seems to be going on." He shook his head. "The doors have been sealed shut."

A scruffy-looking man clad in dark chainmail beneath a sweat-stained shirt stepped up beside Elric.

"Everyone, I'd like you to meet Orris Fen, a blade-brother acquaintance I've been traveling with."

Arlin subtly shifted to stand behind Wil as Orris's gaze briefly slid across the group. Vera noticed the odd behavior but forgot all about it when Elric introduced another newcomer next.   A young woman walked up from where she'd been lingering behind Orris.

"This is Rose," said Elric.

The girl stepped forward and drew back her hood.

Belford gasped. "Claire?" He rubbed his eyes in disbelief. "How are you here…? Is it really you?"

The girl stood guarded.

"This is amazing! You're here!" He was absolutely ecstatic. He rushed forward at her with arms wide seeking an embrace.

She met his advance with a swift right hook to the jaw.

Belford collapsed to the ground like a sack of potatoes. He was dazed by the blow. She'd landed a solid strike that sent his head cracking backwards.

"I don't know who you think I am, but don't you dare touch me," she said sharply.

Belford picked himself up quickly, rubbing his jaw and prodding at his teeth with his tongue, checking for looseness. "You don't know who you are yet, do you?" he asked. "I had the same acute amnesia when I first returned. You must recognize me at least a little bit! It's me… Aaron…. Aaron Levy…. We met a millennia ago during the Arcadian Project…. We used to be able to talk to each other with our minds… share memories… sensations… everything. The connection seems to be gone, but so is the Power right now, too, so I don't know…."

The girl's face stayed stern. "What do you want me to say? I have no idea who you are."

It was an awkward exchange to watch. Belford grimaced. Vera could tell the lack of recognition in the girl's eyes hurt him deeply. His face quickly grew red and puffy as if he were about to burst into tears. He made another sudden move at the girl, yanking up the sleeve of her riding dress.

The Mark of Kings was etched into her skin, clear as the bright day, high on her left bicep.

Vera had seen the intricate marking enough times on both Ethan and Belford for her to recognize it immediately.

Orris grabbed Belford by the wrist and twisted it around behind him.

"Did you not see it!?" Belford grunted. "This is Claire, not Rose. She has the Mark of Kings!"

Orris released Belford's arm and pushed him away. The blade-brother turned back towards the girl. Confusion was etched upon both his and Elric's faces.

"May we see it?" Elric asked.

The girl made a heavy sigh. "This is really no one's business but my own," she said. Despite her words she soon gave in to all the gawking stares. She pulled up her sleeve once more and gave everyone a good look.

"I knew it, the moment I saw you! Even with your dyed hair! You may not remember me yet, but I know you're my Claire!"

Shiara patted Elric on the back. "You're just a regular Mark-of-Kings magnet, aren't you?"

Elric stood flabbergasted.

Orris sank to his knees, worshiping prostrate at Claire's feet.

"I've got a mark too, buddy," said Belford, "you know—next time you think about putting your hands on me."

"So this is Claire?" asked Shiara. "You should know that Aaron here has been searching for you for a very long time. He's been quite incessant about it, really."

"I don't care who he is—don't let him come at me like that again!"

The pain in Belford's eyes made Vera feel like she'd been punched in the gut. Belford was getting all misty-eyed over a girl who wanted nothing to do with him. The emotion on his face, as heartbreaking as it was to see, also made Vera feel like she might as well not even exist. She'd thought she'd seen true affection in Belford's eyes. He'd been a gentle lover for her when she needed him to be. Still, a part of her couldn't help but doubt he would have the same reaction if she were ever to reject him so callously.

Claire had leveled an emotional beating. Belford—*Aaron*—took it all on the chin as surely as he took her punch.

"You'll remember everything eventually," he said. "Don't worry. I know you will." He continued to study her face for a long moment before his eyes drifted down her body to her stomach. He clearly wanted to say something more, but he stuffed the words.

"You both need to go speak with Queen Havorie," said Shiara. "There is much to be reported." She turned towards Elric. "The palace may be sealed, but something tells me they will let these two in at least."

"And I'm not going anywhere without my swordsmen," said Belford as he extended his hand to Elric. "Come on, we can go find Javic once we're in there." Elric grasped his hand in solidarity. Claire followed along behind him, a begrudging scowl on her lips. Arlin rounded out the invited entourage heading off to the palace while the rest of the group remained behind.

Vera watched them leave, feeling an instant twinge of regret. She would have rather gone along as well, but she hadn't exactly been invited. She wasn't needed.

"Which one of you is going to be working on getting me the remedy to my affliction?" asked Wilgoblikan.

Vera and Shiara shared a quick look.

"I've done my part, dragging you all back here alive," he grumbled. "I am going to receive my due reward, aren't I?"

Shiara chuckled. "I sure hope not," she said.

Vera stepped further away from Wil. Grine and Ader could handle the old man. The ex-Goblikan wasn't the only one making her feel uncomfortable with his gaze, though.

Orris was also observing Vera through narrowed eyes. She could feel his pointed stare without even looking back at him. His attention was glued to the Talus Shard blade on her hip. She turned slowly, blocking his view of the weapon with her body. The swordsman's lips turned down into a frown. "Where did you get that blade?" he asked.

Vera remained stiff. She let the tension build inside of her—energy ready to explode at will. She moved only subtly, placing the side of her hand over the gem in the hilt. It was too late to hide it, but her body immediately received the Shard's wisdom.

"All blade-brothers' deaths are scrutinized with serious regard by the brotherhood," he said.

Vera turned to face Orris more squarely. The slender swordsman held his fingers loosely alongside his hilt as well.

"I've certainly not killed any blade-brothers, I can assure you of that," she said.

Orris's fingers wiggled, shamelessly edging further around his grip.

"I killed a Goblikan who went by the name Redbone," she said. "He was no blade-brother. He got what he deserved."

"A Goblikan… then you salvaged this blade from the killer of a brother. For that, I offer the Order's gratitude. But that sword still does not belong to you—it belongs to the Paerto'radam."

Vera's eyes wandered away from Orris and over to the palace behind him for a brief moment. Erratic motion up above caught her attention. The stained glass windows of the palace's façade were all broken out. A struggle was taking place within a high opening.

Seeing her distracted, Orris stepped forward, reaching for her blade.

Vera quick-drew the sword, raising it up like a scorpion's stinger. "Try me," she said.

Orris let go of his sword's grip and bowed his head in submission. Behind him, a man screamed as he tumbled from the palace's high opening. His long fall was silenced by the rough cobblestone below.

Shiara bounded past Vera and Orris, rushing towards the palace.

Vera glanced back at Grine.

"Go on," he said. "Ader and I will keep our eyes on Mr. Grumpy!"

Wilgoblikan scowled.

"I think the queen may need our help," Vera said to Orris. "Are you capable of working together?"

"Like *together*, together?" asked Orris.

Vera flipped her blade around, pointing the glowing gem in its hilt towards the swordsman.

Orris nodded in understanding. He drew his blade slowly, twisting it around to bring their Shards together. The gems worked their magic, pairing their intuitions. They raced in step after Shiara.

CHAPTER
55

Duty Calls

The sun-kissed freckles on the side of Salvine's nose that Javic had always found endlessly attractive had been erased from her face. Her new skin was rosy pink and impossibly smooth, only marked by a spattering of dark bruising. The tiny red pinpricks had arisen all over her body like a rash—a slight misalignment of her blood vessels after her full-body transformation. Doctor Crane said not to worry, that the mild schism would heal itself over time, just as her hair would grow back in, but Javic could do nothing else. Salvine had yet to maintain consciousness since he'd dragged her from her dream-prison in the clouds.

Cale wasted no time in reclaiming the brass spyglass Artifact when Javic was done with it. He left the lab after a brief "congratulations" and a little wave.

Javic kept his focus on Salvine. He worked with Doctor Crane to move her to a nearby room that held a bed where she could recover more comfortably. Without all the blubbery flesh of a Whune, she was left much skinnier than Javic had ever seen her before. Her ribs and hips were sharp to the touch. She weighed barley anything, but he still worried he was bruising her further as he lifted her in his arms and placed her onto a gurney. Her eyes fluttered open just once, but she slipped unconscious again without so much as a word.

Doctor Crane insisted she just needed her rest. Javic could see she was in a tenuous state. Her body was emaciated. While transforming her, neither Crane nor Cale had bothered to add any fat to her physique. She was dangerously scrawny. She barely resembled the girl Javic remembered at all!

Holding her frail frame in his arms nearly made him burst into tears. When the moon set, the sudden disappearance of the Power left him feeling hauntingly empty inside. The thought that he could still lose her all over again gnawed at him. There was nothing more he could do to help.

He'd already processed the loss of Salvine and started moving on. He'd given up on her…. He wasn't about to make that mistake again.

"She'll need calories once she wakes, but not too many—that could kill her," said Doctor Crane. "I'll go back in tomorrow and grow a little meat on her bones—don't worry, I know the female form. I won't make her fat."

Fat?! She's become a frail sack of bones!

Javic held back his biting fury for the traitorous doctor. Crane had betrayed the Crown by helping Lord Ethan Inhibit Havorie as a child. Somehow he managed to prove himself even more despicable with every remark.

Javic was glad when the doctor left him to lie by Salvine's side on a spare cot. The miraculous girl had been all the way to hell and back. Javic believed her dead for so long, he didn't want to take his eyes off her again—not even for a moment!

Despite his intentions, he soon found exhaustion and the comfortable cot working together to tug at his eyelids.

He awoke a good many hours later, groggy beyond reason. A distant rumble roused him from his slumber. Salvine was still beside him, unconscious, mouth agape with drool running down her cheek. The Power had yet to return so he didn't think it could have possibly been too long, but it felt like he was awaking straight out of a coma!

The lights were off in the room, but the ones out in the hallway flickered as the rumble intensified.

A sudden bang at the door made him jump halfway out of his cot. General Aldune burst into the room.

"Where's Doctor Crane?" he asked.

Javic shrugged.

"Ah! No time!" Aldune turned to leave again but then spun back around. "Hey, don't you still work for the queen?" he asked.

Javic nodded slowly, rubbing the sleep from his eyes.

"Then you should get your ass up and over to the palace right now!" Aldune screeched at him. "Didn't you notice the Power disappeared? The moon's up! This is no Echo! We're under attack!" He hurried back out into the hallway just as quickly as he'd appeared.

Javic remembered his duty to Havorie like a wet sock in the face. He gazed over at Salvine once more. Even General Aldune's ruckus hadn't roused her. He quickly grabbed a wash rag and used it to mop up her drool before tugging on his boots and heading out after Aldune.

The general was climbing into a peddle-cab when Javic exited the building. Aldune frowned at him, but then waved him over. "May as well get in," he said. "We're going to the same place."

Javic nodded at the wide man before hopping in beside him. He would have much preferred to walk but he couldn't really refuse the general's offer. He just hoped he wouldn't make small talk. Javic had no trust for any of the commanders of the Ver'konus at this point. Lord Ethan's treason poisoned the ranks. The charter Ethan signed when he first formed the Ver'konus years before claimed the organization's highest directive was to protect the Crown and country. Instead they'd done the job of the enemy! Javic wasn't even a Phandolian citizen, but the blatant corruption disgusted his principles. He cared for Havorie on a personal level—enough to share a ride with General Aldune without batting an eye.

"A helluva day to quit drinking," Aldune grumbled.

Javic didn't comment.

"Could you peddle any slower?" the general barked at the driver. "It's not like anyone's lives are hanging in the balance or anything."

Javic shrank into his seat. When they finally reached the palace, Aldune shoved past him on his way out of the cart. He ran up the steps and burst in through the anteroom door. Javic knew it was bad before he even passed through the opening. Shouts rang out from within. The anteroom had seen a slaughter. Guardsmen scrambled back and forth across the blood-slicked tile. Splatter and bits of bodies covered the pillars and walls.

Javic had no idea what had transpired. The Power was still absent. He continued on through the mess, following after Aldune down the long hall towards the Charisms chamber. The security chamber was even more gruesome. The ceiling still dripped with the men who'd been on duty. It looked like a bomb had gone off, though the box of orbs sat undisturbed.

In the hallway beyond, the most unexpected sight befell his wary eyes.

"Grandfather!"

Elric looked up from where he was hunched over Damian Sarvo.

The guard captain was injured. He sat propped up against the wall in a daze with a bloody smear behind him.

"Javic! Praise Mast! I feared the worst!" Elric exclaimed.

Javic ran to him as Aldune moved in to check on Damian. Elric was looking scrawnier than Javic liked to see. It felt like everyone around him was wasting away! They clasped hands and then shoulders in a tight hug.

"Have you not been eating?" Javic asked, tears already streaming down his cheeks.

"Not hardly enough," said Elric.

A pretty lady in a ragged riding dress with a scowl on her face was watching them with folded arms from the foot of a spiral staircase. "I can't hear Orris anymore," she said. "They've moved on ahead."

"What's going on here?" asked Javic.

Elric shook his head. "I found Claire," he said with a shrug and a shake of his head.

"I'm still Rose," she said.

Elric puffed out his cheeks. His scruffy beard had become so wild.

The pale girl glared back at them both.

"Belford is back as well," Elric continued. "He went on ahead with the others to try to save the queen from… whatever's happening…."

Across the hall, Aldune managed to rouse Captain Sarvo with a vial of smelling salts. Damian coughed and sputtered back to his senses.

"What can you tell me?" Aldune asked, holding the guard captain up by the front of his shirt.

Damian winced. He braced his ribs with his arm. "Assassin… just one… decked-out in Artifacts…" he said. The words made him cough even more. "He came in straight through the walls!" He shook his head. "His ring—it threw me with a kinetic force." He spotted Javic, lingering beside his grandfather. "You, boy," he pointed at him. "Come here."

Javic stepped over to his captain.

"I've half a mind to fire you from the queen's service," he said.

Javic grimaced. He knew he'd skipped a shift. He'd had his reasons, but no excuse would be good enough for Captain Sarvo, especially not after the attack….

"I will reprimand you later," said Damian, "but right now, I need you to take my sword and go defend the queen." He held up his blade.

Javic hesitated. "I'm not really much of a swordsman, if I'm being completely honest..." he admitted.

"Don't worry about that," said Damian. "This sword knows enough for the both of you."

Javic raise a quizzical eyebrow. Damian's pressed the hilt into his palm. Javic gasped as his fingers curled around the leather wrappings. He felt the perfect balance of the weight at his fingertips. An unexpected calmness washed over him. "What is this?" he asked.

"A Talus Shard," said Damian. "Let it guide your hand."

Javic looked back over at his grandfather. He didn't want to leave him again.

"Which way did they go?" Aldune asked.

"Follow me, I can show you," said Claire.

"It's alright," Elric said to Javic. They both knew he needed to go.

Javic felt the pull of the blade. It sensed that combat was near. Javic clasped his grandfather again on the shoulder before following after Claire and General Aldune up the spiral staircase.

CHAPTER 56

Malignant

Bits of bodies and blood splatter marred the royal hallway where guardsmen once stood. Belford had seen such eviscerations before, committed by the Crimson Stalker back in Tavallon. He'd rushed all this way to warn the queen, only to find the assassin had been one step ahead of him all along.

At Belford's side, Arlin eyed the gruesome scene with his blade already drawn. They'd passed through a string of grizzly sights just like it since stepping into the palace's anteroom. Belford insisted on leaving Claire behind with Elric as he and Arlin forged ahead down the path of carnage.

"This is his work," said Belford, "the *Crimson Stalker*, I know it—it's the same thing he did at the pyramid."

Arlin glanced over at him.

"We better hurry…" said Belford.

Arlin raised an eyebrow.

"I'll be fine," said Belford, reading the concern in his eyes. "Honestly, I'm more worried about you. I still have the anti-Power gob-stopper in my gut."

They continued on more quickly, dashing around the bloody spots on the tile after Belford slid briefly on the toes of his well-traveled sneakers. His rubber soles scraped through a layer of shattered glass dropped from the broken inner atrium windows. They skirted the edge of the walkway, both of them avoiding looking down at the drop, a mere step away.

The last time he fought the Crimson Stalker he had Arlin's blade to help calm his nerves. He wished it was in his hand now. His head was lost to a sea of doubts. Arlin's heroic guidance drew him onward. All he knew was he couldn't leave his friend to face this shadow alone.

The door to Havorie's chambers stood ajar. Belford feared they were already too late. They slowed their approach, listening intently for anything—signs of danger, signs of life—anything at all. The room ahead remained quiet apart from a whistling draft blowing in through the shattered-out windows of the palace's façade.

Arlin stopped at the entrance and used his blade as a mirror to spy into the forward chamber. Belford only caught a glimpse of overturned furniture. Arlin soon signaled that it was clear. They moved into the room, eyes searching for either motion or remains but finding neither.

The room had been ransacked—heavy furniture was flipped and dashed, every tapestry torn from the walls. The Crimson Stalker hadn't left a stone unturned.

A crash of glass sounded from further back in the next chamber.

Belford and Arlin stayed low, positioning themselves behind an overturned sofa.

Arlin used his blade as a mirror once more. Belford scooted closer alongside him to see through its reflection. He got a quick glimpse of the Crimson Stalker through the far doorway. It was definitely him. Belford hadn't a doubt in his mind. The same gray eyes that haunted his nightmares scanned across the chamber. He recognized the evil man's flustered expression— it was the same face the assassin had made when he realized Belford had him bested within Garrett's throne room.

The man's search for the queen was perhaps not going as smoothly as he'd hoped.

Belford could see a canopy bed through the doorway. The mattress was gutted and flipped askew. White feathers floated upon the draft in the air. Belford and Arlin both ducked down lower, bracing their backs against the upholstery as the Crimson Stalker emerged from the bedroom.

They couldn't see what he was doing. He wasn't moving— just standing quietly.

The man let out a wordless sigh. "I can hear those heavy breaths over the howls on the wind."

It was the first time Belford had ever heard the man speak.

"It will all grow silent with time," said the Crimson Stalker.

A flash of blue briefly lit across the wall—the assassin's ring shined brightly as it activated. Arlin, with his back still up against the sofa, suddenly went stiff and slipped over onto the floor. It was too late for Belford to do anything. Arlin slid out from behind their cover. The Talus Shard blade skidded from Arlin's fingers, agonizingly out of reach and under scrutiny of their adversary. The Crimson Stalker was up to his old antics. The spry older man could see Arlin now from his vantage point. Belford remained still, holding his breath, though his pulse pounded in his ears. The silver marble Artifact had done its job again, protecting him from the motion-locking attack. He didn't think the Crimson Stalker was aware of his presence yet.

A shuffle at the entry doors brought all eyes towards Vera, Shiara, and Orris as they burst headlong into the chamber. A static tingle crackled across the air as Shiara's firestone earring hungered for energy. It would have been a smart attack, possibly, had they gotten the jump on the terrible man, but neither Shiara's Artifact nor the Talus Shard blades did any good as another flash of blue froze them all in their tracks. They tumbled to the hard tile, still rigid, like mistreated department store mannequins.

Belford could see the Crimson Stalker's shadow as he turned away from the neutralized threat.

I need to get my hands on a weapon!

No sooner had he considered diving for Arlin's blade than it began to scrape across the floor even farther out of his reach, tugged by some magnetic pull. Belford remained still. The Crimson Stalker snatched the sword cleanly out of the air as it flew up to him.

The assassin was deadly fast, and now he had a Talus Shard.

Fan-fuckin-tastic.

Belford felt like his capillaries were about to burst as his growing trepidation made his pulse pound even harder. He didn't let out his breath until the Crimson Stalker finally walked away, disappearing once again into Havorie's bedchamber.

He knew he only had one chance to do what was needed. That troublesome ring had to go! He was certain it was the ring that was causing everyone to freeze. He'd seen it glow back in Tavallon as well, whenever the Crimson Stalker had channeled a kinetic force.

Knowledge that the malignant man could have shredded his friends into pulp if he wasn't so distracted by his search for the queen pushed Belford from his meager hiding place. He was grateful for his rubber soles to dampen the sound of his steps as he tiptoed first to Orris and then to Vera, releasing each of their grasps on their blades before stalking after his stalker with two Talus Shards in hand.

His fears melted away as the blades extended from him, perfect instruments to enact his will. The Talus Shards seemed to almost vibrate against his palms, coaching his body, starting with the finesse of his grip against their bindings.

Ever since the Crimson Stalker first invaded Belford's dreams, he'd felt an eerie connection to him. Looking into the man's dull gray eyes was like staring into a void. He was a silent killer, out to cause chaos. The scary part was just how very good he was at his work. Back in Tavallon, he'd left Belford to watch Arlin bleed out with a slit throat and then gone on to tear Garrett apart limb-from-limb so gratuitously that it felt oddly personal after the precision and efficiency of his other kills. To Belford, he was the boogeyman—an enigma wrapped in a mystery. At this point, he didn't even care to have the answers. He just wanted to stop him.

Somewhere between a dash and a tiptoe, Belford pattered softly across the foyer. He paused just outside the queen's bedchamber with his back pressed against the wall. He knew what he needed to do—he just needed to choose his moment.

The Crimson Stalker had overturned a writing table and a bookshelf, and was working his way around the room towards a wide wardrobe of finely decorated mahogany.

Belford stepped into the chamber silently.

The Crimson Stalker paused. "So it comes to this," he said, his back still turned.

Belford didn't waste a step. He lunged forward fast on his feet. A flick of the man's wrist sent the overturned writing desk aloft and flying straight at him. He deflected the furniture with minimal contact against his shoulder and continued forward, focused on his goal.

Arlin's sword was quick in the man's hand. White sparks flashed as Belford struck against it with both of his blades simultaneously. The force of his strikes pushed the Crimson Stalker back on the balls of his feet.

Belford leaned into his advantage, driving forward even harder with his braced blades towards the older foe. The Crimson Stalker was not so easily knocked from his feet. He returned similar force, pushing the gap between them wider. The assassin ate up his limited floor-space during the maneuver, shifting the fight further into the corner of the chamber. He used the brief gap to shore up his stance.

Belford didn't want this fight to become drawn out. His muscles weren't actually tempered for such combat like Arlin's were. His swords seemed to forget his humanly limitations as they urged him to attack.

Belford struck out again. The Crimson Stalker parried the blows. Belford didn't relent, raining down a whirlwind of strikes that made his opponent flow through an intricate dance of defensive postures. He was burning through his energy, but he only needed to land one blow.

He pushed the Crimson Stalker back until he was restricted by the fancy wardrobe behind him. With gritted teeth, he worked his blades faster and faster, building momentum with every swing. The swirling swords flashed with each blow. It was like a speed round of chess as every move was met by a counter. Suddenly, Belford saw his checkmate in the form of predictable posturing when he performed an offhand upward strike timed just so after a heavy slash from the right. It was a gap in his opponent's flow. He did another heavy right, followed by the offhand upward strike. The Crimson Stalker repeated the same mistake.

He could barely see the gap, but his Talus Shards knew it was there. He did the combo again, but this time he shifted the arc of his next blow to strike the opening. He swung straight down at the crown of the Crimson Stalker's head.

Just before making contact, a flash of blue burst from the assassin's ring. Belford's sword froze in the air, mid-strike. His hand continued moving without the blade as it was wrenched from his grasp. He realized his other blade was frozen in place as well. It wouldn't move no matter how hard he tugged at it.

A slight smile cracked the Crimson Stalker's thin lips as he stared Belford down. The assassin had been toying with him from the start. Just as he went to raise Arlin's sword again, Belford saw one more opening and immediately went for it. He released both of his blades, position-locked and useless as they were, and instead drove his shoulder forward into the

Crimson Stalker's jaw. The man's left hand predictably came up to push Belford back, but just as he did so, Belford tucked his chin. He lowered his head searching for the Crimson Stalker's ring finger.

The digit extended up. Belford hooked it with his mouth, and immediately chomped down hard with his jaws.

He held the little blue ring in his teeth for a brief moment before fully severing the Crimson Stalker's finger with the Artifact still attached. A hiss of pain escaped the man's lips. Belford spit the ring across the floor. A burning rage consumed the Crimson Stalker's contorted face. He shoved Belford back with his mangled hand before gesturing with his bloody nub towards the canopy bed.

To Belford's chagrin, the whole bed exploded sideways at him despite the Artifact ring having been removed from the assassin's person. Belford crashed into the far wall of the chamber as the wooden frame splintered around him.

The Crimson Stalker wasn't merely using Artifacts—he had control over the Power. Whatever the ring did, it had not been what gave the killer his abilities…. Belford's blades were still trapped in place in the air by the assassin's powers. Belford had been so terribly wrong with his assumptions. Removing the ring did nothing but make the man angry.

The wind was knocked out of Belford by his flight across the chamber. He was unarmed, exhausted, and possibly a little concussed. He wasn't sure if the sound of footsteps approaching the chamber was real or not, right up until the moment Javic clamored in through the open doorway with a gleaming blade clasped in his hand. General Aldune followed immediately in his wake, huffing and puffing from a run.

The assassin gestured again. Another flash of blue shined out from the fallen ring on the floor as the man channeled. Javic and Aldune froze in place, just like the others before them. The ring wasn't enacting the effect, but it was certainly glowing in unison to the channeling.

A detector….

Belford couldn't catch his breath. His rattled diaphragm wheezed for air. He was stuck, sprawled out on his back. The Crimson Stalker approached him from across the chamber, his hand still bleeding profusely. He trudged right past Belford to the severed finger, scooped it up, and reattached it on the spot with a blue and white glowing aura. He flexed his reassembled hand, making a fist several times before refocusing in on Belford. The man placed the heel of his boot on his chest and crushed the air out of him even harder. Several ribs popped under the pressure. Belford grunted out in intense pain.

The Crimson Stalker tossed Arlin's sword aside before reaching into his pocket. He withdrew his straight razor. Belford had watched him use the simple blade to kill too many people before. The assassin unfolded the razor slowly, keeping his scowl locked on Belford as he knelt down and placed the blade right up against his throat.

Another sound at the door drew the Crimson Stalker's gray eyes up. Claire stood within the doorway, an expression of timid curiosity etched upon her pale face. Her lips pinched into a tiny frown as she took in the chaos before her.

The Crimson Stalker's pupils enlarged, eyes growing wide as they fell across Claire.

The blade was still at Belford's throat, but the Crimson Stalker's hand held steady for the moment as his attention floundered. Belford saw the door to the mahogany wardrobe crack open slightly silently behind the killer. A thin leg emerged, feeling for the floor before the door shifted open any further. Queen Havorie, terrified but beautifully prepared, swept out into the room like an enraged banshee. She had been hiding within the large cabinet the whole time. She ambled the few steps that separated her from the Crimson Stalker, a syringe of clear liquid clasped in her fingers like a dagger.

She jumped on the man's back without hesitation and jabbed him in the neck all in one motion.

Shock turned to rage on the Crimson Stalker's face.

Javic and Aldune unfroze, grunting and gasping for breath on the hard floor.

The Crimson Stalker threw Havorie off of him. He spun around, slashing at the queen with his razor blade. Havorie cried out as the blade sliced viciously into her arm.

General Aldune was first to his feet. He tackled the Crimson Stalker to the floor and wrestled the straight razor out of his hand.

"He's Inhibited!" cried Havorie.

Aldune continued to pummel the assassin with his fists until he lost consciousness. He immediately went about stripping the man of all his trinkets. He slid the straight razor into his pocket along with the little blue ring before pulling the clothing right off of the killer's back.

Javic nodded to Belford as he hurried past him to Havorie's side. He snatched up the Crimson Stalker's shirt from the floor as he went by and used it to tie a tourniquet around the queen's wound.

Belford propped himself up higher on the wall, still trying to catch his breath. He knew he had several broken ribs, but that was a pittance compared to his life.

Across the chamber, Javic spotted the kit from which Havorie had gotten the Inhibitor. It was sitting in a pile, just within the base of the wardrobe. He smartly snatched it up and put it in his robes, keeping any antidote contained within far from the Crimson Stalker's reach.

Claire stepped into the room. She approached Belford slowly before sliding down the wall to sit beside him on the floor.

Belford wheezed with shallow breaths. His eyes remained focused on the Crimson Stalker. He still didn't understand how the man was able to use the Power while everyone else was blocked.

"I do remember your face," said Claire.

It wasn't much, but it was enough to make his heart swell. He felt tears beginning to well in his eyes.

"I just thought you should know," she said.

Belford tried to turn towards her, but his cracked ribs made him wince.

"Good talk," she said, hopping up unceremoniously and heading back towards the exit.

Belford was alit with the spark of hope as he wheezed and sputtered upon the floor. At the end of the day, fate had brought them back together.

CHAPTER
57

Forbidden Love

Havorie's blood was already soaking through the makeshift tourniquet. The slash on her forearm ran deep. The tips of her fingers tingled with numbness. Her short life had flashed before her eyes while the assassin was splattering her guardsmen. She realized ruefully that of all her lofty aspirations she had accomplished absolutely nothing. Javic clasped her uninjured arm tightly as he led her out of her chambers. Other than Javic, none of her rescuers were her guardsmen—everyone on duty had been destroyed.

"Don't look," said Javic as they stepped out into the hallway. He pulled her to his shoulder to shield her eyes from the carnage. He didn't know she'd already seen it all unfold through the silver film of her Artifact scroll.

Havorie had watched the assassin search for her while she stood crouched low on her feet, hands trembling softly. No

438

one had been able to stop him. No one but her. In the end, she'd fought the heaviness in her feet to brave death. She realized the only way she was going to live was by jabbing Inhibitor into his neck. She felt like she'd been possessed by a spirit braver than herself. Her heart still pounded in her chest.

Calm down.... Just breathe....

She needed to lower her runaway pulse to slow her bleeding.

Javic escorted her through the trail of remains over to the east wing of the palace. He brought her to a small infirmary near Lord Ethan's residence. He stayed with her as the Power-less Ameliorators resorted to manual methods for sewing up her wound. They numbed her skin with anesthetic but the pressure of the needle still stung terribly. The pain refocused her mind. When the doctors were finished, she could still barely feel her fingertips, but the bleeding had finally stopped.

In a bed beside Havorie, Captain Sarvo lay on his side facing the back wall while the Ameliorators worked to dress his wounds. He'd been punctured all the way through his chest.

"Is that you, my queen?" he rasped upon hearing Havorie whimper.

"I am still alive," said Havorie. "I hope that isn't too much of a disappointment."

Damian was lively enough to scoff back at her. "What exactly are you implying?"

Javic ushered the Ameliorators out of the room as soon as they finished wrapping Damian's injuries. He closed the door behind them and stood by with the captain's blade in his hand. Havorie appreciated Javic's ability to understand her wishes without always having to utter an order.

It was time to press for answers.

"Tell me, Captain Sarvo, how did you avoid being blown to bits like the rest of your men?" Havorie asked pointedly. "What exactly happened to you?"

Damian coughed out a rough chuckle. "Funny story—I was approaching the Charisms chamber when a piece of one of my men shot through my chest. A little piece of skull, I believe. I've been told it's still embedded in the hallway."

The queen stood up and walked around Damian's bed so that she could look him dead in the eyes. "You were rushing to protect me?"

"I was the one who issued the alert...."

Havorie nodded slowly. "If you care about my well-being so much, then why, when I was a baby, did you allow me to be injected with Inhibitor? Hmm? Were you the one who threw my mother from the south tower?"

"That's... that's absurd..." Damian stammered. "I didn't...."

"You didn't what?" asked Havorie. "You didn't know? You didn't want to do it? Are you going to claim you were forced? Somebody made you do it?" Havorie crossed her arms in front of her chest and cocked her head.

"You are terribly mistaken!" exclaimed Damian. "Inhibited? I don't see how that could even be possible! No one ever had access to you as a child. Your mother—Mast bless her soul— would never have allowed it! A conspiracy like that would implicate—"

"—Everyone?" Havorie interrupted. "Doctor Crane. Lord Ethan. Councilman Cresdale."

Damian's mouth hung askew.

"Did they ask you to push her?" Havorie spat. "You are the secret suitor—her nightingale—are you not?"

"What are you going on about?" asked Damian.

Havorie raised an eyebrow. "You're going to play dumb?" she asked. "You made Madam Jusair vanish after you overheard me speaking with her about this. You locked me out of the south tower—threatened Javic and Ervia!"

A small frown realigned Damian's jaws.

"You're not going to tell me Tannel Cresdale was the suitor," Havorie ranted on. "I can't imagine that blockhead was ever attractive enough to woo my mother!"

Damian's eyebrows arched up. "Tannel had nothing to do with Queen Nestra's death!"

"Then who was it!?" Havorie shouted. His denials only served to infuriate her further. "Lord Ethan wouldn't have dared sully his own hands with such a task! I know you know what happened!"

Damian shifted on his hip, suddenly sitting up on the side of his bed. Havorie didn't shy away as he leaned forward with his palms against his knees.

"Nobody pushed her, you insolent child!"

"I am your queen!" Havorie screamed. "My mother did *not* fall!"

Damian blinked, his eyes growing glossy. "She did not fall," he said softly. "But neither was she pushed."

Havorie glared into his teary eyes. "Stop speaking in riddles!"

"She jumped…" Damian swallowed hard against his gravely throat. "She took her own life. She couldn't stand to be separated from the one she loved."

Havorie shook her head slowly. "You made her love you."

"Not me, my queen," said Damian, his voice trembling. "I was not her nightingale…."

"Then who!?" Havorie felt like she was running in circles.

"Valyne Jusair," said Damian. "Nestra was in love with Valyne. Obviously the controversy would have been too vast—the pain of her forbidden love ate away at her."

Havorie fell speechless.

"And Madam Jusair is not dead!" Damian spat. "I'm not that close with the woman, but I believe her sister recently fell quite ill. She left the palace to take care of her. If I'd known you thought she was dead I would have said something to you! It's Valyne's business, not mine."

Havorie didn't know what to make of it…. She had to admit Damian actually did sound genuine to her ear.

"I was away from the palace the night Nestra died," he continued. "I'd traveled up north with *this one's* father." He gestured behind him at Javic with his head.

Javic's gaze was locked upon Damian's back, eyes sharp like a falcon's.

"I met your father long ago while training at the Elswani Monastery, Javic. When your mother and her sister were captured by Garrett's men, Bartan came to me asking for my aid in a rescue attempt." Damian gave a slow shake of his head. "We couldn't save them… and neither could I save your father in the end."

Javic stayed behind him, listening intently. He couldn't see the ache of remorse in Damian's eyes.

"But that is why I was away from the palace…" he said, staring wide-eyed straight into Havorie's soul. "I should have been by your mother's side—I knew how terribly depressed she had become." He lowered his weakened body back down to his bed, slumping over on his side again. He shifted with a pained grunt, rotating just enough to catch Javic's eyes. "I trust you will keep my blade sharp while I recover."

Javic clutched the Talus Shard so tight that his knuckles turned white. "Sir," he grunted in response.

Damian shifted his eyes back to Havorie. He reached into his pocket and pulled out the missing heart-shaped locket. "I believe this is what you have been searching for." He held it out for Havorie.

She took it and immediately opened the clasp. Inside, a youthful image of Madam Jusair was on one side, with a picture of her mother adjacent. "But how?"

"The one your people found was a duplicate. I planted it to throw them off—I beg your forgiveness for the ruse. I confess I feared you would be wounded by the truth."

"The truth…."

"There's been no conspiracy. I aimed but to save the reputation of a glorious queen. There is no grand bogeyman to blame for her death—only the prejudices of society."

The truth hurt worse than any fiction ever could. Havorie left Damian to recover as she began to wander the palace with Javic by her side. Her restless legs needed to keep moving. She hoped Damian could forgive her misplaced accusations. She felt incredibly foolish for having levied such words at him.

At least I found my answers.

Ever since reading her mother's journal Havorie had dreamt repeatedly about tumbling over the south tower's railing—the wind in her face; the ground rushing to meet her—that grave drop always ended in darkness before she climbed out of her pillow.

From Nestra's words, Havorie knew she'd been desperately in love with her nightingale. In the end, she'd been so stricken with passion that she never made it up for air.

CHAPTER
58

Arlin's Duel

A stirring in Mallory's womb fluttered to the surface: The first signs of life kicking from within. All the commotion had kept her tense for far too long. She pressed her hand across her small bump, feeling for another wiggle. The baby had been teasing her all morning, only moving when she didn't have her hand in place to feel it.

Ervia had given Mallory the key to one of the guest apartments usually reserved for foreign diplomats. The chambers were lavishly furnished and decorated to impress. Once she lied down on the supple mattress, she never wanted to rise again. Despite her worry for Javic, she did her best to find rest. When the shaking started late the next morning, the bed bounced on its stilted legs, threatening to throw her to the floor. It rumbled halfway across the bedchamber before the earthquake finally subsided.

Mallory knew it wasn't a typical quake. The sounds of window panes shattering all across the palace spoke to the severity of the violent tremor.

When the earthquake stopped, a silent alert flashed with a red light from the voice box panel in the apartment's foyer. She stayed in her room while guardsmen clamored down the hallway outside towards the palace's entrance. She didn't want to get in anyone's way. She only knew for certain that there had been an attack after it was all finished.

Ervia stopped by, wide-eyed and jittery. "The queen is alive!" she exclaimed before Mallory could even inquire about the situation.

"Was that in doubt?" Mallory asked with a furrowed brow.

"Very much so," said Ervia. "An assassin broke in and killed a bunch of guardsmen—he's been captured. Word is Aaron Levy is back, and he and General Aldune saved the Queen from certain death!"

It was a lot for Mallory to process.

If Belford is back, that means….

The voice box buzzed beside the open door. Ervia answered for her, accepting the connection with the press of a button. "Who's calling?" she asked flatly.

"Charisms chamber," the voice crackled. "We've got a blade-brother down here inquiring after a Mallory Worvon."

"Arlin!" Mallory squealed.

"Yes, ma'am, he's nodding."

"I'll be right down!" Another flutter shook her womb. She gasped at the sudden pressure.

Ervia raised a drawn-on eyebrow.

Mallory grabbed her hand and pressed it to her stomach alongside her own. The baby wriggled once more against their combined touch, finally giving her a good feel. Ervia's eyes lit up as she felt the motion.

"Alright," said Mallory after the moment passed. "I've got this."

She left Ervia behind as she hurried to the stairs and down to the first floor. She couldn't restrain her legs as she jogged the final hallway to the Charisms chamber. Without Arlin, it had been an emotionally difficult winter. Ever since he'd left with Belford, Mallory had felt like a ship with a pulled anchor. She'd been tossed about, lost to the mercy of the winds and tide. She missed Arlin's steadfast resolution. Before he left on his mission, he told her he was going to go put an end to King Garrett's madness. She never doubted him—not for a moment!

Upon rounding the corner, the gruesome scene outside the Charisms chamber put a hitch in her step. She slowed as she spotted fragments of bone protruding out from the blood-splattered walls in the hallway.

She spotted Shiara first, walking slowly alongside Belford and another dark-haired woman with a guardian blade strapped to her hip. The Talus Shard in the hilt glimmered with an iridescent shine that sparked an inkling of concern in the back of Mallory's mind. Arlin shouldn't have been around any of the Paerto'radam—not after having killed one of his own to free her....

"Where's Arlin?" she asked. All eyes across the hallway turned towards her as she spoke.

Strong arms suddenly wrapped around her from behind. The wordless embrace startled her only momentarily as the hands caressed her waist, cradling around to hold her belly.

She turned to face Arlin. They both already had tears in their eyes as she peered up at him. A white scar that hadn't been there when he left ran the width of his neck. She frowned at the ominous injury before throwing her arms around him and falling deeply into his tight embrace.

"My liege," she whispered into his ear, "you've come back!"

Arlin rasped an uncomfortable breath. "I've missed you," the wheeze barely escaped his throat.

She could tell it hurt him to speak.

He clutched onto her even more tightly as he spun her around in a wide circle. Mallory laughed as her feet lifted from the floor. After she settled back to the tile she leaned back slightly, studying his sun-touched face. His piercing blue eyes shined happily back at her.

"You've succeeded?" she asked.

Arlin's grin widened.

That meant King Garrett's reign really was over! Mallory buried her head in his shoulder. Her bump pressed up against his tunic as he squeezed her back.

A sharp scream filled the corridor. Shiara was crying out.

Arlin grunted, tensing up against Mallory. A piercing pain entered Mallory's abdomen. She gasped as the unexpected sensation bit into her like fire. Arlin went weak, collapsing against her. A man at his back withdrew his blade from the both of them.

Arlin tumbled to the floor beside Mallory. Her mind couldn't process the pain she was in as she clutched her belly. Blood ran through her fingertips, soaking her dress. She grabbed onto the neck of Arlin's shirt, covering him in her blood as she pulled him back up against her. His gaze drifted askew as his eyes grew distant and hazy, quickly glossing over.

Mallory sobbed out a wordless howl as she held him to her. She could hardly breathe through her anguish. Soon, the corners of her vision began to grow dark. The world slipped away as she fell from consciousness.

CHAPTER
59

Cardinal Crime

In the days that followed the attack on the palace and the slaying of Arlin Calary by the cowardly Orris Fen, Queen Havorie spent much of her time reflecting upon her rule from a modest bench within the central gardens. With the Power still absent, the Ameliorators weren't certain whether Mallory or her pregnancy would survive. Other than learning of Lord Ethan's sudden demise during his return journey, it had been one sorrow after another as the dead were counted. Even Ethan's death was bitter sweet. Havorie would never be able to stand up to him for having conspired against her. She hoped she wasn't making the same mistake as her mother by instilling Aaron Levy as the new commander of the Ver'konus. She hadn't told him yet, but that was her plan. He'd helped save her life, but she was wary to trust anyone with such power.

From the gardens, Havorie could see a massive crack running up the side of the south tower. The insides had completely collapsed during the intense shaking. The unnatural vibrations had been brought on by a tiny tuning fork—one of the Crimson Stalker's Power Artifacts. All of her mother's stored possessions were shattered into rubble at the bottom of the tower.

Nothing was salvageable.

It felt like her whole childhood had crumbled away. She ached under the weight of every fallen plank. It crushed her heart. She'd always felt closest to her mother when she was amongst her things. It was all gone now. She'd been holding onto something that no longer existed.

Nothing was unbreakable.

Havorie made her way to the throne room. Orris's trial awaited her judgment. It was cold within the judicial chambers when she entered. With all the windows broken out of the palace, it was impossible to keep the place heated.

An audience of witnesses met her gaze as she stepped down the aisle towards her seat. She picked up her oak gavel from the central podium as she went by. Once she was settled upon her throne, Orris was brought before her, his wrists and ankles bound in thick chains. Damian had been in her ear all week begging her to release his fellow blade-brother. Havorie insisted on a formal hearing.

Damian hobbled into the chamber, his injury not stopping him from throwing his support behind Orris. He found his place at Havorie's side. Javic stood opposite him.

Old Resoldo was the last to arrive. He was to be her bailiff for the proceeding. The soft spoken steward stepped up to the podium and cleared his throat. "Today, Orris Fen stands before us," he said. "Orris, you are accused of murder with premeditated intent of one Arlin Calary." It was a simple charge. "How do you plead?"

Orris had a sour expression on his face from the moment Resoldo started speaking. "As I've already tried to explain,

Arlin was marked for death by the brotherhood for killing another blade-brother. I only acted on my duty to the guild when I slayed the traitor. It is not murder to enact the law!"

"A simple 'not-guilty' would have sufficed," said Havorie, already fed up with the man. "Although these are official proceedings, I think I would rather not mince my words. I shall speak to you plainly."

Orris watched her through narrowed eyes.

"While I do recognize your extended rights as a member of the Paerto'radam, the word of your law states that a duel should have been held over your allegations. In that way, the superior swordsman could have been given the chance to prevail. It is my understanding that you just went right up to him and shoved a blade in his back...."

Orris grimaced. "The duel you speak of is more of a formality, not a requirement," he argued. "The spirit of the law is straightforward. Arlin Calary was a traitor, and it was my duty to end him. I would have been negligent had I allowed him to escape once I recognized him for his cardinal crime."

Javic's face was a pinched up mask of poorly concealed rage.

Damian approached the throne out of turn. Havorie sighed. She already knew what he was going to say. He leaned in and spoke quietly so that only those closest could hear him. "You must release him, my queen.... The Paerto'radam has sovereignty over prosecuting current and former members, even within your realm."

"Says who?" Havorie snipped back.

"Says a thousand years of legal precedence! When it comes to internal matters, the Paerto'radam need only answer to the Monastery. Need I remind you, this guardian also rushed to save your life, risking safety and health in service to the Crown?"

She could sense Javic staring daggers at her from her other side. She already knew where he stood on the matter as well, given his friendship with the deceased.

Havorie intentionally did not restrain her volume as she responded to Damian. "Do not speak to me like a child! This is *not* merely an internal matter! On the day an assassin nearly tore the palace to the ground, Mr. Fen chose to add to the chaos! I take this matter very seriously, as should you! Murder is one of the most egregious crimes a man can commit! It squelches from the world untold potential, and in this case, it has deprived Aragwey of a genuine hero! Arlin was acting as an agent of the Ver'konus when he was killed." Her eyes swept across the assortment of witnesses before landing on the defendant. "His life was not yours to take. Orris Fen—your cowardly crime of slaying Arlin Calary in cold blood with a blade to the back may not be at my discretion to prosecute—"

Damian exhaled audibly beside her.

"—But!—And need I remind the witnesses!—Mr. Fen in his carelessness did not only kill Arlin. He also pierced the belly of a pregnant woman!"

"I did not mean for that to happen!" Orris burst out. "I was only carrying out my solemn duty to the Order—"

Havorie banged her oak gavel.

"—Under the eyes of Mast, I swear it was an accident!"

"Silence!" Havorie shouted back at him. "Speak out of turn again and I shall take your tongue!"

Orris turned sheepish white at the threat.

Havorie stared at him for a long moment, daring him to test her resolve. He smartly stayed silent. She continued on with her ruling. "I formally decree that you shall be locked away until further notice—and Mast forbid, if either the mother or child dies by your wound, I *will* have your head on a pike!"

Damian leaned into her ear again, speaking in a harsh whisper. "You cannot threaten that! You rule a civilized realm!"

"I can do whatever I please!" Havorie bit back. "Perhaps some heads on pikes is exactly what is needed around here! It would certainly send a message to my enemies! I will not balk nor buckle!" She did not speak quietly. Across the chamber, the witnesses all watched on with stern expressions. Their reports to their various masters would speak of a queen who was not to be trifled with. That was the message she wished to send. She turned back to Orris Fen. "Do not mistake my ruling as perfunctory. It is also not a threat—it is a promise. Your fate rests on the fates of those you've afflicted with your negligence." She slammed her gravel down once more, marking an end to the proceeding.

Damian held up his hand to stop the guardsmen as they approached Orris Fen to take him back to his cell.

"Are you aiming to join him in his accommodations, captain?" Havorie quipped.

"I cannot jail the man for this, my queen…. It would break my own oath to the Order." Damian wrung his hands together. "I must insist you rethink your position."

Havorie stared Damian down. He did not flinch under her glare. "You may not like what I *rethink*," said Havorie. "Split loyalties do not become you, captain. You can serve only one master. I suggest you choose wisely."

Damian's jaw tightened. "I serve Mast."

Havorie had heard enough. "*Captain* Elensol, relieve Damian Sarvo of his duty!"

Javic stepped up to do her bidding. He was getting quite the promotion out of this! Damian continued to stare at her in disbelief. He puffed out his chest, but did not resist as Javic led him from the chamber.

Old Resoldo looked on in a horrified demur, about ready to pull out what little hair he had left on his scalp. Havorie knew he despised it when she lost her temper or acted emotionally. Whatever he thought, she was not acting on a whim. Too many people had tried to minimize her rule. Damian Sarvo had so easily lied to her throughout her whole life about her mother's truth. It was time to clean house. From now on, she only wanted those who were truly loyal surrounding her. It was all she could do to feel safe after everything that had transpired.

Javic and the other guardsmen led Damian and Orris out of her sight. She wished it hadn't needed to come down to such extreme measures, but both men had made their choices. Havorie stood resolute as the witnesses departed next, murmuring amongst themselves. She hoped her ruling would stand as a warning. She'd just kicked a rat's nest. Now she had to wait and see what would come scurrying out.

CHAPTER
60

The Most Dangerous Path

Weeks after setting out on his own into the mountains in search of his little brother, Cormick Gansly stumbled across the first marker in his grueling climb to the Lost City of Sultrim. The ruins of Barhele sat concealed just within the tree line of the Arid Hills. It was now a spattering of stone outcroppings, once grand buildings, fallen and masked by a forest of black spruce and birch trees. To Cormick it was a glorious sight—it meant he was on the right track!

All the journals and old texts indicated that Barhele should show the way forward. Unfortunately, there were many different ways of which one could choose to go forth from the ruins, and his resources didn't exactly agree upon where to aim next. Cormick had several tomes of research he had yet to pour through, but he did not want to slow his progress.

On one particularly fair weathered morning, he left the packhorses hitched to a tree and set off on his mount towards the seemingly most accessible path forward. By midday he

454

found his way unceremoniously blocked by an impassibly steep skeet cliff. The dangerous loose rocks would kill him within thirty paces if he dared attempt a crossing—he'd read of several such accounts already in his notes.

While returning to base camp, his horse, Norman, took an unfortunate stumble and broke a hind leg.

Cormick cursed his luck. Norman had belonged to his father's good friend. He'd promised to take excellent care of the healthy beast when he first set out to retrieve Rylin's reportedly dead body from the Glowing City. After not finding a body to claim, trusty Norm had carried him a very long way. Cormick felt terrible that the best he could do for the steady steed was to slit his throat before the wolves could pick him painfully to death.

By the time he arrived back at his base camp, the packhorses had already received that less-pleasant fate….

Cormick shouted out in pained frustration. In his haste to move forward he'd diminished his own chances of survival significantly. In the nights that followed, he kept a fire burning bright to keep the wolves at bay whilst he flipped through the various tomes of accounts of travelers' past for more clues. While none had been successful, it was accounts of companions gone missing in the night that most irked him.

An odd thought occurred to Cormick. He decided to check which possible pass forward had the most reported vanished expeditions.

Strapped with all the supplies he could carry, Cormick set out with little more than a hunch and an ever elevating fear as he climbed the most dangerous path. He dared not light a fire at night. He was high enough to be free of the wolves, but one of the accounts he'd read had him nervous about the possibility of bears—as odd as that sounded at such high elevations. He nearly froze to death each night from that decision, but the stories… people would vanish at night when they were easiest to spot from their campfires.

Several days into his harrowing climb, a long ridge he'd been following rounded over to a steady climb that led to a quickly flowing river. Cormick discovered his worries were extremely well founded. A bloodied mound of fur and flesh bigger than a carriage with thick arms and claws like daggers lay at the river's edge. Cormick stumbled upon the hulking beast beside a large boulder that had halted the creature's descent down the fast moving waters.

It wasn't dead, but it barely moved, huffing from extreme exhaustion on the riverbank. Cormick needed to pass by too close for comfort in order to continue on with his trek. The matted fur undulated with heavy breaths. The hairs on the back of Cormick's neck stood up as the creature suddenly lifted its brow and spoke with clear words. "Aid me, human," it rasped with a deep voice. One of the creature's eyes was burned out of its head.

Cormick pointed at himself, as if he were not the only human in earshot. "What…? Who…?"

Wide fuzzy membranes flapped up at the creature's sides— massive wings that stretched out against the riverbank. "I am Tanuk. Aid me, and I will not eat you."

* * *

Deep in the halls of Sultrim, the silver rings of the Great Device began to slow. The contraption had finally completed its function. The hum of the hoops changed pitch as the rotations diminished. The air crackled with the release of a built-up static charge.

At the center of the chamber, a man from another age awoke—body built anew from the flesh of another.

As the machine powered down, so did the network of Artifacts masking the Power from beneath the lands of Aragwey. All across the nation, the ability to channel returned at once to those who had been afflicted by the power-hungry process.

CHAPTER
61

Upheaval

One week after the Power vanished, it returned again in a flash as if some sort of switch had been flipped. Belford felt the buzz of the computer's tendrils as they caressed his mind— an electronic handshake. Its presence brought a sharp breath of relief to his lungs that made his badly broken ribs twinge in instant regret. He grasped onto the connection at once, harnessing its ability to mend his body. In seconds, he was healed.

He jumped out of bed and rushed across the infirmary to Mallory's bedside. Her skin was pale and clammy. Her tears had long ago cried out, but her sorrow was still etched into her face. He could feel the infection within her wound with his mind—the computer informed his senses of the festering heat. There was no way he was going to leave her treatment in the hands of the Ameliorators. The Ver'ati doctors were not inept, but Belford trusted his own knowledge much more.

He reached inside of Mallory with his thoughts, envisioning a psychic tool with a straight edge. He scrapped across the inflamed area, removing the ickiness like shaving cheese from a block. He peeled back the compromised layers of flesh with precision, stripping away all the sickness completely before sealing the wound back up again. His work did not leave a scar like the rough seams he'd seen left behind by other Ameliorators.

When Belford was through, Mallory sat up, clutching her abdomen. Her eyes leaked with a waterfall of fresh tears. She thanked him through renewed sobs.

If only I could have saved Arlin as easily....

Belford was getting better at regulating the energy-drain of his cellular work. This time, he'd taken steps to mitigate the metabolic slump he tended to impart upon patients with his healing touch.

"What time is it?" asked Mallory. "Can we still make it to the service?" She hurried to her feet and began stripping off her thin robe.

Today was Arlin's funeral, already commencing without them.

Belford turned away, giving Mallory some privacy as she redressed herself into an outfit that had been dropped off earlier in the week by Shiara. "It's already started, but we can make the end if we hurry!" Shiara had left a fresh pile of clothing for Belford as well. He made his way over to the outfit, folded neatly on a chair beside his bed.

Belford dressed himself quickly, but Mallory was faster. She rushed past him just as he finished buckling up his pants. He threw his arms through the sleeves of the fresh shirt and snatched up his favorite embossed leather jacket. He hastened after Mallory, chasing her down the long corridor, still fumbling with his buttons.

Arlin's funeral was a joint service—shared by Ethan and all the other members of his team who had lost their lives over the course of their mission. The gathering was being held across the Queen's Boulevard at the Arcanum Cathedral. Councilman Tannel Cresdale had organized the whole service and opened it up for the public to view so that he could show off just how dead Lord Ethan was—Queen Havorie was to deliver a eulogy.

When they arrived at the grand cathedral chamber, the afternoon sun was shining brilliantly through all the tall panes of colorful stained glass. It cast a kaleidoscope glow across the lines of packed benches. Upon a stage, Arlin's plain coffin sat alongside Ethan's more elaborately decorated empty casket. More empty boxes were on display beside Arlin's to honor Thorin, Lieutenant Canbel, and the Arcanum steward, Sarbin Raiger, who hadn't made it off the Rosa Marsa.

They'd already missed Tannel's speech, but Queen Havorie stood in wait, about to go up next. The guards recognized Belford and allowed him and Mallory through to the front of the audience. Once there, Belford spotted Vera seated next to Grine. Belford and Mallory were able to slip in beside them, right at the foot of the stage. Shiara was currently up in front of the caskets. She laid a bloodstained cloth in Thorin's box before joining them in the audience. She hugged each of them in turn before settling down for Queen Havorie's eulogy.

Belford spotted Javic off to the side of the stage dressed in his new captain's uniform. He gave Belford a subtle wink, trying to remain professional in his duty watching over the queen. He'd been in visiting with Belford and Mallory all week at the infirmary. He looked relieved to see them healed and well now that the Power was back.

Havorie approached the podium in front of the caskets. A hush fell over the audience as if everyone was holding their breath. The queen's eyes shifted slowly across each of the officials in the first dozen rows. Members of all thirteen houses were present, along with the leaderships of the Ver'konus and the Arcanum. Everyone who was anyone within the Glowing City was out for the occasion. The hush did not falter as Havorie's gaze shifted across each of the notable attendees in turn.

Finally, she began....

"Esteemed guests—" her words boomed across the acoustically sculpted ceiling, filling the entirety of the large cathedral with her thunderous voice. None could miss her harsh tone. "These men, honored before you today, should be revered as nothing less than heroes. They died in-action, defending the Phandolian values of honor and freedom."

Belford glanced over at Vera. She had her dark green eyes fixed upon Ethan's empty casket with an unreadable expression.

"They fought for the rights of every man, woman, and child across these blessed lands to live an equitable life. They made the ultimate sacrifice to stand against oppression—against the evils of tyranny, and while they could not save themselves, they succeeded at making this world a better place for the rest of us." Havorie's eyes continued to sweep across the silent crowd until they settled upon Councilman Cresdale, seated in the front row at the far right of the chamber. "Well, at least that is true for these four men," she gestured to the four lesser coffins that flanked Ethan's. "Lord Ethan was not like the other men laid to rest before you." She continued to hold Tannel with a steady glare. "For you see, Lord Ethan was a traitor."

Gasps sounded across the crowd.

Havorie raised her voice above them. "He was a traitor to the Crown! He conspired to have me injected with Inhibitor when I was just a babe!" A fiery rage exploded from her.

More gasps and a hissing murmur filled the echoey chamber.

Havorie silenced them all with a raised hand.

Tannel rose to his feet and began walking along the outside of the benches towards the nearest exit.

"Sit back down," Havorie's voice boomed across the crowd, speaking directly to the councilman.

Tannel paused in his escape but did not return to his seat. Several of Havorie's guards armed with pikes stood between him and the outside.

Havorie continued: "To honor these four fallen heroes requires that I speak in earnest about the corruption I have recently uncovered. It darkens even the highest offices of our beloved institutions. It has gone on long enough—I shall cast it out now!" She gestured at Ethan's coffin.

The whole casket lifted up off its dais and rocketed through the air.

Screams echoed across the hall as the casket crashed through a stained glass window and soared out into the distance.

"I am Inhibited, no more!" Havorie's shout cut through the uproar. "Lord Ethan did not conspire alone! Queen's Guard—arrest Councilman Cresdale at once for treason!" Javic stepped forward to answer Havorie's order.

Tannel shouted back at the queen: "How dare you levy such an absurd accusation?! I am the leader of the Arcanum—you do not have the authority to arrest me! Especially not in these halls!"

"You *were* the leader of the Arcanum. I hereby strip you of your title. Your council can choose a new head to speak to me, for *I* rule these lands and your head is now *mine*. You are nothing more than a traitor to the Crown—may Mast have no mercy upon your wretched soul!"

A deep shade of crimson consumed Tannel's pocked face. His dark eyebrows were drawn down in a deep frown. Lieutenant General Cale Fisman approached Tannel from behind, a syringe of Inhibitor clutched in his hand. He injected the clear fluid into Tannel's neck as he turned to flee. Tannel gasped as the chemicals entered his body. It was clearly a planned ambush.

The rest of the Queen's Guard stood firm as Javic and General Aldune approached Tannel in unison. They were an odd duo to see working in tandem. They each grabbed one of Tannel's arms and walked him from the chamber in shamed defeat.

As shocked as the crowd was, no one stood to challenge Havorie. Her eyes shifted back across the audience, this time landing upon Belford. "Furthermore, I would like to take this opportunity to declare Aaron Levy as the new Lord of the Ver'konus. May Mast's light shine ever brightly upon him and through these hallowed halls. That is all." She made a small curtsy and then set off up the aisle with an escort of guardsmen surrounding her.

Belford swallowed hard as everyone seated in his vicinity turned to look his way. He'd assumed the appointment would be coming eventually, but he hadn't exactly prepared a speech for the occasion. He stood up and waved awkwardly to the huge audience. "Uh, thank you, Queen Havorie, for that… enlightening… eulogy—"

"—No need for a speech," Havorie interrupted him, speaking out over her shoulder as she continued towards the exit. "Truly. Just pay your respects, and leave—that goes for the lot of you!"

Belford's eyes went first to Vera—a worried frown was punctuated by a furrowed brow. Shiara, seated beside her, was masked in silent consternation. Mallory was even more of a mystery to him. Her eyes were fixed back on Belford, studying him. It was clear all three of the women had their concerns.

Belford wasn't particularly skilled in politics, but it was obvious even to him that Queen Havorie was making a power grab against both the Arcanum and the Ver'konus.

How do I fit into her plans?

The queen's formidable display of the Power had rattled more than a few funeral attendees, Belford not the least of all! A wild energy filled the air within the long chamber. It wasn't until after Belford exited the Arcanum Cathedral and was back outside under the clear sky with the moon perched high above him that he realized why he was feeling so unsettled: The Power had only just returned while the funeral service was already underway. Havorie couldn't have known the Power was about to allow her to perform such theatrics during her speech. To Belford, that indicated an unplanned moment of emotional outrage. He knew all too well how easy it was to lose control when such vast possibilities were a mere thought away.

Rooting out corruption was all fine and well, but Belford had been around long enough to know that every action had rebounding consequences. Behaving spontaneously was never the safest choice. Whatever the outcome of Havorie's antics, it was too late to change course. Belford was clearly to be dragged along for the ride.

Vera stepped up behind him, surprising him with a hand on his shoulder while he was staring out at the palace's gilded façade. "It's good to see you back on your feet," she said. "I've brought you something."

Belford realized she had Arlin's blade sheathed beside her own Talus Shard.

"The Arcanum officials handed it over to me. They must think I'm a real Paerto'radam," she said.

Belford accepted the sheathed blade. They embraced each other wordlessly for a long moment. Belford's eyes stung. A silent tear ran down his cheek. He blinked a second one out from his lashes. He hadn't properly grieved the loss of Arlin, too dosed-up on pain killers all week in the infirmary. Only as he sunk into Vera's arms did he allow himself to feel the bite. Vera hadn't known Arlin like he did, but she knew him well enough that Belford felt commiserated in his tears. She stroked the back of his head with her fingers as he let out a cathartic sigh. He was so sick of losing people.

When he finally climbed out from her arms, Vera planted a small kiss on his damp lips. "Do what you'd like with that sword," she said. "But it would honor me if you would allow me to use this one to continue to protect you and your interests going forward."

It took Belford a moment to realize she was asking to be his protector. He'd always felt drawn to taking care of her—he knew she was quite capable, but it was strange to consider having her be his sworn defender.

"Don't make me beg!"

Belford chuckled gravely. "I just don't want anything bad to ever happen to you. You know better than anyone how dangerous it is around me."

"That's not your fault!"

"It doesn't matter whose fault it is—it's just a fact! People die."

Vera frowned. "You can't say no! You would have to send me away entirely. I won't hear of it!"

Belford made an exaggerated grimace. "I wasn't trying to make you leave...."

"If I'm already going to be here, I might as well have the means to protect us both, don't you think?"

Belford realized she thought he meant to give her sword to someone else. "I suppose if you stay really close...."

Vera squealed in delight. She kissed him again. "You won't regret it! Now you just have to figure out who else gets to be on the team." She eyed Arlin's sword. "Mallory seems nice."

Belford pursed his lips. "I suppose the blade should belong to her, regardless."

"A piece of Arlin is still inside of its crystal," Vera agreed.

Belford hadn't the slightest clue how memory crystals worked, but the tech was certainly a bit uncanny. He had felt Arlin's presence within him when he gripped the handle, though that had been when Arlin was still alive. The Talus Shard transmitted the guidance of all its previous wielders—all their experiences with the blade were recorded into the instruments instinctual memory.

Shiara and Mallory were just walking out of the cathedral as Vera stepped away, continuing back towards the palace. Belford waved them over to him.

"Can you believe the queen turned their funerals into a circus?!" Shiara exclaimed.

Mallory saw the tears still lingering in Belford's eyes and stepped up for another hug.

"I've just received Arlin's sword," said Belford. "I think it should be yours." He offered the sheathed blade out to her.

Her eyes went straight for the memory crystal in the hilt.

"Do you know the powers of the Talus Shard?" Belford asked.

She gently brushed her hand across the hilt for a moment, but then pulled away sharply. He could see in her eyes that she had recognized the echo of Arlin within.

"I'm not even supposed to eat shellfish or soft cheeses anymore. What makes you think a Power Artifact would be a good idea?" Mallory shook her head. "I do appreciate the gesture, but I must decline. Keep it. At least for now while I'm pregnant. I don't really feel like I deserve it anyway."

Belford blinked. "What do you mean? Of course you deserve it!"

Mallory grimaced. "Before I met Arlin, it's no secret that I was taken by some very unsavory men. One of them happened to be a blade-brother." She reached out and touched the hilt once more, not recoiling this time. "Rescuing me was what marked Arlin for death." She released the hilt again. Tears were welling up in her eyes. The first bead streamed down her cheek as she backed away. "Maybe one day," she said softly, "but not today." She smiled at him through her tears.

Belford's emotions welled up again.

Mallory gazed off to the west. "I need to go feed my cat," she said. "Poor Buttercup's probably skinny as a mouse by now without me supplementing his hunting."

Belford's heart ached for Mallory. He lowered the sword back to his side as he watched her go. When he turned around, he was surprised to find Claire standing behind him.

"I was watching you from across the way," she said. "I just wanted... now that the Power is back, to see if the connection... but never mind."

She turned to leave again but Belford leapt ahead to stop her. "What did you say...?" But then Belford realized what she meant: Their connection had not returned along with the Power.

"We're not really them," she said. "I'm not Claire, just like you're not Aaron. I'm a homunculus—an echo from a past age of some woman. So it makes sense that what they had doesn't exist for us. We're just copies."

"Her memories are inside of you too," said Belford, "even if you don't remember them yet."

"Who cares? I have some of them, but the memories are hers, not mine. This body didn't live any of that. That age is dead and gone. I'm Rose now, just like you're Belford, apparently."

"That argument is just…"

"Were you about to say 'ridiculous'?" she interrupted.

"Asinine," said Belford.

"Oh, a synonym."

"Absurd! Outrageous! Delusional! Hell, most of your cells are completely replaced every seven years of your life, but that doesn't make your childhood not your childhood. You're the same person! Your memories matter!" He felt himself becoming increasingly incensed.

"Maybe that matters to you."

Belford scoffed at her. Her callousness gouged at his heart. "You're carrying our baby…" he said.

Her eyes narrowed.

"I'm carrying *a* baby. It's immaculate conception as far as I'm concerned." She turned and ran off down the sidewalk.

Belford was left bristling with anger. Dissociative behavior was perhaps to be expected after all she'd been through, but now she was just being cruel. She wasn't acting anything like the woman he remembered. He grasped onto the idea that her views would change once she remembered more. If she was anything like him, she probably found the bad parts easier to recall. She'd experienced a lot of trauma. It was no wonder she was afraid to dig deeper.

Another thought occurred to him as Shiara patted him on the shoulder: If Claire was unwilling to do the mediations to help foster her memory recovery, she could remain suppressed for a very long time… possibly even indefinitely.

His eyes burned all the worse as his emotions continued to flow out of him. Claire returning to him was all he'd fantasized about since awaking in Aragwey. He felt like he was losing her all over again.

CHAPTER 62

Freedom

The silence in Salvine's head felt wrong. She'd spent so much time bantering with Ash; it was strange to think that she was really gone. Salvine suspected that Ash had always been with her in some form or another throughout her life. Before she was a Whune, Ash was a repressed portion of her personality—an entity of primal rage; an internal protector— she split off when Wilgoblikan twisted her mind. He'd coaxed her out as an alternate personality and given her control. Ash had continued to fight for their joint-body until the bitter end. It was Ash that kept them alive through all the pain and despair of the past months. The silence within her never felt like peace. She dripped with untenable loneliness in her weakened state.

While she rested like a withered old hag on her deathbed she had a lot of time to think about how fortunate she'd been to survive her transformations. Her skin and organs were rejuvenated and young. She was getting a new turn at life. It was a miracle after all the damage her body had accumulated while being a Whune.

She couldn't find enthusiasm for any of the good news. She just felt hollow.

She could still sense Wilgoblikan—his direction, but not his direct thoughts like she once could. He was still Inhibited. The sensation manifested as a tickling tug, like a string tied behind her navel that drew her tired mind towards her old master anytime she let it wander.

Javic stopped by to offer a few words of encouragement, but he wasn't able to stay for long. He had many new duties at the palace. One could wonder how the place ever managed to function without him. Javic told her Doctor Crane was still considering his best options for surgery to put some muscle and fat back on her frame. She would remain weakened until then. Her old Whune body would never have let her down as terribly as her current malnourished skeleton. She felt like a living corpse. She couldn't even hold the plates of food that were brought to her without dropping everything all over herself.

Before Javic left, he promised to check in again soon. "I'll come back once I've hammered out the new watch schedule, I promise! It's no joke being short-staffed!" he exclaimed. He leaned in close. She thought he meant to plant a kiss on her cheek, but instead he spoke out a rushed warning: "Be cautious of Doctor Crane," he whispered. "He's not to be trusted. The queen needs him to look into the Crimson Stalker for her, but she knows he's not a good guy...."

Salvine had heard chatter from the Ameliorators discussing the man who attacked the palace. He could control the Power when the moon was down, at least before he was Inhibited. That meant more experiments for the sadistic doctor to figure out what made him tick. Salvine didn't know anything about all that, but she did know exactly who Doctor Crane really was. He'd enjoyed causing her and the other captured Whunes unending pain and torment.

She closed her eyes, already feeling the drain of exhaustion upon her eyelids.

She awoke suddenly to a rustling at the curtain that divided her room. She hadn't realized she had a roommate until that moment—she wondered if anyone had heard her whimpering into her pillow earlier when she'd thought she was alone....

A smooth hand of light-pink skin pulled back the curtain. The scrawny man it belonged to stood before her, frail body wrapped in a medical gown. Salvine knew him at once. Miester Creany wasn't quite as emaciated as she was. He was able to walk slowly under his own volition.

He looked so different... but she knew it was him from his sunken eyes. The skin on his face was tighter and younger looking than before. Despite a vast difference in his waist size, Salvine couldn't mistake him for anyone else as he fixed her with an amused grin. It was the same infuriating expression he'd made while flicking her in the back of the head as he led her off into the woods to be sold to Wilgoblikan.

"I dunno if ya remember me," he said, "I used to be much fatter." He pinched at his scrawny hipbone.

A tightness enveloped Salvine's chest as she stared back at her old captor. He'd treated her worse than his dog.

I ate that dog.

"Ah, so ya do recognize me," he said upon taking in her expression. "Well, that's good. I wanted to apologize, ya see? For my role in what's happened to ya...."

Salvine was completely cornered as he limped nearer to her bed. The weight in her chest grew heavier. She was frozen in place, unable to move or speak at all as he leaned in.

"That man isn't me anymore," said Creany. "I had to kill him so I could wake up from my nightmare. I defeated my shadow—cut him right out, removed all the cruel parts entirely and left 'em behind." He spoke so nonchalantly. "Really, I feel downright awful for havin' caught ya and all them other kiddos for Wilgoblikan."

Salvine felt like she was trapped in the back of his carriage again as he invaded her space. The pressure in her lungs made her feel like she was about to burst. She may as well have been drowning in the tide again. She imagined it lapping over her nose and mouth.

Miester Creany bent over her, lowering his face to her ear. He spoke in a harsh whisper. "I see yer still scared of me," he said.

She could tell he was sniffing her neck as he hovered over her.

"I'll convince ya yet—imma changed man—there's nothin' to fear anymore. I'm too frail to be 'fraid of now anyway!" He chuckled as he nuzzled against her in feigned weakness, exhaling his breath upon her.

Salvine wished she could melt into her mattress.

"Mmm," he moaned softly. "We've both got such nice new skin." He caressed her arm with his fingertips, seeing how far he could go without any pushback. "So, I was thinkin'," he said. "Once we've recovered more, I could bring ya back to Taris with me—when yer ready to go home, of course. It'd be my pleasure. Who knows, maybe you'll enjoy havin' me 'round—I'm not such an old man anymore—the doctors reverted my age—What a gift!—I guess we're the same age now."

Salvine knew everyone else would believe his gross lies. She twisted towards him with all the desperate energy she could muster out of her diminished muscles. A Whune claw in her fist was the perfect weapon. Ash had saved the severed digit on her body for months, ever since escaping from her confinement the first time. She'd kept it hidden beneath her body during her last transformation. Salvine used it like a scalpel, drawing its sharp edge across Miester Creany's neck. He tried to pull away, but Salvine sat up with him. An arterial spray soaked her gown as she slashed at him repeatedly, making sure to finish the job.

"There are no good parts of you," she growled in his ear. A vast sense of calm fell over her at once as Creany collapsed to the floor and quickly bled out. His miserable life was finally over. There was no room in this world for filth like him—not while she had the means to end it.

To her, it was obvious he was lying about being changed. Salvine was changed, but she had not lost her sense of self. She was hardened by her experiences. She'd gained the ability to be ruthless, though she worried at what cost to her soul.

It's a bit late for a moral crisis, don't you think? The words resonated through her brain.

Ash? You're alive?! Were you guiding my hand?

A buzz of amusement fluttered across the back of her mind. *No. That was all you. I can't move a muscle.*

She was overcome with a joyous rush. Ash had returned to her! *When you fell, I thought you were gone forever....*

She could feel Ash bristling with pride.

Javic wouldn't have let me survive any other way. But it turns out falling in dreams only tends to wake one up.

CHAPTER
63

The Gray Mortuary

Beneath the palace's foundation resided an old slate-block chamber that spanned the length of the central gardens. The series of narrow crypts had started out as Calvenite like the rest of the palace, but with no structural necessity the blocks had been allowed to fade back into ordinary stone over the long centuries since their formation. The dusty corridor was better known as the Royal Crypt, but Havorie's mother had referred to the tomb-lined hall as the Gray Mortuary.

The place where Nestra used to sneak off to be intimate with Madam Jusair, her lady in waiting, was now her final resting place. With the south tower internally demolished, the crypts were where Havorie could feel the ghost of her mother most strongly now. With the setting of the moon, Havorie forged into the underground passage.

The soft vibrations of the electric power turbines constructed years ago by Lord Ethan could be felt more strongly here than anywhere else within the palace grounds. Only the occasional whistle of a draft cut the deafening silence of the isolated hall. It was the perfect place to pace about and reflect upon all that had befallen her beleaguered reign. It had the added benefit of being a location nobody would suspect her of hiding out.

Short corridors branched off from the main tunnel every dozen or so paces. Each contained at least one fancily engraved sarcophagus on a raised block. Every royal body entombed within the crypts was a blood relative of either Hannah Davis or Emily Fox. Havorie, interestingly enough, was related to both of the famed queens—most directly to Emily Fox through her mother, and tangentially to Hannah Davis on her father's side. There was no question where Havorie would have ended up had the Crimson Stalker succeeded in his aim. She would have never thought to hide away in such a dreary place had it not been for her mother's encoded journal giving her the long-ripened tip.

She now knew Damian had been the panther Nestra wrote about, not her nightingale. In retrospect, she should have known—he was always prowling the halls. Havorie had Damian locked away in a cage not too far beneath her feet now.

There were no glowing orbs within the passageways. Havorie carried a tall candle with her. She lit up each sconce as she stepped past, contributing to the rising sanguine glow of the narrow corridor. She had stopped only briefly at her mother's tomb, preferring to keep moving as she let her mind wander. Going deeper into the vault was like treading backwards through the bowels of history. All of the tombs had been placed in sequential order, the oldest at the end.

All—with the exception of one.

Hannah Davis had been laid to rest beside Emily Fox. Hannah had ordered Emily's tomb redesigned to hold two caskets before the end of her long reign.

Havorie had never visited the combined grave before. The darkness and cobwebs had frightened her too much as a child for her to ever wish to venture past her mother's chamber. When she reached the final crypt, she was surprised to find the two stone rectangle caskets inside were placed identically beside one another with no markings to distinguish one from the other.

She'd always assumed since she first heard the story of Hannah's burial that the move had been made in order to jump the line—to show supremacy over Emily and her lineage. As she looked upon it now, she thought the placement more aptly resembled the resting place of cherished lovers, rather than rivals in fame—as ridiculous as that sounded given the three-hundred year gap between their reigns....

Had she been less distracted, perhaps she would have noticed the figure poised in one of the dark corners to her side more expediently.

"Pardon my intrusion," came a raspy voice.

Havorie nearly collapsed to the floor in fright. The man shifted from the shadows to stand between her and the exit. It took her a moment to place his face as the candlelight flickered across him. "Ambassador Cromwell?" she asked. "What in Mast's good name are you doing down here!?"

She wasn't yet convinced the Gravish Ambassador didn't mean to put a knife in her ribs.

"Do not worry," he said. "I needed to meet with you off the record."

"How did you even get past security...?"

"You should be more cautious," he said, stepping closer with a nonchalant gait. "There are many dangers in this world."

He only stopped advancing when Havorie took a step backwards and her heels bumped into the stone slab.

"I come with a vital warning: Your actions against the blade-brothers have displeased the Ek'radam monks," he said. "It may already be too late to prevent them from rescinding their support in lieu of a fresher choice."

Havorie narrowed her eyes. "Their support… you mean for my reign…? Are you suggesting they wish to replace me?!"

"Rumors are already abound—and not just about you tossing corpses through the streets—"

"—That was one empty box!" Havorie interject with a roll of her eyes.

"Nevertheless, rumors purport a new Mark of Kings is upon us—a woman, destined to become the next Queen of Phandrol."

"You speak of sedition! How absurd!" exclaimed Havorie.

"Is it? I beg your pardon, but there is a firm precedent for such a lawful turnover just to your back—the great Hannah Davis took the throne in the third cycle. The Mark is a powerful political phenomenon. People believe it is prophetic. Such suggestions cannot be so easily swept under the rug."

Havorie didn't know what to say. He wasn't threatening her, but she certainly didn't like the proposition he was touting.

"I hope I have not upset you," he said. "It wasn't my intention to caused you distress—there may yet be a solution if you tread lightly with the blade-brothers you hold in custody. Follow my advice going forward and I can help steer you clear of this storm and the many more that will follow. Now that you can channel, there are those of us who believe you to be the superior choice."

"Do you speak for the Kingdom of Graven, ambassador?"

He smirked, though Havorie could barely see the shift in expression on his shadowed face. "No… not today. This goes far beyond such regional politics. I represent a more *global* initiative. Do not fear, at least not for my allegiance. An evolved man does not spoil that which he has only just spawned. Understand what I say: There is a reason you are so formidable with the Power—your pedigree was crafted for you, just as it was for your parents and grandparents before them. You are the product of many centuries of powerful intentions all coalesced into such fair and supple flesh."

Havorie flinched. His words undressed her to the core.

"The slipping blood quantum will be rejuvenated by your offspring—a new age of Power anchored within this region for years to come. Much has been invested and will continue to be invested to see that the proper outcome is achieved."

Ambassador Cromwell stepped back towards the dark corner he'd emerged from. He reached his hand into a crack in the wall and manipulated a hidden lever.

"Do not fret," he said. "As long as you listen to me, I am confident you will prevail."

A grinding sound behind Havorie caused her to turn about. The stone slab holding the caskets was shifting slowly forward at her. Behind it, a hole opened up, revealing a hidden ladder that carried on down through the floor.

"I'll be in touch," said the ambassador as he stepped around the slab. "This extra Mark can be dealt with. It doesn't have to be your undoing."

Havorie was left reeling with countless questions as the unassuming man disappeared down the long ladder and out of sight into the Erotos Underground.

Continue reading for a special preview of:

Tides of War

Book Four of:

The Arcadian Complex

Paul James Keyes

CHAPTER

1

Leviathan

The usually calm Northern Sea surged with a quickly brewing storm. The horizon was blackened by dark clouds, thick as charcoal. Lightning and fat balls of hail crashed down to the bubbling waters off the coast as the strange convergence met with the Aragwian continent. Captain Artimus "Bundles" Gupree had never seen anything quite like it in his long years upon the water. Had his dearly departed Rosa Marsa still been afloat, the oversized chunks of ice would have left dents the size of dinner plates on her rusty-brown hull. Bundles watched from the shore, keeping his eyes on the horizon as all the fishermen along the coast turned towards the inlet to flee the fast approaching ice storm.

The late August heat the region was otherwise experiencing made the ice all the stranger of a sight!

Captain Bundles wasn't really a captain anymore. Without a ship or a crew he was just a man with no place to call home.

His sea-legs felt unstable on the dry ground. He much preferred being out on the water, though he was grateful to be on shore for the worrisome weather today. His son, Eben, and the lovely Coriva Lethos, were all he had left in the world as he toiled to unload another man's catch with a few other day laborers before the dangerous storm could make landfall.

The obvious fear that the weather was unnatural—spawned by wizards—was set partially at ease when Bundles spotted a contingent of Arcani Navigators sailing northeast along the coast towards the storm front. The sleek warships were Propelled by skilled Aerologists who brought their own winds and currents at they backs. The ships' red and black flags flapped counter to the greater prevailing winds. Bundles counted eight ships altogether—two larger command strikers and six small wind-darters in escort positions. It was the Imperial Gravish Navy, back again patrolling the shores. If he didn't know better he might have thought the ships were being sucked into the weather system by means of a vortex from the way they moved rather than being steered there intentionally. He assumed they aimed to dissolve the storm before it could reach land.

"It's just like the ones that hit the coast out west!" exclaimed one of the other day laborers to Bundles' left. A pair of fish dangled from the hooks in his hands as he stared out at the massive wall of clouds. The whole crew was so distracted by the impending storm that they risked not emptying the catch in time from all their gawking.

Bundles had heard the rumors circulating amongst the fishermen: This storm wasn't the first anomaly of the summer. The kingdoms of Graven and Taris had each received a targeted gale of a similar nature. Each had done substantial damage, battering roofs and sinking ships in the respective regions.

"Work faster!" grumbled the foreman that hired the team.

Bundles pierced his hook through the gills of a particularly large sea bass and dragged it up from the hold. The muscular fish was tired and gasping but not quite dead. It gave one last flap, nearly shaking free of Bundles' strong grip. He got it back under control with a thump of his baton.

His eyes wandered back out to the Gravish armada. They would reach the gray of the storm soon with their quick sailing. It had become common to see the Gravish Navy within Kovani waters for the past few months now. A truce had been signed by all of the kingdoms of Aragwey in the wake of the barbarian invasion. Over the course of the last five months, Kovani forces rallied around their new Priestess Queen to push back the barbarian siege straight into the sea. The razed towns on the coast were just starting to rebuild from the damage of the first wave. It was said that many of the invaders had chosen to turncoat, joining the priestess's ranks rather than die. How odd to think that Bundles had been the one responsible for ferrying Livian Niern to Tavallon last winter. Her acquired soldiers were fanatically steadfast in upholding the strict new civil laws of the land—of which there were quite a few too many for Bundles' taste…. There wasn't much room for an old smuggler like him under the new rule. Criminals captured for any infraction were immediately conscripted and sent off to Tavallon for reeducation.

It was like the people were being dared to sin. Livian wanted them to fail. She needed more foot-soldiers for her growing army. Once a man was reeducated, it was said he did not stray from her fold. Bundles had yet to see any of the folks who had been taken ever return.

After aiding the Ver'konus in changing the nation, the irony was not lost on Bundles that he had been left sunk and penniless and now had to work all day everyday unloading an endless bounty of fish while barely earning enough coin to feed and house his tiny displaced family. He had a plan to escape the toil. It did involve a little bit of smuggling, but first, he needed to acquire a new vessel—nothing fancy, just one big enough to hide a small cache of alcohol or some other such newly illegal luxury. He already had the contacts he needed, but he couldn't get a contract without owning a boat first. With so many vessels destroyed elsewhere along the Northern Sea by the storms, the cost to purchase a small vessel had risen just out of reach right as he'd nearly saved up enough to make an offer.

As he watched the Gravish armada reach the tip of the bay, a signal horn blared from the lead command striker. The distant bellow was carried far across the water by the advancing winds.

And then something changed....

Bundles didn't know what he was seeing... the ships just dropped away.

The waves rose up sharply to meet the dark clouds. The water rolled off, leaving behind a mountainous shape in the mist. It was a titan of massive proportions—a spiny sea-beast the size of a monstrous god....

All eight ships were consumed entirely by its gapping maw. A tidal wave rolled off its scaly back as it crashed down to the churning sea. Bits of debris fell from its spiked jaws as the behemoth chomped down on its catch. The fearsome beast stayed at the surface just long enough to let out a gut-clenching ululation, then it submerged back into the waves, vanishing from sight within the storming sea.

A Note from the Author:

If you enjoyed my novel, please consider leaving a **review**! That, along with telling your friends and family about my books, is the best thing a fan can do to give back. The more attention my novels get, the lower the financial burden of writing them will become (it takes years). I will continue to share my stories, one way or another, because that is what I love to do!

About the Author:

Paul Keyes was born and raised in Washington State between the beautiful waterways of the Puget Sound and the always majestic Cascade Mountains. Fascinated by the political and social workings of the world, he obtained degrees in both creative writing and economics from the University of Washington. In his spare time, he is an experienced pianist and composer, which has helped him bring a heightened sense of rhythm and emotional resonance to his written passages. Over the years, he has traveled everywhere from China to the Mediterranean, soaking in the many diverse cultures and histories. Throughout it all, there is no place he would rather be than back home, drifting on a boat somewhere between the San Juan Islands and his home port of Edmonds.

You can follow Paul on Twitter (X) **@PaulJKeyes**,
TikTok **@PaulJamesKeyes**,
or visit **ArcadianComplex.com** to become an honorary Arcadian!

9 781952 872044